MW00831711

Destroying the Tangible Illusion of Reality;
or, Searching for Andy Kaufman

T. Fox Dunham

PMMP

Perpetual Motion Machine Publishing
Cibolo, Texas

Destroying the Tangible Illusion of Reality

Copyright © T. Fox Dunham 2015

All Rights Reserved

ISBN: 978-0-9860594-2-1

The story included in this publication is a work of fiction. Names, characters, places and incidents are products of the author's imagination or are used fictitiously. Any resemblance to actual events or locales or persons living or dead is entirely coincidental.

Without limiting the rights under copyright reserved above, no part of this publication may be reproduced, stored in or introduced into a retrieval system, or transmitted, in any form, or by any means (electronic, mechanical, photocopying, recording, or otherwise), without the prior written permission of both the copyright owner and the above publisher of this book.

www.PerpetualPublishing.com

Cover Art by Luke Spooner
www.carrionhouse.com

In this surreal road novel, Anthony searches for the father he's never met: Andy Kaufman, the legendary song-and-dance man from the '70s. There's a few problems here, of course. Andy Kaufman died in 1984, and thanks to a recent cancer diagnosis, Anthony doesn't have much longer to live, either. However, new evidence has come to light that questions whether or not Kaufman is actually dead. Could he be in hiding, after all these years? Anthony is determined to discover the truth before his own clock runs out. During his travels, he will encounter shameless medicine men, grifters, Walmart shoppers, the ghosts of Elvis and Warhol, and the Devil himself.

These are the most important words I've written, and if you don't listen, your life is an illusion. I was the tenth person in the world to be diagnosed with composite lymphoma—a rare combination of large cell lymphoma and Hodgkins. The survival rate didn't exist. I came through it. I don't know how. Friends tell me it's amazing I did. No. It's just some shit that happened to me. Chemo wrecked my body, then daily radiation for five months to my head, neck and chest devoured me slowly. People never ask me what dying was like. They don't want to know. People live in the false pretense that they are immortal. Death happens to people on the news.

This book is what it felt like to die.

I bonded to Andy Kaufman in spirit because he shattered the illusion of reality, though losing himself as he did. Reality is a construct, created by humans to give value to a system, to provide meaning to their lives. When you're dying, meaning drains out of much of it, and you realize you created and fed into forces like fear.

Love is real. When I was burned down to nothing, a stub of my life, all I had left was love. And now I face it again as it grows in my neck, and everything all the source of this back burns anew, dragged along the hot coals until it ignited.

Read this and understand death so you can know how to live.

Fox

I dedicate this work to Deborah Drake.
Ever faithful. Always on my side and on the side of
those I love even when I fear them. Always able to
talk me out of my den when my fur is up. Never met
you, yet you toasted me at my wedding.
Friendship understands not distance.
BESTIES Always.

SWEET JUMPING BEELZEBUB

JEBEDIAH T. CINDERFIELD sped through the Burger King drive-thru and nearly clipped the fat ham hock of a woman dragging herself across the parking lot. He'd craved sweaty and greasy meat on a flat bun, ripe with sugar and sodium. He'd suck it down his throat and into his guts, absorbing the cow and dying a bit every time he ate. They'd fed boiled shit, oatmeal and moist chicken in that fucking place, and not even the shots of Thorazine and diazepam made it palatable. He threw the steering wheel of the rusty ice cream truck into a hard right just in time to miss her. The truck's heater blew full blast, even though Philadelphia broiled in the hot summer heat—one of the hottest days on record in several almanacs, reaching close to 105 degrees. Cinderfield pulled up to the drive-thru menu, buttoned his yellow trench coat, tightened his scarf, and yelled into the fat mouth of the facial burger.

"Ah shit. I'm looking for Wilma. Christ. Have you seen Wilma?"

"Welcome to Burger King. Try our nice Iced Coffee Lattes to cool off. How may I take your order?"

"Blast. Don't you listen, shit for brains? Is Wilma back there? You can't keep me from her. JESUS CHRIST! Where is Wilma?"

"Sir. I'm sorry."

"Yes. So am I. I only speak the name out of professional courtesy. No one ever bothers to employ my name in times of stress or conflict. Never an 'Old Scratch' or 'Sweet Jumping Beelzebub in a hot red Cadillac'! Just once. Just once I'd like to feel it vibrate my spider web strings. I'm in the phonebook. I've got a toll-free number!"

"Sir. Did you want to order something?" The kid sounded bewildered and clearly not trained or capable of handling a paradigm or situation that did not conform to the usual protocols for ordering at a fast food eating establishment.

"This . . . is . . . simple . . . as . . . shit. So, I will say it again. Oh, how I lament the educational system of this country. I had nothing to do with that, but *they'll* say I will. Jesus Christ! Professional courtesy. Anyway, I've lost my train of thought. Oh, aye. Sweet Jumping Beelzebub! Where the fuck is Wilma?"

"Uhh. Dude. Wilma doesn't work here."

"You're shitting me. Blast. You are shitting me up a shitfield."

"Are you going to order something?"

Cinderfield heard commotion in the background, the adolescent panicking, probably wondering if he should call the cops. He had no trouble dealing with the local constabulary. They'd just think him a demented old man and give him the name of some local shelters, with no motivation to put him in the slammer and have to deal with fits of terror and tears and changing diapers and baby food and other errands of care for the human elderly. No one wanted him for a problem, and he sailed through eternity without hindrance or interference.

A saucy voice took over. "Sir. If you're not going to order anything, then you have to leave." She spoiled for a fight, and Cinderfield adored her. Feeling horny, he wondered if she'd slap him or flail about if he grabbed her fat hot thighs. A voice like that always sprung from juicy legs. He'd lay her down in a sandbox in some abandoned playground, below a jungle gym and the watchful eyes of the Boss in the clouds, strip her out of her uniform and that little Burger King cap, snap off her bra with his shattered teeth shards and then climb up her bulging waist like ascending a hill, grabbing and squeezing her titties as he went.

"Baby. Relax. I'm just thinking."

"Then think fast."

He licked his thin dry wafer lips. "I don't care to dine el fresco. Think I'll come in and enjoy all the delights your fine eating establishment has to offer."

"Whatever."

He pumped the gas, and the old truck roared forward, burning the air and mixing it with black, oily smoke. He spun into a handicap spot at an angle impossible for any mortal driver and jumped out of the car. He balanced on his the balls of his feet, strolled into the fast food dump and queued up. He saw her—black as obsidian and gorgeous—probably born in Africa. He thought he'd detected a bit of Uganda in her voice. Her fat breasts bounced when she walked, not wearing a bra, keeping those beautiful jugs free and happy.

"Oh, honey. You almost make me forget about Wilma." He ran his long fingers through his pointed beard like crows picking worms out of the grass. He'd just waxed the beard and his eyebrows that morning, wanting to look sharp in case he caught the wandering eye of some ill-tempered fast food store manager. She didn't grin, didn't even look up at him from the register. She'd not be trifled with today.

Cinderfield spun his head and examined the few

patrons eating a lunch late in the day, late in the year, during the late life of the old world—the old weeping world. They marched to the orders of their clockwork brains and coiled hearts, following old commands, serving childhood bred fears, lost in the delusions of their spurious realities, created by a malfunctioning mind. And he had come.

The manager looked up, and her pupils dilated. "Mother Mary."

"Same office. Different floor."

"I know you from somewhere." Her hand shook at her register.

"Oh, yes. Indeed. But, I promise you, honey. I'm greatly misunderstood." Cinderfield examined his pristinely polished black fingernails, finding a chip in the paint on his thumb. He'd touch it up after.

"Umm."

Not this one. No. She was too far gone. Maybe he'd come back in a few years when he passed these parts again. Time wound oddly for him, and he could turn back and forth, putting the Caddy into reverse or forward, riding up and down the highway against the flow of traffic.

"Coffee, please."

"Iced?" Her voice crackled.

"Hot! Hot as the lake of fire. I want to burst into flames when I put my lips to the dark and evil brew."

"Just coffee?"

"You got it, sugar. Bring it over to the table? Daddy's got to work."

She nodded and never charged him, didn't touch the register. She labored at the coffee machine and poured him a cup. Cinderfield strolled into the restaurant and mingled among the diners. He surveyed the mortals— couple of punks with skateboards, an old lady in the corner already far gone, but he spotted a large man with a beard slurping up a Whopper. Sauce poured down his fishing shirt, and he shielded his eyes with a trucker's cap. He probably owned that piece of shit pickup outside.

This one. Yes. This must be he. Mr. Cinderfield sat down at the table with him. The trucker's eyes shot up, surprised and perhaps secretly delighted for some company. He stank of acrid cig' smoke, that old tar that gets into your hair and soaks into your clothing. Yellow nicotine stained his fingers.

"I can only assure and comfort you that you will not remember this encounter."

"You a Russkie? I hear Russian on your voice. Damn Reds."

"That's neither here nor there."

"The hell it is."

"Shhh, now." Mr. Cinderfield put his finger to the trucker's lips. The large man quieted like a comforted child, an infant in his arms.

"Rejoice!" Cinderfield said. "I come with glad tidings. I emancipate you. You may not survive. In a few months, you could be rotting in the dirt, food for worms and birch trees. I sometimes dig 'em up and watch the squishy worms wiggle."

"I . . . I don't understand."

When he touched the trucker's lips, his fingers worked into his mouth, down his throat, elongating and stretching, until it fed into his brain. He plucked at the brain's memory centers, reaching deep, into the repressed thoughts and feelings. There it was: a runner, like them all. The whole damned human race ran from darkness to darkness. "Come home now, Franklin Smith. Your father can hurt you no more. Know my gift and be free. Love men as you wish to. Nature matters not. Only

5

your spirit in the wind. Free bird flying." Cinderfield pulled his fingers out.

The trucker wept, tears spilling down his face and drenching his stained shirt. "I can't," he said. "Please, shut your mouth. Your tongue keeps flapping. It's stabbing me in the chest, Bub."

"The chest. Yes. Smoked your whole life, did you?"

"Just like my daddy."

"There, then. Yes. Just a slight touch, not a heavy dose of my medicine, my magical elixir brought from realms far and times long dead. Here, now. Shhh. Just a touch, a dose." Cinderfield pressed his forefinger over the left ribcage and fed it into the skin. Black ink pulsed from his painted fingernails, staining the trucker's skin. It seeded and wormed through the flesh, drawing deeper, pulsing hard and fast, infecting cells, driving them faster, harder, into careless division. Mr. Cinderfield sowed his field, pulled his finger out and grinned.

"There, now. All done. Best to see a doctor early. Hope you have good insurance, mate. Not really my department, you see. I just start the fires, but I'm not a bad fellow. I'm just terribly misunderstood."

The manager carried over the coffee. She couldn't break her gaze of Mr. Cinderfield.

"I better have that to go, honey."

She nodded.

"And Jesus fucking Christ. Has anyone seen Wilma?"

THINKING DIRTY ABOUT ANDY KAUFMAN

Anthony shut the door to the cubicle, set the sterile plastic cup on the edge of the sink, dropped his trousers and boxers and then wrung his soft cock, motivating the scared fella to grow. He rubbed up and down the base of the pink head, and it only elongated slightly, not erecting to its usual and healthy length.

"Shit. Come on. Don't let me down now, soldier."

A pipe jutting out of the wall dripped from a corroded joint into a mildewed bucket in the corner. Drip. Drip. Drip.

"God damn it." Still, his gentile's genitals refused to engorge with blood. The nurse waited down the hall—at least he hoped she was a medical professional, though those sequenced boots didn't denote it. Christ. She might have gotten this job after being fired from a fast food restaurant, and he was just going to hand off the vital seed of his loin to be entrusted by this fry cook. He should have demanded to see her credentials, but there wasn't time. They needed to start chemo tonight, so this had all been rushed. His oncologist didn't want to waste a precious minute, a lost second.

He tried to clear his mind, overflowing, drowning in wild thoughts of the cataclysmic changes that had rocked his private and internal ecosystem. His whole world came apart. He pushed it aside and tried to remember that porn video he watched the other night online, the one with the girl in the black thong. He centered his mind's eye on that thin, tight piece of string, and his manhood responded. He doubted he'd get signal to watch porn on his phone. He sighed and washed his face, then spotted a copy of *Hustler* rolled up behind the toilet. He reached down and swiped it up. His long, dirty blond bangs fell over his eyes, and he blew them from his face with a stream of air from puckered lips. He opened the magazine, but the pages felt sticky to his fingers and weirded him out. He chucked the magazine and checked his phone, hoping to find a stray signal from a network with a careless operator who had not installed a password.

"Shit."

Anthony just needed a push, someone to help him get outside of his head, to distract him from the complex, knotted thoughts: cancer, cancer and more cancer and cancer baked in a goddamn pie. She might do it. He dialed Cynthia, sitting in the waiting room. She'd promised to come with him, keep him calm.

"You done?" she said.

"Remember how you promised to do anything for me?"

She hesitated. "I may have said that."

"I need you to come back here. It's . . . a medical emergency."

"Oh, God. What's wrong?"

"Just come back. Go right through, make a left and come to room 14. Knock on the door. Shave and a haircut. Hurry. For the love of God, hurry, Cynthia Marie Angelo."

She hung up the phone. He pulled his bangs away from his eyes and waited, wondering if she'd get stopped in the hall. She knocked on the door.

"Shave and a haircut . . . "

"Two bits!" he sung. He cracked open the door.

"Are you okay?" She yanked on the hoodie strings on her pink sweater. Her skin bleached white, and it stung him a bit. He hadn't meant to upset her so, but more than that, the seriousness of his situation, the threat of mortality, displayed on her face. This morning, he'd noticed the skin inflamed around her crystal green fields of eye—fields wet after a sweet summer rain—and he'd asked if her sinuses had bothered her, offering some over-the-counter meds. She'd been crying, and he felt like dumbass. She'd been crying over him. He pushed the thoughts away.

"Look," he said. "I know there are some things we've never discussed. Personal things. It's just not talked about."

"What the hell?" Her face screwed up in puzzlement. "What's wrong?"

"I need you to talk dirty to me."

"Oh, goddess." She rolled her head. "You scared the crap out of me."

"I wouldn't ask you, but it's an emergency."

"Planes crashing into a skyscraper are an emergency. My best friend dying of cancer. You're a sick sick man, and I'm going back to the waiting room."

"Look. Wait. It's the nurse. She's timing me. I can't do it. A man's sexual ego is fragile, and if I can't make a deposit to the sperm bank, she'll tell all her friends. And it'll spread. I won't be able to show my face in public."

"If you don't do this, what happens?"

"The chemo they want to do kills fast growing cells like cancer, but it doesn't discriminate. I suppose that's very P.C. of it. It'll kill off all fast growing cells, like my hair follicles, my stomach lining, white cells . . . and sperm."

She reached out and played with his long locks, braiding them. Her eyes dampened again, the tears glistening. She brushed her arm over her face and pushed them away. He huffed; relieved he didn't have to watch her weep for him. He wouldn't be able to take that. He'd run like hell, just hit I-95, stick his thumb out, and drive off anywhere and to forever.

"But, your hair will grow back, right?"

He nodded. "But the treatment might make me sterile."

She ran his hair between her fingers and sighed.

"Don't laugh." She checked down the hall, watching for nurses who might interrupt. "I've never really done this before."

He waited. Cynthia would motion to speak, but the words failed her. She paced, and he leaned against the door, hiding his manhood behind the doorframe, cupping his head.

"Goddess," she said. "I can't do this. I can't think of anything."

"Okay. What turns you? Who gets you hot?"

"Easy. Andy Kaufman." She grinned, curling her lips. He should have known. Since meeting her again as a volunteer at Bloom, she'd educated him of the messiah and performer of the '70s. At night, chatting on Skype, she'd go on about his mad exploits and how it changed the nature of what it meant to be human—something about wrestling chicks.

"Pretend I'm Andy Kaufman and talk dirty to me."

"You look like him. Short nose. And your dark hair curls up when it's warm. When I saw you in the theater department at Bloom, I thought you were his ghost, haunting us. I nearly squealed."

"I've never seen him before, really." He curled his

10

upper lip ever so slightly, revealing the bottom of his front teeth.

"See. There. Andy did that. Like a little chipmunk. If you had sideburns, that would just kill me. I swear you're Andy Kaufman reincarnated—or maybe you're just playing us all and had plastic surgery. He did stuff like that. Goddess, he was sexy."

"Good. Then get me hard, so I can do this."

She blushed. He hadn't meant to be so vulgar and ducked back into the cubicle. Sometimes, he felt like Cynthia was a kid sister tagging around, and at times, he'd forget her age and apologize for swearing or doing something prohibitively adult.

"I'll try." She giggled, and his penis shrunk. Anthony, however, could not fault her. Even as a woman in her late twenties, she carried a young girl's innocence and purity. She'd probably only had a few sexual partners in her life and could not speak about sex without turning red and laughing. He admired that in her, as if she'd protected something sweet, a pink pearl wrapped in a clam's protective shell.

"Okay. Okay. I can do this." She inhaled deeply, paused, then exhaled. "Oh baby. You make me so hot. I want to—" She burst out laughing.

"God damn it."

"I'm sorry," she said among giggles. "Look where we are!"

"I know. Believe me. I know."

"This just isn't something I thought I'd ever have to do. I'm trying. Believe me. I wouldn't do this for anyone else."

He patted her on her head, sliding his fingers down the round bun of dark hair spun around the back.

"You want children?" she asked.

"I've never really thought about it. I guess. I wouldn't

mind exercising my natural gift to procreate. God help my poor kid though, coming from this mind, these thoughts. I wouldn't wish this to anyone."

She paused and considered. "Just relax. And tell me about your first time."

"This is the first time I've ever frozen sperm in a sperm bank because I'm about to start a round of chemo that may or may not work. I've never been dying before."

"No," she said, getting fussy. "I mean—"

He nodded. "Yes. I know. Ryan."

"Your girlfriend?"

"I think so," Anthony said. "As much as we can profess to possess another. We worked together at the campus bookstore at Bloomsburg. You ever see her?"

Cynthia nodded. "Yep. I think so. Another Q-tip. Goth, too. Really pale, always wore black skirts." She grimaced, bending her legs to the side. Her spirit just hung over, and she pushed her body into a crack in the universe and tried to hide it—not long like taffy but a bottom round that rings like a bell. Her eyes cast down in shame of her weight, and she yanked down the sleeves of her long shirt, tugging at them with her fingers.

"Ryan was beautiful, and lethal." Anthony looked off, seeing her again, fog suffusing through his eyes. "An opera singer beauty, and I'd get a stiffy whenever I saw her. She spotted it one night, poking through my jeans, and that's how we hooked up."

"You dated?"

"Screwed. A lot. Don't think we actually engaged in a romantic relationship, no commitment. I thought we had. I thought that's what it meant."

"What was your first time like with her?"

She heard nurses talking outside the cubicle. Cynthia tapped her knee-high boot from anxiety, probably expecting security guards to rain down on them from ripcords with parachutes. She calmed herself when they were clear.

"I told her I'd been with other women, and I had—but I'd never had intercourse. Other stuff. I wanted to wait for someone special. Remember when you believed in innocence and love?"

She nodded and grinned, but her eyes displayed a sad aspect.

"She pulled me into the student lounge in the campus building after we closed the store. It was 3 A.M. I had finals the next day. I told her I was tense. We made out for a while, and then she bit my lip, chewed on it 'til I bled. She even licked the blood off my chin."

"Sounds like a freak," Cynthia said.

"She had a vampire fetish. Goth girl. Dark hair. Torn stockings."

"Yum."

"Oh, yes," Anthony said. "She stuck her hand down my jeans and grabbed me. I was already so hard by then."

"Hold that thought," she said. "Do it."

He rubbed on his manhood, finding it hard in his hands. It pulsed from his touch.

"She pulled down my jeans and led me to the couch. Then she slid up her skirt and pulled her thong to the side. I was shaking by then, and she asked me if this was my first time. I nodded, and she cooed. She thought it was so sweet—plucking virgins. She'd never been anyone's first, having sex at fourteen."

"Goddess." Cynthia shook her head. That wasn't her world. Anthony couldn't tell if she was sheltered or preserved, but found himself pleased at her sexual inexperience. "So, what did you do next?"

"She climbed on top of me and slid down on my dick.

That first feeling . . . so good, like biting into a ripe, juicy peach."

He rubbed himself faster, harder, and quickly built to climax. "Oh, shit!" He shut the door with his foot and ran to grab the sterile plastic cup on the sink. He aimed himself, holding the container, and discharged, filling up the bottom. It looked like a good amount, in case the judges were ruling based on quantity. He cleaned himself up with wet paper towels and pulled up his khakis. Then he closed the lid on the cup and hid it in his suit jacket pocket. He didn't want Cynthia to see it, feeling the need to protect her innocence, to not see any component of his sexuality. Their relationship had gone back to a gentle time before puberty, when girls and boys could be friends without the interference of hormones.

Cynthia walked Anthony out to the nurse's station.

"So, what happened with Ryan?"

"One night, I walked into the student lounge with candles and flowers, to prepare a romantic evening. She was screwing some guy from the early shift. I ran away and cried."

"Awww." She rubbed his shoulder.

"I didn't understand."

"Hush." She pointed at the container. "That's the past. The future lives in there."

Anthony shrugged and hid his sperm behind his back is if he'd been exposed naked.

"It's fine," Cynthia said. "Just life." She giggled. "Bring it here. I want to bless it."

He hesitated at first, and then held the plastic specimen bottle out to her. She raised her palm over it and rubbed her necklace with her other hand. "Goddess. Bless this new potential, the seed of life, that it will bring Anthony hope and renewal—and share this light with the woman who will carry this holy seed in her womb. So mote it be."

"What is that? Magic?"

"Well . . . it's hard to explain. It's more about metaphor. You use symbols or metaphors to represent change, then you act it out through ritual."

"So, you believe that humans possess the facilities to change the cosmos through will?"

"A matter of faith."

He sighed. "The cosmos keeps spinning, with or without us. We're just fleas on the lion's back." He curled his lip into a grin, and she squealed at the gesture, her eyes lighting.

"So cute," she said.

"God. Get out of here."

Cynthia giggled, then exited into the lobby, and he set the container on the counter at the nurse's desk. A chubby old matron took the bottle, wrapped a label on it, smiled, and then took it back to cold storage. She came back out with a clipboard and pen.

"Okay, darling. Please fill this out."

He wrote in his information, address, phone number, and at the bottom, he paused at the section asking for information on authorized handlers. He tapped the pen, dabbing blue dots on the paper.

"That's for who you authorize to withdraw your sperm. Your wife. Your family. Your boyfriend."

"My mother died. She'd just given birth to me, and they were driving home from the hospital. An ice storm. Route 1 was slick with ice. Miracle I survived."

"Honey, you need to put someone down."

He stuck his head out the door into the crowded lobby, full of nervous men. "Hey, Cynthia. You want to be authorized to handle my sperm?"

"I . . . guess."

"Cool." He filled out her name, then handed the nurse the clipboard. He joined Cynthia in the lobby, and they both left to catch the SEPTA bus to his oncologist's office by the Oxford Valley Mall.

"Whatever happened to that Kaufman guy? Is he doing late night infomercials, selling juice machines?"

"He lives forever," she said and paused, watching the clouds float by on high. "And only that."

He nodded, and they walked the avenue, by the burned down bowling alley and weeded vacant lots. In front of the thriving liquor store, they sat on the bench, kicking away a broken crack pipe. A dead cat cooked in the road, fur soggy and rotting, stinking the corner with a sweet, putrid smell.

"You've got Pookie?" he asked.

"He's in the purse."

"Fantastic."

"Just curious," Cynthia said. "Ryan is the only girlfriend you've ever mentioned."

"She wasn't really a girlfriend, at least not exactly. I created that. I saw what I wanted to see."

"If some dude was doing me every night, I'd assume we were an item."

The SEPTA Bus road in on all fours and slowed in the traffic.

They climbed aboard, mounting the stairs and took a seat in the middle. The bus rode light, customary for that time of day. They sat silent and waited for the bus to take him to the oncologist for his first round of chemo.

THE STORY OF ANGEL

I n his bedroom in Great Neck Long Island—the land of wealthy movie and music stars who come to build houses and escape the fury of Hollywood, all Jewish of course—a young boy discovered movie cameras behind the plaster of the wall. Channel 5 of Great Neck New York rocketed online with four hours of programming everyday—music bandstand, comedy shows, horror afternoons—all the characters performed by one boy actor, and his characters populate the world that thrives and pulses inside his tiny body. How many souls can fit in one child?

We shall call this child Angel, for he is pure, outside the dross of the human world, and he is legion. Many daffodils will grow from this child, and each will blossom in unique fashion. Each will glow in the sun.

This child frustrated and mystified his average parents, as all special children do, born outside the cast mold of what's expected of the youth of the 1950s, born of soldiers who destroyed the Nazi monster to give their offspring. His father sells custom jewelry and often works away from the home, traveling the road for months at a time, and his mother tends to her family and home, perfecting the Better Homes and Gardens Life expected of her. This is not the America our leaders promised, when we survived the depression, when we sent our sons and husbands across the seas to fight the Japanese and Germans. They promised a world of peace, ripened and opened for American goods and way of life, a Pax Americana, assured by our military capacity and atomic firecrackers.

And yet, the war continues, never ending. Our partners against fascism defy our philosophy. Great Britain crumbles, and the Soviet Empire devours Europe; its atheistic communism worms through the earth, infecting far countries like a disease. And still, we send our sons and husbands to wars that will contain: wars without end.

Angel knows nothing of wars or nuclear capacity, the fleets and follies of man posed ready to destroy. The world beyond the Channel 5 studio of his bedroom doesn't report the news, and only the audience lives beyond the walls, who tune in everyday to watch his programming.

Angel disturbs the slow, steady temp played by his well-meaning parents. He jumps on the bed of life, bending the springs and pounding the floor. He hides from his mother, leaping out at the last minute, to her bewilderment, or hides in a neighbor's tree house and tweets the wrong seasonal birds to frustrate bullies. He dances and sings and lavishes in the attention of his grandparents and lives the greatest star in the world.

And his father comes home and imposes his need for order. He assigns his checklists and admonishes Angel— yelling, always yelling. Yelling-io. Yello-o. When his father comes home from the road, selling plastic baubles to the stores, he yells.

He loves his Papu Cy. He tells him stories and makes him laugh, and Angel never cries when Grandpa visits. Then Papu Cy stops visiting, and Angel waits at the window, watching for the old wizard to come. His parents tell Angel that Papu Cy has gone on a long trip and won't be coming back.

Why didn't he take me with him? And his stomach rumbles. He buries the anger deep, because he doesn't want to be mad at Papu Cy. Angel knows hurt now, and he doesn't care for it much. Then his parents tell him that God took Papu Cy on a long journey. Who is God? Someone in his audience? He sees his grandpa riding down the highway, and God just picks him up with two fingers and takes him to Heaven. His innocence allows no concept of a supreme being. He only knows a Heaven and Earth at peace.

Death is when God picks you up with two fingers and takes you to Heaven.

Angel escapes the creeping, intruding world through a magic box. To his parents, the crystal screen is the face of a new world, the evolution of the talking boxes they grew up with, the wireless sets that spoke and sang and babbled but never listened—the birth of an era of new creatures that comforted but declined to listen. This box will change the world and what it is to be human. Its great and varied powers will both wound and aid the development of society, casting both emancipation and enslavement like all great technology does. In Angel's world, televisions broadcast new worlds and fusion bombs threaten to destroy them.

The glass does not divide; it swings like a doorway, and the people, animated characters and puppets, live and breathe as flesh and blood. Angel, in his purity, fails to understand deception, the spurious nature of programmed reality. The characters must exist, for they are Angel's friends, his companions each morning, his preachers and teachers, educating him in the way of behavior, interaction and love. They know no hate. They dance and play, cast on strings, and so shall he all through life, never letting go his embrace on the crystal screen—to dance and place and sing cast on string all through his life. And when cold reality intrudes, he will lift his arms, and God will pick Angel up between his two fingers and drop him into the monochromatic fields beyond the television screen.

Angel goes to school, and he hides in the wood to perform his programs, acting out all the characters. He has no friends, but he knows a solution: he creates them. Then, his parents and teachers take them away. He lives in the world of the made. What is reality? What defines fiction? God makes people, builds souls, so why can't Angel? Everywhere he goes, he sees the crystal screen, but no one else can. The world plays on a wide television screen, bigger than his house, wider than his school—a screen that stretches out on the horizon and to the stars. People are just characters, and their souls are the actors, playing different parts through time and space. Angel watches from the moon, far away, outside the show, creating and creating.

And one day, Angel rises with sleepy eyes. He dreamed again of his fame and stardom. He'll be the greatest star in all the world one day, and he writes of meeting himself in novels written by a child's hand—the great star he'll one day become. Andy slips downstairs to watch the house's idol, the new face of divinity, and he turns the dial, seeking out Howdy Doody, his favorite character and best friend.

Instead, he only finds one show broadcasting in strange chromatics, broadcast on the black and white set. He recognizes the man on the screen. He looks like his father a little, but Angel shares his wild eyes. The man Angel sees is a great star of movies and television, and he sees his audiences made flesh beyond the plaster walls. The man has no hair, and his pale skin sags. He looks like he could use one of his mother's plentiful meals. He reminds Angel of his brother, bearing a similar face or even his father if he were younger. Angel watches on and realizes the man is sick. He coughs all the time and blood comes up, and the man cannot lift himself from his chair. In his eyes still lives and dances all the characters he'd created as a child.

The man gazes back into the screen, a record player and pair of bongos at his side. Angel loves his record player and could work it as a child, playing his favorite songs. The man stares through Angel, and Angel stares through the man; and the sung world falls away around them like a collapsing stage, for what is the world but an ending song?

Don't be scared. God will pick you up between his fingers and take you home to be with Lassie and Howdy Doody.

The man does shake in fear. He can no longer see the great screen of the horizon. He has passed beyond it, and pulled up the roots and wires of the world, setting it free. His breathing slows. Angel finally recognizes the man; it is not a screen but a mirror.

Angel sings him a song, his favorite song, "This Friendly World," one that would never depart his thoughts.

THAT OLD BLACK MAGIC . . .

The human brain is like that. One can see patterns everywhere, in random nature, fluctuations of cosmic radiation, a poem written out in a bowl of Alphabet soup. We call that God."

Nurse Clumsyhands drove the needle into the sensitive flesh on the back of Anthony's hand. His skin ripped like yanked fabric, and he clutched onto Pookie, gripped in his right hand. The poor plush seal's eyes bulged. She jiggled the needle, sliding a bit in and out, searching for the elusive vein.

"Son of a whore!"

"I'm sorry," Nurse Clumsyhands said. "You've got tiny veins. We can't use a butterfly." She brushed away her long blonde curls from her sight and pulled out the IV stick, then pressed down on the bleeding hole with a cotton bar. A wasp continued to twist its stinger.

"One more stick, then I'm going the hell home."

Cynthia rubbed his shoulder, and the bulky purse she carried banged into his side. She grabbed it. The nurses had set out a chair for her, but she stood, and paced, and stood. "Calm down, Anthony. It's not her fault."

"Then who the hell is sticking me with a goddamn needle?"

"He's just nervous," Cynthia said. "It's his first chemo treatment. I know that can be really scary."

Anthony poked Cynthia in her round hip. "Don't you dare. You can go home if you do that again."

Cynthia looked stunned and stepped back to watch from a comfortable distance. She fiddled with her necklace, then her hair, then her necklace. She emitted a small sob, then drew it back, sucking on her lips. She held her Goddess icon dangling from her necklace—a fat woman's body, swollen in hips and womb, missing its head—and she whispered:

"Lord and Lady. I ask that you heal Anthony and guard his body during his first chemo treatment. Please . . . " Anthony cut her in two with a hatchet look, and she mouthed the prayer without voice. She finished it and said, "So Mote it Be."

Nurse Clumsyhands grabbed his arm and turned it, examining it like a butcher at a meat market. She yanked on it and slapped his soft flesh with two fingers then wrapped a rubber tourniquet below his shoulder. At first, she hesitated, holding the IV needle above his flesh. She inhaled deep, propped his arm, and drove the needle hard into his muscle.

"God damn it," he said. "There's going to be a lot of this." The top of the IV filled with triumphant burgundy, and the nurse taped it down. She slipped out the needle and secured the line.

"Sixth time's the charm," she said, grinning.

"God damn it," Anthony said. "Someone get me out of here."

"That your little friend?" The nurse pointed at the filthy seal.

"He's an escaped spy from Berlin, and the Russians are after him."

She nodded, not really listening. "My little Charlotte has a stuffed dolphin. She calls him Elvis."

23

Cynthia grinned.

"Oh God," Anthony cried. "Not that bloated excuse for a performer who wiggled his hips into a revolution of poor style and taste. How can anyone listen to that walking ego? He set back human culture fifty years and died a fitting death on his porcelain throne."

Cynthia shot him a dirty look. He shot one back like an old western duel. The nurse didn't comment, just moved on.

"Okay. Let's get you going here." The nurse slipped back into the supply closet. Cynthia hovered there, her lips shut tight.

"Look. You can talk. I've just got bees swarming in my head."

Cynthia sighed and lowered her shoulders. "You shouldn't talk to people like that."

Nurse Clumsyhands returned with a saline bag and line. She sung quietly to herself, joining the song playing on the intercom: "That Old Black Magic".

She hung it on the built-in IV pole on the mechanical chair, ran the line down then connected it to Anthony's line. She pulled a syringe from her lab coat pocket and flushed the IV, shocking Anthony's arm with an icy needle that moved up into his shoulder. He shivered.

"Winter in my body," he muttered. "Winter's hiding in my organs."

Nurse Clumsyhands shot Cynthia a glance of consolation. She nodded for the nurse's kindness.

"God," Anthony said.

Two other patients piloted the mechanical chairs in the chemo suite at Doctor Helsinki's suburban office. The chairs composed a circle and reminded Anthony of plane seats: complete with movable table, arms, footrest and, as an extra for those passengers who'd prefer to take their Vodkas intravenously, an IV pole.

"This won't be so bad," Cynthia said.

"How do you know? I mean, really. I know you were a volunteer at Penn when we bumped into each other again, but did you ever sit in on a chemo treatment before?"

She looked out the window and studied the contours of a birch tree, watching the coils of silver paper flutter in the winds. Anthony caught a whiff of apple, and his nose led his eyes to the refreshment table in the corner of the room.

She looked around, saw the nurse coming. Her tears built in her face like a geyser gained pressure, and she ran off down the hall. The purse banged her side as she jogged.

Anthony didn't call after her. He couldn't endure her weeping. It made it real. Christ. This was real. They were going to pour toxic swill into his veins and burn him, burn him to ash, to smoke and vapor. There'd be no trace left of him, and everyone would forget his name, push him from their minds so it didn't hurt. That's how he'd be remembered; his memory would sting, and they'd be rid of him. That's what humans, especially Americans, did with pain: they erected memorials and assigned dates and numbers, burdening stone and calendar so they could forget. They'd carve his eyes out on tombstone to chisel his name, and he'd gaze out from the prison, through the letters, denied mouth and words or even visage to express. He'd have so much to say to the world, and no one would come and lay flowers on his empty grave and listen. All sans Cynthia.

Then, he missed her. Nurse Clumsyhands returned with a tray of heavy syringes and slipped on a pair of rubber gloves. The acrid rubber odor burned Anthony's nose. She picked up the first, held the nipple of the saline bag, and injected a clear fluid. "That's the first of the CHOP." Her hands wavered over the needles and grabbed a round syringe filled with crimson chemical. "Here we go."

"Wait," Anthony said. "Don't. It's going to burn me up. Huff and I'll puff and I'll puff."

Nurse Clumsyhands rolled her eyes, then glanced back at the hall. "I'll get the doctor."

Anthony sighed. He swallowed down a lump in his throat and nodded. "Just get this over with."

The nurse inserted the round syringe into the IV port on his arm and pushed the plunger. The line glowed red as she drained the toxic chemical, pushing the huge dose into Anthony's delicate body. There was a bitter chemical taste right away, and a sickness overwhelmed him, fatigue pushing into his muscles and stomach churning.

"I feel poisoned," he said.

"Yeah. Sorry kid. This is rough stuff. You'll pass it pretty quickly though, but it'll have done its work."

"When will I start throwing my organs up?"

"Depends. Some patients never feel nauseous at all. It'll take several hours for the rest of your stomach lining to die. That's usually when it starts. We can give you a shot of Zofran before you go, but it will only take the edge off."

"Burn my stomach, then move up to my lungs and heart, spreading outwards like a wasp swarm. What other joys can I expect? Intense and erotic dreams with old lost loves who worked at the campus bookstore?"

She unbuttoned the top button of her blouse and sat down in the empty torture chair next to him in the circle. A headache pierced his right eye but it mollified—the first couple of shots.

"It's a three week cycle," she said. "Though symptoms vary from patient. I had a lady who used to eat peanut butter on bread after chemo and never vomited."

"I'm allergic," Anthony said.

"Right. You'll start vomiting tonight, and this is a lot of the stuff. You'll probably vomit for the next couple of days, maybe a week."

"So, no sushi?"

"I wouldn't."

"That's okay. I don't like sushi."

She nodded and folded her hands. The silvery dolphin ring on her finger glinted in the sterile light of the chemo room. "It'll end. You'll be vomiting one minute and then it'll just be gone. And you'll be so hungry. By the next week, your hair will start coming out. The chemo damages the hair follicles. A week later, your white count dies, and you'll have to come in for blood work and Neupogen shots to boost your white cell count. I'll be honest with you. It's going to be bad. Your symptoms will range anywhere from bone pain to hallucinations. Enough of the prednisone, and you'll go mad or suffer rage."

"So, I should cancel my trip to Vegas tonight?"

She giggled, got up and buttoned the top button on her blouse. "Do you need anything, honeybun? I'm going to go smoke a cigarette."

"I'm cool."

She slipped out of the room, leaving Anthony alone in the universe. House sparrows chirped outside the windows, but Anthony felt submerged in a submarine and so far away from the song, wishing he could rewind time and not ask after his fate. The anticipation made it worse, and he clutched Pookie to his chest, seeking comfort, absorbing the gentleness of the seal as he had as a child, scared in his room at night in the dark, calling to his grandmother but never being heard. He got up from the torture chair and walked the length of his plastic tether to the saline bag, his body innocently sipped like a fiery

Martini with no olives. Anthony gazed out onto the parking lot and watched the traffic race by on the highway with no care or appreciation for foreign and estranged events transpiring beyond the comfort and protection of the vehicle's armor. Their whole cosmos—worlds, moons, stars and dark matter—orbited within a circumference of five feet, and they closed their minds to all the souls being born and dying just beyond their selfish gravity. In the sky above, an ashy cloud—the kind born from despair that promised murdering rain that drowns and wind that shatters homes—hunted the sun, caught the edges of the golden eye and swallowed slow and steady, matching the pace the chemo dripped into his veins.

Anthony returned to the torture seat and reached into his khaki pocket, found his cellphone. He started typing a message to Cynthia, asking her to come back, but he didn't think he could endure it if she'd already gotten on the bus, halfway back to her makeup store in Lansdale. He shut the phone. Anthony could do this alone. His grandparents had taken care of him after his mother had died in a car accident on the day he was born, but they'd always been distant to him, tending him from a sense of the obligation of blood, of family. He always thought they'd blamed him and treated him like a dirty relic of their daughter's choice to wreck her own life. They never spoke of his mother—or his father. At first, Anthony accepted that he didn't have parents. His family structure felt normal—though, what really makes a family? It had only been recently, in this time of trial, that he wondered about his father; however, just talking about his late mother to his grandparents caused enough consternation. He just called it a mulligan.

As much as he tried to block it, Cynthia had comforted him and grown so close, even though their friendship had only renewed this last year, meeting again when he had surgery at the Hospital of the University of Pennsylvania, where she volunteered. They'd lost touch during the senior year at Bloomsburg, and destiny had brought them together again in the oddest of places. She'd taken care of him while he recovered, bringing him junk food, sneaking in cheesesteaks and comic books. Not a night went by when she didn't text:

H+K. (Hugs and Kisses)

He never understood the attachment. Cynthia did anything he asked, something he tried not to abuse, though it tempted him. She was so innocent, never betraying a vulgar thought, yet if Anthony asked, she'd talk dirty to him. She'd taken to him with atomic bonds, the kind only great bodies of gravity like suns could defy into fusion. He'd fallen into this bottomless well their first day, and Anthony filled up her every hour, minute, second. She orbited him, and he'd both grown addicted to her company and resentful of her constant cosmic presence. What the hell was she doing here, anyway? Cynthia had won a national award and recognition for her play, "The Secret Life of Truman Capote." The theater department worshipped her, and last he heard, she was writing a play about Andy Kaufman. Anthony assumed she'd be living it up in New York, going to all the openings and attending the swanky cast parties, not running a makeup shop in Lansdale that leaked money like the Titanic. Still, some spirit of those youthful days must've lived in her; she volunteered at the community theater, where she sometimes directed or acted. Something had rained and buried her alive. Some dark night of the soul had befallen Cynthia.

The saline bag dripped into the plastic vein, draining into his arm, and he grew sicker, like his body filled with mercury, quicksilver running through his arteries, clogging his muscles and filling his brain. The apple donut wrecked his stomach, and he burped acid and jelly. He flipped through a Sci-fi entertainment magazine and dozed off in the chair.

An angel hung over him when he opened his eyes, and he assumed it was his mother. Her white robes hung open, exposing her round belly, thighs and breasts hanging like sacks of sand. She opened her arms to him, and only then did he notice, as she floated in the air, that she gazed through him but possessed no eyes, just two empty caves in her face.

He jumped awake.

The sun set. The sparrows quieted. He woke alone to an empty room and flat saline bag, feeling like he swallowed a bottle of Drano.

"You looked so peaceful sleeping," the nurse said, brushing away her blonde hair from her eyes. She reeked of cigarette smoke. "You're about done, anyway. I have that Zofran prescription for you."

He stretched, and a cramp in his arm groaned. He rubbed his shoulder. "Do you have any free samples?"

"Umm. Sorry. I don't think so. Want me to call the doctor?"

"Does he have any free samples?"

"Sorry." She detached the IV line then yanked the tape around the port on his arm. He cringed as she meddled with the inserted needle. She tugged it out then pressed a cotton ball to the stinging wound.

"Call us if you have any of these symptoms." She handed him paperwork. "The doctor will see you on this date. Your friend gone? Is anyone here to take you home?"

"I don't know. I'm surprised she lasted this long."

The nurse nodded and didn't ask any more questions. She drew the curtain between them, keeping out of his personal life. The nurse didn't take her work home with her.

"What's your name?" Anthony asked.

"I'm just a nurse," she said, and carried the discarded saline bag and tubing into the backroom.

Anthony sighed, gave the fraudulent magic painting a nod then left through the side door. Most of the buildings in the generic complex had gone dark, and headlights flashed in a bright line down Route 1 to the left of the parking lot. He checked his phone—still had time to catch the last bus at the mall. Ahead, he saw a figure sitting on the edge of the sidewalk.

"Cynthia?"

"Hi." A chilly wind blew, even in summer's heart, defying the season. She shivered and rubbed her shoulders.

"How long have you been waiting out here?"

She shrugged. "A while, I guess. I've been counting the leaves on the maples. I got to three thousand and—crap."

He smirked. The chemicals overwhelmed his body, and he felt gravity tugging heavier on his frame, pulling on his bones, dragging him into the earth. His head spun, and he nearly fell. She jumped up and grabbed him, fitting into his body like the proper puzzle piece, built to fit. The union comforted him.

"If I fade away, will you find me? Will you pick at the dirt with tweezers and find every last mote? But toss out the heart. Leave those bits on the dusty earth."

"Oh. Don't say that, Anthony. Goddess. Please don't say that."

"You loved madly once?" he asked. "Didn't you?"

"Shhh, Anthony. We need to get you home."

She helped carry him across the parking lot and crossed the Oxford Valley Mall service road, walking half a mile and continents to the bus stop. They reached the Macy's just as the chemo overtook his final defense, and he leaned against the wall. The Number 5 pulled up.

"Come on now, sweetie. Just a few steps." She lifted his shoulder, wrapping her arm around him. Her baggy pursed slapped his bum, propelling him forward, knocking him up the three stairs. She led him to a seat in the middle, where he collapsed and placed his head on the cool window. The bus lurched forward, and the mall melted behind them as it turned onto Oxford Valley Road. She sat close to him but gave him a border of space and sang quietly. The bus rocked and turned, stirring Anthony's stomach. His mouth salivated from nausea, and he swallowed hard again and again.

"You shouldn't be alone in your apartment tonight. I'll stay over."

"It's fine," he said. "I'm going to stay in my old room down the street at my grandparents'."

Her face screwed up in surprise, then her eyes slanted with disappointment. He felt the pressure of her sadness, and it choked Anthony. "My grandparents don't work anymore, so they don't mind watching me."

"I'm just . . . surprised."

"It's the closest link I have to my parents, and though they've denied me any knowledge of them, not one lost hair or photo around the house, I still feel closest to my mother there, in the house where she grew up."

Cynthia nodded. "So what next?"

"Three chemo treatments, then some scans. Doctor Helsinki will review the films for any shrinkage of the tumors."

"And if there isn't?"

"It's a crapshoot. The odds are in the house's favor." The bus rolled again. "Oh God. I'm going to puke."

"Oh no. Oh honey."

His stomach convulsed, and he tasted bitter bile and apple jelly. It pushed up into his nose, filling his sinuses. "Oh God."

"Baby. I didn't bring a basin. I should have. I can be so stupid." She looked about, then dumped the contents out and handed the purse to him just in time. He wrenched open his mouth and emptied his stomach, throwing up bits of apple donut and coffee from that morning. His vomit had a metallic taste that stuck in his nose. He gagged, swallowed back, and when he thought he couldn't throw up anymore, his stomach let loose again. This was just the beginning. Finally, he wiped his mouth with his sleeve.

"I don't know if I can do this," he said.

"You can. You're so strong, even if you don't know it yet. And you have me."

She reached down and picked up her wallet, makeup kit, hairbrush, keys and detritus from the floor and seat, then took the handle of her purse. His vomit washed around in the bag. "Do you still need this?"

"Who sent you?"

She grinned. "It's here if you need it."

The bus roared on, stopping, letting off an old black couple, and continued its way to Lansdale. The bus driver never made a noise, and Anthony wondered if God had given him a face. Sometimes people never look, and there could be a race of the faceless running about, able to conceal all emotion and work nefarious plots or never be hurt in love.

"This might not work," he said.

"Hush now. It's going to." She hesitated and rubbed her eyes with her fist. "We're slaves to reality. Gods. What do we do?"

"Easy," Anthony said. "We change reality."

Cynthia watched Anthony step off the bus at the Townmart shopping center. His grandmother waited with her Lincoln Town Car, idling in the parking lot. She waved, but he didn't notice, and she nearly dropped the vomit bag. It sloshed around, and she gagged when she got a whiff of the sour reek.

Even in the seconds of time and feet of distance since he'd slipped from her aura, disconnecting his physical presence, she ached through her body, digging a sinkhole in her chest and groin. She recognized the pain, knew the sensation from before she'd met Anthony again after his surgery at Penn. In those early moments when they'd found each other, disconnected after college, his ocean poured into the crater that had been left in her when she'd been thrown away and lost. At first, she wondered if she could do it all again and thought it best to stop volunteering and just hide, run far, far away, but they started texting, and she fell into his black hole and fell hard.

The SEPTA beast groaned and slowed into a Rite Aid parking lot several blocks from the Yardley residential section where his grandparents lived. She grabbed her purse, slipped off the bus and dropped the bag into a garbage can outside the darkened store.

She wouldn't bother him. She respected his wishes to be alone. She knew that's how cancer patients got from her own experience with them, though she never understood it. If she were fighting that monster, she'd never want to be alone—and would always suffer solitude even surrounded by parades of other humans.

By the Goddesss, she was pathetic.

She'd stroll up to his house but wouldn't knock on the door, wouldn't bother him. She'd hide out in the front yard and be there with him, sharing her energy, even if he didn't know it. It would help. She did it for him.

She lied.

She was doing this for him and would only stay an hour or two. She didn't want to be alone and far from him.

She felt him running, and a sob choked her throat.

ELVIS DIED ON THE TOILET FOR OUR SINS

At 3:15A.M. Anthony finished erupting green ichor out of his throat and into the trashcan at the side of his old bed. His stomach muscles ached, and his throat had swollen after three days of the torture.

The chemo burned from the inside, hollowing him out, and by the second night, it distorted his thinking, suffused a chemo-fog through his brain, drowning clarity and logic. He'd retreated to Plato, reading of the five elements of the universe, secure in the logic, praying the words like bishops with the Lord's Prayer. Still, the beast hunted, and piece-by-piece, in small motes that don't seem important until tallied, it devoured his sanity.

He fell. Dark matter exploded. Dark energy imploded. M-Theory cracked open below him. The fabric of the universe tore, and he was falling. It stretched him into spaghettification, pulling him into threads.

Anthony washed his mouth with a damp washcloth, sucked on a mint and picked up Plato's *Republic*. His eyes refused to focus, and he guessed at the blurry words that composed the old master's philosophies—none of which mentioned ghosts of dead country virtuosos, which Plato didn't feel fit to mention in his synopsis of the mechanics of the cosmos. Nausea curled like a snake in his stomach and started to shift again.

The bloated singer sat on the edge of his bed, his cheeks bulging from under his sunglasses. "Aww. Come on man," he said with his southern drawl. "You got any donuts? I haven't had a bite in decades."

Anthony held up the book between them, building walls of words and logic to block out the old ghost—the wild hallucination brought on by the bitter chemicals burning his system, pushing him close to death but never over the edge. The crooner had shown up the second night after Anthony suffered his first chemo treatment, but he refused to acknowledge him while throwing up every thirty minutes. The vomiting had slowed to once an hour, and Anthony felt grateful for the relief, but between regurgitation, he had no diversion and became vulnerable to the ghost.

"God. Will you just let me read? This is Plato. He founded civilization. You diminished it."

"That's cold, man. But that's all right. I know you're just surly and down because you're sick. Would a song cheer you up? I know it used to pick up my baby girl, Lisa Marie, when she got a cold. She's my pride and joy, my baby girl. I'd show you a photo, but they don't let us keep them. But that's all right. Hey man. I can still remember her as clear as a crystal river as a little girl. Here. I know which one."

He picked a guitar out of a black void below the bed and cradled it atop his white outfit decorated with sequins, laying it on his swollen gut. He wore sunglasses even in the darkness of Anthony's old bedroom, and candlelight licked along the black lenses, flaring down his pale face of chicken skin. Elvis dangled his fingers over the strings, tuning at first, plucking the right chords and singing the notes. Anthony pushed the book closer to his face and climbed through the words, the black hills and valleys of ink, fighting the fatigue in his head, the cloud over his mind that poured from his ears and smeared the old bookshelves and dresser and bed. The dark mist suffused through the air, distorting the sea green painted walls, greasing the old photos of him in Little League, the trophies and newspaper articles—no more after the age of eight, when he finally told his grandfather he wasn't having any fun playing.

"Okay now. Here goes." He played the strings, ringing chords, playing somber song. The soft lullaby flowed through Anthony, and a chasm ripped wide below him in the glacier on which he slept; he fell deeper into the crevice and flailed about the bed, padding around the flannel sheets, feeling the firm matter, but still he clung on to the bed, afraid he might fall. He clung to Pookie and held the white seal like a life preserver. The music leaked into the holes in his soul, through the cracks and forgotten mouse tunnels. His grandmother had never sung him a lullaby, and Anthony forced the rush of summoned emotion back, burying it in the yard like he used to as a kid—digging holes deep into the earth with the garden hoe then lying in the hole, letting the earth absorb the blackness, grounding it like lightning. He'd fill the hole before his grandparents got home from work. Sometimes he tried to bury himself.

"Please. King. Just don't."

"Just singing my songs, man."

Anthony reached to the guitar but didn't complete the circuit, terrified he might actually feel the wood, the lacquer, the residual vibration moving through the instrument from the singer's soft midnight melodies—and know he had fallen off the edge of the world.

"You're just a phantom. A hallucination. My body is going through such shit right now. Goblin, be gone!"

"From my end, man, you're the hallucination."

Anthony shut his eyes and focused his thoughts on far-off points, on the house cabin in Maine where his grandparents had taken him for summers on Highland Lake. He dove into cool water, feeling the wet seaweed slither along his toes as he kicked and filled his ears with the lake, blocking the music. He opened his eyes, and Elvis sang.

"I can't control you. You're like a dream."

"Nothing's real," Elvis said between lyrics. "We're not the dreamers. We're living the dream, man."

"Please stop singing."

Elvis began the song again. His hand fell like wind on the strings. The sweet melody pried a door wide, and Anthony leaned against it, struggling to keep it shut and locked.

"If you stop, we'll chat," Anthony said.

Elvis holstered his guitar then slicked back his dry black hair, smearing grease on his hand. He curled his upper lip and smiled. "Well that's all right, then."

"If my grandmother hears me talking to air, she'll have me committed," Anthony whispered. "She's afraid of me now. I hear her hovering outside my door sometimes, but she's scared to come in."

Elvis got up from the bed and sat back on the computer chair at Anthony's old desk, and his bulbous body nearly snapped the handles from the frame. He adjusted his sunglasses.

"I can't stand your music," Anthony said.

"That's fine, man. That's America. Land of the free."

Anthony nodded. "The old dream. You can't control dreams. I try not to dream. But it's getting harder. I feel something coming for me like a comet or cosmic ray blast. This treatment is torture. The Gestapo wants info, and they're burning me every day, breaking me down."

"Do you believe in God, son? In the good Lord Jesus? I prayed everyday for him to take care of my baby girl. I prayed to the King in Heaven. The real King. I'm just a pretender, man."

"That's the only thing my grandparents ever told me about my mother. 'She's in heaven with the angels.' I know it was a car accident, a truck crash on I-95. She was bringing me home from the hospital after I was born."

A wave of nausea twisted and squeezed Anthony's stomach, and he curled up, taking the position. His throat and ribs ached from the marathon vomiting, and he clutched the garbage can, aiming his mouth. He tasted more green bile, and his throat pulsed.

"Aww, man. Hey, I'll let you alone for now. Take it easy, man."

Anthony waved at the hallucination. "A goddamn phantom telling me about Jesus," he said between vomits.

Cynthia held the rusty razorblade to the sickly beams in the dim and broken streetlamp. She'd found it in her father's stuff after he'd taken off for the last time, re-upping in the Navy, sailing off to sunny shores off the Philippines or some sweet, sultry, sun-sinning port, seeking his bliss. Cynthia had maintained the blade over the years, sanded the creeping rust, polished the stainless steel and sharpened and sharpened it again, shortening the blade by near half an inch. She gripped its edge, just able to hold it now, and pushed up her pink sleeve, exposing the soft underflesh of her arm. Scars intersected along the bone-white skin to the base of her elbow, along the fields of freckles, each carefully spaced an inch, meticulously planned and designed like a tattoo or body piercing.

Cynthia leaned back against the streetlamp, hiding in the shadows, keeping along the exterior of shallow light. The lamp flickered off, casting her in darkness, and her body eased. Then it shot back on and cast her back to the whiteness of the world. In the neighbor's yard, she spotted a baby robin squirming in the manicured grass. She set the razor down to retrieve the bird, probably fallen from a nest high in the mulberry trees that grew in front of the extended houses, some of them as large as castles, housing the wealthy of Bucks County. She crossed the lawn, hoping she wouldn't trip a motion detector and get arrested, then Cynthia knelt before the weak creature, admiring gray feather stubs and smooth head, and reached to save him. Wait. If she got her scent on the poor thing, its mother might not take it back. It was dead, though, if she left it. Foxes roamed these streets by night. She'd seen one on the second night, flashing its green eyes in moonlight. She pulled back her arm. The poor blind infant gave a feint howl.

"Please. Please. I can't." She rushed back to her hole to the left of the shallow light from the broken streetlamp. She found her razor and held it to the prescribed location on her arm.

She should go to him. He'd said to stay home, that he'd be fine and didn't want to be seen like this. He was lying. Cynthia knew it. She understood Anthony, recognized his stoic shielding. In the silence between denials, she could hear him shouting to her, sans words, begging her to come in, but she had to respect his wishes. Still, she could be near. She'd climb that maple tree to his window, just to see him, to know he was okay. Days gone without seeing him raked over her in a stream of nails.

"Goddess, forgive me," she recited, matching her ritual, and pressed the razor into the cotton flesh, slicing from equal sides of the bone. The sensitive flesh burned, and the pain spread down into her elbow and up to her wrist. Relief traveled with it, and she sighed, exhaling all her held air, until her lungs ached. Cutting felt like closing a circuit from a lightning rod to ground, and dirty water, drowning her, cleared. She could see again.

She urged to do another line, but she'd hold it in reserve, just in case she couldn't make it through the night. Cynthia sighed and whispered a private prayer, standing below the streetlamp outside of Anthony's grandparents' house: "No one will love this body. I rot. Goddess." She gripped the necklace dangling down her neck. "Forgive this fat idiot. I won't let you die. I promise this to my Goddess. I'll keep you breathing and your heart beating. You'll fly. We'll fly so high."

A few days—or centuries—burned up in a dry, wild burn. The old people in his house had carried him somewhere: a pale, white room, that reeked of plastic and chemicals and stale coffee.

"My name," he said. "I lost it somewhere." Fire burned his head. He set sail in a firelake. His body roasted and dripped savory juices. He lay alone in the isolation room at Saint Mary's Medical Center. Only a moment ago, he'd been lying in his bed, then he just materialized there. Heavy, green paper gowns and masks draped over the nurses, hiding their human identity, erasing their mouths. Did they even wield mouths? Each carried melancholy eyes, emphasized when they'd concealed the rest of their faces.

"You're not human!" he yelled at one of the nurses. She carried a syringe.

"This is Neupogen. It'll boost your white cells."

"Don't you dare. Bad medicine. It'll rip away my soul. My head's falling off and rolling away. Where's Doctor Elvis? Gods, I hate that shit."

He tried to fight her off, but had no strength. The fever burned his eyes blind. She stabbed his arm, and an ache shot through his muscles, merging into his chest.

"Worms! You shot me full of worms. God damn wasps eating me."

His hands morphed to flippers. His body stretched and bleached white. Whiskers grew from his fat jowls, and he honked. He turned into a seal and swam into the sea with the fish and the sweet, malicious little otters. Plato waited for him below the sea. Plato bled Aether.

Bobby Darin sang to him of a place beyond the sea, crooning from the darkness. Pure darkness. Smooth and starless. He'd come home to oblivion, and the pain had floated to his skin and evaporated. Sweet, mother dark.

On Sunday, he put on his best suit—black jacket, slacks and leather shoes. His grandmother kept coming in to check on him. She wobbled into the room and held out a bandana.

"Anthony. Hair is everywhere. It's like we have a cat."

Bare spots exposed the back of his scalp where he'd rubbed his head on the pillow. It hadn't fallen out like he'd thought it would—loose and easy. The hair still clung to his scalp, but the bond had weakened. A little tension would yank it free, and he'd been shedding everywhere, covering his pillow and bed.

"You just can't go to church like that," she said. "Wear this."

He took the red bandana from her and wrapped it tightly around his head, feeling silly, like one of those Russian old mothers, a Babushka.

"When we come home, I'm cutting that mess off." She averted her eyes when she held out the bandana, careful not to look at him. She hadn't made direct visual contact since he'd come home weeks ago from his first treatment. Anthony dressed. They piled into his grandfather's minivan and drove to Saint Joseph's the Worker—where they'd taken him every Sunday, to listen to the talking priests and to drink the talking wine.

They sing of death. Apostles built a faith that worshipped the world to come, the life beyond life. They couldn't comprehend. How could they understand? Before, arrogant Anthony believed he'd understood, that death existed and could consume any second, to darkness, oblivion, but he hadn't, really. A device in the mind blocked true understanding to prevent madness. Now, he understood true, and it drove him insane. He heard the flutter of angel wings.

The power and the glory.

They stepped into the church, genuflected before the tabernacle and bowed before the altar and crucifix hanging above with some poor bloke nailed to the wood. The Romans did that from time-to-time to people they didn't like, but not all of them got worshipped two-thousand years anon. Father Gabriel stepped before the altar, his hands out, palms open to heaven, and the church broke its foundations, snapping its moorings, and took flight. It hovered and chugged, struggling against Earth's gravity, and the people prayed and believed against logic, fueling its engines, feeding it wafers and wine to be transformed to flesh and blood. The temple gained power and broke its earthly tethers. The parishioners sang in praise of the engines.

Glory to God on the highest.

"The power and the glory," Anthony recited like a trained parrot.

They sang and hummed and chanted, falling to their knees, sitting, then standing, following a choreographed dance in worship. Stars flashed by in white, streaking pulses, that shined through the stained-glass windows of angel wings and slinking devils, of hoary gates and red pits that fired.

"We're flying to Heaven," Anthony said, his voice sweet and childlike.

"Shh," Grandmother said—adorned in a flowery dress. His grandfather wore a brown suit, probably the one he'd be buried in.

Anthony joined their song, and the vibrations of their merged larynxes pulsed through him, filling the hollow the chemo-torture carved. He recognized many of them, knowing them as he'd grown up in Yardley, many of them friends of his grandparents. Grandmother smiled sweetly at the community, accepting them all in visage, but he'd heard her at night on the phone, gossiping, telling secret stories of affairs and clandestine alcoholics and rowdy children in jail. Each of them sinned and felt little remorse; yet, each Sunday they came as he'd come to recite the incantations, to press the buttons, jump through the ceremonies to do maintenance on their immortal souls with the same dignity and reverence as taking their SUVs for an oil change.

They believed, here and now, and sang of a man who

rose from the dead. They screeched for a sky-god on heaven, high, who'd sent them his only son, a man who died on the cross for their sins and cheated by coming back. Christ had battled the forces of darkness, spit in Satan's eye, come back on Easter and then ascended. They believed in a superhuman, the apotheosis of their qualities, who dwelled and controlled the vacant and massive cosmos—full of other worlds and playgrounds of physics. They believed they'd be rewarded for their faith with eternal life, but Anthony had never seen Heaven on a star map.

As a child, Anthony had fought to believe. He'd snuck away comic books under his bed, so his grandmother couldn't find them—Superman, mostly. At night, when he was supposed to be praying and reading from the Bible—one passage a night—he'd sneak his DC comics and find more faith in the Man of Steel than the Man of God.

Yet, they believed. Had they willed this God into life? Had humans created the concept, like an empty bowl, then bled life into him through centuries of mindless worship, giving themselves over? Was this faith?

Lines queued for taking the wafer, the Host. His grandmother got up, and Elvis sat down next to Anthony. The pew groaned from his girth.

"Hey, man. Got to church, I see. Good for you, man."

"Oh. You're back. God. You're not real."

Grandmother returned to the pew—now full of new life and redemption, having swallowed her weekly ticket to Heaven. "Are you talking to me?"

"No," Anthony said. "Not you."

She nodded and didn't inquire.

"I was real," Elvis said. "Why can't I be real now? I'm a spirit, and is my existence any less probable than the existence of the living? Just because you can't always see what's invisible—"

"I'm trying to pray. You died on the toilet, you know. Fat and full of pills."

Elvis ignored him. "Hey, man. I'm writing a new song about dark matter. You want to hear?" He pulled his guitar from behind his white cape. The sequins glittered in the low-hanging lights—the eyes of the God, watching. Anthony choked on the sweet innocence:

"Oh, Stephen Hawking!
"I feel the cosmos burning.
"Spinning and spinning.
"Those particles keep on flying.

"Dark, dark, dark,
"you're gonna balance the forces.
"Dark matter, forming.
"No eyes can see you a'glowing.

"Darkened, darkened,
"dark matter."

"I like it, but I just don't dig your music. And you're not real."

His grandmother sighed and whispered to his grandfather, something about taking him home. Anthony bowed his head, ashamed for embarrassing his grandmother. "Why are you bothering me, Elvis?"

"I'm as real as you are, man. You've just decided I'm not. But, if you believed. They all believe in him."

Anthony remembered what Cynthia had said about magic, about how metaphor, infused with belief, could change reality. He didn't care for that logic, since reality would become a personal responsibility. Yet, it felt relevant, the more the thought rattled around in his head

47

like an acorn, easing his spiritual torment, naming the void opened in him when the torture had slowly devoured his mind. He'd found new philosophy, built on his suffering. So it came to be, and he didn't quite understand it yet, as all good religion needs time to grow daisies and daffodils. A sign would come, and he'd be enlightened.

"I'm not real," Anthony whispered, folding his hands in prayer.

"Elvis died on the toilet for your sins," the priest conducting Mass said.

"Come on, Anthony. We're taking you home." His grandmother led him to the door, making apologies to everyone. "He's having chemo," she said. "Not right."

"Elvis has left the building!" Elvis said.

THE SCARECROW WATCHING

I'm falling," the stranger said. His face had burned away, leaving a cake of ash. The ash blew away, evacuating a hole. Then the hole vanished into another hole, creating a paradox. The paradox sucked time and space, drawing it into a nether zone, an empty place that cannot exist. He lay next to her in the field down from his sick house, where he died several times, losing himself, being burned away.

The void explained the effects of the chemo:

The chemotherapy is designed to kill fast growing cells. This is a special cell type in your body. Cancer is a fast growing cell. Alas, it kills all fast growing cells, even the normal ones, the healthy ones that you need to live. Your hair falls out because the hair follicle is a fast growing cell. You vomit out your insides because your stomach lining is composed of fast growing cells. Your sperm dies, so you're not making babies. And your white count vanishes, so you have no protection against disease.

Someone watched them from the fields, a man with open arms, hidden in the darkness. A nebulous night occluded the silver orb. The man watched her with judgmental eyes, and she felt it criticizing, passing judgment, casting down verdicts on Cynthia. It gazed at her stomach—her fat, bulbous stomach making her hideous. She scratched at her arms and heavy gut. This shirt always made her look huge. She wanted to shed this body, try again, cut open her arms and spill out the putrid liquid that filled her. He was dying because she wasn't worth being loved. God had decided. If only she wasn't so fat and ugly. The man in the field judged, calling her unlovable, unworthy.

The empty-man's hand shook. Cynthia reached to take it, but he pulled it away. "I don't want to be touched." It kicked her in the gut, but she sucked back her tears, trying to be strong, handling his mood swings.

"Why won't you take my comfort?" she asked.

"I'm a void," the emptiness responded. "You can't comfort a void."

"You could, if you wanted to. I could help you. Why did you put up a wall?"

"I didn't."

"That's a damn lie."

The void nodded. "Truth is dark matter. It's gray matter. We're all a bunch of gray matter, pooled up together."

"But, you're a void."

"And a contradiction." A cloud passed from the face of the swollen moon, shedding its stolen sunlight down on the abandoned and derelict wheat field. Farmers had forgotten the dirt. The crops grew wild, without a hand to harvest. The light illuminated the burlap face of a scarecrow. It wore a flannel shirt and old khakis. Straws and sodden newspaper fell from the gaps of its outfit. Old, metal hangers framed its body. A scarecrow had not been required in this field for decades. No one cared if ravens fed upon the wheat and corn, yet the scare-man, the wormhead, appeared freshly made, newly woven of clothing, only slightly worn. The crows ruled these forgotten quarters and winged the cloisters at liberty, sans interference. How does one disrupt a creature of the sky?

"When is your next chemo-treatment?"

He'd gone through the cycle, throwing up for days. She'd been over to see him a few times, but most of the time, Anthony didn't want company. Sometimes, she just waited below his window, hiding behind the bushes, in case Anthony called for her, so she'd be there. Cynthia didn't know if it was for him or more for her, Cynthia's own need, her desperation. She had taken a straight razor with her, her old favorite, the one she used in high school when the darkness overwhelmed her, strangled her. A few times, in her need, she had pressed it to her soft flesh but hadn't cut. She had grown up from this, hadn't she? Still, it comforted her to hold the soft blade, to feel its cool metal between her fingers. Cynthia needed it and allowed herself the indulgence. She also had a small bag of pot in her purse. She kept texting Anthony that he should use it for the nausea, but he wouldn't respond.

Then, the vomiting stopped, and finally he texted her. They watched new episodes of *Doctor Who* together. He'd been saving them. That night, Anthony burned with fever, and she called his oncologist. They ordered him to the hospital and admitted him. His grandparents were tired and went to sleep, instead, and she took care of Anthony. Why couldn't he see how much she loved him? For four days, he lingered in reverse isolation, not allowed to be touched. Cynthia had to wear a mask and gloves and a paper apron every time she went into the room. Tonight, she'd picked him up at the hospital after they'd restored his white count medications. He didn't want to go home, and instead, they got off from the bus then walked to the field. He looked improved, stronger. The color had returned to his face, but his dark hair had thinned. She could handle that. Then, he reached to his forehead and rubbed his eyebrows off his skin. She could tolerate it to that point.

Its mouth moved—Mister Straw. "It's the Autumn People!" Cynthia said, grabbing a tuft of grass, pulling up wild onions. The stench burned her eyes.

"Who are they?" the void asked. How did emptiness have a voice? Why did it seek knowledge, have curiosity? She wanted to be a void. Then, she'd slough her feelings and fly with the ravens, on wing with the black feathers, the flying ambassadors of night.

I see you. She felt the scarecrow watching, judging. It had always been there, in many fields, existing in many planes.

"They exist in-between. They live in all the dark places. They dwell in the autumn. They're lost people. Fading. Don't you see it? Did the cancer blind you, too?" She pointed at the scarecrow.

"It's too dark," the void said. "I can't see anyone."

"You're making that up! You just don't want to see him."

The void sighed, showing he still had breath. "I don't want to do this anymore."

"I can take you home. You should sleep, anyway."

"No. I mean. I never want to go through that again."

She reached for the void's hand again, but Cynthia thought better of it. Why set herself up to be hurt . . . this time? "I know, baby. It's rough. I've seen you. I can't imagine how hard it is on you."

"No. You really can't. They all tell me how strong I am for going through this. My grandmother says she couldn't do it."

"I don't know how you are doing this. I know I couldn't. I'd just let myself die. I admire you so much."

The words sounded false as she said them: bad dialogue in a play written by a child. She couldn't help saying it, like someone had pressed a button and played a recording. She protected herself with the words.

"Please shut your fucking mouth," he said and jactitated, twisting on the ground. "Stop. Just stop!"

"What?" she asked. "What did I do? I thought that would help."

"It's not what I want," the void said. His face returned. Eyes focused. A nose defined. Lips grew on his mouth. She recognized Anthony again, her long love and need. She nearly got up and ran. It was easier when he didn't have a face. It didn't hurt so much, then.

"What are you talking about?"

"The *chemo*. It's a long shot, the whole goddamn thing. And it hurts. It hurts so much. I don't want to spend my last few months letting them burn me. I'll never forgive me."

"I'll never forgive you," she said.

"I don't care," Anthony said, and Cynthia hoped her friend was lying. "You don't have to live this way. I do. And not for much longer. I want to accept this. I'm struggling. It hurts, Cynthia. And I'm just doing it for all of you, because I don't want to disappoint you."

"Why don't you want to live?"

He paused and considered it. Cynthia tried not to look at the scarecrow. "It's not that I want to die," he said. "No one wants to die. I'm just accepting that it has come."

"But, it's too early!"

"Who says? I mean, who really determines that? What is a good age to die? How many sands are mandatory before you can leave the world? I'm good, Cynthia. I've had some life. There's a lot of matter in the universe that never has that experience. Whole suns are born, then explode, without knowing what it's like to cry or laugh or eat a Whopper or fuck like rabbits."

"Do you want to fuck me like a rabbit?" she asked, pressing her hand to her stomach, hiding her fat. "Would that keep you here?"

"You're not listening to me. Why is no one listening to me? You're hearing whatever you want to hear because you can't handle it."

She played with the razor in her sweater pocket. "I'm trying to tell you you're strong. That you're not like me. You are a hero, like in a legend."

"It's pressure. You all want me to be something I'm not."

"But, you are!"

He jumped up, unsteady on his feet, and nearly collapsed. She got up to brace him. "I'll catch you," she said.

"I don't want to be caught. I've had enough."

"So, that's it?" Her stomach cramped at his words, pulsing down into her loins like she was menstruating. Cynthia bit her lip and looked up, scanning for the Scarecrow. He no longer hung on his cross. Had she imagined him? She might have. Since Anthony had gotten sick, she had seen lots of phantasms and portents of the end of the world. She was becoming positively biblical, which was odd for a lady of the Goddess.

"Yep."

"Yep? You maniac. Son of a bitch." She went to leave him, but paused, giving him a chance to repent, to protect her feelings. He saw Cynthia waiting and said nothing. Nothing. Never. "Son of a bitch," she said, and did her best to leave him without storming off. She just couldn't wait around, watching him die. That was too much to ask, and she left him in the field alone, among the abandoned wheat and sought the scarecrow. She found the straw-man sitting on a bank of white yarrow flowers, hanging at the stalks, ass in the mud.

"You heard?" she asked the scarecrow.

"I am the sentry of the fields. I have watched humans and their farms since you began to plant and harvest."

"Why didn't you say anything?"

"And what could I say?" The scarecrow spoke with a Russian inflection. "I have watched that boy for a long time. I knew him just after his birth."

"So, you've been here, too. When he got chemo. You've been near."

"And it sounds as if you're leaving," said the scarecrow.

"Why do you watch us, sweet Tolya?" Cynthia asked, unmasking him. She knew the rules: you were never to mention names while in character. But she wanted to know his motivations. Tolya had always been a secretive sort, never exposing his plans or motivations; and Cynthia suspected that they ran deep into pain. Something had wounded this man, driven nails through his hands, and he was ever paying a debt.

"I watch the world," he said, with his typical Slavic aloofness.

"That's not enough," she said. "And you play in the world, keeping us in your eye. You're like Touchstone."

"*As You Like It*?" he asked. "I performed it in New York when I was a kid. My first play. I was meant for the part of Oliver, but they said I spoke funny. So, they made me a clown."

"I bet you were happier as the clown."

"Perhaps . . . " And he grinned like a cat with a mouse under lip.

"There's a devil in you, Tolya."

"The devil shows its head in you. You are being selfish."

"Why should I stay to watch him kill himself?" She pulled up a stalk of yarrow. It's what you did in natural places when you were stressed: ripped out the green. It would grow back. It always grew back. The fronds dangled from her hands and rained down onto the bank like Anthony's eyebrows.

"Aren't we all killing ourselves?" the scarecrow asked. "It is just more obvious with Anthony." The scarecrow took off his gloves. Scars crossed the gentle skin of his palms and lumps rose under the surface on the back of both hands. His gnarled hands grew like tree branches from an ancient and dying oak—scaly brown and of rotting bark, spots up and down the flesh.

"He's right, too," the scarecrow said. "There is no limit or standard life. We all have our clocks."

"Where learned you that oath, fool?" Cynthia quoted the play and put her head on his shoulder.

"I'm old and stupid," he said.

"But, just shut your mouth, now. My heart is breaking."

He rubbed her shoulder. "You'll go back to him?"

"I can't leave him."

"Not yet. Not yet."

"Listen to you," Cinderfield said to Tolya. He strolled along the field, glowing in the moonlight, translucent, nearly invisible. Tolya couldn't tell if he was real, but the devil felt real. Somewhere in his heart, he could feel the darkness. Not everyone believes in the devil, but they all know he's real. "Going on like that."

"Just leave me be!" Tolya said. The young lovers,

though Anthony was too blind to see Cynthia, had both left, off to separate corners. Tolya didn't doubt that they'd figure out.

"I can't ever leave you be," Cinderfield said. "I am your fate, your punishment. You won't let me leave. You think I want to be doing this with my time? You won't forgive yourself, so I have to stay. You've given your whole life to this boy. And he doesn't even know it."

"A life for a life," Tolya said.

"Learn to move on, dude!"

DOCTOR HUMINGDINGER & HIS STAGE OF THE WILDS

"**Ja,**" said Doctor Humingdinger, speaking in guttural Dainglish like a stereotypical German character in an old movie. "I'm seeing *gut* progress! Young man. *Ja.* I can safely say you will live a very, very long time through." The doctor stroked his beard, tugging on the edges. The corner peeled off, and the doctor pressed it back to his jowl, securing it. The doctor held a sexy figure for a man, Anthony noticed. Must have been a genetic thing.

"Well . . . I'm surprised, Doctor . . . did you say *Humingdinger*?"

"*Ja.* Doktor Henreich Von Humingdinger. I got my doctorate in medicine at the Berlin Polytechnique in the '60s. I climbed over the Berlin Wall and escaped with my mother and six brothers, all tucked away in a suitcase."

Anthony cracked a smile and stifled a laugh. "Berlin Wall, huh? Far out." A star on high, burned bright, stinging his eyes, and he adjusted the rim of his brown fedora to block it. He'd taken to wearing the hat since his hair had fallen out several weeks ago, giving up that washerwoman bandana his grandmother had insisted on. The Alopecia bothered her, and she'd kept asking when his treatments would be done, anxious to have all that vomiting and sickness out of her clean house.

For the first week after she'd shaved it off, he'd reach for it mindlessly to play in his curls, and it would draw tears when he couldn't find it. Just when it started to grow back, he'd have another treatment and lose all the fuzz. What had been weirder, was rubbing his forehead, and brushing away his eyebrows into fine hairs.

Cancer separated him from the others, and everyday, he felt a little less human or a little more; he couldn't tell if he was coming back or going away, and figured he'd find out in the end.

"Ja. Berlin wall. All very exciting. Before that, during the v'war, we hid thirty-five Jueden in our kitchen cupboard. One day, the Gestapo came—"

"Herr Doctor?" Anthony interrupted.

"*Ja?*"

Anthony smirked again, trying not to giggle. He calmed himself, looking away from the obvious props, out of place, ignoring the wide-open nature of the office. He focused on the desk, the doctor, and tried to take the visit with his new oncologist seriously. "Has anyone ever told you that you're just like a stereotype from an old war movie? It's almost downright offensive."

The doctor nodded. "A little too much?"

"A bit."

"*Ja.* Well." The doctor got up from the desk and strolled around the open office, made up of only the desk, the chair in front of said desk and a couple of rusty file cabinets in the back. A fake novelty phone graced the desk along with a cracked picture frame. He stepped around the side of the desk to the edge of his open office and knelt down by a worn shoebox then lifted back the lid. He fondled the contents as you would a baby, cooing and kissing at the air. The box chirped, and then he replaced the lid. Anthony ignored it, trying to focus.

The doctor came over to Anthony and pressed the mouth of a stethoscope to his back. "Now, breathe for me, young man."

Anthony inhaled deep, then exhaled.

"*Ja. Gut.* Very *gut*!" He returned to his desk, picked up a large envelope nearly half his size, opened it and pulled out transparent x-rays. He hung them up to the ominous lights above, and Anthony's eyes wandered to the trail of curtain hanging in view. He looked away. Live in the moment. Reality is tangible.

"*Ja.* All of your scans are normal. You are a very lucky young man. I'd call it a miracle, if I wasn't a Goethe-worshipping atheist."

"Still offensive."

The doctor's beard peeled away, and he pressed it hard to the cheek. "Darn it," Doctor Humingdinger said, in a lighter and feminine voice. "I didn't have a lot of time to prepare."

Anthony leaned back in the chair and crossed his legs. His left hip ached again, matching the pain moving up into his ribcage. Chemo damaged the nerves, and he'd endured long, burning nights. He slipped a tall bottle of Morphine Sulfate out of his shirt pocket, opened the lid, stuck two white pills in his mouth and swallowed them down with a sip from a water bottle.

"So!" Doctor Humingdinger said, voice returning to its contributed normal. "My diagnosis is that Doctor Helsinki was a complete quack." He cupped his hands in front of his face like a duck's beak. "Quack. Quack. Quack. Not only do I see a complete reduction in the tumors, but also you have a good and strong heart. A noble young man all about, and damn sexy, too. And you can't argue with we Germans. With science, V'e rule da Vorld!"

"I'm not doing this anymore, if you can't take it seriously."

Doctor Humingdinger sighed. The beard cracked again, and he let it fall, revealing a soft chin and gentle lips.

"Sorry, Anthony," Cynthia said. She tugged the rest of the beard away. Her gentle visage revealed from under the spirit glue and hair. "I've never played a German before. I played Cordelia once, but they hanged me in the end. We were trying to go the other way with this one."

"I feel like a fucking moron," he said.

"Anthony," Cynthia said. "This is the heart of magic. Will. The universe has played you a bad hand, but we can change it. We just have to believe in it, create the metaphor and play the ritual."

He scoffed and stepped off his stage. His left leg ached as he descended the few stairs at stage-left, a pain that had started after the last chemo treatment. He'd forgotten to mention it to Doctor Helsinki that morning during his follow-up.

"Maybe it's too soon for you," she said. "You need some time. I know. I've seen it. But you can't believe him. He's a doctor, not a deity."

"He's the closest thing we have to a God." His foot hit the last step, and he toppled to the side, grabbing the stage for support. The morphine bottle slipped from his pocket and rolled on the floor. Cynthia ran to help him, but he snarled his lip at her.

"I should just accept it. Physics is physics. Reality is solid."

"It's all in flux, Anthony."

"God. Don't you ever stop? Fuck."

He picked himself up, and she hovered nearby, ready to assist, but not reaching out. She'd respected his space, and he sighed and leaned on the stage, resting his leg.

"I just don't want to get my hopes up," he whispered.

"Oh, honey. Believe in me. I've seen miracles. Doctors can be wrong. One day, I'll take you through the recovery room to talk to some of the patients who were given death sentences. They kept positive attitudes. They knew that nothing is forever."

"Thermodynamics."

"Sounds like magick."

"Nothing is nothing. Nothing is forever. Absolute zero. Total efficiency."

"Science and magick. They make love. That's so sweet. It's so sad you can't feel it."

He got up and took her arm. "That's just it, Cynthia. I'm starting to. I can feel reality now, like a fabric, a quilt. It can be changed. Fuck it. You're right. It's all leaving me, and I held onto it, sailing a rotten ship. All my life, I believed in a system of rules. I can walk in this world, and see all these other worlds in orbit. I feel like I'm coming undone."

"Shamans believe that." She stroked his shoulder and slipped off her lap coat, then removed the skullcap, setting free her long, thick hair. Heavy makeup smeared her face, still, covering her feminine, gentle aspect. "The tangible nature of reality. Nothing is real. It's just perceived by the human mind, labeled and cataloged. We define the rules of interaction with the world, based on observation, then pass these chains to our children.

He tapped his foot on the stage. "Just molecules, arranged. We can reshape it, cut into it, and this stage becomes a boat. We'd sail away."

She nodded and changed shoes.

"We can make pain go away," he said.

"Make pain go away."

"Find out what's real, beneath it all. The prime numbers that can't be changed. The bones of reality."

"Ja!" she said.

"God, that's offensive."

She giggled. The theater lights came on, revealing rows and rows of empty seats cascading back into the darkness, drawing on ever and ever. She hugged him, wrapping him up in her arms. He declined to raise his arms to hug her back. "We can beat this, Anthony. Reality is tangible."

"You're going to rip me apart."

In the audience, a single pair of hands clapped. "Very entertaining," spoke a disembodied voice.

"It's medicine," defended Cynthia.

"And horseshit."

"Excuse Tolya's fickle Russian soul," Cynthia told Anthony.

The old actor got up from the far seat on the left and limped up to the stage. He grabbed a broom from the front row and swept up the aisle. Even though indoors, he still wore an English wool cap, and the light exposed the grooves and tight skin of his face, as if he'd been buried in the Valley of the Kings, dug up after two thousand years, soaked in pickle juice, then buried for another couple of centuries before Howard Carter dug him up, expecting gold and riches but only getting the old sour Russian actor.

"It's not good acting because you don't believe it," Tolya said. "I know good acting. I starred in *The Tragic History of the Life and Death of Doctor Faustus*. Christopher Marlowe. He was a Russian poet born in Elizabethan English. Very tragic."

Anthony waited for Cynthia to take the bait. They'd argued many nights over poets and Russian literature. Sweat beaded on her face and mixed with the makeup, streaking charcoal down her chin. She sighed, exhausted, and let the mad Russian win this round. She'd be back— ever tenacious.

"Tolya, is the AC fixed?" Anthony asked.

"It was never broken. It's freezing in this place!"

"Must be the Siberian genes in your body."

"Don't mock. I had an uncle in Siberia. He was a male prostitute under Stalin, maybe even *under* Stalin, a family legend says. I think about Uncle Yori often when I drive trucks when the plays are not pay so good. A better life maybe."

Cynthia slipped from Anthony and climbed the stage. She knelt by the box, checked on its contents, fidgeting with towels inside.

"Got an angel in the box?" Anthony asked.

"I do. A little angel." She picked up the shoebox and carried it to Anthony, cradling it like a baby in the curve of her shoulder. A tiny bird, not more than a week old, nestled in a white towel. It studied Anthony with black ink-spilled discs and raised its head in response to the light.

"I didn't know you were pregnant," Anthony said. "Mazel tov!"

"Stop it," she said, giggling. She rubbed its belly along its feather buds.

"Where did you find it?"

She dithered and focused on the bird. Finally, she said, "In a neighbor's yard, lying in the grass. At first, I didn't want to touch it because the mother wouldn't take it back. But, there are foxes on the night streets. The poor thing wouldn't have survived the dawn."

The infant responded to her touch and curled in the warmth of Cynthia's skin and blood, drawing life from her life. She grinned and swayed her shoulders, flickering like a new mother. Anthony backed from mother and child, breaking his gaze and stepping into the shadows of the poorly lit theater. For each joy there was a debt of melancholy, and when the cosmos balanced out accounts, the moon was going to crash on Cynthia.

"You should have left it to die."

"Anthony! What?"

"You're going to bleed. It's going to pulverize your bones and grind your organs. You love it. It's going to kill you."

She pulled the box away in a protective stance. Her eyes sliced into Anthony.

"I know you're going through a lot, Anthony. I'm trying to be patient. But, I've just never heard of such cruelty, before. How could I leave it there to die?"

"Nature is cruel."

"But it doesn't have to be."

"You think you're helping."

Behind them, Tolya plugged in a vacuum cleaner and piloted it up the aisle. He shook his head, listening to them argue. He pushed it by the stage, avoiding a stack of boxes—kilts Cynthia had ordered for a Fall production of Brigadoon. They raised their voices over the appliance's groan.

"My baby will grow strong and take flight," she said. "The Goddess told me. I prayed for days. When I'm not thinking about mundane crap, I pray. I worship in my sleep. Under each breath, I'm begging. If I don't stop, if I keep the record skipping, maybe she'll hear me. If my voice is gentle. If my words come sincere."

"No deity is listening. You're screaming into the winds of Jupiter, praying in the black storm."

Tolya tripped on his bad leg, lost guidance of the vacuum and slammed it into the box row. Several boxes toppled and spilled into the front seats. Cynthia's arm shook, and she quickly set down the shoebox cradle onto the stage, before she dropped it. The still and practiced mountains on her face quaked and shattered. River poured through the cracks and crevices, pooling at the corners before dripping down the peaks. Her stoic visage crumbled.

"Goddess. I was so good. I didn't cry once since you saw Doctor Helsinki."

Anthony cupped his hands as if praying with her, to her, begging her. "Don't, Cynthia. I swear. I'll run. I'll go up in smoke."

She pressed her palms to her eyes, trying to push the tears back in, keep them hidden, save them for another day, long from now, a debt to be paid with thrice interest because of the repression. Still, sobs erupted from her throat, and she clawed her pretty pink fingernails down her cheeks, drawing blood from the scratches.

"You have to fight," she said. "You're acting like a child. So freaking stupid. There's a chance. There's always a chance."

"You read too many fairly tales. I hate that shit."

She hovered to him, opening her arms, seeking, like a frightened child seeks a parent's protection and love. "Let me hold you, just for a little while."

"Stay the hell back," he said, backing away. "This is the end of the bird, the end of everything I know. Get used to it. You're too weak. This life is going to chew you up with broken, sharp molars."

She lurched forward and grabbed him, clutching his lanky body tight. Anthony's muscles relaxed. The tide flowed in, and he let himself fall into her hands, allowing her to hold him up, to lend her strength and stand against the ever-constant gravity pull. She sobbed into his shoulder, soaking his shirt. The cool air from the AC finally kicked in and chilled the moisture, and he shivered. She pressed her mouth into Anthony's collarbone and mouthed each sob, suckling on his bone.

"Tighter," she said. "Pull me inside of you." Cynthia burdened him with more weight the longer she held him, and Anthony steadied his footing before they both collapsed.

He broke the embrace and jerked back. She tumbled and grabbed one of the seats, gaining her balance. "I can't do this," he said.

"I keep thinking of you not in my life. The void. I don't want to go back. You fill me up, Anthony."

"I just can't. I'm not spending my last days comforting the people around me."

Cynthia balled a fist and struck his shoulder, nearly knocking him into the stage. She swung again, and he dodged. His shoulder throbbed, spreading into his chest.

"You've got fucking stars in your head," he said.

"I'd rather be insane than a coward." She let down her arms.

"Oh, you can just fucking go."

"Right." She picked up the shoebox and cradled it under her arm. "Just push me away, like you did with Julie. And all of them, I bet. You want to die alone. That's fine. Have your own freaking way. I'm done."

Nausea twisted Anthony's stomach, and he fell into one of the chairs. Searched for his Zofran tablets and remembered he'd stuck them in the morphine bottle. It had rolled down the aisle. Summoning strength, he steadied himself on his feet and searched for the orange plastic cylinder.

Before leaving, Cynthia opened the box and checked her ward. Her face screwed up, perplexed, and she stroked the infant bird, finding no relief. "His skin has gone to ash."

"I tried to tell you," Anthony said. He found the bottle, took a seat in the front row and dug out the Zofran. He set the pill on his tongue and let it dissolve, the foam pouring down the back of his throat.

"I was reading about the Ark Foundation. They take in wildlife. It's in Newtown, I think." She set the shoebox on his lap, and he kept his hands free of it. "Be there with the bird?"

"It's pointless, Cynthia."

"Oh, goddess damn it! Just do it."

Anthony nodded and didn't say another word.

"I'm going to use the computer in the office and find the address." She jogged out the left exit and into the side hall. Tolya finished vacuuming and started stacking the boxes. Then he stepped behind the stage and rolled the curtains. The heavy, blue drapes extended across the stage, closing the circuit, sealing the portal.

Anthony watched the motherless bird. It looked off into no certain vector with glassy discs, not responding to the changes in its environment. Its hue etiolated, burning to charcoal as he watched. Anthony could sense the life spilling from the tiny thing—so small, so simple, yet so rich with the spark that only nature could summon. He reached to touch the infant, to run his finger along its back, to provide him a last sensation, so the poor, senseless child would know it wasn't dying alone. It had been denied the comfort of its mother, cast off on dangerous field, the careless plane and at the mercy of predators who had no mercy. Nature had been wise not to grant compassion to wild things. As he watched the little thing die, he exchanged places with it, feeling his own life slipping away.

He couldn't endure their pity. The little connection he felt to his grandparents had already eroded. They'd already written off their grandson. Cynthia would spend the next six months choking back sobs, poorly concealing her melancholy pits; and he'd always see through it. She'd fawn on him, needing comfort, reassurance and speaking to him of miracles, of magic. Anthony opened the bottle of Morphine Sulfate and spilled a handful of the little brown pills into his palm. He had nothing to swallow it down with, and some would stick in his throat, but it should've been enough to lay him to sleep.

Anthony had no skills to exist in inchoate states, phasing out and in, stuck half-between. Reality shifted. The doctors had tortured him with the caustic chemicals, the poisons, dissembling him. His understanding of reality had shifted, and he no longer trusted terra firma beneath his toes. He expected gravity to shift any minute, sending him flying to Jupiter. Matter dissipated in front of him, melted, then reformed again, shifting like sand dunes in a windstorm. He'd lost all his roots, the foundation, and flying made him airsick.

Eyes shot fire into the back of the skull. Eyes watched from behind, in the cheap seats, from the darkness veil. Anthony didn't turn his head. He sensed a witness to his final act.

Anthony held the finger of his left hand above the dying bird, swinging it in pendulous motion. He cupped the pill pile in his right, raised it to his face, and pushed the morphine into his mouth. A few stuck to his dry lips. He shifted the pills in his mouth with his tongue, and his saliva dissolved them. Anthony gagged on the bitter juice.

He stroked the bird's back, and the infant, responding to his gentle motion, raised its neck, looked at Anthony and faintly chirped, plucking the high note on a harp string. The bird felt his comfort. Then it died.

Anthony searched the wall for the time. The only clock

read midnight, its gears broken long ago and never repaired. A rushing wave overwhelmed him, a sense of sharp regret. He'd die without ever knowing his mother and lie in the wormy earth with a hole in his soul, unable to move onto the next life. The bird had died unfinished, without understanding its simple destiny. Its seedling soul never had time to mature, and its spirit would not take root in the otherworld; merely melt away and feed into the fecund soil where new souls sprouted. Anthony would just melt away and fertilize nascent spirits.

And he couldn't do this to Cynthia, not on the same day her infant bird left the world. Maybe tomorrow, but not today.

Anthony shot up from the chair, and it folded shut from the release of pressure to its spring. He darted up the stairs, heading for the actor's bathroom behind the stage. He tangled in the heavy curtains, clawing at the fabric, cutting through the sails and pushed into the slit at the meeting point of both drapes. He hovered there, dancing on one foot.

The stage represented the threshold of worlds. The theater existed as mundane reality, and the waves of protean and malleable flowed in and out, over the beach, through the surf of curtains. Humans crossed the threshold and cast off their skins, put on new faces and tore reality to shreds. They worked their loom of words and music, weaving new worlds across the silver veil, the ancient Celtic doorway to the other lands; the islands in the stream. On the stage, one could change the laws of physics. Dancing on the planks, singers summoned new stars and sculpted foreign planets from mental clay.

Anthony hesitated. He sensed the power. He'd fallen the rest of the way into the pit when Doctor Helsinki informed him that the mass in his pancreas had refused to decline. Choosing to stay in the world sent him down madness road. Reality flew apart. Nothing solid. Foundation and structure at his command. His heart sped, feeling the supernova power that surged into his hands and numb feet, pouring into his chest.

He jumped and plummeted through the curtains, breaking the veil, consigning himself to the wilds of the nexus.

It wouldn't be hard to invoke nausea. The Zofran had never really eased it, just taken the edge off, and he spit stomach acid from the glob of pills he'd just swallowed. His stomach threw them back.

Anthony just made it into the tiny, filthy bathroom when his stomach spasmed. He vomited a mouthful of brown motes and tried counting them among the coffee and bile.

He needed more time. God. Please let that be the lot of them. Such a fucking idiot.

Jebediah T. Cinderfield watched the play unfold in front of the theater, hiding in the back row, wrapping his fragile form in the darkness. He bundled up, wrapping the scarf around his neck, tangling it with the folds of gizzard skin dangling from his chin. The play suffered his patience and he tapped his long fingernails on the chair next to him and stroked his triangular beard down his pointed chin. The lead, some young actor, still rough around the edges, swallowed the handful of pills, regretted it, jumped reality and fell through the curtains. Cinderfield clapped politely and hoped Wilma would be on next. That's whom he'd come to see, not a bunch of middle-class white people, ruminating on life and death.

"No. I didn't kill the bird." He spoke to the vacant stage, reciting his dialogue from the darkness. "Not my department. It's not even in the same office building. I didn't invent death." He pointed upwards at the roof, indicating a higher seat. "That's above my pay grade, yet, boy do they blame me. I'm just a scapegoat, honey."

It seemed remarkable to Cinderfield just how familiar he'd found the lead actor, and he pondered whether he'd paid the young and unfinished man a visit on some past round, standing on some yon battlefield.

He watched the stage, sensing the potential energy charge in the curtains, ready to part and issue new vision. Wilma would slip out on stage with bare feet, dancing on her arches. She'd cover her naked frame with a balloon, inflated just enough to fill her edges, and with a little shift, she'd expose a breast curve or the inner, pale flesh of a fat thigh. Cinderfield grabbed the air, stroking those sweet, sweet limbs, running his sharp fingers up her stomach. He waited, and the curtains declined to part.

"Bloody fucking nuggets on a bus with no tires! Put on the Boss-Damn show, already!"

Still, the stagehands did not yield to his demands. One of them, the knobby Russian with fouled miner's lungs, coated with tar and stained amber from nicotine, stepped out from the stage.

"What in the hell are you yelling for?" he bellowed across the vacant theater.

"Wilma! Wilma! Wilma the Tease! Wilma the Snake. Watch her slink and slither. What a bod'!"

Tolya jumped off the stage, landed on his bad leg and nearly collapsed. He righted himself and limped up the aisle. "Get on out of here, you loon!"

"How will they keep the boys down on the farm, once they see those thick juices of Wilma the Snake?"

Tolya sat down next to Cinderfield. "Do you have a pack of Lucky Strikes on you?"

The devil nodded. "Awful sticks. The worst. It'll cost you a secret. That's the going rate for another inch closer to death. One soul-killing secret."

"Sold," Tolya said.

"Here you go, sir."

"Spasibo," Tolya said, plucking a stick from Cinderfield's hand. "I am obliged."

"Yes you are, sir," he said. "Ukraine?"

"'Til the age of five." He ignited the cig. Its red coal glowed in the dark theater, and he blew a smoke stream from puckered lips. "I'll be buried there, too. My ashes laid in potato fields."

"Ashes," Cinderfield said. "Divine." He said the word again, stretching it out. "D-I-V-I-N-E."

"Divine," Tolya recited.

"Pay up."

Tolya sucked down another long puff from the cigarette, then he let it dangle between his fingers. The ash fell off and piled on his leg.

"I was there," Tolya said.

"Yes. Of course. That fits."

"Should I lie? It'll kill him."

Cinderfield shook his head. "That would be kind."

"I won't be here much longer." Tolya hacked and coughed, rising from his seat until the spell passed.

"His soul won't grow if he don't know," Cinderfield said.

Tolya finished the cigarette then bent down and pressed it into the floor, extinguishing the butt.

"Now, when the hell is Wilma coming on?"

73

ANGEL GROWS UP

Angel goes to Kiddie City. The store is a place of wonder, of spirit, where Angel can grow his wings through his songs. What song are you playing?

"'Playing on Me Ol' Guitar!'"

This will make him famous. All the world will love him. Isn't that what all angels want? What they crave?

All the world will love him.

Angel is too young to be on the crystal screen and doesn't know how to get there. So, he makes his own shows, practicing, living his dream. Angel founded Channel 5, beginning its broadcast in 1953 to millions of people, though it was only live to one boy. A camera in the wall gave him to the world, and he truly believed it existed. He acted out hundreds of characters, in all sorts of shows, playing out every scene, saying each word of dialogue for all the characters that possessed him. Why go out and play in the world? He created his own worlds in his bedroom. He went to school, ignored his subjects and played in the nearby woods, playing out his television shows in secret, except for his best friend, Alfred Samuels. The boy was a phantom. Angel suffered secret loneliness. He spoke to his characters but his characters never spoke to him. He had the occasional playmate, but none could match his spirit, his enthusiasm. None of the other kids could understand him. His parents certainly didn't. Only Grandma Pearl cheered the child on, spoiling him.

His father sold cruddy jewelry. People liked to dress up and become something they weren't, hiding their faces, their bodies, distracting others from seeing their beauty— and ugliness. Angel didn't hide himself. He pretended to hide his mind and spirit, making his father yell and mother cry. But he felt different from all the others who wore bad clothing and jewelry. Angel didn't feel like he had a soul, and he made up people to fill the hole. Angels were born without souls.

So, he acted out. His family would take him to Coney Island—the heaven of his youth. He'd kick and scream, pretending to act out, but really, trying to get all strangers' eyes upon him, watching him. His parents would take him on the Cyclone, and he'd scream before the ride ever started: We're all going to die! Angel. Angel. Angel. See the Angel! Then he'd go off to the freak show where he felt at home with the lost, the enemies of society.

Finally, Angel's mother protested, worried about the boy, his secret television show. That's when she informed the lonely child that he couldn't perform without an audience. This was an amazing concept to Angel, and it would change the nature of his existence. For a stick of bubble gum, he could convince his sister to watch his antics and chew and blow bubbles for hours. With an audience, he had to actually have quality to his act, learn how to play his instruments, get the applause and approval of his watchers. He wanted more than attention, now. Angel needed their approval, to entertain them. From then on in his life, in his screaming, singing, dancing and desperate seeking of attention, he would find an audience. Such moments turn worlds.

Why does Dad always yell at Angel? Sometimes he

screams and screams, and Angel hides away behind his own face. Dad was a war hero. His name is Stanley and he won the Purple Heart during the war to end evil. The Nazis were going to come and kill his family, and Dad stopped them. No matter what Angel does, his father is always angry at the boy. He runs and hides in his television story, and the anger gets inside of him, festering, frightening the boy. It'll sleep, then come out one day, wearing a moustache and sunglasses.

But, Angel is excited! Babatunde Olatunji came to Angel's school. He was a tall African, Nigerian, dressed in a dashiki. He could make a drum sing. The drummer came to Baker Hill Elementary and played to Angel's soul. He taught Angel of the drum, of its exotic power over people. It hypnotized Angel, and his fingers tapped the air, hands beat the wind. He had to learn this power. He begged for lessons and practiced day and night, beating a headache into his father's noggin, never allowing peace to come to their house in Great Neck, to his mother or siblings. He beat out his frustration. When he felt no attention from Stanley, Angel's father, he beat until his fingers stung. He beat out the anger from his father.

HOLE IN MY SOUL

Before heading over to the diner, Anthony stopped at his apartment in the complex in West Lansdale, by the park and North Penn School. The manager had taped a yellow flyer to the door, declaring his lease in violation from lack of rent. Anthony hadn't been able to work in months, not subbing for school or at the Barnes and Noble. Matt, the manager, had been cool with it. Anyone firing a cancer patient can't get into Heaven, and Anthony hadn't even thought about bills and rent and food. His grandparents had paid the medical bills and put him up since he had the biopsy on his pancreas at Penn.

He fed his key into the lock, walked into the chaos of stacked books, folding chairs, gaming consoles and dirty dishes. Flies buzzed around the studio flat, and he found a bag and filled it with clothes and a few precious items: toiletries, a copy of the best poetry from W.B. Yeats, a photo of his fiancée that he'd kept to remember and forget. He shut the door behind him and didn't envy the slob who was going to have to clean out all his shit.

If you slipped the short-order chef at Captain Spizzie's Happy Sunday Diner & Latvian Orthodox Church a buck, he'd tip some bourbon into your cappuccino. The owner didn't carry a liquor license, so the transaction had to be conducted in a clandestine manner: a protocol that could only be taught by a comrade already in the know, a member of the private circle that frequented the pizza joint and church by night and weekend. Another reason this was kept secret was because the chef—a Serbian expatriate who fled his country—did not check ID and would tip bourbon for anyone who knew the signal, trusting that it would not be taught to anyone under the age of sixteen.

Anthony and Cynthia sat in the corner booth. She set the box of moribund avian next to her and flipped through the music cards. Each table came equipped with a remote to the jukebox; a miniature jukebox that lit up when you fed it three quarters. She selected a couple of songs from Journey and fed the little slot mouth some coins. The jukebox awoke, glowed white, and "Don't Stop Believing" sang from its wide and many mouths. Gladys, the waitress they knew, brought them two mugs of joe and set them in front of their respective drinkers. "I didn't order the 'special' coffee," Cynthia said.

"Gods . . . My friend . . . I'll have it."

Gladys nodded. "So be it." She set two menus down, and Anthony paged through one of them. The greasy plastic slipped between his fingers.

"I love to order eggs and bacon at night. Pancakes with strawberries. Crepes. I love that."

"We need to bury the little one," Cynthia said, looking at the box. She'd taken the bird's death with dry eye and acceptance, having buried it all again, keeping it secure. "I feel like I'm splitting into two people. I'll pay for it."

"And I'm coming apart."

"We could bury him in someone's yard. Have a little memorial service. Say kind words."

"Do you think God would listen?" Anthony asked.

"We'd listen."

"True."

"Do you think in a few years, anyone will even know the bird will be buried there? I can't take the thought that he'll be forgotten. I'll be forgotten, too."

"I don't even know where they buried my mother."

"You mean you never placed flowers on her grave—not begonias or daffodils? Daffodils are beautiful for the dead. When I was a little girl, and we drove to my grandmother's plot, I always placed a single daffodil. Bright and yellow like a sun."

"How can I sleep easy, not knowing her? I've always wondered. I'll keep wondering through eternity. There's a hole in my soul. I'll be a rotting insomniac. I don't have high expectations for an afterlife, but I was hoping to have a little peace. This is promised."

Gladys came over to take their orders.

"Pancakes with strawberries . . . and hash browns."

"Blueberry muffin," Cynthia said.

Gladys scribbled it down and strolled into the kitchen. Anthony sipped his coffee, and the bourbon kicked his mouth. He swallowed it down hard. He considered the adverse effects of mixing alcohol and morphine, and he still wasn't sure exactly how many pills had remained in his stomach after he'd vomited. Still, he'd not suffered any tiredness nor had it suppressed his breathing. These were the first signs of an opiate overdose.

He looked around the diner, admiring what a marvelous place housed the spirit of God. Over the last few decades, a sizeable Latvian population immigrated to Montgomery County, living in Philadelphia slums at first, saving a little money, bringing over relatives and eventually leaking out of the city for a better suburban life.

Enough of them had gathered to form their own community, and they grew tired of commuting into Philly every Sunday to worship their interpretation of God On Saturday nights, they shut the kitchen at 11P.M. The men came, bringing ethnic food and drink, then they pulled apart the booths and stacked the tables. They unloaded folding chairs from a storage room and set up their altar. Their priest brought all the icons and instruments of holy faith, and after final touches of clothes and even plastic decals for stained glass—depicting images of angels casting demons down into Perdition—Captain Spizzie's Happy Sunday Diner became The Latvian Orthodox Church of Lansdale Pennsylvania.

"We should find your mother," Cynthia said.

"What would be the point? She's dead."

"For your own peace of mind."

"For *your* peace of mind, you mean." Anthony sipped his coffee and enjoyed the sweet aftertaste. The liquor warmed his stomach, and he knew, by this time, he'd be dead if he had missed any of the morphine. "Anyway, I haven't the slightest inclination where she could be buried. For all I know, they cremated her gentle feather body and cast her out over Highland Lake in Maine."

"Can't you ask them?"

"Three things you didn't do in Roman house: Swear, take the Lord's name in vain, and inquire about dead parents. If I kept it up, Grandfather spanked me. He never said much, whispered when he spoke, but he bellowed when angry. Rage woke that man like a sleeping giant. Rage at my mother. She hurt them, somehow."

"There's nothing around the house? Not even a photo or a crayon drawing of a horse she did as a little girl?"

He shook his head. "Maybe. A brown stain on the wooden flooring in front of the kitchen sink. Sometimes

I'd wake up after midnight, come down for a cup of water, and find my grandmother on her hands and knees, altering prayers and sobs from her lips, and scrubbing at the stain with steel wool. She kept asking my grandfather to have it replaced, but he said they'd have to rip up most of the house. She smothered it with rugs, sometimes a new rug a week, when she got bad."

Cynthia played with her muffin, flicking bits and popping blueberries into her mouth. She twirled her finger in the butter and drew clouds on the plate. Anthony managed to swallow another bit of pancake. He stomach eased some, getting used to the chore of digesting, and he followed it up with a forkful of hash browns and another swig of coffee. The liquor relaxed his muscles and eased digestion.

"I'm just spit-balling, here," she said.

"That's a cute phrase. See that on television?"

She nodded. "Before opening the store, I used to temp for All-Team. A lot of it was acting as a conduit for paperwork. Someone handed me files. I scribbled on them or entered data then handed it to the next robot."

"And we all went along to circus," Anthony sung.

"Don't interrupt."

He bowed his head.

"Was your grandfather the type to keep records?"

"He wants to be buried in his paperwork. We're going to pull out all his organs then wrap him up in receipts and bills and invoices. He keeps all that in his office. Even receipts for appliances, like a VHS recorder he bought twenty years ago. He was furious one day because he couldn't find it." Cynthia didn't finish her thought, letting Anthony get it. He curled his upper lip—a chipmunk deep in cogitation. It took him a few moments, but he had been drinking bourbon. "A funeral, even a private one, is a pretty expensive clambake."

"So is a burial plot or cremation," she said. "So, we find some paperwork."

"If my grandfather catches me, he'll kill me before cancer does."

"You really think he'd hurt you?" Cynthia asked.

Anthony sipped down the coffee. "When my grandfather worked in his study, I used to watch TV with the sound muted because I was terrified of disturbing him. The man smoked his pipes, never saying a soft word to me or my grandmother. He either stayed quiet or yelled. Grandmom kept the house spotless and remained obedient. She'd cry during the day when he wasn't home. They both scared the shit out of me."

"And what about now?" Cynthia asked.

Anthony picked up the cup of coffee and sipped it. He frowned. "Too bitter." He picked up a plastic container of creamer but didn't rip off the lid. He squeezed it, and the milk dripped from his fist into the black brew.

"Now? I see them for what they are. A pathetic old man trying to control a universe that can't be controlled and an old woman who lived in fear so long that she lost herself." He dropped the empty plastic, and it hit the floor. "Fuck 'em. Nothing matters anymore. I'm free of this shit, now."

"You don't have your own key?" Cynthia asked.

Anthony pulled up the doormat on the porch in front of the door to the two-story bungalow in Yardley. "Obviously not." Fresh grass aroma with a hint of sweet onion tickled his nose, and he stifled a sneeze. The world flowed liquid, his perception still altered from the bourbon or morphine or a pleasant mixture of both. At times, his vision melted like clay underwater and reformed.

"Whisper, now. If we wake them up, if they catch us."

She put her finger over her lips and Anthony shot her a dirty look.

A plywood painted sparrow dangled from a hook in the front of the door. The bird held a sign announcing the start of 'Blue-Skies & Blue-Eyes Summer'. Cynthia ran her finger down the rough paint, tilting the bird to the left. Anthony adjusted it to perfect center. "And don't touch anything."

"Right. Right." She set the shoebox coffin on a porch chair, and they slipped into the house, silent as burglars, careful as cats. "Take off your shoes and put them next to the closet."

She complied. He checked the runner in front of the stairs to make sure it still aligned to the wall, then pointed at a statue of a young country girl wearing a blue dress and carrying a cornstalk staff—one of those ceramic sculptures sold in sets by greeting card companies. "My grandmother has shelves and shelves of those idols in her sewing room. She always collects the new one. I broke one once, snapped off the arm when I was running in the living room. I went without breakfast, lunch and dinner."

She nodded and rubbed his shoulder. "My grandfather's office is in the basement. He locks himself down there for hours, smoking and sorting papers. It relaxes him."

Anthony led her to a door behind the staircase. It faced the kitchen, and she spotted the lock in the knob. "Trouble?"

"He doesn't always lock it. Why would he? He rules the world." He reached for the knob, hesitated, scanned the house for witnesses, then grabbed. "Shit."

"Locked?"

She grabbed her purse, rummaged about, and pulled

out a wallet. Cynthia handed him her bankcard. "Try that. It works in the movies." He positioned it in the door crack. "It's an old door and looks like the original lock."

"Shit. I mean shoot." He'd corrected his swear by environmental instinct. "Wait. Not your bank card."

"Right." She exchanged it for a credit card. "That one's been canceled for months now. Break it if you must. Maybe it'll be like a voodoo doll, and some corporate president at Capital One will break in two."

He fed the plastic card into the crack. He maneuvered it, and his eyelids tightened, trying to focus. His hands shook as he guided—another side effect of the nerve damage from the chemo, something he'd have to learn to work with and survive, at least for a while. The card snapped.

"My Aunt Judy's rose garden!" he whispered.

"Your Aunt Judy's what?"

"I'll finish that thought when we get outside," he said, holding out his hand for another card. She gave him an old library card, the letters worn near to white.

"Your grandmother was some kind of Nazi," she said.

"Jawohl, Doctor Humingdinger." He fed the next card into the lock, easing it into the bolt and bending it back. "Almost got it." The card snapped.

"Your Aunt Judy's rose garden!" Cynthia said.

"Watch your mouth." He sighed.

"It's not working."

Anthony leaned his forehead on the door, lending it his weight, resting on the walls of his cage. The door popped open, lifting from its hinges, and he grabbed onto Cynthia, nearly taking her with him down the stairs. He steadied himself.

"Don't say a thing," he said.

She shrugged. "Old house."

Anthony flipped on a light switch, and they crept down the stairs, reminding him of something out of an old black and white gothic film: Laurel and Hardy meet the scary Nazi Grandmother. Framed photos of his grandfather golfing decorated the walls, each descending in time, leading from the picture of a silvery haired old man to a young man with blond hair and hopeful eyes, all of them wielding a golf club. Was he traveling backwards in the fourth dimension?

"I wonder if that was before he had my mother? There's something missing about the man now, not that I'd know. I really don't know a thing about my grandparents."

Anthony viewed the office like he had as a child. His stomach cramped, and he hovered at the staircase. Several file cabinets, twenty feet tall, barricaded the walls, sealing the fort, the drawers wide and deep enough to house bodies like a freezer at the morgue. Framed diplomas and documents decorated the walls, speaking of his grandfather's importance and accomplishment as an accountant—feats Anthony could never match, always knowing he was a lesser sort of man, the kind of offspring a broken daughter produced. His corner desk had a flat surface for writing and a side computer setup, and his grandfather had exhibited shelves of various kinds of pipes of all styles and makes. He'd stored several tins of exotic tobacco at the bottom, and the reek of the plant, rich and caustic, burned his eyes. He rubbed them with fists and kept checking the basement door, waiting for his grandfather to burst it open and come barreling down the stairs. He'd yell at him in such fury that hot ash would spill out of his pipe and singe Anthony's soft face.

"He's going to catch us. He'll stop loving me. He'll put me up for adoption."

"Anthony. You're not a child anymore." She kissed his forehead. He shook it off.

"It's this sickness. The past and present have come undone. Getting all tangled up in my head."

She plucked at his sleeve. "Where would he keep the receipts?"

Anthony pointed at the last filing cabinet. He lingered, steeled his face then went over and yanked open the bottom drawer. Neat and filed folders tilted forward, some of the papers spilling out. Anthony knelt and collected them neatly into their home folders.

Cynthia studied the labels. "Looks like a color code for each year." She flipped through them, reaching an orange section. "Your mother died in 1985?"

He nodded. "On my birthday. Check February. Feb second."

She yanked out a folder marked 'WINTER 1985', then sat on the rug before the tall cabinet and paged through the documents—invoices, store receipts and various paper detritus—the wastes of time by a made record keeper. All for lost. Ink faded. Paper rotted. Pulp sank into the soil.

"Goddess," she said. "What a freak. Every supermarket receipt. All the bank statements. Car payments. Even fees for the country club." She searched and picked and plucked, and she tilted her head, reading.

"Nothing about a funeral. But did you know your grandfather rented a storage unit off New Welsh Road three days after your birthday?"

"They've never spoken of it. We've always had plenty of room, either in the attic, the crawlspace or the shed."

She fingered through the remaining files. "He's got a steady receipt for each month. According to the invoice, he'd rented it for—" She paused. "Goddess. Thirty years."

"My grandfather is a serious man and a fanatic with

money. My grandmother must have all my mother's stuff stored—old records, clothing from her adult life and the rags of her childhood, photos, drawings, furniture, the sum total material elements that linger after a person leaves the world. That has to be it. Grandmother couldn't keep it and she couldn't just toss it away and acknowledge the emotional rite of mourning, of admitting she'd brought a life into this world and that life had stabbed her in the ear.

"That's exactly my grandfather. Just get it done. Hire a truck. Pack it all in boxes in one day. Rent a unit. And bury it. Efficient. Disciplined. Always marching to his orders."

"I have the address right here," Cynthia said. "Do you think it's still there?"

"Let's check."

She returned the folder, stood up, and opened the top drawer. She grabbed the closest file in the purple folder, fingered through the pages, then smiled.

"Eureka. Another invoice, sent purely for record, from five days ago." She folded it and slipped it into her pocket. She paused. "Problem. These things usually have a padlock."

"My grandfather would make sure it's a good one, too."

The ceiling groaned from pressure, or maybe the house settled in. Anthony froze, even breathing slowly, folding himself into the shadows. They waited and suffered no discovery.

"He keeps his keys on a chain, usually dropped on his dresser before bed. He has sleep apnea. We even get near their bedroom, and he'll wake up."

"Anthony?" his grandmother's voice, a hollow voice blowing through wide and vacant caves, called down the stairs. "Is that you?"

Cynthia scanned the basement, looking for an exit. Caught like a rat in a trap that's in a basement that's Grandfather's office.

"It's just me, Grandmother. No need to call the SWAT team."

She stepped down onto the third step and didn't dare come farther. "You know you're not supposed to be down there . . . especially with friends." She tightened her blue housecoat then checked the curlers in her gray hair. She rubbed the grit from her right eye.

They obeyed and climbed the stairs. Grandmother shut the door and checked the lock. It didn't catch. "We really must get this door fixed."

"We needed some printer paper," Anthony said. "Cynthia is writing a new play." Cynthia winced. She hadn't written a line since her last play won all that national attention back at Bloom. He'd never found out the cause of her writer's block and never bothered to check. What would he know of such things?

"Well, it's good to have fun hobbies," Grandmother said. "I sew."

It sounded like a compliment, but Grandmother had a method of demeaning with her compliments. Anthony nearly corrected her. Cynthia had been more than just some girl playing writer. She had talent, potential, and she heard the voice of the universe. Her first play about the life of an actor similar to Andy Kaufman was going to be produced on a major stage. Again, he never heard what happened with that.

"Well, why don't I make us some tea?" Grandmother said. "Anthony, come help me in the kitchen. Why doesn't your friend go sit on the back porch? Such a lovely night like this." Anthony tilted his head, signaling Cynthia. Grandmother had evicted her. She sighed.

"Guess I'll go pretend to write some plays to put on in my living room," Cynthia said.

"Very good, dear."

Anthony followed Grandmother into the kitchen. Her left hand trembled as she filled the stainless steel teapot. Her Parkinson's had gotten worse, and she took out saucers and cups from the cabinet.

"I can't get that poor boy out of my head," she said. She bowed her head for a moment, then went back to making tea.

"Which one?"

"That Jimmy what's-his-name. The one who got recruited for the Eagles, starting next season. Drunk driver hit him on the way home from a friend's house. Funeral's tomorrow."

"A lot of people die every day, every moment."

He reached to help her sort the tea out, but she waved him away.

"I'm not some silly old woman, Anthony. I know what you were doing in your grandfather's office." She checked both saucers and cups, then held one of the saucers under the faucet and scrubbed it.

"I have a right to know my mother." He stood and held the back of a chair, refusing to sit.

"I'm your mother. God gave you to me." She set the saucer and cups on the table. "Now, sit down. You're making me nervous." He hesitated, then pulled out a chair and sat. His left leg shook, and he twirled the saucer in front of him 'round and 'round. "Just stop all this foolishness. Karen turned out to be such a mess. You don't want to know her."

Steam poured from the kettle mouth as the water started to boil. Grandmother fetched a tin of tea bags from the cabinet and set one in each cup. She knelt down at the rug in front of the sink, covering the hardwood floors, and adjusted it against the cabinet. "I just don't know what happened to her," she said. "She was such a happy child. We used to go to Maine every summer. She loved Jesus. She prayed every night before bed. Something just went bad in her. The apple rotted." She got up from the floor and turned the teapot, making sure the spout faced the wall, the hand set to midnight.

"I've told Doctor Helsinki I'm done with treatment. He didn't argue with me. He nodded."

"You have to do what you think is best." And it struck him how she didn't argue with his decision, to fight for his life or try to convince him to try experimental treatments. Had he meant so little to her, just another ceramic figurine in her collection, a broken one she'd hid in the closet but unable to break the set and toss?

"When you and Grandfather are sleeping in the dirt, I'll be all that's left of you and your daughter. When I'm gone, the blood ends."

"Maybe it's better that way."

The kettle keened, shooting a steam jet into the air. Grandmother carried the pot to the table where she filled both teacups. She set it down then laid out sugar and cream. Anthony didn't sip. They lingered in silence while the world turned and the sun burned.

"She was crazy, Anthony. The devil climbed up in her. She started sneaking out at night to see boys. We grounded her. We disciplined, but it just got worse. I found a bag of the pot in her room one day while I was cleaning. We went to the church for help, but like the stone in the stream, the words and faith didn't get inside her." Grandmother clanked the side of her cup with the spoon, ringing it like a fractured bell. "And then she got older and started hanging out with those . . . people. She wanted to be some kind of actress. Actress, indeed. Such an unwholesome profession. She was in rehab twice, kept promising us she'd get clean. She broke our hearts. Then, all that wrestling business. She had no sense, no dignity, and humiliated us. We told her no more and told her not to come back."

"You just threw her away?" He gripped the tea cup, and nausea overwhelmed him. They'd just written his mother off, washed their hands of her and moved on with their vacant lives. The wrong people got cancer.

"She made her choices," Grandmother said. "Now, you have to make yours. Put away all this business with Karen. It's like she never existed. Stay here, with us. Your grandfather will make sure you're comfortable and safe. Haven't we always taken care of you, put a roof over your head, kept you fat and warm?"

"I have a hole in my soul. I can feel a blackhole. I'm falling through it. I won't know eternity."

She sipped from her tea. "That's all of us, Anthony," she said. "Keep this up, and you won't be welcome here, anymore. Enough of the past! That'll be it from Grandmother and Grandfather. No more."

He studied her face, looking for a cruel smile, some hint that she hadn't meant it, but Anthony knew. They had done it to their daughter, and wouldn't that just be easier, throwing him away, declining any responsibility for his care? They'd turned away their gaze, so they couldn't watch him die, to spare themselves all that pain.

And he'd die alone. He hadn't been able to work in months. In a few days, he'd have no home. He couldn't imagine dying in Cynthia's apartment, and he knew she suffered enough debt to lose her store, her car, and a second car she'd signed a loan on that she'd gotten rid of two years ago. His grandparents had paid his medical bills, made sure he had his meds. The world scared him enough when he was healthy, and his leg thumped, his fingers raked the table, thinking about dying away from everything that was familiar to him, the comfort of his family and first home. He knew this house, had made secret dens in its walls, a fort in the crawl space they'd never discovered, and on the day his body expired, he planned to crawl in there with his comic books and the crayon picture he'd drawn of his mother, guessing at her appearance. He'd tacked it on the wall and slept there at night. His grandparents had never noticed.

"Peaceful," Anthony said. "Letting go. Pushing my boat out to sea. No fuss. No mess. My mother never existed."

"I'm your mother, Anthony." For a moment, her lips moved, and maybe she was going to say, 'I love you.' If she had, he would have stayed. He would have let this all go and just allowed the circuit of his life to complete itself. She closed her quivering lips and sipped her tea.

"I want the key," he said.

"You understand what happens next?"

"You've made that clear."

"This is your choice, then." She got up from the table, climbed the stairs and returned a minute later. She set a brass and tarnished key in front of him.

"Finish your tea, Anthony, then please collect your friend and leave."

"I'm done, thank you."

His grandmother didn't watch him leave. She focused again on the rug in front of the seat and finally grabbed a rag, some floor polish from the cabinet, and knelt down. She pulled back the rug and scraped at the spot. Even in the dim light of the kitchen, Anthony couldn't see the stain. She scrubbed and sucked on her upper lip, sucking in her throat, gurgling.

"I'm so tired, Anthony. The world is dirty. It's broken. It's all out of place. I'm carrying it all."

"And who asked you to do that?"

"That's the problem with your generation today. You all think it's someone else's problem."

Anthony scoffed.

"She was a mean-spirited child," Grandmother yelled. "I can show love! I can show affection! I'm not a cold bitch. She had the problem. Not me."

He pulled Cynthia's long sleeves from the sun porch.

"I have the key," he said.

"What happened?" she asked, looking back in the kitchen.

"Fuck it."

He led her through the living room and paused at the front door. Anthony picked up the ceramic figure, the queen of May, the goddess of spring. His hand shook as he held it, frightened of damaging Grandmother's precious figurine. Then, he lobbed it against the wall. The figurine shattered.

ISLANDS OF REGRET ON 309

The SEPTA bus rocked by the Montgomery Mall, turning off into a side lane and speeding up, heading for the stop by the Barnes and Noble where Matt promised Anthony his job slinging books and coffee would always be secure—for generations and generations.

Cynthia kept the shoebox on her lap, stroking the lid, comforting the remains, comforting herself.

"You planning to carry that around with you all day?"

"Just a little while longer. We'll bury it tomorrow."

The bus rode light, just Anthony, Cynthia, and a heavy spirit filling the depths of the wagon—the detritus, the reminder of lost souls who left a little of their taint, smeared a bit of their regret, forgotten and dripping, smearing and greasing. They sat as close to the front as they could. Anthony recognized the driver—a squat, black guy with a moustache, a blue cap stuck to his head.

"How's it going, Mike?" Anthony asked.

"Another mile in this bus. Another hemorrhoid bleeding. Doc gives me cream, but I might as well use cake icing. Give my wife something nice to taste once in a while."

"God. You're a sick man, Mike."

He croaked like a frog. "As the Good Lord made me. Yes, sir." He grabbed the mic to address the passengers,

94

playing the part of a guide. None of the passengers gave a shit. "Look to your left now, below the streetlight on the intersection, to 309," Mike announced, adopting the tone of some tour guide. "There it is. Island of regret on 309."

Below the vector of illumination of a streetlamp, just at the triple intersection of 309, 63 and 202—meaningless numbers—a plethora of flowers—roses, carnations, violets and begonias, decorated the pavement and curb, piled over the shards of shattered windshields and torn bits of wire. Mourners had laid teddy bears and plush toys to commemorate the spot, providing not comfort to the dead but to themselves. A photo framed in ornate silver marked the spot where Jimmy Christmas, new starting forward for the Philadelphia Eagles, discovered the universe did, indeed, have a sense of humor, enjoying various pranks and japes, and Anthony wondered if the stern-faced, boxed-head athlete also possessed such a sense of humor and screamed laughter into the wild, wild darkness. They drove below the scaffolding bridge carrying several stoplights, and night flooded back into view.

"Do you want me to stay at your place for a bit tonight?" Cynthia asked.

"Actually, about that," he said, curling his upper lip. "Could I crash at yours? I hate to put you out."

This time, she dithered. "Well, that's kind of a problem."

Anthony recognized the listless look in her glance, like two fishing trawlers broken free of their moorings and thrashing about the bay, free of their ties, abandoned by the land and right to sink. "I've forgotten to pay my phone bill a few times," Anthony said. "It's hard to think of corporeal matters now. It wastes my fine sand grains. You?"

"Business at the store isn't the best. A few days ago, I

came back to the apartment, and found my crap by the dumpster. It's cool, though. I'm doing the makeup at a commercial in a few days. One of the girls said they'd help. Business always picks up in the summer."

Anthony didn't say it, but he knew why. She'd seldom left his side since they'd met at Penn before his biopsy. He knew she'd been letting her life slip, her responsibilities pushed aside, and he should have told her to take care of things; however, truth was, he'd grown accustomed to Cynthia being with him. He gazed out into the darkness through the filthy Plexiglas, watching the trees flow by. He focused on an oak tree that had grown around the base of a power line, wrapping it layer by layer in slow growing bark. To remove the pole, city workers would kill the tree.

"So, we've both officially joined the hobo nation?"

She nodded. "She really just cut you off like that? I don't care how sick you are. If you don't play by my rules, you can die alone on the street?"

"I don't think she's really been alive for years."

She grabbed the seat. "That . . . that bitch."

Anthony rubbed her shoulder. "So, are we sleeping here?"

"No can do," the driver croaked. "The boss would have my hide, covered in cake icing or not."

"Where have you been sleeping?" Anthony asked.

"The theater. I'm not supposed to, but only Tolya knows about it. If anyone notices I'm there, he just tells them I'm in late or early. They applaud my diligence." She huffed. "So, where's your stuff?"

He tapped the bag on his arm. "Travel light. All material goods are illusions, sources of stress. Buddha birthed from a lotus blossom to tell us all that."

The bus approached derelict community theater— concealed behind a Mega-Walmart, the great castle of commerce, the kingdom of clouds and vapor. Mike pulled the bus up to the curb and threw open the portal. Anthony got up with Cynthia, and she held the cardboard coffin under her arm.

"You all be safe, now," he said. "Let Jesus take the lead."

Anthony and Cynthia strolled the vacant parking lot, following the access road, walking in silence until, after a good ten minutes, they crossed the wide desert.

"Wait. Isn't this the office of Doctor Humingdinger?"

She flicked his shoulder. "I admit. Not one of my best."

The Lansdale Community Playhouse crumbled and rotted like an old galley beached in a storm then abandoned by crew to crumble and rot. Wood planks fell at random from the walls, exposing gray plaster behind, which flaked off from the elements. Dressing rooms on the second floor stuck out like an exposed and broke femur from the skin, supported by a bunch of wooden stilts. Tolya added new ones every year to keep the addition on the second level and not crashing to the ground floor. Lansdale Borough had voted to spend community funds to establish the playhouse just after World War II, and if any actual members of the community came to plays, they'd probably vote to rip it down, selling the land to the Walmart Corporation for another expansion. Bats nested in the roof, and they twittered and tweeted as Anthony and Cynthia crossed the woefully inadequate parking lot.

They slipped in through a stage door, passed below the stage through a tight corridor. Anthony lowered his head and smashed several times into the white plaster, bruising his shoulder. He tasted mold on the air, the flavor of rot and decay common to old buildings. They came out from behind the stage, and Cynthia set the bird down on a desk by the light switches, then fetched a bag of blankets.

"I've only got a comforter and a sheet." She laid out the covers on a flat pile of old and faded playbills from shows created, sung and performed over the last half-century, now all memories to the old and forgotten by the dreaming dead. Ropes and rigging swung above, and the worldly curtain shielded the duo from the empty theater and all the watching ghosts still sitting and waiting for a show to begin. "Why don't you take the . . . bed," she said.

"I won't hear of it," Anthony said. "One bed. One blanket. One pillow."

"You want to share?" Her hummingbird eyes flapped tiny wings.

He sighed. "It doesn't mean anything, of course."

She sighed and rolled her shoulders. "Of course. Two mates. Two friends. Two chums."

Anthony pulled out an extra-large shirt from his bag and stepped into the actor's bathroom. He took off his khakis, hung his fedora hat on a hook and changed into the shirt. It draped low over his thin thighs. Anthony washed his face, brushed his teeth. He returned the hat to his head and returned to their new bedroom backstage. Cynthia had slipped on a stained long-sleeve shirt and white jogging pants to hide the girth of her hips and tiny calfs. She'd given up wearing shorts as a kids and hadn't bothered to shave her legs in months. She curled up under the blanket along the side of the pulp bed. Anthony sat on the lumpy books, moving his bum to find secure foundation, then slid under the covers. Her warmth eased the chill on his skin, and he leaned his body closer.

"So, here we are, then," he said.

"Mates. Friends. Chums."

He eased his head back on the fat half of the pillow. Cynthia hung to the edge like a spooked cat clinging to the corner. He sensed the theater slipping its moorings and setting sail on the high seas, a ship carrying old ghosts for cargo, to be delivered across the silver veil.

"So, Tolya's coming tomorrow to take me to get some makeup supplies for the store," Cynthia said. "We have to go early. The post office closes at noon on Saturdays. We could ask him to drive us to this storage area."

"He wouldn't mind? He seems a bit . . . grizzly bear."

"Nah."

"Cool."

They lay in silence several minutes longer.

"Shame about that football player," she said.

"Lord of the earth. King of heaven. Young and vital. Next year, he would have crossed the line and made it, and we would have cheered him on, not for him, but for ourselves, in hope we could make it, too."

"Do you think he thought about death?" she asked. "That it could happen to him?"

"No. He thought he was immortal." Anthony reached and touched her arm, drawing her closer. "You can relax. This is just damn silly." She unfurled her body and turned over on her back. Her left breast brushed his chest, and his muscles relaxed. He felt the progression, the current moving them to the next amorous stage: the hands that reach seeking hands; the mouth that seeks another mouth, a circuit demanding closure and sparking white flares into the wind.

She pulled back her hair from her forehead then brushed her hand along his ribs, settling it on his stomach. He adjusted his position, digging out the book sticking into his bum, and pushed closer. He'd lost his only family, his home, all security. He sailed on Cynthia to keep him from sinking, and he admitted to himself that he didn't mind the company. It couldn't be love; but he shivered and shook, and a cold sweat soaked his shirt from his neck to lower back.

"You poor thing." She touched his damp collar.

"Life with cancer."

They connected, and she turned on her side and wrapped her arm over his stomach, not holding tight at first, testing the waters. She kept it there, and he didn't bite. Her shirtsleeve pulled up, and Anthony noticed two red and angry lacerations above the wrist. As if Cynthia had plucked his anxiety from his body like rotten fruit, his branches lightened, and tonight, he might sleep deep and forgetful, beyond the reach of the ache and fatigue that always nibbled at his bones in sleep. He slipped his arm around her shoulders and cupped her arm.

The darkness screeched, snapping their repose, and Cynthia jumped, ripping back her hand. She returned it. The bat screeched again, then twittered and flapped beyond the curtain. Cynthia wept. The tears burst from her eyes like swollen clouds and rained down her cheeks. She pushed her head into Anthony's shoulder.

"Please don't," he whispered.

"I'm such a dreaming idiot. A fat, ugly moron. I can't help it. My coil is bent. I'm all bent inside."

"I was so close."

"You make this into a feathered bed with silk sheets. This theater into a penthouse. I won't be able to sleep again. Not alone. I don't believe in ghosts. That means their souls didn't get into Heaven."

Anthony lay there, letting her weep until her breathing slowed and she shut her eyes. Then carefully, he untangled himself from her grip, and he slipped through the curtains and down into the seats. He sat back in one of the chairs, pulled the brim of his fedora over his face, closed his eyes, and listened to their constant whisperings, whipping and whistling from the seats behind him—the dead watching the show.

Anthony slept on rocky shoals, and the stones dug into his back. Time slipped by, and in the darkness he summed his thoughts, sure he'd dozed off for a few hours. God stabbed his gut, waking him, fished around his pockets for the morphine then got up from the theater seat and staggered to a water fountain outside the audience bathroom. He swallowed the brown mote and considered taking a second. The pain surged up into his chest, and he lay back against the wall and slid down, curling up on the rug. There he lay, until the cramp dissipated.

A mouse scurried out from a crack in the wall, brushed against his shorts then nibbled on his toe. Anthony pulled himself up, slipped backstage quietly so he wouldn't disturb Cynthia, and found his pants and flipped on his fedora. He'd woken up in mind to run a small but critical errand, and she'd rage and claw and gnash teeth at him for doing it; however, it had to be done this way. Cynthia couldn't let things go. When her cat, Peppermint, died a few months ago, she kept its rotting remains in another shoebox in the bathroom. He'd only found it when searching for the source of the flies. He finally convinced her to bury the thing in the empty lot behind her apartment, but she wept in the morning then wandered around in a fugue state.

He checked the desk for the coffin but found it missing. Cynthia had gotten up in the middle of the night and brought it back to bed with her. She clutched it under her arm, cuddling with it like a bear or lover, and she shivered, finding no heat. He gently took her fingers and uncurled them from the box's edge, then lifted her arm. A recent red slice cut down the base of her wrist, and he slipped down the sleeve.

"Jesus Christ," he whispered. He counted the even slices and scars: nine. And she had more white flesh canvas to cut. Cynthia turned, feeling his presence. "Jeremy," she muttered. "Gonna sleep in a little longer."

"You get some sleep, darling."

She cooed in her sleep, and he grabbed the box then slipped from the stage, exiting through the back fire door that no longer possessed a functioning alarm.

The wet grass shocked his partially numb feet. The tops of his feet chilled, and he felt every lick of wet grass, each stream of dew. The bottoms of his feet felt numb, asleep, like the circulation had stopped, and each sensation pricked pins deep into his limbs. The chemo killed nerves in his extremities, and the less he felt in his body, the greater his soul awakened.

Earthstar burned in full potential, not yet spending any of its finite fuel on this day. Through the residual of dew still suspended in water vapor in the air, the sun refracted, shifting in spectrum: its own unique shade of orange that he'd not seen anywhere else in the world. Only stars possessed this grace, and he stood in the grassy field behind the Walmart and let the light shower him, wash over him, imbuing him with the same potential. He drew down its spirit, and the solar ghost possessed him, moved into his chest and sped his heart, drained into his limbs and pushed his legs.

"She's burned long before I crashed into existence, and she'll keep on burning so very long after," he said to the ghost of Elvis.

"So beautiful is God's glory," the dead crooner responded. "Better love it while we can."

"Elvis, I hate your music, and I'm not religious. But you do wax beautifully."

"Aww. Thank you very much."

The sunflower blossomed in the sky, and the light stung his sleepy eyes. Anthony shielded his eyes from the glare. "It's going to go out one day."

"Can't be helped."

He turned and nearly ran back to the derelict theater, to hide in the basement, to dig a hole deep into the earth. A moment ago, the sunlight renewed him, sparked in his chest and reminded him of the power and the fury of life. Now it stung him, wounded him, a reminder of what was going to be lost. Memorial couldn't sooth him now.

"Take it easy, man," Elvis said. "You've got a job to do."

Anthony focused on his breathing, drawing in the humid air. It calmed the bird swarm in his chest, flapping in his head, and he looked around for a suitable spot to conduct a burial. The sun blinded from the East, rising from the breast of the Atlantic to shower America with fecund light to power the human world.

"She's gorgeous naked," Anthony said. "I will see it no more."

"That's the price, man," Elvis said. "And without that, the sun would grow dull and weak."

"There," Anthony said and spotted a sandy patch of grass. Other shallow dunes marked a diamond. This must have been a softball field at one time. "In the sand."

"That's lucky. You didn't bring any tools, did you?"

Anthony suddenly felt stupid. "Thinking ahead is absurd at this point."

"Not for you, man. For others."

Anthony crouched on the golden sand and set the box down, then dug his fingers into the sand. The damp grains clumped together, and he pushed them aside, keeping ahead of the flow back into the hole. Most of the sand he moved rushed back in, and he worked for several minutes to clear a space big enough for the coffin.

"Should I say something?"

"Yeah, man," Elvis said.

Anthony brushed the sand from his fingers and considered a proper eulogy. He'd never delivered one before, especially for an avian, and he felt the whole business to be silly; however, it would comfort Cynthia, lessen the blow when she jumped him and wrestled him to the floor.

"One of God's creatures," he said. "And the world will be diminished."

"Just beautiful, man."

Cynthia hovered in front of the back exit, pacing back and forth. Anthony slowed when he saw her. Her cross face fired off a shotgun blast in his direction, and he felt molten hot buckshot burning his chest. He slumped his shoulders and met her.

"I'm out of here, man," Elvis said. He pulled open a hatch in the stage that was earth and descended from danger.

"What the heck were you thinking?"

"I'm not thinking. I've given it up. Bad for my health. I haven't thought at all since this started."

"Don't use your cancer to get my sympathy. Remember. I know you. You did a lot of stupid things before this. You're a boy, and boys can be dumb."

"I just wanted to spare you pain."

Her admonishment kicked his gut harder than he'd thought. How had she come to affect him so much? He'd kept her at arm's length, never letting her in too deep, but she'd dripped in like water, finding the cracks and seeping into his hot heart. He nearly knelt before her, repented and begged forgiveness.

"You were just going to leave, weren't you? Just run away, and I'd never find out what happened to you."

This wasn't about the bird and burial. Beneath the hatchet face, Cynthia sucked on her lips. Her face swelled red from tears. She dabbed her eyes.

"I'll leave whenever I damn well please," he said. "I own my death. It's not yours. Elvis can kiss my cancer-ridden ass."

"Don't say that, Anthony."

"No. I'm sick of this shit. It's not about you. You're so goddamn pitiful. I have nightmares that you're going to hide in a closet for the rest of your life, curled up in a fetal position after I'm gone. You'll drown in the hole I leave."

"The hole is bigger than you know," she said, keeping remarkably calm. Anthony flared his nostrils, breathing hard and fast. The pain stabbed his stomach, poking through to his back. It fueled the fire.

"Look. I don't know what this is. Fuck. I can't even think on those terms, anymore. Tangled wires. The mountains stand on their heads. I can't figure love from anger and lust from hate. Why do you do this to me?"

"When you leave this world, a part of me will go with you, and I'll be less for it. We'll all be less."

"I'm just going to go," Anthony said.

"I . . . I have no fucking clue. I'll go find my mother, and we'll be together. She'll tell me my future, and I'll name her liar."

"Mothers always lie to their children. They call it comfort." He turned from her and faced the morning sun. "I have no comfort for you. I'm going."

"I'll come with you."

He paused, hesitating, trying to ignore the agony boiling in his gut. He needed Cynthia to touch his shoulder, but he'd driven her back into the wall and set her flesh pale. She wouldn't reach out, afraid of being bitten. And he might too, clamp his jaw down on her soft hand, add new scars to her ritual marks and grind her bones in his teeth.

"I saw the scars," he said.

"No one's supposed to see them."

"How many of them are from me?"

She didn't answer. She wouldn't speak of it. "They're mine and for no one to see."

He waited, letting them both cool down. "Well, that's it, then. Goodbye, Cynthia. Vaya con Dios. Off into the wild blue yonder."

"Fine. Go to hell, Anthony. Go fuck yourself, too, while you're there." She felt awkward speaking that way to a cancer patient, but he was still her friend.

He grinned. "You still see me," he said.

"You're so dramatic sometimes," she said.

"Yeah. I am. What about the stuff?"

"Tolya will be here in an hour. We'll pick up the makeup supplies then drive over to the storage area."

"Cool. But then I've got to jet."

"Sure."

"I'll leave soon as we're done," he lied.

ANGEL'S GOD IN SEQUINS

In his life, Angel would seek gods to worship, someone's beauty and power he could venerate and pray to. He never had much use for an ethereal being, a divine power. You can't hear God laughing when you sing and dance, so what's the point of praying to Him? Then Grandpa Paul brought him God in shiny sequins. Angel had never known a greater power than himself. Now he knew Elvis. The Memphis boy was everything Angel wanted to be. With his guitar, he wove wings of music that could lift a room, and crowds around the world cheered and swooned for the troubadour. Angel remembered his days in the recording chamber. He reached his hand into a boy in Great Neck Long Island and showed him what was possible.

One day, he would steal the singer, borrow his soul and imbue himself. He would use his majesty and spirit to purloin that applause—the angel thief. Angel would surprise people, and he would lose himself into the impresario, becoming him at times with the world cheering at his rhinestone boots. Angel owned all of the King's records, playing them again and again, lost in the songs. He studied the King of Nations and Heavens, watching his lip curls and hip turns, never missing one Elvis show or movie. He studied his teacher in awe at his gift of seducing women with his songs, seducing Angel, drawing his worship and prayer. Angel would drain the King's essence—master of females, lord of sex, always getting the girl with his gyrating legs and wavy hair.

Women were the great mystery, and Angel longed and conspired to be in love, to possess and be possessed in return. Angel desired to know desire. He misunderstood the nature of coupling, and he picked random girls—always the awkward, shy ones, females in his school he'd never even spoken to—with whom to fall in love. He arranged his classes to their classes, adjusted his scholastic schedule to pass them in the hall, living each day for those brief smatterings of romance, when his knees would wobble and heart beat fast into his ears. Then the girls would pass away into their lives, never seeing the young Angel, never noticing, and he could enjoy his infatuation without the burden of having to give love to be loved in return.

Women would always be a mystery, and Angel didn't believe that he could ever give of the sacred vessel of himself to love as one was supposed to love. Angel didn't think he could give himself like you were supposed to when you loved another. He enjoyed his own energy too much to ever want to share it, jealous of the attention, always needing to be the center of the hearts around him without enough room for others to share his.

Angel's body grew, and he began to enjoy sports, running, and wrestling. He grew out of the shy boy who performed private programming in the woods and began to perform more for his friends, acting out fake fights or playing the school jester. Eventually school bored him, and he ignored his studies, letting his grades lapse. He learned to escape, hiding out in the open areas, the happy hunting grounds of Great Neck. Or, on special days, he indulged his lust for action, for the masses by riding the Long Island Railroad into the jeweled city of Manhattan.

You could be anything you want to be in New York—it didn't matter. This became Angel's battle cry, and he drowned himself in the great city, escaping from gray Great Neck and himself, clawing out of his boring soul like scratching through a wall. Angel visited his cousins, and together, they'd play in Central Park or visit museums, see concerts, poetry readings, indulging in the beatnik life. Angel mobilized a hippie menagerie of players, wild friends who worshipped similar faiths of indulgence and escape, which he called F-Troop, based on the television comedy. This new church became notorious in the Manhattan neighborhoods, and they were never separated, surviving in the unkind year of 1964 together. An evil war brewed in a hot jungle across the world, testing the soul of America, exposing the darkness in its nature. Kind kings had been killed, stolen from the people. The old ways that united the country had broken, and even the bonds of family suffered. Angel and his minions indulged in mind-altering talismans, smoking plants or licking sugar cubes, swallowing magic pills. Eat me. Drink me. They sought new dimensions of thought. He even compelled his flock to drop acid and listen to Elvis, to see his true divinity, much to the annoyance of his clan. They played pirates on the State Island Ferry or smeared Bleecker Street in a mess of rainbow paints, fighting color wars. The vagrants panhandled in Central Park singing Elvis or his silly songs and slept in abandoned warehouses, seldom returning to his nest in Great Neck.

Angel would be famous one day. He believed in his own destiny, his own greatness, his gravitas. He often told his flock that one day he would rise among the dull and ubiquitous, the boring grazers and breeders. Angel knew it. Elvis assured his ascension.

Angel longed to grow his wings like all the other Angels God loved in heaven, and sometimes when he was high, he nearly believed he was soaring. He longed to fly—but not to feel the wind under his arms or soar close to the sun. He needed all those of the pitiful ones on the ground below to look up and see him, to steal their eyes and fill their spirits with jealousy. He wanted the masses to see him and burn.

By all rights, Angel should have been drafted. He didn't understand the war in Vietnam. It seemed like such a faraway place, a distant fantasy jungle, and nothing shown on television was real, right? His doctors declared him 4F, labeling him as deranged, mentally ill. This relieved Angel. He knew he could never conform to an army: a soulless mass where you surrendered your identity. Angel could never kill. He only wanted to summon smiles, laughter, and stun. So they called him sick in the mind. Others would be harmed or hindered by this diagnosis, but Angel wore it like a badge. He had been deemed different, unique, not a faceless member of the masses. This inspired him to defy and rebel. Angel didn't have to be like everyone else.

PLAYING WITH CURSES IN THE VALLEY OF THE KINGS

The explorers hiked through the individual tombs buried in the Valley of the Kings. Beneath the sand, laid buried spirits of time, of history bottled up and trapped where neither sunlight could fade or wind could erode. The tombs stretched beyond sight, far beyond the horizon of this century. Slaves of the era placed each brick with reverence, expending their own life to worship the expended spent lives of kings and queens, who would forever exist in greater wealth, comfort and security, rotting in the opulence and protection while each slave toiled his muscle to grit and labored his days in service to the dead.

"This place is cursed," their Russian servant said. Professor Roman had found him while lecturing at the University of Yalta, and he'd become his faithful bodyman—though long in teeth and snarly like a grizzled wolverine. "If we stay, we'll be cursed, too."

"We came here to find the lost queen." Anthony adjusted the brim of his fedora to guard against the eye of Ra. The sun baked the bricks and pavement, roasting the desert valley. Sweat rolled down Anthony's neck.

Lady Cynthia, lovely in her white sundress and sandals, arms still draped in long gown sleeves, twirled and danced as they strolled. She held the artifact in her hand, the ancient key to surpass locks sealed in antiquity, bypassing the walls of the old and soon forgotten, the unlocked and emancipated treasures of the mind that would initiate the birth of stars—if the old legends of Pharaoh magic were to be believed. She referred to the faded papyrus—the scroll they'd liberated from its vault in Arabia, facing the biting and snapping jackals of Anubis. She studied the script, decoded the old numbers and pointed the way.

"Unit 713." She led the way, passing through the rows of uniform crypts. Each portal glowed orange, capturing the light of Ra and summoning to stand shield against the eroding claws of time.

Tolya growled under his breath. He squinted his tiny eyes, emphasizing the tight Slavic features of his face, then spit a wad of stinking tobacco on the pavement.

"Our bodyman protests," Anthony said.

"This is a fool's mission," Tolya responded.

"I don't do any other kind."

"Time moves forward to cure and relieve," Tolya said. "The past is the absence of sunlight."

"I wish to be complete," Anthony said.

"Another illusion. You'll only find agony in the past. People hide these things in the dark, far from the sun. They pack them away and hope never to find them again. You're a fool."

Anthony nodded. "Fair enough."

The sandy valley receded, and the tide of new and vibrant interpretation flowed. Anthony felt the heat through his sandals, radiating from the baking blacktop. He leaned his hat over, blocking the sun's angle as they navigated King Valley Storage Lots of Lansdale. Cynthia followed the designated numbers and led them to the far side of the lot. A fence divided the property from Sunny Response Cemetery, and beyond the chains and barbed wire sealing its top, the hoary memorial marble decorated the rolling grass. The white monuments glowed along the horizon. Nearby, a funeral procession gathered, pulling up in limos, following a hearse, while a crowd of mourners gathered, resplendent in their midnight black outfits— silent of lip and pale in face, sickly and hunched over. A Channel 10 News van pulled up at a polite distance, and a mobile crew got out and started to unpack camera equipment. Anthony turned his gaze away. "That's because that football player's funeral is today. Damn shame. So young."

"What's the cutoff age when it isn't a shame anymore?" Anthony asked.

"I just meant . . . "

"People are so ignorant sometimes," Anthony said.

"Lot number 713," Cynthia said, ignoring him. The storage cell faced the cemetery, and Anthony kept his back to the repository. She beckoned for Anthony to release the portal, to shed the gate of closed Eden and let in the light. "Why are you waiting?"

Anthony slipped out the key from his pocket and held it to the padlock, not feeding it into the mechanism. Tumblers waited. The ghosts slept sound.

"Maybe Tolya is right."

"Anthony," Cynthia said. "We're here. It's now."

Gravity forced back his hand, sucking it to a singularity drawing in ravenous need from the cemetery. Grandmother had offered him peace, and he'd told her to stick it. Had he been rash?

Tolya nodded and spit a wad of tobacco. It splattered on the brick wall. "Best to just let things be. This is the world. This is the statue of gardens."

"Your mother deserved more, Anthony," Cynthia said. He nodded and fed the key into the lock.

"Hold up there, folk!" a man yelled from down the avenue between storage areas. The walrus in the gray suit wobbled over, landed on his paws and spoke, spitting from two white tusks of bucked teeth. "Now, take that key out of that lock. Cease and desist."

Anthony slipped out the key. "What's all this about?"

He pointed at Tolya. "Hold up. Who is this gentleman? Are you Gregory Roman?"

Tolya shook his head, and Anthony sensed the loss of an opportunity.

"I'm Bob King. I'm the manager."

"Congratulations," Anthony said, grinning. Cynthia kicked his sandal.

"I just got a phone call from Gregory Roman."

Anthony sunk, slumped his shoulders and leaned back against the cool brick, keeping his eyes in the shadow, averted from the cemetery. "And my grandfather instructed you not to let us in? He's coming up right now with a truck, isn't he?"

"You're quick, slick. His is the only name on the lease. He's the boss."

"You don't understand," Cynthia said. "His mother is in there."

"There's a person locked up in there?" The Walrus shook and blustered.

"No. His mother is dead."

"There's a dead body in there?"

"No. Wait. It's all her stuff, like her final belongings. Anthony is dying."

Anthony scoffed. "Don't Cynthia. I swear. Don't you dare."

"He never met his mother—"

"Well I'm sorry about your dealt hand, slick, but the man who is on the lease has got the gold key. Life ain't fair. Now, if you can work this out with your grandfather, I'll stay open late for you. But that's all I can do. I'll pray for you, if you think it'll help."

"Probably not," Anthony said. "But it never hurts to try."

"Now, I'm sorry about this," he said. "But I've got to take that key off of you."

"And if we don't give it up?" Cynthia asked.

"Then I'll have to call the police. Your grandfather said you stole it."

"Of all the crap!" Cynthia yelled.

Anthony grabbed her arm. He curled his lip in his chipmunk thoughtful face, signaling to her that he had an idea. "We don't want any trouble," Anthony said. "Mind if we wait here for my grandfather, maybe talk to him?"

"Well, I don't see any problem with that." The manager held out his hand. Anthony dropped the key. "I need to head back to the office." He turned and looked at the event. "What a beautiful day for a funeral. It's a golden day. Feels great to be breathing." He turned around and waddled back up front to the main office building.

"You just gave up," Cynthia said. "Why do men always let you down?"

Anthony sucked on his lip, his eyes flashing. "Cynthia. All that makeup in the car. Now, if my grandfather is following his usual routine, he's opened his coin shop on State Street for Saturday morning collectors and antiquers. He never alters his routine."

"What are you getting at?" Cynthia said.

Tolya picked up on his plotting, and he shook his head. "I don't know anything about your grandfather," Tolya said. "Never met him."

"Chances are, never has that guy, either," Anthony said. "We could pull this off. But we only have maybe ninety minutes."

"A rush order," Cynthia said. "Come on." She tugged on Tolya's arm. The old Ukrainian huffed, shoved a wad of shredded tobacco into his lip and nodded. He just melted from her touch. She dragged him back to the parking lot.

Anthony leaned his back against the brick and slid down, crouching in the shadows, among the cigarette butts, dirt and spider webs. He listened to the priest reciting Latin, conducting the funeral for the fallen football player. In his head, he took apart the familiar, yet foreign incantations, finding their rhythm. Wailing carried over the wind, and he pushed his palms to his ears, blocking out the keening.

"I got you some tea if you need it, slick." Bob stood over him, offering him a cup in his fat paw. Anthony gripped the plastic cup of tepid brew, sipped with parched lips and swallowed against his sandpaper throat.

"There, now," Bob said. "A little tea in the morning has you jumping up and about."

"Do you think I'm a child?" Anthony said, sipping the tea.

"Can't help it, slick," he said. "Afraid I might break you."

"It's fine. You brought me tea, and I might break. I'm falling into Earth's gravity, smashing into the atmosphere and breaking up into bits of stone and fire."

"Like you said, slick."

Meanwhile, The funeral continued with the eulogies. The incline sloped down from this point of perspective, giving Anthony and Bob a clear view of the proceedings. An older fellow, in a suit too small for his large frame, stood by the silvery coffin and bellowed the songs of the God of death. Another news van had pulled up and filmed the ceremony from a distance, disconnected from reality.

"Shame about that," Bob said. Then he studied Anthony, measuring his light, the pallor of his skin, the spark in his eye and calculated his duration of life, as if it could be read like a water meter.

"How 'bout you?" He pulsed out a tiny flask from his jeans pocket, uncapped it and drank some of the liquor. He offered it to Anthony, and he waved it off.

"Who measures the tides? How many photons bombard the world?"

"Shit," Bob said, taking another pull of the liquor, probably to soothe his damaged spirit after encountering the walking dead. He felt his own mortality. The fog parted. The self-delusion receded. Anthony reminded them all, the majority living in the forever fantasy. Consciousness shall never end. Bob tipped back the bottle and emptied the remainder. "What the hell do you say to that?"

"Hire a thousand writers. Enlist a thousand priests of all religions. Give them one rolling sheet of papyrus and a nearly empty pen. Set them to work. I'm fading. I can't find the words."

"Nah. None of that philosophy bullshit. Can't stand priests, either."

"Then what is to be said?" Anthony asked.

"Shit, slick. Just sucks."

The eulogist broke into a mountain of wind howls and collapsed onto the coffin. He banged on the silver aluminum then banged on his chest, smashing his coat in projected frustration. He cried for the boy now mulched to earth. He cried for himself.

"Yep," Anthony said. "Just sucks."

"I wish I could do something for you, slick. Your grandfather sounds like a real S.O.B."

He finished the tea and scanned the avenues between the cement tombs. Noon drew on. Then he spotted Cynthia leading a patent senior, guiding him like a doddering old fool who couldn't maintain his balance. Oh no. Anthony shook his head. Tolya looked like a demented Rabbi escaping for a Bar Mitzvah: long curly beard, bad wig, black-rimmed glasses molded out of plastic, and to top it off, probably to remark on his many years of experience in a violent world, a scar sliced down the side of his cheek. It reminded him of a job done for a school play, but he couldn't fault Cynthia, since she'd had merely minutes to create the character and only the backseat of Tolya's car for a dressing room.

Damn. He should say something, maybe distract Bob from the obvious forgery. "Grandfather." Anthony stood up. He set the cup on the concrete. "You are . . . looking well today."

"I feel bloody tired," he said. "Bloody hot day. Bad for the arthritis." Oh, God. He'd adopted a British accent to cover his Russian tones, and it sounded like a child imitating an actor from a bad English movie. Anthony covered his mouth with his hand, pretending to cough, trying to hide the sudden spout of laughter.

"Yes. It is hot, Grandfather. How is your war wound?"

"It was a trucking accident," Tolya said and rubbed his left leg, forgetting his character.

"No. The scar on your face."

"Oh! Only hurts when it rains."

"Good morning, sir." Bob offered his hand. "Bob King. I'm the manager here. We spoke on the phone earlier." Tolya wavered, then extended his hand.

"Yes, we did. And I'm pleased to say I have resolved any differences with my son—"

"Grandson."

"Yes, he is. My grandson. Right pain in the bum, sometimes. But a good lad. He's going to help me go through the unit. My back, you see, and my gimpy leg."

"Very good, then," Bob said. "Now, if I could just see some identification."

Tolya looked at Cynthia. Cynthia looked at Anthony. Anthony gazed down into the cemetery below. A woman in a pant suit read an official comment over the coffin, reciting from a clipboard.

"Blimey," Tolya said. "I forgot my bloody wallet."

"Is this really necessary?" Cynthia asked.

Bob chuckled under his breath and shook his head, then met Anthony's eyes and cracked a little smile. Anthony sucked on his upper lip and said, "It's okay, Grandfather. I've got a feeling. Show him your license."

Tolya hesitated, and Anthony touched his arm. He spit a wad of chew, not accounting for his new beard, and it caught in the bristles then dripped down his chin. Cynthia found some tissues in her pocket and dabbed it up.

"He just suffered a stroke," she said.

"A stroke," Anthony said. "That's good. That's very good. But it's okay, Grandfather."

Tolya shrugged, pulled out his wallet and showed his license to Bob. The manager didn't even glance at it.

"All's good, Mr. Roman. Here, let me give this back to you." He handed Tolya the key. He hunched his shoulders and looked ready to collapse.

"I'll be in the office if you need me, but I've got to warn you folk: If something ain't on the up and up, I'll have to call the police."

"Right," Anthony said. "We shouldn't be too long."

"Good luck with your search, slick," Bob said. "I'm sure your mother was a fine woman." He strolled up the avenue. They waited for him to part before speaking, as if they still had a cover to protect.

"Why did he do that?" Cynthia asked.

"'Cause life just sucks, and he had it in his power to make it a bit easier for us."

They heard Bob howling with laughter in the distance.

"What a motley crew," Anthony said. "If we're going to keep fucking with reality, we're going to have to practice."

"I think you ruined this beard," Cynthia said, still fidgeting with it. Tolya shrugged at her, then handed Anthony the key. He popped the lock and heaved the gate, pushing the slats into the roof.

Anthony checked his phone. "We've got maybe forty minutes, then we'd better haul ass. Bob warned us."

"I can't watch this," Tolya said, his accent returned. "I'll go listen to the game in the car."

"Tolya." Cynthia handed him her phone. "If you spot trouble, warn us."

"Da, Comrade General." Tolya vanished into the uniformed rows.

Anthony might have imagined the scent. The sweet aroma lingered under the sour stink of mold and mildew. Old paper smelled woody or like a wet autumn—common to attics full of books sentimentally valued and perhaps needed at some future point. The pages turned to dust at the touch. He thought of his grandmother's perfume, but she scented with musky draughts. It could have been kin to Karen's sandalwood lotion and possessed a spicy and not-subtle character that would be immediately detected. Was this her gentle impression? It seemed familiar, perhaps his first sensation from outside of her womb, the scent of his mother. He locked onto it like a bloodhound, and it guided him through the precisely arranged boxes placed in the four corners of a coeval cross. Cynthia hovered in the light, waiting permission.

"Only a few minutes to know a lifetime," Anthony said, and beckoned her into the tomb. "It's near here. I'm sure." The boxes were stacked five high, and he set the top one down and pulled from its junior. A stain blemished the pale cardboard, and he knelt by it, pulling back the duct tape sealing.

Cynthia toured the boxes, reading the dates—each properly marked in the bottom corner with block digits. "This is like your grandfather's filing cabinet."

"Control," Anthony said. "The universe can be discovered, refined, accounted, tallied, and deposited." He imagined his grandfather the day after his mother died, handling the arrangements, discharging his paternal responsibilities, encoding and processing the emotion. He'd gone down his checklist, sparing or blocking his wife from any grief, keeping her sealed off behind his doors like a doll buried in a closet, forgetting the sigh of the burning orb.

Vertigo rocked Anthony's body, settling in his head. The mold burned his throat, and he choked. He focused, concentrated, resisting the pressure to deny, to run away, to just let his grandfather cart all this stuff off to the dump and strip his mother of identity, weeding her existence for the space-time record. Who would remember her? Who would care? Best to just erase it like it never happened.

"When I was a kid, they'd fight," Anthony said. "Not loud. They never yelled so the neighbors could hear them. Couldn't make a scene."

"I know people like that," Cynthia said, sorting through the boxes.

"I was playing alone in the living room with my cars. I

never had friends over. I'd ask, but Grandmother told me I was coming down with a cold or the flu and shouldn't be around folk. I always had a cold."

Cynthia nodded. "Poor thing."

"They were fighting over where to move the dining room table—just a matter of a foot. Grandmother was adamant, wanted to move it away from the kitchen door, but he said its end would stick too far out in the kitchen. They argued for some time, and I pushed along my little cars, driving them into the kitchen. Grandfather stopped talking and stroked his chin, thinking about something she said. Then he raised his arms like a Baptist praising Jesus and brought them down on her face, the back of his fists smashing her cheeks."

"He hit her? I despise that jerk."

"Next morning, Grandmother's face swelled up and turned black and blue. I asked him if she was okay. Know what he said? 'Your grandmother is just fine. She has no bruises. It never happened.' And she agreed."

"Abusers do that. They have to erase the incident."

"But it was more than that. He believed it. His eyes went wide, and he had no idea what I was talking about. He didn't like his behavior, what he'd become, so he simply vetoed it and removed it from his recollection of reality."

"But he can't do that."

"Why not? It's all human recollection. Reality is perspective, memory. It is what's recorded. He decided to delete it from the record of his home, and thus it never happened. Eventually, my grandmother's eyes healed, and life went on."

"But you remembered?"

"I defied the bastard," Anthony said. "I burned it into my head, but after a few years, it felt more like a dream.

And I wondered if it even happened. I had no record to confirm it, and even records can be disputed."

"Please stop, Anthony." Her voice quivered. "I don't care for this. I feel less . . . real."

"I've not felt real since Doctor Helsinki informed me I was dying."

"But, you are real, Anthony. And if you feel like you're slipping away, I'll hold onto you. If you try to fly, I'll hold you to the ground, even if you rip my arms off."

Anthony managed to tear the tape and pulled free the sallow newspaper. He paused to check the date on the sports section: February 10th, 1985. He pulled out glass and plastic bottles of various creams, perfumes, soaps, and lotions. The cap had popped off one of the containers, and a white cream encrusted it. Anthony pressed it to his nose and breathed in, sucking down the aroma. The crust flaked off and stuck to his mouth, and he licked it, tasted the bitter soap, the ripe perfume flowering on his tongue, then swallowed it down, tasting his mother, reveling in her flavor, to make it indelible.

"All my life, I've known this scent," he said. "It's come home to me."

She picked up some of the bottles. "I adore lavender. I wear it sometimes."

"In college?"

"Everyday."

He nodded.

"It looks like your grandfather packed it all chronologically. Your mother's life starts there, at the back left."

"I feel like I'm on a game show." His blood pressure rose, pouring warm water into his head.

"And there's a ticking clock," Cynthia said. "It would take a month to go through all this."

Anthony curled his lip. "Then we only open the boxes buried deepest, the ones my grandfather would want to remember the least."

They moved to the first quadrant and dismantled the symmetric squares, shifting the boxes and digging deep. Each square composed a cube of five-by-five, and they aimed for the epicenter, pushing away the rest of the boxes. He dug out the root and pulled the tape from the lid, then went through the folded baby blankets decorated with cherubs. Anthony pulled out a little pillow. Tiny white motes of porcelain sprinkled from its lip, and he collected the baby teeth. He stuck one in his mouth and sucked on it. Deeper below some baby clothing, he plucked out a dirty plush seal.

"Oh, my Goddess," Cynthia said. "Where did you get yours?"

"I found it in the crawlspace below the house when I was a kid. My grandmother tried to take it away, said it was filthy and would make me sick. I cried all night, and she finally gave in. Sometimes, I could make her change her mind, especially if I wailed loud enough for the neighbors to hear."

"Should we take him with us?"

Anthony looked at the white seal. The left side of its face had faded, probably from infant suckling and a later oral fixation. He'd suffered the same issue. "No. She needs it. I have the brother, anyway." They returned the contents to the box and sealed it, then they moved onto the next quadrant in order.

They followed their prescribed methodology and dug to the heart of the stack.

"Youth and adolescence," Cynthia said. Anthony pried open the box. His fingers ran along white silk sealed in a transparent bag. He lifted out the gown and displayed it to Cynthia.

"Pretty dress," she said. "One of the sacraments, I bet. Holy Communion. Confirmation. I love the lace."

"She was a child, my mother," Anthony said, remarking on her formation in his head, the missing components filling in the timeline. "She was born and grew into a young woman."

"And buried away and forgotten like Mary Magdalene."

"What made you say that?" Anthony asked.

"Felt like what it was."

Anthony dug through the contents and found a watch box. He opened it.

"A Mickey Mouse watch!" Cynthia said. "Goddess. These were so popular. I remember when I was a little one." The remainder of the box rattled, and he dumped the contents onto the cold concrete: broken alarm clocks, the clockwork species, of various types and designs. He counted at least ten.

"And she grew up," he said. They moved onto the next satellite of boxes.

The third box contained mostly clothes: torn shirts, punk gear, Doc Martin boots and chains. Some records had broken, mostly old Sex Pistols, some metal, too. He handed Pink Floyd's *The Wall* to Cynthia.

"This freaked me out," she said. "Classic stuff. Marching hammers. I can't imagine this stuff in your grandmother's house. That must have been a circus."

Anthony pulled out a cardboard box and opened it, revealing small wooden birdhouses and key ring holders. He found a full set of tools, the kind needed for a shop class. His mother liked to build and work with her hands, and he couldn't recall one piece of homemade craft that decorated the house growing up.

Anthony dug under the records and pulled out a

wrapped barrette wrapped in red bandanas. He unwrapped it and held the silver raven to the frail light. The light glinted, and the raven flapped its wings by shadow trick.

"Gorgeous," Cynthia said.

"Please have it."

"No. I couldn't."

"She would have given it to you," Anthony said. "I feel that. I know it." He offered it to her, and she held it to her chest.

"Your mother was a sweet woman."

Stuck at the bottom, Anthony recovered two framed pictures. The first showed a young woman with dark hair, sharp eyes and a long nose standing with his grandparents, both younger and animated at some sort of sports meet, maybe soccer. His mother looked around fifteen with early breasts growing from her chest, ripening and swelling. She wore shorts and a jersey depicting the number '47'. Below that, Anthony found another framed photo. He reached into the shadows to retrieve it, and a glass shard slit his thumb. He grabbed the frame by its side, set it on his lap, then sucked the salty blood from the wound. The picture showed another family portrait, this time with an older woman, maybe seventeen, her breasts fully grown and a line of cleavage exposed from the short top of her black dress. She wore a white corsage on her wrist and a white headband. Glass shards spilled from the picture, and to refuse any theory that the glass had shattered while in storage, two thick black Xs blocked out his grandparents' faces. An angry hand had drawn them with a Sharpie marker.

"Let's give it a moment before we open the last," he said. "It's all coming too quickly."

"Your grandfather will be here soon, and I hope to be long gone."

He nodded and steadied himself. All his days, he'd wondered about his mother, constructing one fantasy to the next, fashioning her as a nurse, or a teacher, or a young friend, anything he required at the time. Her spirit became protean, and he sculpted her into the remedy needed to soothe the current illness or pain.

"I'm always going to be running out of time, now," he said. "But then, so are you. You just don't realize it."

She flinched at the observation.

They found the last box, a larger set than the rest. Grandfather had stacked her dresser, chairs, box spring, and mattress along the back wall. An oval mirror reflected sparse sunrays. They struggled to lift out the covering boxes, unsealing the keystone, then finally separated it. He sensed the dense contents amassing gravity and bending space around it ever slightly into a gravity well.

"Why are you waiting? The lawnmower is coming. It's chewing up the ground."

"I know," he said, fingering the flaps, bleeding on the cardboard from his sliced thumb. "I can hear the motor. I can feel him chomping. We're dead. She's just . . . not what I wanted. I've fantasized for years."

"Our heroes are never what we imagined them to be."

"Just another illusion. Makes the world."

"Now, honey, come on."

He pulled back the flaps on the box and drew out the top layer, a bag of clothes: old torn jeans, tattered shirts, Bob Dylan t-shirts and combat boots. A lot of hippie stuff.

"I love this chick," Cynthia said.

"I think these are journals," he said, pulling free dusty notebooks. He tore wide the first, eager in eye to read the words and consume her private thoughts, taken from her mind and recorded on the flaky paper. "Son of a bitch." A black line redacted every sentence from page one to the last. Anthony paged through the next notebook and the next.

"Goddess," Cynthia said. "He's insane. He didn't throw the journals out, but he went through and crossed out every line of prose? He's a lunatic."

"It's perfect for him. He erased her, and these journals existed, representing her deletion from reality. While this tomb buries her possessions, her soul sleeps in the dirt, chained from freedom, sealed off and starved. It's like your magick, the metaphor. He was thorough. He enjoyed this labor, crossing out every word, each sentence, bricking up her thoughts, ripping them from the ether and sealing them from eyesight. This is an act of torment. This is torture, slow and deliberate and careful."

"Then it's a good thing he's coming to throw all this stuff out. She'll finally be free."

Anthony pulled out a dry-cleaning bag and pulled the zipper, revealing a pristine black leather jacket. "That's gorgeous," Cynthia said. He took it off the hanger and wrapped it around his shoulders. He detected a meager scent of sandalwood and cigarette smoke in the leather.

Below the journals, he discovered a hymnbook, dusty and torn, then a plastic bong, cracked down the side, packed among books on Buddhism and transcendental thought. He continued digging down through the records and pulled out a scrapbook that also served as a photo album. A black raven in flight drawn in pen and ink decorated the cover.

"Maybe she's been reborn a raven," he said. "I'll be born a raven of her nest and fly beneath her wings."

Cynthia brushed away a tear and scratched her eyes, probably irritated by the mold.

He paged through the journal, admiring the various constructs of paper and decals and plastic motes. Photos adorned some of the pages, some faded or stained. The few that depicted clear scenes suffered blackened faces. His grandfather had been thorough.

"What is that?" Cynthia asked.

"It looks like a wrestling match." Anthony examined the photo—a wrestling ring, a professional arena filled with screaming fans. It looked to him like some kind of joke. "There's a guy, but this can't be right. He's wrestling a woman. You can see her dark hair around the black mark. It doesn't even look like a wrestling uniform." He showed her the male wrestler, obvious from his features and flat chest. He wore a white set of long underwear and gray shorts. His dark, wild hair flailed from around his blackened face. Memphis, April 1982 labeled the bottom of the Polaroid."

"Oh my Goddess," Cynthia said. "Let me see that." She tugged the album out of Anthony's hand. Some folded letters dumped out of a secret compartment in the glue between pages, hidden behind embroidery. Anthony pushed them back into the slot. "I know this. I've seen this scene before. Memphis?"

"Are you and the angels going to tell me?"

"Look at her hair. See the raven barrette?" Anthony studied the photo and spotted the decorative piece in her hair. He could have had wings, maybe a bird or butterfly.

"So, you're saying my mother did do some amateur wrestling?" He recalled his grandmother mentioning this, but Anthony didn't understand it.

"No," she said. "Well, yes. But, it's more. The guy she's wrestling . . . remember what I said when I first met you?"

"'Hey dude, you're sitting on my hand?'"

"No. After that."

"You said I looked just like that comedian. Kaufman." She pointed at the photo. "He wrestled women. It was a gig. Really upset people. He loved playing the villain wrestler."

"My mother knew Andy Kaufman?"

She flipped through the pages and studied more shots of the match. "It's got to be. I studied it for the play I wrote. This is Andy Kaufman." Then she looked up, her eyes wild and flapping wings. "Go into the light, Anthony."

"What?"

"Just, please. Humor a mad woman."

He got up and stepped back closer to the door.

"Take off that hat, please."

He hesitated, then removed it, feeling bare to her. He held the fedora at his side and rocked in the dirty light streams.

"Goddess," she said. She stroked his round cheek, ran fingers along his chin. He moved back from her, feeling his stomach twisting. The glare in her eyes spooked him, and he nearly backed out of the storage unit. His phone plucked a harp string, snapping the moment. He grabbed the phone. Several messages had been left from Cynthia. Tolya had her phone. He quickly called back.

"Tolya?" he asked. "What's the skinny?"

"Where the hell have you been?"

"It's the brick walls. We must not have had any signal. Shit."

"Well pull up your goddamn socks and get out of there," he yelled into the phone. "Your grandfather's come with all the hosts of hell at his call. He went in, talked to the manager, came out, sat in his car, and now a Lansdale police cruiser's pulled up."

"We're gone. Pick us up in front of the cemetery." Anthony shut the phone. "Grab the book. We've overstayed our welcome."

She closed the album and held it under her arm,

130

careful no more papers fell free. He held her hand and tugged her into the light. A police radio squawked around the side of the building. Their boots registered footfalls on the concrete.

"My hat, please."

Cynthia offered the brown fedora, and he tilted it over his forehead, keeping the sun from his eyes. He studied the fence, looking up at the barbed wire. He sucked on his upper lip then ran back into the storage unit and grabbed the wire clippers from the box of tools.

"And off we go dancing." Anthony prepared himself for a feat of exertion and steeled his body, summoned the required fortitude. He could still pull off moments of strength but soon ran out of steam. He grabbed the grooves in the chain link fence and pulled himself up, careful not to rip his new leather coat. His arm muscles ached, but he held on.

"Anthony!" she whispered. "I can't climb a fence."

"You mean you've never climbed a fence before?"

"I'm a girl," she said. "I always used the gate."

The fully uniformed officer turned the corner—a young guy with black hair—along with his grizzly partner. He heard his grandfather talking to them: "I want them arrested for trespassing and theft."

"No, hold on, sir," the young one said. "Let's just see what's going on."

Anthony offered his hand and braced himself. "And I bet you've never been in jail, either," Anthony said. She looked back at the cops, sighed, then grabbed it. He stretched his arm and helped her climb the fence. She mounted the link and pulled herself up, catching her shirtsleeves on the links. She yanked them free.

"So, what about the barbed wire, Indy?"

Anthony smiled, his eyes glinting in the sun. "Taken

care of." He climbed another foot, reached up with the wire clippers and snipped twice. The spool of barbed wire spun free.

"Sweet," she said. She leaned over and kissed his left hand.

"Hey. Stop." The cops dashed for them. They barreled over the top and dropped down the other side, then darted down the incline, nearly falling from the sudden angle drop. His feet almost tripped underneath him, and he couldn't control his vector. The cop's radio squawked behind, and he heard his grandfather raising holy hell.

"That's the last of him," Anthony said, holding his head high in the sun, then breaking right through the remaining funeral procession. He bumped into the crowd, hitting the priest in the back and knocking him into the aluminum coffin. Several of the female mourners squealed, and he toppled over into the fresh marble marker. The news cameras recorded the whole faux pas.

"Excuse us," Cynthia said, able to control her descent. "He's not well. He has cancer. We were visiting his mother's grave, and he fell ill."

Anthony sensed the vacuum of the cameras, sucking at his soul. They drank in his spirit then exhaled, flowing out, tempting him with the power. He commanded the attention of the city, and his heart raced from the realization. This time, real humans populated the darkness in his bedroom, a true audience, and the urge to dance, to revel in their attention set fire to his limbs.

"And I needed to dance," he yelled and whooped. "Oh, do I need to jig and waltz on the graves of the sleeping and the dead. Everyone, now. Let's dance on the graves."

The crowd's collective jaw hung open, all of them mortified.

"He's very sick," Cynthia said, picking him up. "I'm taking him home."

"We're all going home, one day," Anthony said. "So dance dance dance like a madman who can't stop dancing." And he sung it as they walked away from the funeral, free of foot and Cynthia's face glowing red. They met Tolya off the highway, eluded the police and made their getaway back to the Lansdale Community Theater.

OTHER PEOPLE LIVE IN ANGEL

Other people lived in Angel. Elvis became real to him, a voice in his head. Angel became the King, dressing like the performer, talking, staying him, and pretending to be Elvis. He also excised the other people who invaded his mind, using them like vessels, sailing to new worlds. He loved playing foreigners, and a simple voice began, a simple accent—a humble gentleman who came from a faraway island in a faraway sea, taking Angel faraway. Angel moved from soul to soul, face to face, gyrating his hips as Elvis, being a happy and silly idiot or playing the bongos as a foreign islander from an island that sank. Over time, the foreigner's spirit intensified; he loved folk music, the bongos, and always wanted to be a comedian. Then Angel would speak in tongues, creating variations of words, spouting nonsense with grace and sentience:

Sebenye metitemya yaderni nidee terma.

He knew what each word meant, yet listeners pondered, spending their priceless attention on Angel. He craved it.

Finally, Angel fell in love. Glorious! Gloria. He heard about a school for entertainers in Boston—Grahm Junior College. There, he'd find his way and build a life with her.

Since his youth, Angel had worshipped the mighty crystal screen, the great saying, the wizard of his eye. This was his god, the source of his spirit, his élan. He sought the secrets of this altar, decrypted its mysteries, sought its soul. How could he find his way to the other side of the screen to trade places with the performer? The viewer had no power, but the performer on the other side controlled the world. At Grahm, they held this power: studios, cameras, editing equipment. Angel would no longer need to beg on the street for audiences or play to his siblings. Now he could create his own crystal altar, hang his religious icons and give the other personalities a forum, a place where they could prosper and expand. Grahm was a progressive temple, a place where his antics were seen as education, exercises. He thrived when he performed, yet failed at the mechanics of production, of the disciplined crafting of the visual arts.

Gloria, still in high school, came to see Angel, and together they worshipped creation, inception and conception. Let's make a young Angel! Why not? We'll bring a life into this world without oversight, responsibility. That's what flesh does. Why fight it?

But he sought a world beyond the flesh, and in Angel's studies at the college, he discovered a new way to expand the horizons of his mind that did not require limited and transient substances. Transcendental meditation became his new means of living. He performed this magic mental trick every day, taking it like a prescribed medication, and this new method brought Angel a force he'd never truly known before: stability and a connection to his own personality, through the stormy seas and choppy waves of the other voices who possessed him. Angel played his bongos, seeking the heartbeat of the life force, and he surrendered all drugs, giving himself to this new religion, the old religion as a pilgrim or zealot. Meditation didn't calm the fires or mediate the rage, but allowed him some peace, to know himself and perhaps control the forces that threatened to rip him apart. It caged the tornadoes, contained the storms and allowed him to even use the power, channeling it into his performance, creating a controlled madness that he could tame then even create.

Angel found the penultimate in art, a usage of raw spirit, of essence that he could generate into new people, carving new faces from his own given and finite flesh. He knew a power that only belonged to the gods and time. He grew a new womb in his soul, a forge of personalities, characters at his own center, which he built brick-by-brick through his meditation, each day unlocking its design and operation. He created new people, controlled them, summoned them when he performed, and now he had the facilities to put this power to its potential, employing the visual artistic equipment of his school. Angel lived in a fantasy world, yet he could function in reality, living in society, and this changed his status from mentally unstable to sane and profitable. Angel found a way to live in his disease and adapt, and this would take him to greatness.

Gloria's womb flourished with his offspring. She was eight months when he left on a holy journey to Vegas, to see his King, to show Elvis his new novel. The life grew in her body, and Angel didn't notice. He'd created so many people that it had become mundane. He was a many-father to many people, and he'd eventually ignore this child also, not truly understanding that he'd created this life. Their families allowed this because he was different, and no one called him selfish.

The baby was born to the eighteen-year-old Gloria. She and Angel had hidden this pregnancy from both families, who were shocked and furious with the young couple. The family immediately took the baby away, arranging the little girl to be adopted. They discouraged Gloria from touching her daughter, in fear of building a bond. Her family gave her no choice, and she called Angel the next day from the hospital. Angel had gone out west to seek his mental wave. Angel was sweet, kind and disconnected, treating Gloria like a distant cousin who had given birth to a child he'd never meet, always polite.

Hi! Hi!

And they took Angel's daughter, hid her away, put a curse on her so she would never know her father; and it was all fixed. Angel never had to pay a dollar nor any thoughts to the life he'd created. What was one life among the several in his head? It wasn't very entertaining, and it didn't help his own journey of becoming. Children were born all the time, and he couldn't afford the attention. The world had to look upon his light, and Angel refused to share.

WIND-SONG OF THE DEAD

Anthony paged through the scrapbook and searched the blurred photos and three-dimensional creations, seeking its secret spirit, its sincere nature. Reveal your heart to me. Buried deep, beyond the distortions of time and his grandfather's desecration, detailed his mother's soul. She'd created it here with photographs and stickers and beads and colored paper, creating a proper memorial stone as if she knew her fate—*Remember me. I lived once. I existed. Matter organized and created my identity in this world. Remember me if but for a short time. Stars are born and die, and I took but a fraction of the light.* She'd hidden her secrets here and time had buried them deeper, but they could seek them out, recreate them, bring his mother back into this world.

"You're awake," Cynthia said, sitting next to him in the theater audience chair. She gave him a cup of hot tea, and Anthony held it below his chin, letting the vapors pour over his face, warming his skin and eyes. He blew on the brim of the dark liquid and stirred the sugar until it dissolved.

"I was going to let you sleep all day," Cynthia said.

"What time is it?"

"Almost eight. Are you hungry? I cooked some hot dogs in the microwave. I'll make you one."

"I've got clay in my stomach." When she mentioned eating, Anthony became aware of the pain pinching his gut. He'd sensed it in his sleep, nearly waking him, but after this morning's exercise and police pursuit, his body took the rest he needed. He had to get used to the changes in energy. Even the smallest tasks required three times the effort, and it frustrated him. He burned his youth in a bonfire, and it was probably this youth that had kept him alive this long, slowing the cancer and strengthening his resistance. It wouldn't last.

"What was he like? Andy Kaufman?"

Her eyes clouded all dreamy, and Anthony saw her lover's look—her true love, dead now many years, but just as real and alive to her heart. A twinge of jealousy pinged his chest, and he shook it off. None of that now. Jealousy was for the long-living.

"A genius. Sheer genius. And mad. He lived ahead of his time, and I doubt he'll be truly recognized for generations, if anyone remembers."

"I confess I only know him from you—and that movie where Jim Carrey played him. I watched some of it one night, but I was half-asleep and don't remember much."

"Andy challenged reality," she said. "He knew something none of us did. He messed with people's heads. He hated being called a comedian. Song and dance man, a performer. Credit wasn't important to him, and he never took it for many of his creations like Tony Clifton and the bad guy wrestler. To this day, him and his friends claim he wasn't Tony, and they both played the part of the nightclub singer so he could appear to be a real person. He wanted to shock people, to knock them out of their complacency. He liked to wake people up."

"Are you sure that's what he wanted to do? He sounds like some frantic flailing warrior philosopher. You sure it wasn't just for fun, that he liked fucking with people?" He sipped the hot tea, and it singed his tongue. He blew to cool it.

"Maybe," she said. "But even if he hadn't planned it, that's what happened. You're probably right. I doubt he thought about it much."

"What happened to him? You said he died."

She didn't speak for a few minutes, sucking on her lips. "I don't want to talk about it. Not like this."

"Come on, Cynthia. Why the hell do people think they're going to upset me by talking about death? You think I don't know it, that you're going to ruin the surprise? I think about it all the time and feel guilty when I bring it up."

She sighed and took a sip from his tea. "Lung cancer. He never smoked. God's joke. He had chemo, even went to faith healers. Maybe he burned the world too hot, and the universe had to balance itself. That was a line from my play."

He nodded and felt the circle turning, putting all the variables together in his head. It had to be this way. He played a part in a script written at the beginning of time. All the world and sum of human existence watched.

"Honestly," she whispered, scared of invisible spies or the devil listening in the background, "I don't even know if he's dead."

"How do you mean?" He sipped the tea then quickly threw it up onto the floor. She reached out to take his hand. "Leave it be," he snapped and wiped it up with a napkin. Little signs showed his worsening symptoms. He could no longer hide it as well. They continued.

"He talked about faking his death. And he was getting more and more extreme, trying to top himself, shaking up the world. He created so much negativity, especially with the bad guy wrestler, and played it so perfectly that most of the audience couldn't tell it was a gag. And sometimes I don't think it was. He got lost in his characters. He created new lives, and they became so powerful that he'd get sucked in and not always be able to find his way back."

"Do you think I could fake it? Make it unreal, somehow? Short out the circuit. Balance the equation."

She took his hand in hers and kissed it. "I don't know, Anthony. I'm not just going to wait and let this happen. I can't do it anymore."

Anthony opened the journal to the wrestling pictures and traced the outline of the woman on the mat, touching her hair. Even blacked out, she still exhibited such youth and life and fury. He felt proud of her, even if he'd only known her briefly from the inside. He could sense the same fury burning in him and understood why his grandparents had feared him so, keeping him at a distance.

"And he wrestled women?"

"Oh, yes. It was a good bit. But caused problems. He wanted to be a bad guy wrestler, but he wasn't physically inclined."

"They'd beat the shit out of him," he said.

She nodded. "So, he decided to pick on women and created this infuriating sexist character. He talked trash about women, getting the crowd riled up. He created so much negativity—but it wasn't him. Just a bit. He worshipped women, emotionally, physically, and spiritually, and was the kindest soul in love. A gentle creature. The crowd didn't see that, though. He'd invite women into the ring and wrestle them."

"And that's how my mother got in there? How they met?"

"I don't know. Maybe. I swear that's him. He had a

unique presence and wrestling outfit. All designed to stir up the crowd."

He ran his fingers along the pages and felt the bulge of the hidden letters. "Oh, damn. I nearly forgot these, in the police chase and all." He plucked them from their secret cavern, folded into the paper sculptures glued to the pages. "Letters."

"Love letters," Cynthia said. "They have to be. The ways of a woman."

Anthony hesitated at the folds of the first document, then he unfolded the paper.

Dear Mr. Kaufman:

You are a pig, sir. And I want to grind you into the dirt. I am not a professional wrestler, but I have more spirit then you can deal with. To prove to you that women are not inferior, I will drive out to California just to meet you . . . and destroy you.

You're a pig.

Big fan.
Karen

A faded Polaroid fell out of the batch of love leaves. It showed Andy Kaufman wearing his long underwear and black shorts holding down a woman on a mat. Anthony recognized his grandmother's eyes and chin.

"Your mother," Cynthia said.

"I've only seen her picture a few times. My grandmother won't keep them around the house. I found one once in a copy of Salinger's *Nine Stories* that was in the basement. She burned it. She actually lit a candle and burned it. It was almost ceremonial."

"They were in love for a little while," Cynthia said.

Tolya snapped Anthony from reading, stepping in through the theater side door. "Need to take care of the sink in the kitchen. Don't let me disturb your acts of futility."

Anthony waved at the old bastard and returned to reading.

"Sounds like your mother hated Andy and loved him. But that was pretty much Andy. People didn't disregard him or ignore the guy. You adored and despised him. He provoked a reaction."

"So, my mother sent him a letter."

He dug through the letters and found a closely dated one:

Dear Karen:

I thank you for your letter, and I hope you'll come wrestle with me at my show at Berkeley University. I hope I have not offended you with my song and dance. It's all show business. I'm getting the crowd all riled up.

You're from Pennsylvania. I grew up in Great Neck, Long Island, and my family still lives there. Give my agent, George, a call when you get here. I've included his card. I can find you a place to stay.

Andy Kaufman

"He sounds like a decent and sensitive guy," Anthony said.

"A lot like someone I know," Cynthia said. The letters

were polite responses, single pages, some with flowery doodles all over the parchment. The papers turned violet and pink and were written in casual style. You could see from the letters that their relationship moved from impersonal to amorous. Some of them were dated and stretched over a month. Envelopes showed postmarks from across the country. His mother must have hitchhiked across America, riding her thumb.

"My father was there," Cynthia said. "He went with your mother. I think a group of friends went. He's talked about it when he's been drinking. He always talks about your mother when he's had a few beers."

Anthony came to the last letter:

Dear Karen:

Come soon. I'm sending you the money to fly out. Stay with me. Our souls have sought each other. I have something to complete with you. I don't understand it. I feel it. Bob says I'm crazy, but I don't care. I need you here.

Tony is jealous. I have not told him you're coming.

Andy

"They hadn't even met, yet," Cynthia said.

Tolya stuck his head into the theater. "You two mad persons!" he yelled. "Come to the kitchen. You're on the news."

"Beg your pardon?" Cynthia asked. Tolya ducked out, and Anthony returned the papers to their hiding spot and shut the scrapbook. He got up, bending over from the sudden pain, and steeled himself to push on. He fed another morphine from its bottle and sucked it down dry. Cynthia followed him to the kitchen on the lower theater level in the back.

Tolya sat at the small kitchen table and turned up the volume on the small color set. An anchorwoman with bad hair spoke:

"Two fugitives wanted by Lansdale Police for questioning in a break-in at King's Valley Storage early this morning interrupted the funeral for high school student and football star, Jimmy Christmas, in Lansdale today."

"The cameras," Anthony said. "Oh, fuck."

The news showed Cynthia and him running through the crowd and banging into a few of the mourners and hitting the coffin. They didn't play any sound, narrating above the footage. It reminded Anthony of the end chase scene in old episodes of *Benny Hill.*

"One of the duo, as yet unidentified, demanded the crowd to dance and desecrate the graves. Spokesman for the Lansdale Police Department commented, saying, 'Use of recreational narcotics not only hurts the user but the whole community.'"

"I'm not on drugs!" Anthony yelled. "Oh, wait. Well, I am on morphine. But. Fuck. I'm dying of cancer."

The news replayed the footage again, zooming in, clearly showing their faces—easily identifiable.

"On YouTube, the video has already reached ten thousand views. Users are voting on the message, and so far, the comments are evenly positive and negative. Some proclaim the message, calling this man a prophet. Others say he should be arrested for disturbing the solemn occasion. Users are calling this man The Death-Dancing Prophet."

"How does it feel to be a prophet?" Tolya asked.

"Reluctant prophet," Anthony said. "Like I've been kicked in the face."

Cynthia watched, her face mortified, her jaw hanging wide. "We're wanted by the police?"

"That's just the news, Cynthia," Anthony said. "They would have stormed the place with a SWAT team. Relax."

"Easier for you to say," she said. He may have been leaving the world and no longer cared about what humans could do to him, but she had to stay and didn't want to go to jail. Cynthia's phone twittered. She stuck it to her head.

"Yes. Well. Sure. I guess. See you in a bit." She shut the phone and dropped it on the table. "That was the theater chairwoman, Ms. Sanders. She needs to come over and talk to me. She didn't say goodbye."

Tolya shook his head.

"It'll be fine," Anthony said.

Cynthia rushed out to the bathroom and washed up, then ran back to the stage. Anthony followed her. She gathered up the bedding and sheets, then dragged the piles to the corner of the stage. Anthony helped dissemble her makeshift bedroom. They picked up around the theater, and a tall woman in a pant suit stepped into the theater. She wore her gray hair pulled back into a bun, and Anthony wondered when the last time was that she'd really gotten laid—not just a quick, complimentary fulfillment of the obligations of marriage, but when she'd been propped up on all fours and taken it from behind until she howled?

"Hello, Cynthia," she said. "I didn't realize you had company." The left side of her face stuck a bit when she talked, perhaps the result of a stroke or Bell's palsy. She walked stiffly, with reverence, the way an executioner leads the inmate down death row.

"Just Anthony. He volunteers here at the theater."

"Among other things," Ms. Sanders grumbled, and Anthony shut his eyes.

"Let's just go, Cynthia," Anthony said. "Say goodbye. We don't need this place."

"Well, I'm sure you saw the news tonight," Cynthia said. "But, I can assure you, it's a complete misunderstanding. Taken entirely out of context. It's actually quite a funny story. Total, total misunderstanding."

She stuck her hand up, interrupting Cynthia. "Well, I'm sure you have your reasons for upsetting that family during their time of mourning. You may have even been innocent in it, but that's beyond the point, now. It's all about perception, Cynthia."

Cynthia slumped into the chair. "Really. It was an accident. Completely lawful. We were running from the police after conning a manager and breaking into a storage unit." She bit her lip. "I'm not helping, am I?"

"Nope," Anthony said.

"Regardless, it's about what the public sees. This community theater only exists from the generosity of our patrons, and many of our usual donors are starting to doubt the cultural validity of live theaters. We're struggling to keep them, and at this time, it's uncertain whether we'll be able to pay operating costs for next year."

"I understand completely," Cynthia said. "We can tell them what happened, explain it. It's actually quite funny and lively. I can imagine Andy Kaufman doing the same thing—"

"Here it comes," Anthony whispered.

"Let me be clear, so I can save us both time and embarrassment. What you did was simply unacceptable, and the board of directors had an emergency meeting on Skype and agreed to revoke your custodianship of this theater. I expect you to fetch your things and leave the keys with me, tonight."

Cynthia opened her mouth to speak. Anthony knelt by her and took her hand. He didn't say anything, just rubbed the back of her fingers. "I said kind things for the bird this morning," he said. "I spoke them for you. It's time to let go."

Cynthia sighed, releasing a lungful of air. She rubbed at her eyes and stretched her face, fighting the tears. Anthony's heart dropped into his stomach.

"With dignity," he whispered.

"Of course. And I hope this rectifies the situation. I apologize for any inconvenience." Cynthia slipped off behind the stage and grabbed her stuff. She had a few boxes, and Tolya helped her pack his car. His noble and grizzled face never betrayed any feeling, but he'd been ready to help without needing to be asked.

"Good night," she said. They left the theater, exiting through the side door.

Anthony turned around, quickly. "Bitch."

Cynthia smacked him, and they piled into Tolya's car. He drove them to their last refuge: the makeup shop in Lansdale where he left them to plan their next move.

CINDERFIELD SHUT UP. PLEASE!

Tolya unlocked his apartment door. Twin roaches, perhaps family-born of adjoining eggs, rushed out from under the door, scattering into the hall then making for the apartment across the way. Louie's stereo pulsed into the hall, and Tolya considered banging on his door for another round of drunken threats. He couldn't, tonight. He threw open his door and slammed it, protesting the noise in some small fashion.

He stumbled in the dark, knocking into the folding chair in the corner. It tipped over and hit the television tray, knocking into his small flatscreen and PlayStation. He flipped on the light switch, exposing the barren walls and cracked window. More roaches scurried under the sink.

"Go on, you little buggers. Live the short time you have and not know pain. Eat and shit and lay eggs."

He took out a pack of hotdogs from the fridge, and the reek of old and moldy food assaulted his nose. He brushed it off and rubbed his nostrils, then dropped the hotdogs onto a chipped plate. The meat had expired last week, but he figured they'd be good for a while longer. He stuck the pale sticks into the microwave and cooked them until they curled and darkened to a sickly brown. He got out plates from the cabinet above the sink while the dogs cooked.

Tolya carried them over to the table and set each broken and mismatched plate at the seats—father, mother, son, daughter. He returned with cracked tumblers and set them by each plate along with silverware and napkins.

"Lord loves a big family," Jebediah T. Cinderfield said.

"Should I set another place?" Tolya said.

"You know better than that. You've already done me fine, just fine. Good hospitality, suh."

Tolya stepped to the microwave and yanked out the plate of cooked dogs then set them on the counter. He grabbed a bag of stale hot dog buns, picked out the moldy ones and fit the remainder to the four hotdogs. The grease burned his fingers, but he disregarded the pain.

"Fuck off," Tolya said. "I'm tired of you, devil."

"That's rude. If you didn't have me, you'd have no one to talk to."

"I'd rather be alone."

Tolya distributed one hotdog to each plate. An adventurous roach dropped onto the table and crawled to the plate edge. Tolya let him linger.

"No one wants to be alone," Cinderfield said. "So, when's the fam' coming to eat this sumptuous banquet?"

"They'll be home soon." Tolya sat down at the table and picked the hard bits off the bun. He played with his food, then reached under the table and found a half-filled vodka bottle on the rug, where he'd knocked it over last night while heading to bed.

"Any minute, huh?" Cinderfield said. "Come running through the door to this mansion. 'Hi, honey!' 'How was work?' The children follow behind her, come in and kiss their father, and you all sit down to a family meal. Don't forget to say grace!"

"Fucking grace."

Tolya took a bit from the leathery dog and gnawed his

broken teeth on the meat. His back molar screamed in pain, and he nursed it with vodka.

"Oh. But wait. You don't have a family. You left them, didn't you? Just went and took off to find your bliss. Or punishment. And everyone else had to suffer, didn't they?"

"I'll fucking kill you!" Tolya grabbed a knife and pointed at his own sternum.

"Tch. Tch. None of that now. You do have a debt to that sexy girl, don't you? The old wandering eye."

Tolya bit off another hunk of dog, chewed it on the other side of his mouth, avoiding the bad molar, then choked it down. It firebombed his stomach.

"It wasn't my fault," Tolya said, lying to the devil, lying to himself. "Bad snowstorm, that February."

Twenty hours on the road driving dresses and pants and boots for the distributer in New York—straight shot from Florida. Tolya had called his wife in South Carolina, told her he expected to be done by the morning and was hopeful for breakfast. She'd make him crepes with beer batter, then he'd sleep the weekend and see his kids in the evening. Sylvia lost a tooth and was excited to be getting a dime from the tooth fairy.

1985, he'd driven a truck. This summer he scored a role in a play in Philadelphia. He'd finally been given a part in the iconic play of writer Anton Chekov: Uncle Vanya. Tolya was cast as the doctor, Mikhaíl Lvóvich Ástraf. He'd longed, since boyhood, to wear the country physician's brooding face and desperate eyes because of the doctor's wasted potential being stuck in the country. Tolya understood that burden, and though the part would only enforce his Russian stereotype, he'd play the noble role with deep passion. His participation in such a high profile performance should finally get him the attention of an agent. Fuck trucks. No more long hauls. No more lonely days and nights on the road, tempted by truck stop waitresses and the usual whores who frequented gas stations along the interstates. "The I-95s", he called them, though on the really long drives he might pay twenty dollars of his travel expense and get a quick handjob in his cab. All the drivers did it to help relax.

The suspension buckled a bit on the left side, so he compensated, keeping a steady pass on the interstate. He'd make Philly in twenty, and the 95 should have been clear with the storm. He'd crashed into the Nor'easter coming out of Delaware and hoped to clear it before the storm dumped too much snow, grounding him. Management had been clear about being late. He'd get her through. That's why they'd given this load to the mad Russian. He had a reputation of getting through and never speaking of it, just lighting up a cigarette and asking for the next load.

He pulled up to a service station just outside the city and filled the tanks. He didn't want to have to stop before New York and get stuck in some iced-over parking lot. Snow and sleet mixed, shelling the pavement, sealing it in ice. He trusted the weight of the truck, the momentum to keep him grounded, and public works had already started salting the highways. He'd keep his head high and see her through.

"Yo. Mister. Can I get a ride?" The bird had flown out from behind the truck. She tapped his soldier—a hippie chick, even though it was '85, with hair tied in braids and beads. She wore a leather jacket, brown with flaps and tall-laced boots. Her swollen breasts poked through her t-shirt, which read: I COME FROM HOLLYWOOD. He nearly told her he couldn't accept passengers, but he felt his manhood twitch. He nodded, and she jumped into the cab. The hippie girl carried something low, wrapped in blankets at her stomach, probably her stash of pot. He didn't smoke that shit on the road.

Tolya finished gassing up, climbed up into the cab, and pulled out onto the highway. The tires slipped, and he adjusted, keeping cool speed. The truck would see them through. The girl rocked the blanket, and her swollen breasts bounced under the tight shirt. He felt himself harden in his blue work pants.

"Do you believe in a loving God?" she asked. She sucked down a sob.

"I believe in a suffering world."

The truck veered to the left, and Tolya yanked the wheel, keeping her steady. Sleet pelted the windshield and splattered across the screen. Wind raked the snow, and he focused to see the three-lane highway. Philly's blue scrapers rose high over the city, standing sentry and warning. He drove into the heart of the Nor'easter.

Tears pooled at the edges of her eyes, and she rubbed them away with her fingernails. The truck rocked, and her breasts bounced. Tolya had gone a week without seeing his wife and had held off on the whores at the service station. His cock pulsed, rubbing against his pants, and he let go of the steering wheel and reached for her leg, massaging her inner thigh with his finger.

A cry sounded from the bundle—an infant's sob, hungry and small. The hippie chick pulled down her shirt, exposing a rose blossom and fed the child's mouth to it. It quieted and suckled.

"Is that your son?"

She nodded. "His father died today." She grew a fresh bouquet of tears. "I miss him."

Tolya didn't pay attention. He shouldn't have picked

her up, shouldn't have given into his loins to commit adultery against his family and children. He should have just kept driving. He didn't see her reach in time, lifting her arm. His hand had been stroking her leg.

The only thing he could remember next was the flash, like the world had fallen on him. In the darkness, trapped in the twisted metal, when he finally opened his eyes, his face stinging from sleet, he heard the infant wailing.

ANTHONY CASTOUT ON THE TIDE

W hen I was but a child, I believed the dead sang through the wind." Anthony watched the burdened branches of the birch with silver bark groan and crack under the wind's lashing.

"The wind is all we have, now," Cynthia said. "Bunch of hobos, we are." Cynthia fidgeted with her long sleeves, stretching them down off her hands until some of the seams tore on her purple hoodie.

Anthony grinned—the eyes of a child excited by thoughts of play, of imagined battles with toy soldiers and fishing trips down the canal for black, bloated carp swimming in the still water. Cynthia tapped a pen on the rubber tip of her sneaker; her eyes darted back and forth, following the light traffic that traversed Main Street in Lansdale. Thunder pounded the sky, and Cynthia jumped, dropping the pen onto the sidewalk bordering the front of the Make Me Pretty and Loved makeup shop. The shockwave rattled his chest and struck his heart. Lightning ripped and wounded the night sky, setting the shops and apartments in the two-story brick buildings in a pellucid glow. The electricity spent its brief life force then died, and darkness rushed back into the cracks and fields.

"I know this storm," Anthony said. "I feel its spirit—unique and bold and so very old. It's inflated and deflated beyond counting. It was born a slight breeze—not enough pressure to stir a hair curl on a soft summer afternoon. But it waited. The wind knows patience. It dwelled and gathered in the grass plains at the continent's heart, accumulating with its own, birthing a family of gales. It twirled and whirled and unified the choir."

The wind settled in brief repose then surged again in celerity, composing a beat to his mythic tale.

"Warrior wind of the plains. When finally it commanded the still air of the lands, the thunderheads, the clouds of the sky realm bowed to its power and swore fealty to Lord Ventus. The virgin maiden rain surrendered itself to its power and prowess, and the wind carried its mate on wide shoulders, running fast across the hills and forests and mountains. They locked in constant embrace, a thousand arms reaching and holding white breasts and thighs. Wet mouths sought out inchoate bodies that danced and mingled in carnal exchange."

His narration excited the wind to wild lust, and it pummeled the street, rocking the traffic lights and streetlamps. A banner hanging over Main Street that announced a bike event in town that weekend tore free from its lines, flailed at the buildings and finally settled in clumps in front of Royal Comics. One of the thick limbs of the birch tree cracked, spraying shards of wood and white papery bark.

"Are you doing this? Anthony?"

Thunder roared ahead and drummed the earth. Cynthia grabbed Anthony's arm and leaned in close. He listened to the frantic pace of her breathing and ran fingers through her oak moss. Her breathing slowed to his touch, and he nearly pulled his fingers back. Was this cruel? Encouraging this? The wind howled once more, demanding he finish.

"Where does the lightning come from?" Cynthia asked in a child's voice.

"The union of their spirit. The joining of their elements in coitus. They merge and build to climax, and it explodes in fulgent bursts, slicing across the dimensions, space-time, pouring plasma."

"Thunder?"

"The two lovers crying out, howling to the heavens in their pleasure fury. No body can deny it. No spirit can block it. Such is the power and force of the love-making spirits of the wide, wide sky."

Thunder blasted the town again, thumping the brick walls. Cynthia relaxed her fidgeting, and Anthony heard a light moan, just under her breath. She arched her body, raising her back, and the motion set tingles through his inner thighs.

"Suppose we're sleeping here tonight," she said. "Not much space in the store."

"It'll be fine."

"How can you not be pulling out your hair in worry? Sorry. I mean. You know what I mean."

"I'm beyond it," he said. "Whether I sleep in a king-sized bed at the Holiday Inn or under a highway overpass, I'm still moving away from this world."

"I'm trying to relax. To see it your way. I'm still grounded with deep roots. It sounds so peaceful."

"Sometimes," he said. "And chaos and wind and agony. I touch my flesh and expect the particles to fly apart. The bonds lose their attraction. I turn to mist. I am nothing. I am nowhere. I am everywhere."

She leaned her head against the brick wall outside the shop. Fire sirens keened in the distance, wailing like a miserable ghost tormenting the village. "I doubt I'll be able to keep the store much longer. The rent has been late for a few months, and I'll lose business now that I've lost my position at the theater."

"Let it go, Cynthia," Anthony said. "You can't control these things."

"Let it go? That's what you tell me? Look. I'm sorry for what's happening to you, and it's killing me every moment of every hour of every day, but I can't just drop everything. I have to survive. Let it go, indeed! Bullcrappy! Goddess."

He threw up a little again, and the vomit hit the street. Blood dribbled down his chin, and he mopped it with a handkerchief. His body weighed heavier as if gravity amplified, pulling him down to earth again. The sudden change in motion tilted the balance of his stomach, and nausea warped his head, feeling its pressure behind his eyes.

He couldn't control any of this, not anymore than he could influence the storm. Anthony didn't enlist. Lighting had struck him, and the electricity, the power, surged through his body, his spirit, setting cells growing like weeds and burning out his mortal spirit, leaving the remains—the pure heart, beyond mortal trifles, that rare element infants possessed in the moment of conception, before each second of life, of corporeal influence distorted. The cancer and its emotional animal, its spiritual self, burned away all of earthbound created, seared away the deadwood and fear and loss, refining and smelting it, clearing the dross until only the virgin gold remained—the spark, his soul.

"It can't be my fault," Anthony said.

"It is your fault, you know," she said, pulling from him. "Or wasn't that you dancing on that poor guy's grave? In front of the family? It wasn't enough that you disturbed the funeral. You had to do your preaching. You saw those cameras and couldn't help it. Stupid vanity."

He sighed, and he gazed down at the sidewalk. She had him. With this transformation came the obsession to sing, to preach, to dance the part and show all the world. He'd always suffered the need for attention, since childhood, perhaps the result of a lack of attention from his grandparents. Up in his room, he'd put on little song and dance shows, always performing for an imaginary audience, lavishing in their attention and phantom applause. It's why he'd gotten involved with the theater department at Bloom, to meet some people, find some friends. He always felt awkward with other humans, especially members of the opposite sex. He was jealous of those with natural charisma and social ability, and he longed to be the center of attention. The theater gave him a place on stage to be watched, the ability to step outside of his social anxiety and be someone else. Anthony wanted to warp reality, to change the nature of existence and just change himself. Now, it didn't really seem to matter. "I didn't mean to get you hurt," Anthony said. "I no longer exist."

"I *do* exist!" She huffed and tugged at her long sleeves.

Anthony wondered if he should bring up the scars, whether it was any of his business. "Well, we're homeless, now."

"I know." She curled up next to him and took his arm. Her kind touch signaled a relief to the confrontation. "I didn't mean that, Anthony, what I just said. I've always been terrified of being homeless, like when my mother would take me and my brother away from my father, and we'd live at aunts' houses or cheap motels full of roaches and hookers. I swore I'd never live like that."

"But, you're right," he said. "I'm still here, and I have to try to balance it. This new spirit. This new force."

The wind had blown steady, almost soothing, with a

hypnotic cadence. Then, as if preparing for a sudden moment, it blasted the street, throwing traffic lights, ripping tiles from roofs and whipping them into parked cars and windshields. Several car alarms chirped with worry and warning, protesting the storm's violation of their security, calling frantically to soporific owners buried deep in their apartments from the futile crying. The wind punched the weakened branches of the birch tree growing these last thirty years but mere meters from their position sitting outside her makeup store because he wanted to enjoy the storm.

"The storm's turned on us," Anthony yelled. The heaviest of the branches, reaching out above their heads, moaned from its siege. Cynthia looked up just in time to see the wind rip the branch from its trunk and collapse to earth. Anthony shot up with unusual balance and strength, grabbed her arm and pulled her clear of the fall. The force on her struck a sudden pain, and she yelped, worried her arm might be pulled from its socket. Anthony tossed her to the side, and the tender fingers of the branch drew across her soft cheek, tickling her skin. She giggled, tasting the wooden earthy taste when birch fingers plucked at her lips and tongue like an erotic maneuver. The heavy branch crashed the pane glass storefront, and the window imploded, all the shards flying inward. She considered screaming, but the event had struck so randomly that she couldn't decide through the daze.

Several additional branches launched from the tree, cast free, emancipated from the birch, from their life, serving no more purpose sans a brief moment of demolition—denting cars, bending parking meters and scratching the pavement. Anthony knelt by her, holding her shoulders.

"You're here? Are you bleeding? Did it hit your head? Cynthia? Damn it. Cynthia?"

"A bit dazed."

"My last tether. I'd float away. I'd float out into space, break Earth's gravity and turn to gas, filling Saturn up. Shit."

He helped her up, and she examined the damage to her window. "It'll be the landlord's problem, now," she said. "I'm just going to clean out the shop and one of the girls can store it at their house. The heck with it."

"Just leave it all behind?" Anthony asked. "Then what do we do next?"

"You have to know the truth to be whole. I have to know, too. I'm seeing it even more, all the time. You have his childlike face. The eyes. The spirit. Friends called him the purest soul they ever knew. I think that's your soul, too. You can know your father, your mother and know yourself. You need to be whole. Pure soul."

"How?" Anthony asked.

"We could do a paternity test," she said. "DNA."

"Andy Kaufman is dead," Anthony said. "We can't go digging up his body."

"But, his family isn't," Cynthia argued. "There's always some controversy going on between his heirs and old friends. He came from their blood."

Thunder crashed in cacophony. The burdened clouds could suffer their weight no longer and opened their eyes wide, pouring ponds and lakes onto the thirsty world. It drenched their clothing, and they clung to the edge of the building, jogging through the alleyway that divided their building from Royal Comics, and slipped into the shop through the backdoor. The wind howled through the broken window, and the rain soaked the rugs.

"We have canvas in the back. Extra curtain." She led him to the back and opened a large steamer trunk. He helped her lift the curtain, and they dragged it to the window. She grabbed a stool behind the counter, accidentally banging it into the shelves of boxes and makeup kits, past the wig wall and all the fancies of illusion that filled her art.

"Goddess," she said. "It is a long, long trip. We've got no dough."

"We'll work cheap jobs. Wash dishes. Buy gas and bus fare."

"I have no idea where we can even find his family," she said, struggling with the curtain and climbing up on the stool. She tried to hang the edge from one of the hooks that held some of the props hanging in the window—all blown away in the store somewhere.

"We'll ask questions. Play detective. Figure it out."

"People love their privacy, especially the families of celebrities. I bet they get their fair share of kooks. Like us."

"We do have a resource, one we can perfect," he said, hanging the curtain from a far hook. "We can make people. Play God. They're no less real than we are, and for the time we need them, they'll live and breathe and exist."

"Then we murder them when we're done?" she asked. "That's cruel."

"No, Cynthia. They're going to murder me."

She nodded. "Maybe Tolya . . . "

"There's something more to that mad Russian," Anthony said. "I sense it. Something of the angels. The essence of the devils."

"Anthony, I'm sorry," she said. "I can't do this. I need familiar things. I know this town, and especially now, I need the security of what's familiar."

He hung the curtain from the last hook, and it shielded against the wind and rain. It blew open from the bottom, and they pressed two chairs against the base, keeping it firm. Thunder rocked the building.

"Oh, my store. I loved this store. Everything's changing. I hate change. I feel like the ground is falling away under my feet." Her confident tone started to change.

"You used to write," he said.

"Yes."

"I have to do this," Anthony said. "You understand that, don't you? I can't be whole until it's done. I need the vector. If I can find my original, then I can calculate my path to the next world."

"Oh, Goddess, Anthony. Don't ask this. I've already lost my store and my theater. I'm losing you. I thought we could do this, but I'm scared. I need my familiar world to stay centered. I can't go with you."

"But, it was your idea," he said.

"I'm sorry."

"Then I won't ask."

Dad was coming off a night shift. He still wore his uniform and sat at the kitchen table, pouring milk into a bowl of Lucky Charms. Cynthia stepped into the greasy flat. More of his black hair had gray, and a bald spot spread over the back of his head. She read the date on the milk from behind him.

"That's three days-old," she said, slipping into old rhythms.

"I just got that."

"There's probably a new one, still," she said. "You never threw out the old one."

He read the date on the carton, sighed then dumped the cereal into the sink. She got out the milk and made him a new bowl. He dunked his spoon and dripped milk on his moustache. His radio squawked. She always hated that thing as a kid, when Dad would come home for dinner and leave it out on the table, listening for a call. He could never be home with just his family. The job always came first over Cynthia and her mother. He'd always promised her he'd make time for her school plays or art exhibits, and then he'd just leave in the middle to respond to a call even when off duty. The job thrilled him, gave him meaning. He got a high off being a cop and not from his family.

"So, why are you here?" he asked. "I thought you . . . needed to figure some crap out on your own."

"I'm going away. I wanted to check in." She went into her bedroom, grabbed some clothes, a suitcase, a box of tampons she forgot she had. She tore through her closet but everything she found, she hated. She'd often buy a new shirt or maybe a skirt but then grow to hate the way she looked in it. It just piled up. Finally, she found some stuff she could tolerate. She tossed some old dresses and shorts into her suitcase. It was all she had now to wear.

"Well, where are you going, baby girl?" She twinged when her father called her that.

"I'm heading north with Anthony," she yelled from the bedroom. Cynthia gathered her stuff and carried it out to the kitchen.

"I saw his grandfather golfing last weekend," Dad said. "The man said Anthony was just fine."

"Sure. Just fine."

"No," Dad said. "I make my living by knowing when someone is lying. The cancer's going to kill him, isn't it?"

"I'm going," she said, grabbing her bag, heading for the door. Then, she paused. "You're an insensitive jerk." Cynthia censored herself, holding back worse language. "You never cared about Mom's feelings and you don't give a damn about mine."

"I just call it like I see it."

"That's not an excuse!" she said.

"You don't have the right to judge me," he said. "I did the best I could as a father as I understood the role. You always liked being on your own, in your room reading or going for your long bike rides just by yourself. One day, you'll have a child and know what it's like to never be able to please them."

"I'm too fat," Cynthia said. "No one will ever want me."

"Oh, stop it with that self-pity shit. You know you're the most beautiful girl in the world."

"You don't mean that," she said. "I'm just your fucked up, broken and huge daughter. Remember how you always told me I needed to exercise more? That guys don't really like pleasantly plump?"

"I never said that," he said. "Damn it. I'm tired of this shit. I'm going to bed." He got up, taking off his shirt. His grizzled face paled, and she noticed more of his hair had grayed. She'd never quite seen him looking so old.

"Well, I'll be gone for a while. You'll have to find the milk by yourself."

"Wait," he said. "You're looking after him?" He truly sounded concerned.

She nodded, calming a little.

"I've got some muffins," he said. "Sure you don't want to stay for breakfast?"

"I'm not hungry," she lied. She was starved but couldn't let herself eat.

"I'm glad you're taking care of him," he said. "That he has a friend. I loved his mother. We could have been something. Don't get me wrong. I loved your mother, too, but Anthony's mother was my first. I was young and crazy in love."

She set down the bag and then sat on the couch across the room from him. A roach scurried to the wall, dislodged by her motion. "You never told me this before." She couldn't recall ever seeing her father this way. His face changed, sweetened, and he smiled when he spoke. He had been young once. Cynthia couldn't imagine it. Her father had always been a distant man, and he'd always treated her like a child, even though she was a grown woman now.

Now he spoke to her like a friend. "I didn't always want to be a cop," he said. She waited for him to elaborate. "I wanted to be a comedian. Act in comedies. I wanted to be Robin Williams. Andy Kaufman."

"And that's why we used to watch all of Andy's stuff together," she said. "Why you got me into him and Robin Williams and Steve Martin?"

"I was so in love with Anthony's mother. We had a comedy troupe. Improv. Wild life. We all ran away together, went west. Then Karen met Andy. They wrestled, and I lost her. How could I compete with Andy Kaufman? He was a god to us. I came back here."

"She left you?" Cynthia asked, feeling a familiar sting.

"She never even saw me. I screamed at her, told her I never wanted to see her again. I was too passionate back then, and I wounded my best friend. My father let me come home only if I enrolled in the police academy, following in his footsteps."

"Why did you give it up?"

He grabbed a beer from the fridge and started taking off his uniform. She could read the pain on his face as well as he could read hers. "She called me and said she was coming home, that she needed me. That she had lived a dream. I didn't know she was pregnant. I never knew who the father really was. I didn't want to know. I would have gone to her. She was back in town a few weeks. She wasn't ready to tell me. She wanted to have her baby first. My love never made it home from the hospital. I was training with the Lansdale Police Department. We were the first on the scene of the accident. Some foreigner was driving. We always suspected he'd been drinking, but the blood-alcohol level was equivocal."

"That's why you gave up comedy?" Cynthia asked.

"It took me years to be able to watch anything with Andy Kaufman, and then I was able to move on. I found it all again, and I wanted to share it with you.

"I've got to go, Dad. Things aren't right between us, but we can work on it when I get back." She went to him and kissed his cheek.

"Cynthia. Don't abandon him like I abandoned his mother. It's going to be a knife in your stomach. But don't."

"I'd never, dad. I can't ever leave him." She grabbed her suitcase and left. His words haunted her, and she wondered if she could really handle it. Cynthia wanted to be able to, but she really wasn't sure. Why did the Goddess have to make her so weak?

ANGEL'S EEMATATIONS

And so began the *eemetations*.

"A field of silence creates a thrill," said the Maharishi, Angel's master in transcendental meditation. He teaches Angel balance, how to generate the field between commonality and oddness. Many souls flow like streams within Angel, and he cannot balance them on his own; so, he learns to meditate each day, keeping the rivers from flooding him. He has been so many people, spoken with diverse voices that, sometimes, he cannot remember what his own voice sounds like. He feels his mind cracking, breaking into pieces, and Angel falls off a cliff into a chasm. It takes him days before he can come back.

Meditation brings him back, centers Angel, otherwise he would fall off the world and never return. His teacher shows him a new way of existing, of letting go of the self, and it frees him to become others, to turn protean and adjust to changes in life. Most people demand that life be static, but Angel knows how to be flexible, that reality itself is a construct, an illusion. What defines a person, but a mind? And a mind can be re-written. A person is nothing more than the substance of memories, the sum total of their experience, and Angel possessed the power to fill his recollection with new memories, the little nuances. He does more than create new people. He becomes them.

People are born into him and fill him like a vessel, an ark. He nurtures the new souls like offspring, children, and he grows them, planting souls like bulbs, then raising the daffodils.

Angel invests his energy, his élan, into the crystal screen, into implanting himself on the other side for millions to see as he did as a child: his escape. Angel is called upon to make appearances for real shows, not just programs in his imagination, such as *Comedy World* and *The Steve Allen Show*. Real people, beyond siblings and school friends, will be watching—strangers. People will know his many names, but he will not know theirs. Isn't that fame?

"I am very nervous because ees my first time on TV. So, you know, last night ees very hard to go to sleep." The Foreign Man soul wears blue-olive coat, oxford shirt, white socks and brown loafers. He keeps his arms rigid at both sides—stiff and nervous in presence. He taps out a rhythm, mocking his efforts, pretending to pretend a performance, turning reality in on itself. The little man from a sunken island is terrified to be in front of strangers. His eyes boil likc cggs.

Correspondent of comedy, Barbara Feldon, introduces this international waif on *Comedy World*: "I can't think of a single performer I'd rather be watching than this absolutely adorable young man from the Caribbean Islands . . . "

He speaks in a nasal voice, uncertain and wavering. He pauses, rolling his eyes, creating a disaster on stage, perfecting his imperfection, imbuing awkwardness into his audience. We all cringe watching the art of the perfect disaster. The Foreign Man is so desperate to be loved, and this he shares with Angel. All must be watching him all the time and know his life, the glory and truth of his power. Love me. Love me.

Love meeeee!

He mocks the comedians he finds so tiresome and intimidating. Angel has tried to tell jokes, to be funny, but he just likes to dance around, sing his barnyard children's songs and do his voices.

"Take my wife . . . she is terrible. Please." Snort. Snort. "No. No. I love my wife." There lies resentment in his act—and fear. He does a poor eemetation of de President Neexon, throwing two Vs into the air. "Let me make one ting clear. I am de President." And tells a story of two brothers dragging a cannonball up a hill. His audiences are traumatized, and yet he carries on—a foreign man finally getting his chance to perform to a major audience, showing his vulnerability, casting his hopes and dreams to the judgment of strangers. The audience feels sorry for this man, but he has no concept that his act is terrible. Who is this idiot? Is he for real? The audience can't tell. Angel plays them, tapping into deep feelings of sympathy and revulsion, in that motivation in all people to persecute the inept, the inadequate, and distract the attention from their own personal failings. Angry mobs form in concerts, stirred up by this faux performance. He summons pity, laughter, criticism, hate, and Angel flies above it all, whipping it, pouring petrol on the fire until he's created a frenzy, a furious mob.

"Tenk you veddy much," he'd say and receive silence from his bewildered witnesses.

And this is how the experiments with reality began. Angel didn't seek this forum to entertain, to draw laughter. He wanted to disturb, infiltrate thoughts, to upset the human's quaint understanding of reality. It was through these means he began to adjust and manipulate what it was to be human, to distort the human design. The stage became his laboratory, and this is how he processed his emotions: not through expression, like normal people, but through re-creation. He was an unsettled young man, nervous, anxious and unsure of himself, desperate for fame and confused by the wants of the modern comedy audience; thus, he created it in his act, his characters, showing his feelings, making a person from them. Later, his father's anger, manifested in Angel, would show through his other characters. And Angel entertained himself, always taking his act one step further, excelling from his previous scenarios.

And now, to destroy their perception of reality. Then he does his final eemetation, De Elvis Presley. By now, he's convinced the audience that he is a buffoon, a fool, and they've written him off. He opens his record player and puts on a record: *Also sprach Zarathustra*. Angel turns his back, strips his foreign man outfit, combs his hair back and snarls his lip. Then he faces the audience again, gyrating his hips. He has morphed into Elvis—the King, *his* king. He performs for the audience, singing classic Elvis songs, his gospel since his youth. Angel's performance stuns the audience—so lost in their judgments and preconceptions, the false reality he's implanted into their minds.

This would be his obsession. He needed people to understand that reality was tangible. It could be played with, altered, and so much of it – what people believed was real – actually depended on perception. He offered emancipation, freedom, enlightenment—and he had fun fucking with their heads.

A DIRECT TELEGRAPH TO GOD

T his shit wouldn't have happened if you'd drive on a highway!" Cynthia yelled. "We'd be in Long Island in a few hours, talking to the Kaufman family."

"The turnpike steals your soul," Tolya said. Cynthia kicked the restored grill of the ice cream truck. The red and beat face of the devil painted on the side mocked her.

"Don't kick her!" Tolya said, racing to clean the dirt from her sneaker. "She's cherry."

"I don't believe in the devil," Cynthia said. She hated driving in the truck, having to switch off to sit on the bench in the back. Tolya still stocked cones and sandwiches, and the fattening cream threatened her. She'd already eaten two during the ride, and the ice cream made her fingers sticky.

"The devil is the reason we're on this trip," Tolya responded.

"Then your devil should have possessed you to drive on the highway," Cynthia yelled back, walking up the dirt road. "They have gas stations on highways."

He refused to drive through any major cities, claiming the traffic would make him go catatonic. Driving towards Scranton in this manner would take days, but it was the only way Tolya would take them. He drove the country routes no faster than ten mph. Every time a squirrel scurried across the empty road, he stopped and had to calm himself down. They passed few gas stations, and finally the car dried out somewhere in the middle of rural Pennsylvania.

"We should have taken the bus," Anthony said.

"We didn't have money for tickets," she reminded him. "My account is overdrawn, and your grandfather kept control of all your money. Anyway, he sounded like he could do it. I didn't realize he was this nuts." They hiked up to an old barn on the route, hoping to find a farmer with a gas can. She stuck her head into the barn after hearing some coughing and crying. A flustered old lady dashed up from her bench, nearly fell over, gathered herself then stopped them at the door.

"Reverend Racecar Ritchie Richland rises." The old lady adjusted her flowery dress and fixed the back of her hair. She, nor any of the congregation filling the old barn church, couldn't have bathed in days.

"We just need directions," Cynthia said. "Our driver, Tolya. He won't use the major highways, so we're figuring our way through the backwoods. I'd been to the Poconos as a kid, but I can't remember the roads very well." None of them had phones. They couldn't afford the service, so she navigated the old-fashioned way: by the stars and a map . . . and hope. "Now, the map says—"

"We can no longer speak of the damned human race," the old lady said. Sweat rolled down her flat bust. She held herself up on a bench, and her head wobbled as she spoke. She looked like she hadn't eaten in some time. "Y'all best go on out of here before the Reverend pulls himself up out of the cold earth, sticks his hat on his head and finds you here in these solemn proceedings. He'll snatch you all bald."

Anthony studied the portrait at the back of the barn,

probably the aforementioned Preacher that had captivated this congregation so much in life, that he still held them, even in death. His hawk-bearing chilled Anthony, even from the two-dimensional oil painting, the way a pigeon must feel when he looks up and spots the angular configuration—the sharp eyes and razor beak, of the face belonging to a bird-of-prey—bearing down upon him from high. The painting displayed a wizened face, grown wild in oak moss, black strokes down the many creases and wrinkles of his visage, bulbous nose and draped in a simple parson's outfit of black, complete with stringy bowtie. He possessed the congregation, gazing on them from the oil painting.

They sat in the benches in the old barn, standing on the sodden straw while the wood dry-rotted around them. Sometimes they sang hymns of His coming or prayed quietly. The old woman, of relation to the preacher, Anthony could guess, kept them in line, spoke for them, compelled them to pray and remain, even though the small crowd had also not eaten in days and sipped from the few remaining water bottles distributed among them. This old woman had identified herself as Mattie Dot, and she'd determined to go to heaven at the hand of their old preacher; and no outsider would interrupt or prevent her ascension.

"We just need some directions, then we'll be out of your hair. We're trying to get to Scranton."

"Begone! Jezebel!"

Anthony buckled over laughing. "She sure told you, Jezebel."

Cynthia fiddled with her long sleeves then clutched her swollen goddess necklace.

"Excuse me, ma'am," Anthony said. "Begging your pardon. How did your preacher die?"

Mattie Dot gazed upon his countenance and ran a finger over her eye, stifling a sob. She shook her head then her flabby neck and moved it down until her whole body trembled and wobbled. This must have been some kind of local ritual to drive out the devil, as the shaking looked to be intentional and not the result of a neurological condition, at least not a physical one. "God guided our Preacher Reverend Racecar Ritchie Richland in the driver seat of a Ford Bronco. And it was God who put the bottle of Jack Daniels in his ever-loving tender hand. T'was time to come on Him, so he could rise again and bring the good news to his children."

The congregation, those still able to stand, rose to their feet, waved their arms in the air and cried out, "Praise God." Those who did not fall back onto the wobbly benches, eased themselves down.

"And Ma'am, please forgive my ignorance, as we are city people and ignorant of your blessed ways," Cynthia said. "Yet, we do wish to be saved, and I believe it must be Providence that led us to your door. Who was it that decreed that he would again rise from the grave?"

"It was the good Reverend Racecar Ritchie Richland. One day after his burial, God would then pull him up by his ears and set him again on the earth."

Anthony read the rotund woman; the way her eyes sought every crack in the old wood or whistle by the fresh wind. From the manner in which she held herself together, keeping her body and spirit from shattering into pieces, he perceived her deep and wrenching need. Even three days waiting in this hothouse, this rotting barn, she'd applied fresh makeup, touching up her face, pausing in their conversation to renew her lipstick, with aid of a little mirror from her purse. She watched the barn gate, eyes never drifting, looking for the Reverend to rise and renew her faith, validate her heart.

"You loved him, didn't you?" Anthony asked. "Your body's gone cold like an oak in winter, and all the leaves have fallen away, leaving you bare and naked against the wind."

Dot's lips quivered. Her cheeks blushed—roses dried out in drought. She waved her arms in the air, and her flab flapped. "Go on out of here! Interlopers. Behold! There is a stranger in our midst."

The senior members of the congregation watched with dazed eyes, suffering dementia from their prolonged stay. The women and men held firm, their faces strong in the foundations of faith, waiting for a miracle, determined for it to be true. The children played, bored, mostly stripped of their clothing. Babies wept, hungry, anxious to grow and live. Anthony spotted a young woman grinning from a back bench. Her faded Metallica t-shirt exposed her midriff, barely covering her pregnant belly. She reached behind her head, tied her straggly, black hair into a tail, then fanned herself with a bible.

"Leave now, heretics!" Mattie Dot called. "Be gone and leave in peace."

"Promised land," Anthony said. "It's always so close, isn't it?"

Some of the stronger men rose, crossing their arms in warning, ready to throw them out into the world. Anthony tugged on Cynthia's long sleeve. "Time to go, Jezebel."

"But—"

"We're not real to them," Anthony whispered. He led her out the barn gate, and they walked down the hillside to where Tolya had pulled off the road. The hills rolled on—verdant hills, levels cut by patient glaciers that sculpted the mountains and lakes. In the winter, the northern peoples came here to ski. In the summer, they came to fish and enjoy the clean air. They'd driven through Jim Thorpe on the way to Lake Naomi, following the Pennsylvania highways north and passed the mausoleum of the great athlete made now into a park and tourist attraction.

"My grandfather worked at a steel mill near here in Scranton," Cynthia said. "The fires went out. My father mined coal up north. The coal mine closed. They turned it into a museum." She thrummed her Goddess necklace. "We have to help those people."

"They don't want to be helped," Anthony said. He knew the type: resistant to discourse, closed to new thoughts and change. It threatened their sense of stability, and Anthony both ridiculed and resented their faith. They exposed his vacancy, hollowed him out and demonstrated his meager, thin soul.

"If we don't find a gas station soon—"

"They won't listen to outsiders," Anthony said. "Did you see the portrait? Formidable."

"He reminded me of your grandfather," Cynthia said. "He terrified me. The only way they're helping us is if that cult leader tells them too."

Anthony curled his upper lip and stared back at the barn on the hill. His eyes lit up like a child's when he's given a new toy. "Do you think you could?"

Cynthia grinned, nodding at him. "The oil painting gives me a vision, something to copy—the extremes and grooves. All that gray. We packed plenty for the trip. Oh, shoot. I don't exactly have a parson's suit."

Anthony beckoned to the property by the barn—a clapboard farmhouse with few clapboards left, exposing the plaster and foundation. Chickens cackled from a henhouse built of wood and wire. "I suspect the good

177

Reverend Racecar Ritchie Richland wasn't buried in his only good Sunday-come-to-preach outfit."

"We can't break into someone's house!" Cynthia said. "They'll call the police."

"Why?" Anthony asked. "The world is ending. Remember?"

Cynthia burst into the barn, disturbing their scratchy and weakly sung version of Amazing Grace. She'd run up the hill without resting, so she'd gasp for air as if she'd witnessed the shock of her life.

"What is the meaning of this?" Mattie yelled. The young men stood up again without prompting.

"My sincerest apologies," Cynthia said. "I see the light. Oh, Lord, I see the light!"

"More city tricks," Mattie said. "They've come to test our faith. Throw them on out of here. He's going to rise soon. I feel it. I see the signs. I see angels, pure and full of wind and harp songs. Oh, yes. Angels come and carry him by his toes."

The men walked to her, ready to toss her out. She put up her palms. "You don't understand. I have seen him."

"More trickery. Foxes walk about our lands."

"Your Reverend. I saw him rise from the dirt like a born baby."

Mattie held her hand, halting the men. They looked at her with puzzled faces. "What do you speak of, child?"

"We wondered the hills, searching for . . . " She had to make this good, the confession and testament of the redeemed. "Pot and booze. We're city kids and we came to party."

"And so they came among us, to sow their sinful ways, to lead us into the arms of the devil." Mattie whipped up the congregation, and their paleness and fatigue evaporated.

"We found a grave with fresh dirt to have unmarried sex."

"And where was this grave?" Mattie asked, her right eye shutting and stared at Cynthia with the clear left. A vein in her neck pulsed.

Cynthia hesitated, dithered. Anthony waited outside, away from sight. He nearly whispered to her. It would be near, not in any cemetery. He watched the scene through a hole in the barn wall.

"By the farmhouse, off to itself," Cynthia said.

Mattie paused, then nodded. "We buried our beloved by his childhood home, never farther, as he said. If we buried him in a public grave, it would hurt his renewal."

"At first, we thought it was a groundhog digging up . . . turnips or potatoes. Dirt was thrown into the air. I'm ashamed to say we laughed. Forgive us. How ignorant we were." The congregation shuddered collectively. Cynthia could take it. She'd walked out onto stage in front of hostile or intoxicated audiences and drew them deep into her world. She had a gift to make worlds and build doors in those worlds. "When we got closer, to taunt the poor earth creature, we saw it wasn't a creature at all but a hand digging at the dirt. I thought it was a trick on us city kids, but he struggled and pulled at the roots and grass. We watched as he dug himself up. He reached his arm for a hand to hold—"

"Lordy. Lordy! I must go to him! He reaches for my hand." Mattie stumbled out of the barn, and Anthony figured that was his cue. He centered himself at the door, unsteady in his new shoes. The tail of the frock coat hung low around his legs, and he liked the feel—the outfit of a Philomath. He tightened the bowtie at his neck and slipped a hat on the gray, modified wig Cynthia improvised out of the set she'd stowed in the trunk. He threw open the barn gate, standing in the midday sun, and the light set his white makeup and black crease wrinkles glowing. He lowered his voice, remembering every preacher he'd ever seen in movies, especially Robert Duvall in *The Apostle*. These people starved and ached and would probably not notice any of the differences in character, but just to be sure, he'd keep in the shadows. That's what folk did: they'd taken this preacher and dressed him to satiate their needs, their unfulfilled faith, creating a spiritual scarecrow, a walking and talking totem. Anthony didn't have to act vehemently; he only had to wear their expectations, and he wondered if he'd suffocate under their weight.

Some of the congregation fainted on their benches, rolling off and sprawling out on the straw-ridden floor. Others leapt to their feet; howling and reciting imagined recitations in tongues they created in this hysterical moment. Mattie threw her arms up and praised the air. She nearly ran to him, but she held her place, as she'd probably been trained. The crowd hushed, once their surprise passed—each shocked with wide eyes, exposing the spuriousness of their true faith. Not one of them really expected for him to return, and Anthony hid his smirk beneath the flowing moustache. The makeup weighed heavy on his face, and he concentrated on ignoring it. He remembered what Cynthia always said. *Just feel the part. Say what they expect you to say.*

"My people," he said, in a voice spoken through the hole of a creaking oak tree, blown to the grip of its roots in a windstorm. "I am risen and come with good news."

"Halleluiah!"

"I come carrying many summers in my coat. It's always summer in heaven, and I've come to share them." Anthony considered his gospel. He sensed the chance to truly touch these people's lives, to set them free. Their deep fears created their need, and they held to the preacher's coattails like frightened children. Cynthia told him to just feed into them a little, get them to give directions, then slip away for a bit and not return. She said it wasn't right to upset their faith, but Anthony felt a deeper calling, especially now, wearing the outfit of a preacher, a true prophet. He faced the void, saw death running at him, and these people had to know. He couldn't address it slowly. They'd never listen. He had to shock them out of their complacency. It would sting. It would hurt like hell, but it would be the only way it worked.

"What is the time, Reverend?" Mattie asked.

"About a quarter-to-twelve," Anthony said. Mattie flinched, and he realized the true spiritual depth of her question. She held her arms to him, trying to grow them to close the distance and connect the insulator between them. He sensed the valleys of her love, of her need, and Anthony wanted to stay there, to swim in that lake, to wade in its maternal channels. Her void of love joined his, carved out from his grandmother's glacier, deep and wide, and he stumbled off the edge of the cliff, falling deeper into the chasm.

"Yes. Forgive me, my children. For I have traveled far into death and returned," the Reverend said. "It is the appointed time. The end has come."

The crowd praised, relief melting their faces, easing their backs and spirits. The weight of the human world—of empty bellies, crying children, and hard labor—lifted from their backs. Anthony walked forward, holding the lapels of his frock coat. "God is in his heaven, and we are free."

Mattie couldn't contain herself any longer and she rushed forward and swiped up the preacher in the flabby folds of her arms. She pressed her cheek into his neck, and he turned his head so the makeup wouldn't smear on her face. Her rolling fat warmed him, protected him, and kept him secure. She drenched him in her heavy sweat.

"Will you take us home, Reverend?" she asked.

"We *are* home, my dearest," Reverend said. "Earth will be the new heaven, and it will be faithful to those who remain."

"You will stay?" she asked. "You hurt me so bad," she whispered into his ear, then kissed his lobe, shooting chills down his neck. He curled and flinched.

Cynthia stepped down the aisle. "He told us as he climbed from the grave that he could only stay a short while. He has only come to bring the good news of the new world. Forgive him. He gets lost."

The preacher raised his arm at her and pointed. "Do not listen to the lies of heretics and city folk. Forgive them for they do not understand and shut your ears to their deceptions." At his words, the stronger men stood again and readied to remove Cynthia.

"What are you doing, Preacher?" she asked. "This wasn't what was supposed to happen."

"This was the plan since the Lord created time," he said. "He has raised me like Lazarus, and I will stay and live with my people and grow in their pure love."

"And abandon us?" Cynthia asked. "You're a bastard, Anthony."

"Remove her!"

"I can understand it," Cynthia said. "Why would you want to be Anthony anymore? And I'm sorry." She raced to the preacher and yanked off his fake beard, smearing his makeup down her hand. The spirit glue tore away, and it exposed Anthony's young and smooth face, contrary to the old and weather-beaten visage. "You're really gone, aren't you?"

Mattie looked over his visage, released her arms and backed away. "No!" Anthony said. "Do not be fooled by the illusions of the devil. It is me. The racing racecar of the Lord. I've come back from the dead to bring you all salvation. I've got a direct telegraph line to God. He hears all prayers when I tap the button."

Mattie collapsed into a bench and rubbed her palms down her face, tracing a lipstick line down her chin. She wobbled weeping. "I really believed it," she said. "You'd just leave me in this world like that. It had to be God's plan." The crowd waited for her orders, but she quivered and shook. No one reached out to hold her, then Cynthia took her hand.

"It had to be done," Cynthia said. "I need him, too."

"Just go," Mattie said. "You've done enough."

With this revelation, the crowd rose from their benches or helped those earthbound to their feet, and they filed out of the barn, their faith snapped. "Time to go on home," one of them said, exiting with the same lack of enthusiasm as if leaving a mediocre high school basketball game. Only the pregnant chick in the Metallica t-shirt stuck around. She held her swollen belly, feeling for movement. Cynthia grabbed Anthony's arm and yanked on it, pulling at his frock coat.

"Is it you?" Cynthia asked.

He shook his head, then raked the remaining makeup down his face, peeling off the slight prosthetics. "I went away for a little while, and it felt good and warm and I could rise from the dead. Cancer didn't give me the willies no more."

She pulled him into an embrace and wrapped her arms around his neck. "You scared the crap out of me."

"Yo, guys," the pregnant chick said. "Think you could give me a lift? I know how to get the hell out of here."

"You'll guide us north? We need gas."

"Fuck," she said. "I need a cig'. Yeah. I'll guide you. Like the north fucking star. I'll kick in a few dollars. You're not driving to Manhattan, are you?"

Cynthia counted their current funds in her head: about thirty dollars they could scrounge together. The money would help. "Why Manhattan?"

"That's my name."

Cynthia took Anthony's hand and led him out of the barn, leaving the congregation ripped open, sending them on a new journey of seeking, the true one that never ends.

"You saved my ass back there," Manhattan said.

Anthony sat next to Manhattan in the back seat and applied cream to his face. He scrubbed the makeup off with a rag, and Cynthia reached from the front and handed him sterile wipes. He liked the frock coat and kept wearing it, adding to his wardrobe of black jeans and a button-down shirt.

"What were you doing there, anyway?" Anthony asked.

"I got a ride with some kids. I didn't want to go south. Tito's south. My boyfriend. So, I got off in that shitty little village. You guys heading through Scranton? My mother lives there. I need to stop and get some shit."

"Guess so," Cynthia said. She handed her a water bottle, and Manhattan nursed half of it down, gratefully.

"Three days," Manhattan said. "Waiting for that old man to return. He felt me up once, when he claimed to be laying hands on me. First preacher I ever knew to use his cock to heal the sick. Dirty old freak. Someone in town said they had food and would take me in. They did but they talked shit about me—the sinner. Those bitches looked down on me."

"Welcome to the ship of fools," Anthony said, offering his hands.

Manhattan took it like a lady, gripping his fingers. "Awesome sauce. The right ship for me. You had a pretty good con going there. They would have gotten down on their knees and worshipped you. Bunch of freaks."

Anthony handed up the latex bits, beard and wig, showing his bald head. Cynthia cleaned the gear and packed them into various satchels. "The worst of conmen," Anthony said. "We're not looking for cash. We're after souls."

"Cool," she said. "Vampires."

Tolya sat in the car with his shirt off, still alongside the road. "Idiocy," he said, breaking his vow of silence since the trip began. Anthony knew that eventually his distaste and disgust would compel to break his reticence. "Now a new moron joins this band."

"That means 'welcome'," Anthony said.

"Idiocy. Right." Cynthia snapped her head and stared at Anthony, axing him with a look only a woman could employ to the proper temper. "Like what you did back there? Goddess. What's wrong with you?"

"I'm dying of cancer," Anthony said. "And it's slow."

"Cancer?" Manhattan said. "And it's killing you, too? Fucking sexy."

Cynthia sneered at her then returned her attention to Anthony. "You're losing it. You were just going to abandon us. You were going to forget about me. We've made all these promises for you. Given up everything."

"I told you," Anthony said. He found his fedora in the floor well, grabbed it and scrunched it with his hands. "I'm not going to spend the rest of my life comforting others."

She composed herself, breathing in deeply, her nostrils flaring. Her beauty soured with her anger, and Anthony looked away, finding her entirely unattractive. Every woman had an ugly-face, and all the cute drained.

"Well, just don't forget about us on your quest for a mad orgasmic martyr's finish," she said.

"We're all martyrs," Manhattan said. "Most of us just don't know it."

"Stay out of this," Cynthia responded.

Anthony sighed and slipped on his hat. "I felt like I was floating. And the story proved so attractive, hypnotic. I fell into the preacher and really believed for a few minutes that I could truly rise from the grave. Blame me if you want. I couldn't give a shit."

She turned around. "How far until we hit a gas station, Manhattan?"

"I remember one just up the road. How far are you going, anyway?"

"To Long Island to find proof that Anthony is the son of Andy Kaufman. Then we'll convince his family to do a blood test to prove it."

WALKING THE FIELDS TWILIGHT

YOU Sticking With these chumps?" Cinderfield asked. Tolya pumped gas outside of the Cheese Barrel Store— a crappy little store decorated with Dutch paneling and hex marks where the locals sold boxes of Honey Nut cereal to tourists at a sixty percent markup. The closest supermarket was probably fifteen miles down 73. The place stocked-up on beer and wine and cigarettes, and a clapboard sign hung over the door:

WE SELL LIVE BAIT. AND IT'S WIGGLING!

"Live and wiggling," Cinderfield said, ignoring Tolya's attempts to ignore him.

"Just leave me be!"

"Never. Never. Never. Oh what fun! Twiddle-dee-dee!" Cinderfield clicked his heels. "You're playing chauffer to some kids. Didn't you try this before, once? Didn't work out too well, if I recall."

Tolya gripped the gas pump, and his knuckles bleached. "What if I fell to my knees right now and prayed? Grabbed my palms and begged to let Jesus into my heart? Would that be rid of you?"

Cinderfield clapped. "Then you'd have two sons-of-bitches whispering in your ear day and night. Be my guest, sir. My poor relations with corporate HQ have been falsely reported. I really am quite misunderstood, but that seems to work the best for my job."

Tolya yanked out the gas nozzle and let the petrol pour down his legs. Then he ripped out his matches, pulled out a stick and pressed it to the sandpaper strip.

"I'll burn my skin and bones before you can have my soul."

Cinderfield clapped and giggled again, his eyes alive with child-wonder. "Go on, then. Light it up, you coward. What a show it'll be. We'll rip off our clothes and dance around you. Whooping and hollering!"

Tolya put away the matches. "I have to finish this out. I have to see those kids get where they're going. I owe it to him."

"Just as I thought," Cinderfield said. "WHOOP WHOOP WHOOP. LIVE AND WIGGLING!"

Cynthia watched Tolya as she sat on the bench in front of the store. She pushed her skirt down to her knees to keep it from bunching up, and her hand tangled in spider webs under the bench. "Who the hell is he talking to?" Cynthia asked. "Is there someone behind the car? I see a shadow. Do you think souls give off shadows?"

"The shadow came first," Manhattan said. She puffed on a cigarette without regard for her pregnancy, and ash trickled onto her gut hump, catching it on the faded Metallica shirt.

"You shouldn't do that to your baby." Why should this chick get to be a mother? She and Anthony would have such beautiful children, but the hope was moot, now. She just couldn't see it with anyone else; and Manhattan didn't care about the gift she'd been given, probably never would.

"I've cut back," Manhattan said. "I was once a two-pack-a-day-bitch. Down to three cig's a day, and that rammed my ass. The only way I get through it is thinking of monster trucks driven by old vampires from the movies. Fucked-up, I know. But, shit. It works."

Cynthia sighed and looked up to Anthony for support. He leaned against the oak tree built into the foundation of the country store and played with acorns dangling from the twigs.

"It's good for him, anyway," Manhattan said. "This planet is full of fucked-up shit. I'm not setting up my kid to get kicked in the chest by the real world." She puffed. "Moment my womb evicts him, he's going to choke on the smog and drink the mercury in the tap water."

"The state should take your baby," Cynthia said, no longer concealing her bitterness.

"It's not a perfect world, and I hate it when mothers lie to their kids."

"Every mother does," Anthony said. "It's not for the kid. It's for themselves, and they might believe it just a little while." Anthony stepped handed a bottle of water to Manhattan. He hadn't asked Cynthia if she wanted anything.

"Did your mother lie to you?" She put out the cigarette on the bottom of her Dr. Martens.

"My mother taught me the only truth." Anthony strolled off from the parking lot and broke the threshold of some birch wood growing in silvery bark at the edge of the road.

"What does that shit mean?" Manhattan asked.

"His mother was killed," Cynthia whispered, "on the day he came into the world."

Manhattan's face twisted in fright, breaking the mascara stream lining her dark eyes. Then she shrugged. "At least she got it over early."

Tolya hung up the spout and stepped through the puddle of gas in the parking lot. He got into the car, and drove it into a side parking spot. "We going?" he yelled out the window. Gas fumes wafted through the car window.

"Goddess," she said. "Did the pump break?"

"Mind your own fucking business," Tolya said. "Let's haul ass."

"Looks like Anthony's gone for a walk," Cynthia said.

"Jesus H. Fucking Christ," Tolya said, then stuck a tobacco wad into his lip.

Cynthia's stomach gurgled, and she'd begun to feel dizzy. She couldn't put this off anymore, and she stepped into the store and bought a stale hotdog from the vendor, added relish and ketchup then walked out to the parking lot. She looked at the processed meat and felt huge, ugly. Anthony didn't want her. This Goth Q-tip shows up, and he's all over her, even though she's pregnant and with some guy. Cynthia couldn't make herself eat. She nearly chucked it, but held off. She wondered how long it would be until she could eat again.

"You hungry?" Cynthia asked.

"Always . . . carrying around this load. Why? You want to buy me a steak?" Manhattan asked. "I could swallow a whole cow right now. I had the practice with my last boyfriend." She caught Cynthia off guard, and she snickered. "Those cult-freaks fed me wheat pancakes for a week. I know I shouldn't bitch about it, but those things are fucking bitter and hard as hockey pucks." Cynthia gave her the hotdog instead of wasting it. At least she'd done a good thing with the food. "I've got a friend who'll put me up in New York," Manhattan said. "I'll just have to keep my mind focused on monster trucks and vampires 'til I get there. How far are you guys going?" Manhattan asked, sucking down the meat.

"'Til the end of space and time," Cynthia said.

"Shit. You've got to eat. Let's forage."

"Like . . . in the woods? For real?"

Manhattan shook her head. "Yeah. In the woods. God. It must be nice to be so innocent, all sugar and spice." Cynthia flinched a bit. It sounded like an accusation, and she nearly reported all her experiences with the dead and the dying and everything she'd lost, but then she realized Manhattan just burned that way and not to take offense. She tugged on Cynthia's shoulder, and she got up and followed Manhattan into the store.

The door jingled when it opened, smacking chimes hanging from the ceiling. The air twitched Cynthia's nose: a mix of coffee, old fish, and musty mold. An icebox hummed next to the door and boasted the largest live bait selection in the Poconos. The shack sold a limited selection of grocery store goods, mostly stale or beyond its expiration date. A Stetson hat nodded at them from behind the counter—and a golden-rod of a man with silver hair growing down his head and lip nodded under the hat. He dissected them both with scalpel eyes, and Cynthia crossed her arms over her chest, not sure if the hat-man enjoyed filthy thoughts or just didn't trust city girls.

"Damn," Manhattan said. "Like a hawk, probably a hunter. Stores in the city are easy. The clerks couldn't give a shit, but this guy hunts deer, probably out for days at a time, just waiting." Manhattan pointed at the several sets of antlers decorating above the counter along the wall. "I've done worse, but I'm off my game."

"You mean? We can't!"

"You want to eat?"

At moments of crisis such as these, when the rigid frames of her conscience—the dimensions and borders of her upbringing and social experience—pulled on her, protesting, Cynthia found herself looking to Anthony for advice, no longer trusting in the reality that had so harshly betrayed her twice. Anthony must be wise because he walked in fields at twilight, in the in-between places: life and death, reality and unreality, Philadelphia and New York City. Stealing would have normally sent her into tantrums, but they needed supplies if they planned to make it. And Anthony needed this. Who committed the injustice? Peasants starved in Russia, and the Czar locked the grain houses to feed his barbaric soldiers so they could be strong when they butchered. Babies starved in the row houses of Philly, and McDonald's sold from a dollar menu. Though she paused and considered. You could justify anything you wanted. She stood on the edge of a deep pit and knew it, understood the dangers she faced with her subjective logic. Still, she'd only let herself fall a little, far enough where she could pull herself back up when the journey ended. Reality had become so tangible, and it was easy for Anthony to exist in such a variable protean way. He wouldn't be around to face any of the consequences.

Manhattan slinked over to a wide cylinder of beef jerky on the far shelf, by boxes of donuts and candy bars. She grabbed a few stalks and examined them, studying the rough crimson beef. "Shit brings me out in a rash," she said, and let them fall from her hand back into the can, still holding several stalks and lifting them with a magician's precision and stuffing them down her pants. Her shirt fell back over, hiding the evidence. Cynthia blinked, deciding whether she had seen such an event moving at quantum speeds.

The old hawk in the hat never took his eyes off of them. "Perfect," Manhattan whispered. "Ain't nothing going to get by him—not a bunch of city girls. He just can't believe his eyes might fail him."

Cynthia nodded, feeling dizzy. Reality wobbled. It felt like a game. Manhattan led her to the deli meats in an open chilled case. The hawk's gaze followed, and Cynthia felt him drilling into her back, watching his prey, ready to pounce and drive his talons into her neck. She shivered.

"He's going to see us," Cynthia whispered.

"Shit, man," she said. "If he catches us, I'll just blow him. Not the first time."

They examined the packs of lunchmeat. "This shit brings me out in a rash," Manhattan said. She dropped the bundled but held it with her fingers. When she turned to walk away, she slipped it under her shirt from a side angle. They strolled along the shelves, harvesting the old food. Most of it had expired anyway and would probably give her food poisoning to serve karma.

Anthony popped his head into the store and yelled to them, startling Cynthia. She squawked. "Sun is setting to the west," he said.

"Just got to get some cig's," Manhattan said, and Anthony left for the car.

Cynthia studied Manhattan's lower curves, checking for outlines of the small supermarket she currently transported concealed by the circumference of her unborn son. It blended well, melding into the holes and ridges.

The old hawk picked apart their atoms and searched for any guilt. He didn't feel as a man felt—more an angel, come yielding white sword, an angel of vengeance on earth to serve God's justice. He sliced through Cynthia, and she fell into vivisected chunks, spilling out onto the filthy floor of the market. He reminded her of Father Pierce—the wild-eyed old priest at their church, St. Joseph's the Worker, where she attended as a child. He'd scream of hell, never of heaven, and swore to them all that not a soul in his Parish would ascend and sit at the table with the Lord, nor drink from his cup.

"He's going to send me to hell," Cynthia said. Manhattan jabbed her in the leg, and Cynthia tugged on her long sleeves, hiding her deepest sins. "To burn in the lake of fire."

"Cool it, chickie," Manhattan said.

They walked the thousand miles to the counter, and Cynthia wrung her sleeves, nearly exposing the red and swollen slices up her arm. She tried to force the thoughts from her mind, but the harder they pushed, the more they squeezed out between her fingers. She composed a little poem:

Hawk in the hat flying in the air;
Little mouse crawling, have a care,
He's never going to love you.
Death is never fair.

Shit. Her eyes soaked in tears. Manhattan pressed on.

"Pack of Marlboros," she said.

"Yep," the hawk in the air said. He turned his back, but somehow his eyes still fixed on the girls, and he dropped a pack on the counter. He studied Cynthia, focusing on her eyes, and a hot tear dropped from the left and slid down her cheek.

"Why are you crying?" Manhattan asked.

"Your baby is born to a broken merry-go-round."

Manhattan dropped a few crumpled dollars on the counter next to a collection bottle with the picture of a happy child on the label, who apparently was also dying of cancer.

"Now, you girls don't think I didn't see you, do you?" Hawk puckered his dry lips into a tight triangle. His eye lit up with euphoria, the kind of high that comes from killing a noble beast and drawing back that nobility into one's self. He waited and watched their response.

"Don't pull that shit on me," Manhattan said. "Next, you'll want me to blow you so you won't call the cops."

Cynthia fought to contain the howling, clawing cat in her chest, and it popped its head into her throat, choking her. "We're hungry," she said. "You don't understand. I never do stuff like this. I'm good."

Manhattan kicked her foot and furrowed her forehead. Cynthia sighed. She got it. The hawk was just testing them. "Goddess."

"I've had enough of you wild pups stealing me out of my store. None of you know the value of money, just living off your parents and getting fat, bringing this country down. I didn't kill V.C. so you shits could wreck everything that was great about this country. No, suh."

"Goddamn it," Manhattan said. "Just call the police and spare us the lecture. My dad used to lecture me all the fucking time, then he'd go get drunk and beat the shit out of my mother. Your morality's a joke. It's a funny wife-beating gas."

"Maybe so," he said. "But in my store, it's God's law. Now, you both put back what you took, and I'll call the sheriff. No reason why we can't dispense this like civilized adults."

Manhattan yelped, buckled over and clutched at her gut with her hand. "Aww, shit. Not now."

"Now, quit your complaining and take your medicine. We all have to sometime."

"She's not complaining," Cynthia said. "She's pregnant!"

"Father's probably out of the picture, too. Bunch of godless heathens running wild. I turn my back, lest I turn into a pillar of salt." He reached for the phone, and Manhattan gasped and bent over, her eyes split wide in surprise. Cynthia couldn't tell if she was faking, but it didn't matter.

"Only a man would be so obtuse," Manhattan said through her teeth and howled until he put down the phone. "He beat me, you asshole. I had to get away. But just call the goddamn police. They'll send me home, and he'll find me. I'm sixteen-goddamn-years-old."

Cynthia shook her head and studied the chick, her face beyond her long dark bangs. She hadn't seen her youth before, not through the veil of bitterness she wore. She could never have been young, born so old and raked and eroded by the wind and the rain, by the neglect of a careless mother and the rage of a careless lover. She now felt precious to Cynthia, and she needed to protect Manhattan and her child, as if all the hopes of the damned and lost human race beat in the infant's new and tiny heart.

"Now, take it easy, little lady," he said. "It's going to be fine, now." His tone softened into that of a loving father, showing another side of him. Cynthia clutched her shoulder and helped her slide down to the floor.

"I think her water broke," Cynthia said. Before he could look down, she interrupted him. "Better get some towels. And set some hot water to boil. I'll call the hospital on my cell."

"Cell reception isn't always the best up here," he said. "Maybe I should—" Manhattan howled again and rolled her eyes back into her head. Cynthia brushed the long black hair from her face. "Please, sir. Towels. And get water bowling. Now!" She employed a feminine authority, exhibiting her genetic knowledge of childbirth. Like a good man, he bowed and ducked out into the back to fetch some towels. She figured he lived above the shop. Soon as he cleared the shop, Manhattan got up, a bit wobbly from her wide load. Cynthia helped her to her feet. She grabbed some chocolate candy around the register, a few bags of potato chips and bottled water from a little cooler on the floor.

"Move your cute pink ass," she said.

Cynthia raced her out the door. Tolya and Anthony sat in the car, waiting. "Start it!" Cynthia yelled. Tolya, recognizing their flight, turned over the engine. They leapt in the back of the truck, and Tolya pulled out onto the rural route and headed northeast.

"Don't take the highways," Cynthia said. "He'll probably call the state troopers."

"Not a problem," Tolya said.

Manhattan unloaded their gains and good from out of her baggy jeans and shirt. She piled the lunchmeat and jerky and pastries and candy onto the seat—a bounty from the Lord, rich and ripe, to fuel their journey north for sometime.

"You're pretty good at that," Cynthia said.

"Growing up, that was a trip to the market. Helps carrying around this bowling ball. I can carry a lot more. Call it my contribution to your journey into madness."

Cynthia paused before asking, worried about stepping on a sore toe, but Anthony would ask. He wouldn't care about upsetting anyone. Reality had to be disturbed. He'd taught her so much.

"Did your boyfriend really do that?"

"What?" she asked, and tore open the plastic wrapper on a beef jerky stick. She bit off the top and chewed it down, hardly pulping the meat before swallowing it and biting off another piece.

Cynthia knew that world of abuse existed, had seen it

enough on television or listened to the laments of scared friends stuck in such vices as she held their hand and leaned their heads onto her shoulder.

"Oh, yeah. He beat the shit out of me. Sometimes I took it because I'd done something like scratched his motorcycle or smoked his meth. He would have hit me anyway, but I felt better when I'd done something to aggravate him. Gave me some control."

"That's . . . "

"If he finds me, he'll kill me. I left 'cause of the kid."

Cynthia laid back, no longer hungry. Bile filled her gut and pulsed into her throat. She watched the birch trees pass. Signs said fifty miles to the Delaware Valley Water Gap. As a child, Cynthia's grandparents had taken her to Bushkill Falls up north in PA, and the waterfalls flowed over her spirit, cooling and assuring her. They drove farther and farther from the falls, heading north to Scranton.

ANGEL'S FRIENDS

And like all sources of light, Angel drew other fireflies to him. He went before the masses, on stage, an audience at church, worshipping the word and the song, and he gathered allies, friends, companions and fellow high priests before the altar. Many of like spirit and mind were drawn to Angel, who thought him wild and untamed, at first. They didn't understand the child at play, making his funny voices, acting out, loving a stage even without pay or little applause. When he stepped off the stage or away from the microphone, he seemed to shift out of this world, from our reality. Angel didn't feel right until he returned to stand before the crystal screens in their eyes or the eye that projected onto the crystal screens. It was such that he didn't feel real until he stepped into that fantasy world where he could play and process. Angel wasn't complete with crowds watching him, joining him, finishing his body.

And so arrived Angel's high priest . . . the lion, the zoo-master, his spiritual soul mate. They felt each other's thoughts, knew each other's rhythms. The two minds came together like a match touching a pool of gasoline. His new companion, his counterpart, would become a sounding board and enabler, helping Angel summon his diverse and disparate voices into unique personas, then unleash their terror upon the hapless and innocent world. His friend's name—a real person and not a fictional character created by Angel—was Bob, and one day, he would become Angel's mourner. Bob had been woven of star matter and given a soul to support Angel, to give him a home, a trusted friend and then keep his candle lit, to continue their work. One day, Angel would wound Bob, and he would always be broken without his friend.

Angel found a new stage in New York City—the heart of the world, his haven, his playground. Angel had frequented many comedy clubs, catching rising stars as they flew by, and he'd penetrated the crystal screen, but this new stage was beyond the perimeter, the border. He was making it, ascending. The show was hip, for the young people, college students, daring and brilliant, where an angel could truly soar.

He stood on stage, alone, in front of a red curtain, wearing his gray suit jacket. His eyes flashed to and fro, nervous, unsure. He looked terrified—a carefully created appearance. Instantly, the audience pitied him or felt bewildered by his presence. He waited, silent, spreading his anxiety to his watchers, the silent and stunned. They waited. The tension built, tighter and tighter, near to snapping. Angel waits, employing the silence, making the anxiety work for him, using it against his audience, and playing them. Then, his motivation switches in. His eyes light up. Some random idea strikes him, and he reaches for a child's record player setup on a table by him on stage, replacing his usual drums. He opens the case, and then pressed the arm carefully to the record. A tinny orchestra plays, sounding a preamble, a buildup of triumphant music. Angel's face brightens, and he bobs to the music, the theme song of Mighty Mouse. And he waits. The audience watches; again, they are bewildered. Angel is at play.

Here I come to save the day!

He mimes, pretending to be singing. Then stops while the chorus sings again. The audience comprehends. They laugh and watch him. He's not singing or dancing. He's not telling any jokes. He's sampling standing in panic then motioning with his hand for the rare report of Mighty Mouse. The song quickly ends, and he bows. The audience goes insane, applauding and cheering. Angel's won them. His life is born to the wider world. He is ascending.

CLOSER THAN A COMET; NEARER TO A MOON

What's dying like?"

Anthony walked with a birch stick he'd collected along the road. Clumps of silvery-papered birches grew in families along Rural Route 8. He gazed out over the spirited mountains, hummed to the wind that blew from their mouths and danced his feet for the ancient ghosts.

"Can't really tell you," he said. "It's not like something that takes a while. One moment you're tapping your toes or licking ice cream cones, and the next—there is no next moment, I guess. If I can contact you somehow through ectoplasmic communication, if I still have thoughts to think, I'll let you know."

"That's cool of you," Manhattan said. Anthony studied the young woman as she hobbled and wobbled, lifting and balancing the load in her womb. It reminded him of an elephant walking on stilts, and he couldn't fathom why she continued to defy gravity. She looked too young to have a young one growing in her, but nature designed humans this way, before they learned to artificially extend their lives through sanitation, surgery, and vitamin elixirs sold in convenience stores that could do everything from soothing an inflamed prostate to extending an erection.

Tolya bent under the hood. "Koorva!" he said. Anthony assumed Tolya swore in his native tongue, and he couldn't understand the profanity; however, at times, he could match the usage, the vehemence of the language. Humans possessed universals.

"Need some help?" Anthony asked.

"*Need some help*?" Tolya mocked. "I repair tractors as a boy in the fields. I drive big rigs and fix engines when they break down. I don't need help."

Cynthia sat inside the car, leaning her head against the window. She kept her eyes partly open, watching Anthony and Manhattan talking and walking, never looking away or actually trying to snooze. She'd grown pensive the more they'd spoken in the car, and Anthony felt her heavy over them, prowling from her seat and growling. They continued their stroll, kicking the gravel.

"Does this all look different to you than before?" Manhattan asked. "The grass and the mountains and shit?"

Anthony paused and scanned the horizon. At times, he could perceive precision in the contours of the stone peaks, the grand hillsides that trapped and entombed the hot earth beneath. He shut his eyes and ran his chest over the landscape, feeling it tactile—a sense that had improved since his body declined, though not yet declining in noticeable ways yet, except for some pain and fatigue. He could feel each curve as if he touched the foothills—and deeper and deeper yet, diving into the rock and dirt, knowing it like an old relative, someone familiar to him from childhood.

You are ancient. I am your blood. I grew from your spirit. You are the bones of the living earth.

He felt the mountain sigh in its sleep and opened his eyes.

"I can feel the mountain," he said. "Like an old grandfather."

"That's like shaman shit," she said.

Anthony shrugged. "He feels old and wise, like knowing someone. And they sleep. Long, long slumber. Nations rise and fall, and they wake briefly to witness their birth and death. I can see it now. Really see it. All things in nature, those things of identity, possess a spirit. They exist in this plane differently. Their heart. Their aether."

She took his arm, and he could sense the budding rose in the young girl, beyond the child, deeper, rooting in her chest. She sought a protector, and just his voice comforted her.

"Your world is beautiful. I wish I could live there."

"This is a world of peace," he said.

"It's a fantasy, then. A real one, but a fantasy for people." A red-tailed hawk swooped down low over the valley and surveyed the land below. "People only do violence. It's the nature of man."

"But man can know peace, too. It has happened. India. During the Raj. The Mahatma freed his nation through passive resistance."

"That was never real," she said. "They just made it up. They all got together in a room, smoked pot and dreamed that shit up."

He rubbed her hand. "I'll show you. For you and your child."

"Not my child." She lit a cig' with a plastic lighter and sucked down the smoke. "Soon as this little bastard pops, I'm giving it up."

"Is that what you want?"

She hung her shoulders and looked away, then tapped the cig', casting its ash on the road. "What the fuck do I know?" She took another pull. "Best thing for this baby is to be away from me. I fuck things up like with my parents, my boyfriend. I'm just going to fuck the kid up, too."

Tolya slammed the hood of the ice cream truck, got into the vehicle and started it. "Moving out," the Russian said.

Anthony walked Manhattan back to the car and opened the backseat door for her. Anthony helped Manhattan up into the front. She nodded politely and rolled her round load into the seat, sitting next to Cynthia. Anthony took the back bench inside the cabin. Cynthia pretended to stir from sleep.

"You two have a nice walk?"

They pulled off of the road, driving up a gravel path and passed derelict and rotted barns, old farmhouses with their roves collapsed and through a tractor and car graveyard. Old pickup trucks rusted in the open air and moisture, now home to squirrels and foxes. When it rained, their engines leaked oil and stained the grass black.

"It's up here," Manhattan said. "On the left. My dad owned forty acres here."

Tolya and Anthony pushed the truck over a hill, and the transmission grumbled and protested his command. A white clapboard garage came into view. A rusty gas pump leaked water from a nozzle on the side. Grass grew through mounds of gravel in the lot, surrounded a two-story farmhouse. Wild corn and wheat grew in the fields surrounding the house, not cut or tended to in years, now a ward to the wilderness. Creeper vines scaled the filthy clapboards, reaching into broken windows that had been shabbily sealed with cardboard. A light rain washed the land, and even with the light flow, the rain gutters leaked down the side, filled with dirt and leaves.

Anthony gripped the bottom of his seat. Let's be away from this pit, this forgotten hell. He sensed the loneliness, the forgotten spirit possessing the structure and land. It had once been loved and cared for, but the family now neglected it, no longer sharing the dream of the farm, of drawing the raw stuff of life from the soil. He held back. They'd only be here for a short time while Manhattan gathered her things.

"It's exactly the same," she said. "I hoped if I ran away for long enough, it would fall down. There are ghosts at windows. Anthony, come in with me."

Anthony hesitated, then released the chair. "I shall fear no evil."

"Not evil," Manhattan said, opening the door. "Just my mother." Anthony hurried out first and helped her to her feet. "I don't think she's here. Sometimes she goes to stay with my aunt in Bethlehem."

Anthony thought he spotted a brand new pickup truck parked behind the garage. Manhattan didn't notice, so he brushed it off. He just wanted to collect her stuff then get the hell out of there before whatever haunted this place, whatever disease oozed and dripped, infected him, too.

Her mother didn't bother locking the side kitchen door, and mice scurried on the linoleum that peeled up at the corners in brittle flaps. Bananas and apples rotted in a basket on the leaning table, and the fruit flies swarmed the rinds. Anthony bumped into the table, and flies swarmed filled the air before departing for safer bounties.

"I'm going to run upstairs and get some shit. There might be beer in the box. I doubt it, though. My mom usually drinks it all."

"I'm fine." Anthony knew of derelict ships like this farmhouse, and read about poverty, but all his life his grandparents had secured him in a clean yet sterile environment. Grandma would have suffered a coronary if she saw this place, and Anthony kept his distance from touching any surface. Manhattan grabbed some garbage bags from under the sink and dashed through a swinging door into the rest of the house. Anthony gazed out through the window over the sink, looking back onto a collapsed chicken house.

"Who the fuck are you?"

The male voice startled Anthony, and he quickly turned, a little stunned by the aggressive tone. He had to remember he walked in the wilderness. A young man, tan of skin, clad in a 49ers shirt and jeans, stood in the kitchen doorway smoking a cigarette and carelessly allowing the ash to fall on the hardwood floor.

"Tito, I presume," Anthony said.

Tito stomped towards him, beating the floor with his steel-toed boots. "I'll just beat the shit out of you. Fucking stupid breaking into houses up here. These crackers don't have crap." He lurched for Anthony. His heart sped, and he tried to focus through the worlds orbiting in his head. The confrontation shook him deeply, but he loved the energy, wanted more.

"Hold up," he said. "We're here with Manhattan."

"Who the fuck is Manhattan?"

"She doesn't want to see you," Anthony said, realizing he might have said too much.

"Tina? Finally. I've been hanging around this shithole for a week waiting for her to come home. Where is she?"

"Tina and Tito," Anthony said. "Must have loved the alliteration. Soul mates. I bet you can be very sweet when you're not giving into your rage."

"Where is she?" He grabbed Anthony's shirt and squeezed. He stank of beer and cigarette smoke.

"None of this is real," Anthony said. "We have to learn to let things go."

"You're some kind of fucked-up nut job." He pulled Anthony tighter. "Where is she? She's pregnant. I saw it on her friend's page. She has no right to keep me from my son." He twisted Anthony's shirt and tightened the collar around his neck. Anthony resigned not to speak. He couldn't. No matter how hard it rained or the wind howled, he couldn't give into the storm.

"I saw a man rise from the dead," Manhattan said, standing in the kitchen doorway, dragging a black garbage bag behind her. She huffed out of breath.

Tito released Anthony then lunged at Manhattan. Anthony reached to grab his shoulder from chivalrous reflex but missed. His legs trembled, and he nearly toppled over into the table. Tito went for Manhattan, and his face clenched, eyelids tightening.

"Why did you hurt me like that, baby?" He reached his fists in the air and held them there, hovering over her. She closed her eyes and braced herself, didn't raise her hands or run away, perfectly trained. He slammed his fists down on the doorframe, cracking the wood. She flinched and yelled out.

"It's time to go, baby," he said. "I'm going to take care of you and my son."

She hesitated, looking at Anthony. Her eyes glazed over like a zombie's. All the defiance burned out of her, gone to smoke.

"Don't look at that asshole," Tito said. "Get in the truck before I drag you."

"Okay. This has to stop." Anthony stepped forward, still shaky from the physical confrontation. He steeled himself. He had no illusions that he could end this peacefully through communication, but what did he really have to lose? His body failed him, decayed mote by mote, lost to eroding time. Tito couldn't really take anything from him. Flesh was a delusion, a comforting illusion and could only be temporary bruised or beaten. He knew he couldn't physically fight Tito. Anthony had never been a prime physical specimen before he got sick and had no talent for pugilism, and now everyday it took greater will just to stand and function in normal capacity.

"Manhattan."

"That's not that bitch's name!" Tito said.

"Remember Gandhi."

Her eyes shot wide.

"Remember who?" Tito asked.

"You can't have her," Anthony said, closing the distance between them. "She's going to remember who she never was and could always be. I'm going to give her that strength. I'll breathe it deep into her, blowing the wind that the mountains blew into me. And you're going to let her go. She's going to end it with one word."

Tito cracked a smile. "I like your new friend, baby. He's funny. He's a goddamn comedian."

"Anthony." Manhattan touched his arm. "You need to just let us go. I don't know what I was thinking. I can be so stupid, sometimes." Tito tore her hand from Anthony, flung her into the door. It struck her head, and she cried out. Then he hit Anthony's ribs with open palms and pushed him back into the table. The rotting fruit toppled from the basket and rolled to the floor, evicting a horde of flies.

"You're going to hurt, asshole," Tito said.

"Oh yes. I should hope so. I want it to hurt. I want my bones to snap. I need my veins to rip. I'll burn in the sunlight, and I'll crave each moment. When it stops, then I'll be gone. I'll feel nothing."

Tito gazed at his face, not speaking, eyes in wonder like a charmed cobra. Anthony's silence broke the trance. He punched Anthony in the ribs, and the pain seared into his shoulder.

"You can't hurt me," Anthony said, buckling from his hits. "My nerves register pain, warn me of injury. But they're obsolete, you complete ass. You can't hurt me. You have no power over me, what little power you had."

He struck Anthony's jaw. The nerves registered pain, sending signals to his brain. He shut them off. He fired them, laid them off. *You've served me well, but I won't be needing your services anymore. Cheers, mates! We'll rot together.*

"Tito! Stop it." Manhattan leaped forward, grabbing his arm. She tugged at him, a mouse yanking on a tree branch. Tito turned sharply, locked Manhattan in his gaze and rubbed his knuckles. She stepped back, and he bore down on her.

"See? See what you make me do? Cause I love you, baby. I love you so much, and you make my crazy." Tears streamed from his eyes, sheer regret showing through his visage at his body now out of control. He moved down on Manhattan, and she backed into the cabinet. Then he punched her in the head, hitting her eye socket. She cried out then stifled herself. She bowed her head in supplication. Tito wept and rubbed his eyes hard with his fists.

Anthony collected himself, slipping morphine from a bottle in his pocket and swallowing it dry. He told his pain centers that it didn't matter, and that helped take the edge off the throbbing in his chest.

He wept, joining Tito. He cried for the monster, the child among men. He'd been left behind, trapped in an age of physical dominance and rage. He could never love and would never know love's return—and in this, he was both cursed and blessed. Still, the man yearned for more, the hole bleeding in his chest. He couldn't understand why it was denied, and with little experience in processing such complex emotions, he raged, turning to a primal force in his brain, before humans knew of love, seeking control, dominance. Tito lived the old primal ways, and he existed as a throwback in a society working its power to evolve and punish those still giving into their Neanderthal nature. He'd never know a place in this world, always be afraid and lost, and Anthony sympathized with Tito. Still, he'd reserve his compassion. He wept for Tito, because Tito was lost.

"Hit me and burn it out," Anthony yelled. "Strike me. Beat me to a pulp. Snap me in two and make a wish, and I'll pray that it's granted."

"You're some kind of a freak?" He left Manhattan supplicating by the sink. She guarded her pregnant womb with both arms and stood statue-still. "Who the fuck is this guy? Some kind of retard?"

"You can hit me all you want. I'm your punching bag. Hey, folks, it's Whack-a-mole! I'm the mole. Come on, Tito. I'm right here. All that rage. For the mom who never loved you. For all the tests you failed in school. For everyone who left you. Cause you don't feel like you have a soul."

"Shut the fuck up," he whispered, still crying. "I have a soul."

"It's a myth, old son," Anthony said. "Souls are outdated. We've thrown them out with poodle skirts and record players. This is the age of the soulless. You and me. That's our destiny. Our legacy."

Tito rushed him and slammed him against the wall. Anthony took in a deep breath then let it out. He did it again, calming his system, preparing for the assault, the pain. Tito slammed his face, and he felt his jaw crack behind his ear. Maybe not broken, but it screamed.

"Fight back, you retard."

Anthony folded his arms into a shaman's stance, bracing himself for the fury. He would not raise his fists in anger, not to protect himself or anyone else. It's what Tito could understand, the only way he could communicate, and Anthony wanted him to feel alone, to know the world he'd created. Tito hit him again in his forehead. "Fight, faggot. Pussy."

Anthony started to sing the black matter song the ghost of Elvis had sung to him.

"He's a retard," Tito said. "Hit me."

Anthony shook his head.

"Hit me, goddamn it!" He punched the wall. Anthony flinched, but held his stance. Tito's hand bruised like a rotting plum. He must have broken it, but he didn't notice. Anthony looked at Manhattan. She had lifted her head from the bow and watched Anthony, gazed into him, her face lit up in wonder like a child watching a solar eclipse. She studied him, understanding, breaking through her fear, the fog that clouded her eyes.

"You fucking faggot!" He slammed the wall again with his broken hand, then he clutched it, his face twisted in obvious pain. "Do you see what he did to me, baby? You going to let him hurt me like that?"

"He hurt himself," Anthony said. "He's powerless, really. Only the power we give him."

"Baby," he said, rubbing his hand. "Let's go home." She hesitated, looking at Tito then Anthony. Anthony said nothing, just looking at her. He'd presented his case. She had to decide now. "I said get in the truck, now!" He went for her, grabbing at her shoulder. She broke from her statue pose, threw open a drawer and pulled out a steak knife. Its handle came loose in her grip, and the sharp metal sliced into her skin. She held at him. He backed up, putting his hands up.

"You stupid bitch," he said. "Now put that away before I get angry."

Anthony said nothing. He wanted to tell her to stop, that it wouldn't come back to hurt her. The energy we give to the world circles back to us. She'd only cut herself, slash at her own spiritual skin and hurt her child.

Tito lunged for her, and she chopped the air with the blade. It struck his arm, slicing through his sleeve. He pulled it back. "Fucking bitch! I'm going to end your life."

"Are you going to kill him?" Anthony asked. He waited for her to respond. She shuttered, shaking in place, grabbing the knife's bare metal. Blood dripped down her pregnant belly. "Because that's the only way this will end. So go on then. Stab the belly. Strike the heart, but make sure it sticks. Kill this man. Bathe yourself in his blood. And that'll be all. I won't judge you. Not my place."

She trembled, shaking like a birch tree in a storm. Her eyes pendulum swung to and fro between Tito and Anthony. He froze, holding up his hands, exposing the deep bruises along his palm.

"Well, what are you waiting for?" Anthony yelled. "Kill the monster. Right between his fucking eyes. Strike him down for all the men who hurt women. Murder your father and his father. Murder me. I will die. Save me my pain."

The knife slipped from her hand and clattered on the linoleum. She sat and curled up against the cabinet, pushing her palms to her face. "I'm sorry," she said, sobbing. "I'm sorry. I'm sorry."

Tito looked at her, then Anthony. He paused, his eyes considering. "I don't need this shit. Crazy assholes. You just try to survive without me. Crazy, homicidal bitch." He ran by her, out the side door, and a moment later, Anthony watched him peel out on the road, kicking stones from under his back tires.

Anthony knelt down and touched her fingers. "Free now," he whispered. "You are alone, and it is good. We all have to be alone." She sobbed into her hands. Anthony picked up the knife, secured the screw on the handle and washed it in the sink. He placed it back in the drawer.

"We'll stay here, tonight. You'll be alone, but we won't be far. Closer than a comet. Nearer to the moon."

Tolya and Cynthia sat at a picnic table behind the farmhouse. Manhattan had brought them out an old bed sheet from the closet and covered the table with it to hide the layer of white bird crap. They boiled hotdogs in the kitchen from reserves still good in the fridge and cans of beans. He served them on a tray but declined to sit or eat, returning to visit with Manhattan who had taken a turn and hung out in the house.

Cynthia bit off chunks of the meat and stale bread and pushed them around in her mouth, then finally, she swallowed them against the acid wall in her throat. Between eating, she yanked at her long sleeves until the seams ripped. She watched for Anthony to come out of the house and moved between fits where she grabbed the table and moments of depression when she'd lay her head on the table and roll it about on her forehead.

"What's eating you?" Tolya asked.

"It's crap. All this is a bunch of crap. Her boyfriend could have killed Anthony, but he had to go and play the hero. Goddess! He could have killed my Anthony."

"You always loved him?"

She blushed and tried to put her head back down on

the table, trying to conceal her red cheeks. She nearly denied it, started to, but she needed to vent. Tolya wouldn't say anything. He was Russian.

"I think my whole life," she said. "I just didn't know it was him."

"Need can feel like love."

"It's got to be love," she said. "It hurts like love does. It's ripping out all my organs. I devote myself to him, and he won't stop looking at her! I've seen his eyes, the way he gazes. She pretends not to notice, but she curls her hair and exposes her pregnant belly. She's a little bird fallen out of the nest, and he's got to save everyone. It stinks. Goddess."

"And you feel like he owes you something?"

"No. Not owe. Just. I wish he'd notice sometime. Give me a little hint. I'm sure he loves me, even if he doesn't know it." She bit off another hunk of hotdog and gagged it down.

"You've not told him?" Tolya asked.

"It's obvious to everyone."

"Why not tell him?"

She shook her head. "Goddess, no. I couldn't. I don't want to make his life harder than it is. But what if I don't tell him? I'm losing him. I feel him less and less. What happened at the church is just the start. He's playing with reality. He's playing with me." She rubbed her nose on the picnic table and fought her sobs. She needed Tolya to reach out and touch her hair, to comfort her. Instead, he sipped from a beer.

Anthony tapped her on the shoulder. She hadn't seen him come back out of the house. "I need you," he said.

"Oh, honey," Cynthia said. "I need you, too."

"Manhattan is determined to give up her baby," Anthony said. Cynthia's stomach cramped like she'd been kicked.

She sucked it up and hid her anguish. "That's her right."

"But she doesn't really want to. She's just scared, and if she gives it up, it'll rip a hole in her. I can't watch it. I've known too many shattered souls in my life already, and she'll never come back from this one."

"Do you . . . love her?"

He sighed, rubbed Cynthia's shoulder. "I'm no longer like you or her. I'm too far gone, now."

"Okay. So what do you need?"

"A living, breathing and flying angel."

"I'll get the makeup kit from the truck. Find some white sheets and crap."

Manhattan waited for her new crew to go to sleep before slipping out of the house. Anthony slept on the couch, and Cynthia curled up on the floor in a blanket. The weird Russian elected to sleep in Mr. Snowballs, and he seemed fine with those accommodations. Manhattan stepped from the house, down the porch. She ignored the pinching of splinters driving into her bare feet. She wore no clothing or cover against the elements, and her swollen belly jutted out from her body, bracing her small breasts. Her little legs struggled to carry the load, and she had to pause to get her balance.

She scaled the incline up the hillside, following along the stony road, walking into the swollen moon that blossomed like a fat lily over the empty fields and derelict buildings, a wharf of shipwrecked homes and shipwrecked lives. The stones drilled into her swollen feet, and she ignored the discomfort. When she reached the top of the hill, she turned left and cut into the potato fields where she'd dug up the tubers for her family at dinner time, when she'd danced young in the grass, this far paradise where she could play and think and be alone, just among the ground and the trees. She'd frolicked here in her youth, oblivious to her parents' misery, to the drinking. Her mother used to tell her to go out and play because Daddy slept on the couch and felt grumpy. He stank up the house.

She strolled through the grass, careful for groundhog holes. She used to pick violets here and tie them into her hair. She loved being alone, loved the open sky, so far away from the world that frightened her on the news—all the violence and death and crime. Why would anyone want to live in the cities? They seemed like the places where people went to grow old and die.

She walked with ease and confidence in the darkness, stepping in and out of the moonlight, knowing each contour, each rock and blade of grass, mapping them out with her feet. She had drawn the spirit from this place, its life force, moved it into herself. That life force welled in her, and it built her child in its flesh and blood, defining its spirit, moving through its lay lines and glowing. She longed to join the land, and tonight she'd come home to do so.

She treaded the grass and skipped the brooks, and a poem she'd heard in high school recited in her thoughts— prose she'd ignored, forgotten, but the words must have carved themselves into her spirit.

I must be gone: there is a grave
Where daffodil and lily wave,
And I would please the hapless faun,
Buried under the sleepy ground,
With mirthful songs before the dawn.
His shouting days with mirth were crowned;

And still I dream he treads the lawn,

She sat at the edge of the ravine—cut deep and long by the flowing stream a good distance below, the bank covered in river stones from when the stream flowed mighty and proud, pouring from the melt-waters of the mountains in the North. The grass cooled the skin on her bum, and she looked down at her pregnant, swollen body, then rubbed her hand on her womb, soothing the innocent within. She wanted to protect it from all the darkness in the world, including herself and her fear. She'd even planned to give it away but she knew the darkness would find it, hurt the small thing, taint it. It had been the purest gift she'd ever been given, and she'd felt young again, renewed, alive like she had as a child herself. But it would end. The human world ruined beautiful things, and she couldn't allow her child to spoil.

She braced herself on the cliff and wondered if she should pray, but she couldn't remember the words. So she sang quietly to herself, humming the tune to "Amazing Grace". It would only hurt a little while longer.

"If you jump, I will catch you and fly you home," spoke a melodious voice, a violin playing. It startled her, and she grabbed onto onion grass to keep her from sliding down the cliff. The broken plant fiber scented the air with sweet chives and onions.

"What the fuck?" she said, looking up at the angel. His face glowed white in the moonlight, holding its own internal lambent light. His waxy skin glimmered, and his silvery locks dangled like magnolia branches. He draped himself with a white robe that bulged up in the back, perhaps from wings. Feathers poked through the hole at his neck. "Bullshit," she said.

"Mayhaps, so," the angel spoke. She recognized him

through the makeup, recalling his stunt at the temple, but she declined to complete the thought and refused to study the façade closely. She had prayed, and the angel came to her.

"What do you want, cherub?"

"What we all want," he said. "Perfection. To know peace. To not hurt anyone. I've wounded so many, and I carry the guilt heavy. It weighs down my wings, and I cannot fly high or long. Centuries I have been trapped on this world, far away from my hosts and kin. How I long to fly."

"I'm going to fly tonight. I'm going to soar. I'll be free. There's peace in the air, in falling free. Then it won't hurt anymore."

He lowered his powdery hand to her shoulder. "You are beauty," he said. "And it lives in you, even if you can no longer see it. Your child is innocence, and he can show you the way home."

"Why did you come here, angel?" she asked.

He gazed over the cliff. "To fly one last time. To relieve my burden and hope the hand of God catches me. Is that why you came here?"

"I want to fly, too." She laid her naked back in the grass, scratching her shoulder on a concealed thistle. "If I keep this baby, I'm just going to fuck it up. I can't stop smoking. I'm already poisoning its lungs, making it sick. It'll get cancer. I'll infect it."

"Its body will sicken and age. Nothing you can do about that. Even we angels grow old, though slowly. Our bodies do not decay like yours. We slowly turn to stone. So many of my brothers and sisters, my siblings of the high sky, can be found in your cities, on the tops of your buildings and in your gardens. Not many of us remain. So this is the world we've made."

219

"I can't watch that. If I jump, we'll both freeze in time. The world will stop spinning."

"Then we'll jump together and hold hands and know eternity."

"But, you can't," she said. "The world needs angels. There aren't many of you left."

The angel shook his head. "No. It's time. I can no longer endure the ground. I'm so heavy. I'm full of lead and gold."

The angel stepped to the edge and hung a foot over the cliff. He spread his arms like a bird with wings, closed his eyes and leaned forward.

"Don't!" She jumped up, wobbling from her pregnancy, and grabbed him. "You can't. Don't take this from me. You crazy fuck." She dragged him back and grabbed the grass to anchor herself. The weight of her child stabilized her, and she struggled, holding him tight. Her fingers ached from his burden.

"Let me go," he said. "The world will be less beautiful without you in it. How can I fly free when I know you're floating below, cool in the water, gone to ice and wind and waiting, ever waiting for the kiss of the divine to emancipate you. Release me."

"This was my thing. My release."

"And it wouldn't hurt you if I fell?" he asked, leaning back then tumbling onto the stable ground. She released him and rubbed her sore muscles.

"Shit," she said. "I'm trapped. I'm stuck. I just don't want to hurt anyone, anymore. I'm born bad, all broken and damaged. I'm jagged glass. I'm a smashed window. I'm a shattered porcelain doll." White powder coated her fingers, and she rubbed it off on her bare leg.

"But, I love you so, now," the angel said. "If you were not in the world, it would wound me."

"I'm going to fuck my child up."

"Oh, yes," the angel said. "That's for sure. But you'll teach him to love also. You'll teach him that we are fragile, imperfect, and can be redeemed." She sighed and kissed him, holding her breath, stilling her chest. She felt the baby kick in the womb, and she rubbed the spot to comfort him.

"I can't protect him completely."

"No. You can't even protect yourself. It's the way this works. But you've seen something today. There's light in this world."

She ran her fingers through the grass and sprinkled fronds on her pregnant belly. "I'll try it," she said. "For a few days. I'll give you that. I'm not promising anything."

"That's fine," the angel said. "I hate promises. The heart should be enough without need of them."

THE RISE OF CINDERFIELD

I was Touchstone, the clown," Tolya said, remembering his days on the stage, when his planets fell into alignment. "I wanted to act, to be others."

"No one wanted to hear a Russian doing Shakespeare," Cinderfield said, burning him again, always reminding him of his failures. He lay with Tolya in the field outside the pregnant girl's house. A few minutes ago, Tolya watched Manhattan leave the farmhouse, and Anthony, dressed as an angel, followed—playing games, playing games with people's heads and souls.

"What gives that kid the right?"

"Aren't you playing with their lives?" Cinderfield asked. "Hiding your secrets? They love you. Do you think they'd still love you if they knew the truth?"

"Fuck you! Monster. Leave me alone. Where did you come from? Why do you bother me?"

"I'll tell them the truth," Cinderfield said. "Dig up the past like a butchered body buried in the woods, hidden away. Buried bodies. You're a fragment of a man without a past. You're a hanging fingernail. Oh. You make me laugh." And Cinderfield cackled.

"I'll kill you."

"Won't be the first time," the devil responded. "Will you hang me on a cross?"

"Just shut your mouth," Tolya said.

"Never," Cinderfield replied. "I will follow you until you're hung from a cross again."

May 16th 1984

Tolya served four years in jail for involuntary manslaughter and driving under the influence. The judge had called him a menace, a rat that snuck in through the holes in America's immigration policy and even suspected the actor of being a communist agent. Americans didn't care for Russians during the early eighties and with good, though biased, reason; you wouldn't share tea and vodka with a neighbor who pointed a shotgun at your front window day and night. When he got out, he got work on construction sites, keeping under the radar and hoping no one noticed him talking to the devil. So, he drank whiskey to keep the devil silent. The only thing that kept him fighting was the thought of the baby he had saved.

"Fucking loser," Cinderfield told him as they walked along the Levittown Parkway, headed for the small apartment he rented near the lake. "The boss gave you that child to look after, and all you do is kill your liver."

"Don't you ever go away? Isn't there a magic spell I can say?" He quoted: "Thrice the brinded cat hath mew'd."

"You killed his mother. You owe that child something. Remember whom she said the father was?"

"Andy Kaufman," Tolya said. "If she wasn't stoned out of her mind."

"You know it's true. The baby is your destiny. You should find the father so he can look after the babe. For all you know, the child is in an orphanage."

A Ferris wheel spun ahead, dancing and twirling above the church over the boulevard. Saint Mike's fair had migrated back. Tonight, folks would take their tots down to spin on mirth engines, throw money down fixed games and eat shit and junk—such was the American experience.

"When will I be free of you?" Tolya asked his devil.

"You know what be—the sincere way of it, what I am. You'll be free when the child is safe. All you have to do is find Wilma." Reality merged again. There were times when he couldn't tell if Cinderfield was real or just a shadow pouring out of his legs, counter to the light of the sun. Now, he possessed Tolya, just took him over.

Wilma had been hiding. Fuck her ass! Jeb Cinderfield ran into traffic across the Levittown Parkway, crossing to the church grounds of St. Mikes where the Ferris wheel spun and cotton candy choked. Cars screeched to a halt in the road, some swerving to the side. A vendor hit his calf. "Go fuck yourself, too!"

A black dude got out of the Trans Am, grabbed Cinder's scrawny shoulder and socked him in the chin. Cinderfield looked back, stunned. "Good on ya, lad. Hit the bloody devil. Da! Are you fucking Wilma? I think she's running around."

"Fucking jive mental patient," the dude said, and got back into his car.

Cinderfield crossed the rest of the way with no oncoming traffic, all halted at the streetlight down off Rt. 13 in front of the Levittown Train Station. He ran to a mobile stand where they roasted pink tubes of rat shit and pig noses—the perfect food for Satan. A couple talked in front of him, and he listened in to their conversation. The devil always listened.

"He's not dead," the boyfriend said.

"The news said cancer killed him."

"It's one of his twisted games. Andy Kaufman is pulling some kind of twisted-fuck prank."

Cinderfield knew the name. Tolya, the man he'd come to torment on Earth, had seen the young Andy Kaufman doing his act at comedy clubs up north, back when nobody understood what an Andy Kaufman was. Tolya had been an aspiring actor. The world mourned the passing of an angel. Birds flew a bit lower, slower. Clouds beclouded the golden orb. Rain drizzled but did not compel into thunderstorms, just dripped and spit on the face, enough to shock cold but too little to quench the ever-thirsty spring growth of marigolds and honeysuckle. Andy had left the world, and the Earth would always be sadder for it.

Cinderfield crushed a dandelion that had grown up through a crack in the blacktop, then he howled, knelt down and tried to straighten the broken stem, bring it back to the world. Yellow strands of the pollen spread like blood on his finger. The flower popped off in his hand. House sparrows perched on the lighted signs over the concession stands and rigged games. The devil threw up old whiskey and hit the shoes of the couple ahead.

"Yo. Buddy. What's your problem?"

"You're a fucking waste of flesh, and an angel just left the world. We're running out of fucking angels!" Cinderfield picked up the slaughtered dandelion and slipped the smashed flower into his lapel. It flopped, raining yellow pollen down his jacket. The dude in queue kicked his shoulder, knocking him back.

"Time to go!" Cinderfield said, swinging out his broken pocket watch. The clockwork had run fast before rusting shut, showing the perpetual date of May 16th 1984. He'd always believed it his own death date but no longer felt certain. "The best prophecies are the kind you do yourself.

225

Burn in heaven!" Kaufman's death felt like the final omen, the indication that it was time to end this sad existence. Being the Lord of Darkness had been fun for a while, and he loved being defiant, spitting in the eye of his boss and causing trouble in his perfect creation. God was such a control freak, but he could no longer tolerate it. He crawled off on hands and feet, and the couple turned around, ignoring him. Cinderfield crawled through an anthill. The wheel spun behind him, filled with families flying to heights, reaching for the gods. He pushed himself up and stumbled. He could jump off the top of the wheel, but he wanted something more dramatic. These assholes had to awaken, maybe feel something for once, just a frisson, a moment, to mark this. In a few years they'd start to forget Andy Kaufman.

Then, he saw the device of his delivery, the vehicle of his news, as if sent from the Good Lord himself, in Satan's hour of need. It glowed silver chrome and blue in the faded sunlight, surrounded by fluttering flags, set upon four giant rubber wheels. The monster truck preened, sitting on display at the center of the fair. It would take the Philadelphia Spectrum this weekend to devour old cars, crushing the poor broken things to the cheers of the people. One of the crew had started the truck to the cheers of children who watched the new God rumble and shake, spewing dirty carbon and smoke from its fat-ass pipe.

Cinderfield knelt before the monster truck. "Lord. We are not worthy of thy bounty." He sprung up, his body strengthened with holy purpose and vision, jumped into the driver's seat and slammed the door shut, locking it. He'd been too fast for the crew to catch, and they yelled and banged on the door.

"Ha, ha! Assholes!" he said, and turned on the radio. Pink Floyd blasted the cabin. He grabbed the microphone, switched it on and broadcasted to the fair. "Vroom, vroom, bitches!" He popped the clutch, and the truck lurched forward. "Out of the way, ass munchers!" he yelled over the speakers. "Remember today. Burn it into your fucking asses. Bunch of fucking robots." He hit the horn, and a banshee keened, driving the visitors into a frenzy.

"VROOM, VROOM!"

In a few years, someone might remember him as the foreign guy from episodes of *Taxi* or maybe Mighty Mouse from *SNL*. They'd see him, ponder Andy for a few minutes then forget. Cinderfield gripped the wheel, bleaching his knuckles. "Andy lives, assholes!"

He gunned the monster truck, accelerating it into a vendor's stall. The occupant had long since vacated his traveling business, and the truck casually twisted the stall under its front tire, compacting it fast. Cotton candy and popcorn flew out the sides, and the truck spit out the crushed box, tossing it into a sideshow tent and ripping the curtains. Cinderfield pushed on. "Wake up, assholes!"

He drove down an alley between attractions and vendors. People ran out of the way, a dog got loose from someone's leash, and Cinderfield spotted him, turned the rudder and crushed a balloon-dart game. Pink dolls and plush blue smurfs bled under the carriage and fired off like fuzzy bullets. The crew chased behind, and some of them tried to scale the truck carriage, climbing aboard like pirates attacking a ship at sea. They couldn't reach the frame, fell off, rolling onto the blacktop, and Cinderfield cackled. He turned off the parking lot and onto a side lane, following Levittown Lake—a synthetic body of water, a cyst in the heart of the artificial 1950's town of manufactured ranchers and churches. A crowd now chased him. Some of the mob yelled after him; others cheered. He avoided parked cars, swerving, doing not more than fifteen mph.

He spun the rudder, changed gears, used to driving commercial trucks up and down the interstates of the eastern seaboard. People came out of their ranchers to watch the spectacle. Ladies looked up from their spring planting. Children stopped riding their bikes, stunned by the site of the blue god tearing down the lane then chased after the truck, calling and howling at him. He waved and honked for them. Two police cruisers joined the chase, flashing lights and squawking at Cinderfield. More would come. Hell, they'd probably call out the National Guard. He planned to reach the parking lot at the lake where he could get clear access then drive the truck down the steep incline and into the water. Inevitably, the truck would topple over, spin and crush the devil's frail and vulnerable body, the mistake of nature. Why had they been made so fragile, susceptible to physics and cancer?

He approached the parking lot, shifted gears, and pushed for the lot. He misjudged the turning speed of the vehicle, jumped over the curb and hit the brakes before smashing into a sparrow-laden tree. But, too late. The sparrows flew from the danger, but one chose a dangerous vector and hit the windshield. Tiny feathers and blood smeared the glass.

"Fuck," Cinderfield said. He threw open the door and jumped down from the cabin. "This isn't what I wanted. More murder." He searched under the front of the truck. Its engine still popped. He found the limp sparrow and cradled its tiny body, rocking it against his chest and pressing it to his own pumping and thumping heart. The crowd closed around him, encircling him in a barrier of fascinated and dumbfounded humans. The police pulled up and got out of their cars with pistols ready. One of them yelled at the crowd, but Cinderfield couldn't hear him.

"The little fellow has died. An innocent creature. Never

hurt no one. God is cruel. I was his instrument. I should burn with Tolya." He plucked at the sparrow's chest, flicking its brown plumage. The limp bird drizzled blood on his thumb. The sky rained, and Cinderfield saw red drops. The cops pushed through the people who watched the old man weep silently over the death of the sparrow, impressed and terrified by the concern he showed for such an insignificant creature—the tiny screw in the mighty and wondrous blueprints of God.

"Come back," Cinderfield prayed. He didn't mean to pray, yet that's what fell from his lips. When you're the devil, you're always praying in thoughts or voice, even when you refuse such holy incantations to the landlord who threw your red ass out. He rocked, and even the officers felt so taken with the scene that they put their guns away and approached gently. A young officer set his hand on Cinderfield's shoulder.

"It's all right, sir," he said. "You're just drunk, aren't you?"

"I have the power in me," Cinderfield said with tears. "If Wilma was here . . . "

"That's for God and Jesus."

"Then, what the hell is the point?" Cinderfield gripped the sparrow, and it twitched in his palm then curled. It opened its beak, breaking awake from the stun of the truck strike. Its left wing twisted onto its body, broken and in need of mending. Cinderfield felt the bird spark back to life, and he realized it had just been temporarily unconscious. But the crowd, the officers, saw something else. It was only later that Cinderfield really understood: in an era when a cowboy actor piloted the White House and armed for Armageddon, the people of the commons despaired for miracles.

The crowd inhaled a collective sigh then tightened,

reaching to touch Cinderfield, feel the fur of his hot red coat, touch the body of the man who could recite life back into an avian—and perhaps others.

"But I didn't do it," Cinderfield whispered. Even the cops stood in awe. "Am I under arrest?"

"For now," said the young cop. "But we'll tell the world what you did." A reporter from the *Bucks County Reporter* had arrived and snapped photos. One of the pictures would turn iconic and spread to other newspapers. A television news van from Channel 3 KYW pulled up and got out their cameras.

"How did you do that?" the cop asked, helping him up. Cinderfield clung onto the bird, guarding it from the reaching crowd. The throng had swelled as people walked from far houses or the fairgrounds. Some of the crew and fair staff assured the police that they wouldn't press charges and insurance would cover the damage. No one had been hurt.

How could they prosecute the new messiah? No one wanted to be Pontius.

ANGEL'S ANGER

A dark voice spoke from the shadows, from the back alleys and sleazy nightclubs, the lounges and speakeasies. A man emerged in Angel, a new voice, a jerk, jackass and egomaniac, a slimy lizard with a bloated face and idea of his own self-importance.

Angel remembered his father's anger, the way he'd scream in their house in Great Neck, frustrated over work, family, or Angel's innocent and creative antics. His father, Stanley, seethed, always so quick to rage, to yell and scream, sans patience. He frightened Angel, never understanding, always at odds, admonishing the boy. His father didn't understand him and never tried. Stanley just wanted a normal family with behaved children who would become upstanding members of society, productive and law-abiding, mundane and boring. It would take many years for Stanley to appreciate the special child that had been born to him, the spiritual light that burned in Angel's soul. And by the time he did, Angel would be lost to him.

Angel conceptualized that anger, used it as a vessel. He created a face, a flabby body, an entitled bearing and aspect. Tony raged to be born, ripping out of Angel, created from his father's anger, allowing Angel to deal with it, process it: the rejection of his father. He longed for his approval, his applause, his mother's, too, but they'd never quite understand their different son. Their disapproval haunted Angel, who naturally longed for the approval of his audience, who needed the love of strangers to verify his mind, his existence. Tony gestated in that shared rage, the frustration and more so, the desire to disturb, change, upset the natural order, to keep agitating and rebelling against polite society, the calm people, the pretentious and superior. Tony was their caricature. Angel wanted to show people themselves, the worst of their American natures, the conceit; yet, he'd still, on some level, possess kindness, empathy. He'd play Tony as an extreme character, an icon, mythic in essence. Who would really believe he was real? And there was the joke. Tony would become a new man, but everyone would be in on the joke; however, they'd never be quite sure.

So, he found an old pink tuxedo, too small. Angel bought a shaggy wig, put on big sunglasses, and stuck out his chin. In time, he manufactured a body suit, perfectly shaped to his body, showing off years of eating steaks, drinking booze and smoking with abandon, even though Angel existed on health food and clean living. Tony was an antithesis of his nature and the perfect emancipation, freedom to invoke his asshole qualities, to treat people like dirt and upset them, all in the name of entertainment. Nothing inspired an audience's reaction like a villain, and Angel enjoyed playing the devil. His status as an actor, a celebrity, caused people to make certain allowances, to let him get away with being naughty and rude and causing a ruckus.

And so, he unleashed Tony Clifton onto a naïve and comfortable world. Tony was a bad nightclub singer, a lounge lizard who misspoke his words, sang out of tune and humiliated his audiences. Tony traumatized Dinah Shore on her show, trying to cook. He lost himself there, falling into the dark and hairy pit that was Tony, screaming and carrying on. Somewhere in the process of his performance, in his spiritual catharsis, Tony detached himself. Angel played with dangerous physics, old magic, the black arts of dead gods. Tony sought independence, freedom, the will to act and wreck, embodying all of Angel's darkness. Tony infected Bob, Angel's partner. Soon, Bob began to wear specialized gear, makeup and devices fitted just for him to create the perfect replica— not just a twin to Tony, but also a clone. They worked to perfect the duplicate, and soon, Bob took Angel's place, portraying Tony on stage, in shows, in public, and Angel would appear nearby and confuse the audience. Who was Tony? Tony was neither Angel nor Bob. He'd become a separate person, Lucifer possessing. In time, Angel's brother would play Tony, and the nightclub singer would survive death—immortal, with the human race forever or as long as it existed.

Angel had learned about reality, how it could be manipulated, played with, created and shaped. A person could be made. What really defined a human being? Society had its details, standards, paperwork and numbers. All of these could be duplicated. What was a person really worth? They had lived in a world where life was cheap, created in an instant and just as quickly extinguished. Nazis and Communists had shown that people could easily be mowed down in masses, removed from the world and forgotten. All it took was the will and an absence of empathy.

Tony and the other people had become Angel's expression, his truth and gospel. He needed to show humans that reality could be altered, that perception defined humanity and was not as static and safe as people believed. In this, Angel upset the fabric of society, attacked the core of a working civilization. None of this was real. It was all an illusion. Through the creation of Tony and its transferring spirit, he had evolved from performer, entertainer and into a revolutionary, perhaps even a terrorist.

"Ya know, I'm not useta playing small places like this. I'm doing it as a favor! So, if you wanna be a good audience, I'll sing for you, I'll tell you some stories, we'll have some fun. You wanna be a bad audience, I'll walk right outta here!"

He began to upset people, to challenge their preconceptions, and though this truly was the nature of comedy—the modern philosophy of observation—he took it to an extreme. Foreign man was innocence, anxiety, a child. Tony was anger, bitterness, and disruption. Angel existed between the two extremes, caught in twin orbits, torn apart in the middle.

Angel never believed anyone would take him seriously, but his audiences failed to understand. He disrupted without entertaining. He attacked but didn't comfort. Angel, even with his attempt at balance through meditation, turned into a dark being, and he used his tools to challenge life, to change it or destroy it. Somewhere, Angel lost his way, and that's when he began to depart this world. Nothing expressed that more than his wrestling.

THE WIZARD OF WALMART

No wonder you don't want to survive," Cynthia said.

"Beg pardon?" Anthony asked.

"Let it be," Tolya muttered and swerved the Mr. Snowballs to avoid a dead raccoon petrified in the middle of the two-lane country road through North New Jersey. A sign marked the entrance to Flemington down 202, and they passed by generic malls and fields of solar panels. Manhattan ended her short stay with their band, remaining home to give birth to her child. They weren't sure she wasn't going to fuck the kid up or just abandon it, and they figured it had as good a chance of being loved or screwed up as any kid.

"It's no wonder why you want to die. I feel awful about your grandparents."

He turned his head from the window. His eyes crossed, showing confusing. "You think this is my choice?"

"If I was good enough, thin enough like a Q-tip, maybe you'd stay and fight with me," Cynthia said.

Anthony crossed his arms. "Where do you come up with this shit?"

"I'm just sorry that the world has been so hostile to you. I don't mean anything by it. I'm letting you know I'm here."

"Of course you're here." His eyes bulged. Curly hair fell

down over his forehead. "Where the hell else would you be? You're sitting in a car with me."

"Do you want to know where? Out with some cute guy with a nice car, a tan, and a good paying job. I don't even care if he's married. But here I am with you, giving up my life for you."

"This is where they had that Lindbergh trial," Tolya said as they passed into the heart of town. An antiquated courthouse bearing pillars like a roman temple decayed at the center of the American village. "It was a farce, of course."

"Gods," Anthony said. "This isn't a fucking game show. I don't win or lose. I have no choice."

"Of course you have a choice," Cynthia said. "It's all about willpower and positive attitude."

Anthony shut his eyes and pressed his fingers on his temple, shaking his head. "You just don't get it, but how can you? Being on the outside."

"I get it!" Cynthia said, taken back. Tolya stopped short at a red light, and the momentum lurched her body forward. She grabbed the door. "Can you take it easy?"

"You want to drive?" Tolya said. "Go ahead. You drive us to Long Island on this fool's errand. To the Great Neck!"

The trip that should have only taken a few hours had stretched out to days, as Tolya insisted on taking the long roads, off the highways, seeing the world as they traveled. She didn't mind. It gave her more close time with Anthony, and they'd run out of money for gas, or money for food then had to stop and beg, borrow, even steal. They'd gotten lost for hours, driving west in Pennsylvania and north towards Eerie, then turning around and driving the length of I-80 into New Jersey. Whenever she suggested they were driving the wrong way, Tolya would snap and say, *I was driving trucks on this road with Shakespeare pouring through my head before your father's sperm and mothers ovum collided in a travesty we call the human being.* She stopped asking and just went with the flow. They'd aim Mr. Snowballs north and keep moving. Eventually they'd arrive at Great Neck, Long Island, where Andy Kaufman's family lived. The journey troubled them little. Convincing the family to donate DNA for a paternity test would probably be the greatest fight of her life. But she needed Anthony to know his place in the universe. If he felt more settled, then maybe he would calm and see her—*really* see her.

"Well, I think you're going to live and go into the world and have lots of babies," she said.

"Believe whatever you need to believe to feel better, love," Anthony said, employing his prick voice.

"If I believe it hard enough for you—positive thinking. It's the essence of magick. We can shape the universe if we really try."

"You're so damn naïve."

"Why? Because I think you're going to live?"

"You don't really believe that. You're just trying to convince yourself."

"You told me yourself: reality is tangible, an illusion. Why can't you believe in a reality where you live? And we're happy?"

Anthony stopped talking and rubbed his full rich lips. He turned to the window and studied the passing storefronts and apartments. They passed a World War I memorial—a bronzed cannon, old artillery, and writing engraved on a metal sign bolted to a stone pillar. Engraved names filled the bronze plate. Cynthia remembered to say a tiny prayer for the lost soldiers. She mimed one word with her lips, making no sound:

Amen.

"Amen!" Tolya yelled out like a southern preacher.

"I will disappoint you," Anthony said. "I promise. I will let you down. Positive thinking. That pisses me off. The illusion of control. An addiction. A sickness."

"In a few miles we will run out of gas," Tolya added. "That is not an illusion. You two have any money?"

Cynthia searched the pockets of her sweater and jeans. "A couple of quarters. Nickels."

"I've got no dough," Anthony said. "But maybe if we all think positively, God will grant us a miracle and fill the tank."

"Do you have to?" Cynthia yelled.

"Forgive me. I'm dying."

"You are not!" She rubbed her face, blocking her weeping.

"I'm parking until we figure this shit out," Tolya said. They pulled into a municipal parking lot, a few spots in the back beneath some birch trees. Cynthia opened the front door and got out to stretch her legs. Tolya pointed at the parking meter, and she dropped in the last of her change. Her stomach gurgled, and the savory aroma of cooking meat wafting from a nearby bar and grille did little to satiate her hunger.

"Is that a parade?" She heard the percussions and march of a band, recognizing it when she played trombone for the Pennsbury marching band—playing mostly during football games or for competitions. She hadn't picked up the trombone in years. Her feet marched to their own beat. The marching band wearing full regalia, marched like a column of soldiers down Main Street. Men riding horses followed them along with several trucks crawling with locals from various organizations—4H, the Lion's Club, Knights of Columbus, Jaycees. They walked from the ice cream truck and stood on the sidewalk, watching the parade.

"Odd," Anthony said. "They didn't close off the street to traffic. Is it a special day?"

"Might be something local," Tolya said. "One of the town whores has been canonized or something."

Anthony blew raspberries in a surprise laugh. "Very Catholic. Stories of redemption."

"You can be redeemed," she said. She may have worshipped a goddess, and Cynthia would burst into flames if anyone ever dragged her into a Catholic church; however, she could appreciate the very human concepts expressed in every faith.

A woman wearing a blue wig and walking on wide hips led a couple of kids down the sidewalk, following the parade. "What's the skinny?" Anthony asked.

"Where have you been living, sweetie? Under a rock?"

"On the moon," Anthony said. "Mars. I'm the ancient god of death for the red planet. I have rusty dust in my blood."

"Sounds painful," the old granny said. "Stop picking your nose, Thomas!" She admonished one of the children who pulled his finger out of his nostril. "That's just rude."

"So . . . the parade?"

"It's the Walmart," Granny said. "Finally we're getting a Walmart. Fuck Springfield."

"Yeah. Fuck Springfield." Thomas stuck his finger back in his nose.

"That's a bad word, Thomas," she said. "Forgive my grandchildren. Their father is a heroin addict."

"Should I apologize?" Anthony asked Cynthia, whispering into her ear.

"You have a lot to be sorry for," she said. He ignored her. She needed to lighten her spirit and stop punishing him. Cynthia couldn't make him love her, and it wasn't his fault. She felt selfish, but she couldn't help it. He was dying and had all their sympathy and support, but she died with him, her soul exploding like a collapsed star. No one gave her sympathy.

"Why have a parade for Walmart?"

"It just opened! Finally, we can beat Springfield. The parade just happened. It's wonderful. Think of the money we'll save!" She gathered up her grandchildren and pushed them forward, following along as the local war veterans marched in uniform, decorated in badges and medals, carrying their rifles.

"They'd hire us," Anthony said. "Probably the only ones here, too. Lax policies on staffing."

"You want to work at a Walmart?" Cynthia asked. "They're the devil on earth."

"I don't believe in the devil," Anthony said. "Just the darkness in people. Maybe that's old Lucifer."

"Walmart destroys towns. They've set the union movement back decades. It's a sickness. Disease. This town is celebrating its death."

Cynthia studied the birch and maple trees lining Main Street. Oak leaves browned and etiolated like autumn had come early. The bark on the branches dried out. The trees died. Lawns paled yellow. Even the dandelions darkened brown and died. "It's killing this town," she said. "Killing the spirit of the land."

Anthony looked upon the hill, on the castle built and growing, digging its roots into the earth. The sun arched west behind the cinder block building, setting the store glowing like a white phantom, like some wild angel.

"She is beautiful though," Anthony said. "She's the sexiest woman I've ever seen."

The people of Flemington danced at world's end. Comets burned in the sky, promising that their town would soon sink into the ocean off the Jersey shore. The sky smoldered in fire, growing along the perimeters of the atmosphere. Lilith flew over the sky, raining the black strands from her armpits down on the people below—not offering forgiveness or redemption. She offered long pubic hair growing from her crotch, her skin covered with oozing pocks and pimples. She was beauty beyond anything humans could understand, for she gave completely of herself—and her pubic hair.

Three strangers come among the masses from the town, which worshipped at the cinderblock temple on the hill. Strangers had come and given them the temple. They asked for nothing and took everything. The villagers opened their veins and arteries on the temple, painting it brown in their life fluids. They breathed out the wind from their lungs and didn't draw in air. Volcanoes popped from the ground, pouring smoke and throwing brimstone at the temple, and the masses crowded about the building, seeking protection from their commercial and material gods.

A god of clothing and textiles. They worshipped the covering of their bodies.

A god of sparks and wires. They worshipped him with their televisions and DVD players. A god of house wares, dishes and appliances. They filled their kitchens in worship.

They sacrificed the soul of their town. The villagers gave up their hearts, dug them from their chests, popping ribs and bone. The marrow spilled on the dead ground.

The trees died. The soil turned moribund, leeched of nutrients and the gentle stuff of life.

The village celebrated the end of days with a carnival. The impromptu parade marched up Main Street, climbed the hill with heavy breathing and then descended upon the temple. They came to pray, to see miracles and to buy cheap jeans. Popcorn vendors popped corn. Other vendors sold hotdogs. Stands fried burgers and chips. Cotton candy whipped. Amateur artists painted children's faces as cats or wolves or popular characters on television. Jugglers tossed bottles into the air. Children carried balloons on strings. One of the grandchildren, Thomas, let his go for a moment, probably expecting it to be there. The trapped helium quickly ascended, lighter than the air molecules around it, and the balloon shot up into the air like a ballistic missile. Thomas cried, and his grandmother tapped his neck. "You shouldn't have let her go!"

"Happy Armageddon!" Anthony yelled, and the people cheered like a birthday party. They admired the tractors on display outside of the Walmart. Plants grew in plastic pots for garden decoration. Children's bicycles bearing flapping ribbons lined the other side, beyond the automatic doors. Cars saturated the parking lot. Windshields reflected the sunlight. The volcanoes fired lava in streams into the air, and it filled the upper atmosphere to the brim, turning the sky crimson, burning the stone. It suspended above their heads, and they waited for it to fall. It declined.

"This way," Anthony said, leading them inside. The automatic doors opened, swallowing the trio down. Tolya tailed behind them. The automatic door closed, pinching his ass. He swore in Russian.

"We should go," Cynthia said. "We should really . . . go." Stacks of cheap DVDs in bins greeted them along with cheap toys, plastic crap, water pistols. The mass of flimsy goods strangled Cynthia. She choked, couldn't breathe.

"Take it easy," Anthony said. "It can't hurt you."

"Don't even pretend that," she said. "This is death."

The grandmother they met in the street now greeted them at the automatic doors. She couldn't have been inside for more than a few minutes, yet Walmart recruited her fast, fixing her to the infrastructure. Her face grayed, decayed, turning silver to match the doors. She gazed, sans emotion, with hollow eyes. Cynthia shivered when she saw her.

"Welcome to Walmart. The friendliest place on earth."

"That is yet to be seen," Anthony said.

"We need to get out of here." Cynthia sensed her strength draining like someone had punctured her. Her blood thinned. Her heart beat against her ears. "This is a bad place. It's poisoning the earth."

"We'll be stuck in this town without gas," Tolya said. "You want to find Andy Kaufman? We go sell televisions and microwaves."

Anthony led them to the customer service desk that wrapped around the back of the Walmart. Printed applications waited on the counters with a box of cheap pens. He grabbed one, handed a sheet to her and then Tolya. Cynthia reviewed the questions. They appeared simple enough: your basic identification and job history. A groundhog with no college education could get a job here, peddling cheap plastic. Anthony distributed the pens and they filled out the questions. It didn't take long. She had a college education, so that would work against her at the store. They handed them in to a bean-pole man wearing a graph shirt.

"You're not from around here?" A scar sliced up his lip. It looked like he'd had corrective cosmetic surgery on his mouth, perhaps for a harelip.

"Just passing through," Anthony said. "Need to work for a bit. Maybe something in the stockroom?"

"Will you be strong enough for that?" Cynthia asked. Anthony shot her a dirty look, and she shut her mouth.

"I'll process these right away," said the functionary behind the rounded desk.

"You're very kind," Anthony said.

The fellow leaned in to talk to them, looking both ways for spies and whispered. "A wizard lives here. They flew him out from Omaha, Nebraska. A goddamn wizard. He'll take your heart. He'll enchant your mind. You should run."

"I've never met a wizard," Anthony said. "Might be fun."

"You're never going to leave here," the functionary said and processed their applications. He fed them into a scanner and waited. A bell rang. The printer spewed out documents. "You've been approved! You poor souls."

"Poor souls, indeed," Anthony said.

"You can start right away. You go up to the front to train as a register girl." He pointed at Cynthia, reading from the document. "The old one will work in gardening. Customers find old people in gardening comforting. But you're a jerk, aren't you?"

"And proud of it," Tolya said.

"With a secret, too," said the functionary. "Has he told you his secret? It's a big secret. The Walmart computer detected it, and we might not have hired you. But you came on opening day. All sins are forgiven on opening day!"

"All sins are forgiven on opening day," Anthony chanted with the staff member.

"All sins!" he repeated. "And you. You will be a traveler. The wizard of Walmart has detected your

244

sickness. You will sell to the customers. You will tell them that life is short, and they shouldn't save their money. You will tell them of the illusion of control, how they should buy at our sales prices. You are special, and we will only have your employment for a few months." He fed the instructions into the shredder.

"Welcome to Walmart."

"You're very kind," Anthony said.

"Now forget. Leave your woes behind. No more pain here. Walmart is bliss! So says the Wizard of Walmart. He is ancient. He is forever. You will never see his face evermore. He is lost to the centuries. He is no more and everything."

"We just need gas money," Tolya said.

They shook hands, hugged as if for the last time, and departed to their respected stations, to become cogs in the machine, mindless and lost. So, they joined the store, merged to its walls, functioning under its promise.

> *Oh, forget and be lost. Life is nothing more than pain.*
> *We offer truth to action; not love in vain.*
> *Welcome to Walmart, the house of deceit,*
> *Let go your burdens. Abandon your conceit.*

BREAKING THE SPELL

The New America:

They slept in the bunker—an old army base bunker where they built the castle. Engineers piped in air, and the halogen lights sparked and sputtered, casting fast shadows that soon evaporated from the clammy, dirty walls. Voices echoed, but nobody spoke. The commissary served weak cream-of-wheat in the morning.

"I had a name once," the sick one said.

"No," said the Russian. "We never had names."

They stood in line, both carrying plastic trays. The slaves all wore gray pajamas, matching like a sky of shale clouds floating down to eat the watery hot cereal. Spiders dropped from the ceiling. Roaches scurried on the cement floor. A sign hung on the wall that read in electric red letters:

Think Only Happy Thoughts and You Will Succeed!

A kitten hung from a tree and looked out at the slaves with swollen eyes.

"You know that cat has been long dead and decomposed," the Russian said. He'd shaved his head like the rest of the slaves. The sick one hadn't. It reminded him of something. He wanted to remember, but then he stopped himself. He almost liked it here.

"You're a cheerful one," Sick said. "I'm going to call you Mister Smiles."

246

"No names," Smiles snapped. "Names make us unhappy. You know what the wizard says." The other slaves gasped.

"You don't mention him. Ever."

"Yes. Of course."

"Smile," Sick said. "I miss someone. I can't recall. Did we know each other before?" A large black man wearing a hairnet slopped a wooden spoonful of cream-of-wheat in his bowl. The Russian moved up behind him. He picked up a piece of cold and charred toast and dropped it on the tray. They both sat down at an empty cafeteria in the corner, below an air vent blowing chilly atmosphere. His nose burned from the ozone mixing.

"Nothing happened before," Smiles said. "We were born here under the ground. We will die here. They grew us to serve from blood samples and dirty condoms. We are not human."

"We couldn't have always been here. I remember being a child somewhere bright and green. A stern couple who never laughed or smiled. Their eyes grew storm clouds. It rained from their faces constantly."

"Shut up," Smiles said. "No one talks like that."

"Will we die here?" Sick asked.

"No. We will live forever, and they'll kill us soon, once we're no longer useful. We're batteries, and we're going to run out. They'll throw us away and replace us. They'll grow new workers."

Sick swallowed a spoonful of hot cereal, and it pricked his stomach a mix of thorns. Hot acid burned up his throat, and he dropped his utensil. It clattered on the tray, bounced and hit the floor, chiming like a tin bell. All the other slaves frowned at him.

"I saw the ghost of Elvis last night," Sick said.

"Him? He was a dream, too. Never real. There is no world beyond the castle."

A green light contained in a wall lantern lit up, shedding the room in verdant color. An empty woman's voice—she'd lost her passion long ago and probably should have died, too—announced: "All workers for the morning shift please be dressed in your uniforms and take your posts. Announcement: Two workers died this morning. They strangled themselves with bed sheets. Please do not kill yourself. It is a waste of resources and time to replace you. That is all." The green light blinked.

They got up in unison, with Sick a bit slower, hurting their conformity, and dropped the trays off at the receptacle. Then they went to the locker room, dressed in the blue and white uniforms and climbed the ladders to the open air. Clouds gathered over the cinderblock castle. Trucks groaned in and out, releasing their cargo, fueling their machine. The junk would be sold at cheap prices to a population trained to need it. Dew soaked his shoes as they strolled in a line to the store from the bunker buried in the fields.

"The day is a whiskey-soaked cherry," Sick said.

"Where do you get this shit?" Smiles asked.

"Firecrackers keep popping and burning in my head. I have wild thoughts. I think I must be a reject. Wonder if I'll die?"

"Of course you will," Smiles said. "Inevitable. But they'll grow you again. You won't remember, but you'll live forever. There are big freezers where they store our kind. When you die, they will thaw out the next one."

"I had a name," Sick said.

"Blasphemy."

"We were on a mission. Time is being lost."

"Delusions."

"I feel the spirit of god in me."

"Hallucinations."

248

"Then I'll live in the dream. Like the ghost of Elvis said. I'm not supposed to be here."

They entered the servant's entrance to the chaos, below the two windows on the second floor of the building—the dark eyes of the wizard who ruled the kingdom of Walmart. Before entering, Sick paused to feel the spit of rain on his cheeks.

"They're going to erase you," Smiles warned.

"It is inevitable," Sick said back.

"I go to my post in automotive."

"I'm at cash-wrap today," Sick said. "Maybe I'll see her."

"Who?"

"I can't remember."

"Then it won't hurt."

He saw her at the registers. Memories rang in his memory—bell song. His heart flinched. He remembered, if ever briefly, a smattering of recall that surged through his sick body, stirring him back to his life, his humanity, before he'd become an automaton for this company.

He knew it. There had been a world before. But just as fast as the memories rained back, the hot sun came out and burned them to steam. He gazed down at the woman—not unattractive. A bit stocky, but gorgeous hair. She looked back at him, and her eyes fed on him.

"Anthony!"

"I beg your pardon."

"Goddess. You don't remember, do you? I think it's a drug, something they're putting in the water or the shitty cereal."

"Smiles told me that not remembering is freedom. Why would we want to remember all the people who hurt us, abandoned us? This is better. I . . . feel better."

"But you're not yourself."

"You remember?"

"Anthony." She leaned in and kissed him fast on the lips. "Like in a fairy tale. My kiss will wake you from eternal sleep."

He waited for the memories to flood back. He waited for several seconds. "Nope. Nothing yet."

"Fuck," she said. "That answers the question about true love." She sighed and twirled her hair. "Yes. That grin. That little chipmunk grin. You're still there. Thank the Goddess."

"I don't know what you mean."

Customers queued up. The supervisor shot them a dirty look. He didn't want to tangle with the dark creature, the minion of the man upstairs. Darkness oozed from its body. A black veil covered its head. The customers never saw them, and Sick pondered whether he had dreamed them. They moved as nightmares on the wind. "We'll talk later," she said, and broke away from him. "Cynthia. Remember."

"I can't."

"Then you're no good," she snapped and opened a register in aisle three. Sick toyed with the snacks and candy in the aisle. His stomach dropped out of his body. He moved to leave, and she ran up to him fast, annoying her queue of customers. "You're dying, you asshole. And you're wasting your time here."

Dying? Who was dying? We're all dying.

The slaves worked the day, selling the goods for the Walmart Corporation.

"It's all a fucking lie!" the chubby one said. He was ordered to stand with the old man in the electric wheelchair. Guards came and took him away, dragged him upstairs to see the Wizard. "Don't. Fuck. Kill me." One of the plain-faced and barren guards armed himself with an electric prod. Mud ran down from his eyes. They dragged the slave up the grand staircase, hidden behind a secret door in the boys' clothing department. "I want to remember," he said. Then the world ended for him.

"Poor old soul," Sick said to Smiles.

"He's lucky," Smiles said. They hung out on their break in the automotive department. Smiles leaned on the tires. The place reeked of rubber, and Sick's eyes watered. "They'll make him better. The man upstairs will make him happy and forget again."

"This girl at cash-wrap knew me. She said I was still me."

"Stay away from her," Smiles said. "She'll get you murdered or destroyed. There will be nothing left of you."

"I don't remember her. But I feel her. Maybe we were in love once."

"Fuck it. Even worse."

"Probably."

"Just stay away from her. You don't need that."

"There might have been a world before. I can feel it."

"You feel shit," he said. "I see things. I dream things. We are living a dream now. This is better. This is true life. Just forget. You don't want to remember, my friend. You will be happier this way."

"You remember?" Sick gagged on the ascetic scent of rubber. He paused, waiting for Smiles to respond. His heavy eyebrows shot up.

"What does it matter? I dream. I see things in my dreams, terrible things."

"What do you see?"

Sick sensed a supervisor peering around the corner of

the automotive section. It wore dark robes that absorbed the light like a black hole in space. Its eyes leaked obsidian. A dark field emanated from its presence. It oozed onto the floor, leaked across the department. It could sense him working out the truth, and the dark force waited, ready to report to the man upstairs then come for him, to drag him up to the next level.

"They'll come for you," Smiles said.

"Maybe they should."

"Are you in pain?"

"No. I'm actually content. And it feels so wrong. I miss the pain. I don't feel alive."

"Alive is an illusion!" Smiles yelled. His skin paled. The supervisor creature twitched. It summoned night. The lights dimmed: a warning. Don't remember. Forget, sweet child. A poem entered Sick's mind:

Come away, oh human child.
To the waters and the wild
With a fairy hand-in-hand.

"For the world's more full of weeping," Sick said.

"Then you can understand," finished Smiles.

"Tolya?"

"Shit."

The dark supervisor moved. Its robes flowed along the floor, and rats followed. Spiders fell on its body. It extended a long finger at Anthony. Tolya grabbed a tire iron off the shelf and flung it at the creature. It passed right through its incorporeal body. What made it real? His nightmares? It summoned the darkness and held itself together by force of will, of the man upstairs. The Wizard of Walmart.

"Get the fuck out of here, boy!" Tolya rushed the

phantom. It merely had to touch his shoulder, and the Russian collapsed. Anthony struggled with rushing to help his friend or running from the castle. The phantom supervisor moved on Anthony. He backed into the wall and hit a rack of car air fresheners. The castle suddenly smelled of pine and artificial cherry. It mixed with the aroma of rubber, and Anthony nearly vomited. He swallowed back the nausea, choking it down.

"I remember."

"No. You don't." The phantom hissed, a whisper, almost beyond his hearing. The supervisor faded in and out of reality, a wicked ghost, a darkness. "I lived once like you. I dreamed of my life. I faded out. I exist for the store now. The store. Love the store!"

All the nearby slaves chanted, yelling to the cue of the supervisor: "Love the store!"

The darkness reached for Anthony, extended its hand. He backed into the corner. Another supervisor came down the side, looking to fix the problem, exterminate him like a virus that threatened to infect the store. They'd erase him—as good as killing him.

"Hey, baby," said Elvis. He dazzled them in his white sequined outfit. It burned starlight, amplifying the white lights from the ceiling, blinding his eyes. Elvis wore his sunglasses and a pair of knee-high boots. He looked a bit thinner than Anthony remembered him. The atmosphere sucked and shimmered to him, and the earth slipped off its axis, pulled to his gravity. He had a presence that sank you in like a sinkhole, and even the Supervisors shuddered, pulling back from Anthony.

"Fast now, baby," Elvis said, a hint of feminine tones in his voice. "Take this." He threw a CD at Tolya. Yes. That was his name. Tolya. How could he forget such maudlin guilt that expressed on the Russian man's face? He held a

253

secret, one that cut him so deeply. As Anthony slipped from this world, he could sense it, feel it longing to be told. All secrets suffered in the body and longed to sprout from the black earth.

"The hell should I do with this?"

"Play it, baby." Even the charm of Elvis infiltrated the gray and brooding Russian. He actually smiled, probably cracking years of thick clay that rained down in dust onto the floor. He stepped to Anthony, grinning at the Supervisors, and said, "I'm so, so sorry for what I did." Then he gave the Supervisors the finger and slipped past them to the office where the store played its music. The Supervisors stirred and floated, unsure of how to act. When they started to move, Elvis stuck up his arm, pointed at them and said, "Don't move. Thank you very much."

"*Tank you veddy much*," Anthony said, quoting his potential father, Andy Kaufman.

"Rightcous," Elvis said. The lulling muzak suddenly halted. The energy jolted. An earthquake shook the floor.

"The wizard ain't happy," Anthony said, daring his name. "Wizards are out of fashion, gone out of the world. I will not be your slave."

"Right on, man," Elvis said, staring through wide sunglasses over his eyes. Bad makeup smeared his face, and the left eyebrow drooped; however, he knew not to draw attention to it. This was no ghost.

"Burning Love" played over the intercom systems. The air stirred. The shelves shook and trembled, dropping screwdrivers and drills in their plastic uniforms. Tires dropped from the wall, hit the floor and spun, riding to freedom. Elvis extended his arm in a salute to music, pointed two fingers at the ceiling, at the throne of the Wizard who lived above, and curled his lip.

"Wizard on high,
"I feel my heart beating faster,
"Faster and faster, freeing these poor slaves."

Elvis changed the lyrics as it sang over the speaker, chanting to the workers, the slaves and their dark masters. He challenged the wizard on the second floor who looked down below and ruled all.

"Now take me to see this wizard!" Elvis said.

"I'll take you," Anthony said. Tolya appeared from the back after delivering the CD. Elvis enchanted over the speakers—waking and inflicting. Most of the staff suffered, falling over the floor. Customers fled the emancipation. Normal middle-class never wanted to suffer a revolution. Only the impoverished changed the world.

"To the damn wizard," Tolya said. "We'll melt him with water!"

"Hey, man," Elvis said. "I'm a Christian child. None of that." Tolya even looked a bit ashamed, his face burning red down his grey, bristled mutton cheeks. "None of that bad language, now."

Anthony expected a temple to the ancient power. There should have been drapes flowing over the windows, igniting sunlight behind the violet fury. Great fires burning. He could control the elements. He summoned the storms and the snow. He waited. The wizard had always known. He traced the ether with his hands. He felt the burning world with his stomach. So old was he. So old.

"You should probably come in," said the little man behind the counter. Not a strand of hair grew on his head.

He sat squat behind a desk and fiddled with an abacus. He wore a white, buttoned-down business shirt, cross-sectioned with a blue graph.

"Your reign of darkness is over, Wizard," said Elvis. His old songs of America and love played over the speakers. He sang of the old world and the new. Elvis sang away all their woes. He sang away the cement blocks and cheap muck that sold to Americans. "Let us go so we can love."

"But you want to be here."

"We don't," Tolya said, following up the staircase and into the office.

"But, you do. You love it here. We calm your pain. We put you to sleep." He fiddled with the abacus. He played with the beads, moving them up and down in old-fashioned fashion. "I am but a business man."

"And you've destroyed the world, man," Elvis said. "You've killed its forest. You've polluted its air and filled crap under the soil."

"That is bad makeup. Elvis is dead."

"I don't know what you mean, man."

"August sixteenth, nineteen seventy-seven. Under the ground with all our plastic junk. That's where we bury things we want to forget."

"My music lives on."

"But you do not," said the Wizard of Walmart.

Anthony stepped into the upstairs office with Tolya, but they did not sit down. Blinds covered the windows. No light shown through. For all the time they'd been here—days, months, years?—the sun had never come out over the town. Rain drizzled over the warm atmosphere.

"Man, you are no kind of a wizard. Where's your robes and hat? You got a magic wand?"

The W of W opened his desk drawer and pulled out a

television remote, probably the counterpart to the television built into the wall on the other side of the room. Elvis laughed, and his rhinestones shimmered.

"What's that, man? You going to watch Letterman?"

"With one button push, I can slaughter you."

"How's that, man?" Elvis asked.

"There have been mass murderers in this world, some without compare. Genghis Khan. Stalin. Chairman Mao the great, but none could kill the soul, the mind, destroy individuality. Nothing compares to the murder of the soul. What a feat! What a grand miracle. We live in an age of dark and terrible magic. Amen!"

"Amen!" Elvis yelled.

"And one contraption above them all succeeded where men have failed. Not even Mao can overcome its magic. Like a virus it spreads. Like a drug, it addicts. How like a God that is worshipped by the masses. It moves in slowly. It defines. The box that at first waits, and as you watch, it defines consciousness, demands your definitions. Too ugly? The crystal screen defines how you should look. Too fat? All the women are thin and beautiful unless they're objects of ridicule or pity. The men are all strong with defined jaw lines. How should we live? Tell us, crystal screen. Scrye our futures."

"Television don't mean anything," Elvis said. His voice had started to slip, sounding more feminine. "We're all special people. All beautiful."

"That's because you're a fat chick that no one will ever love."

Elvis buckled over like he'd been kicked. His wig slipped to reveal pinned back hair.

"Son of a bitch," Anthony said. He clenched his fists.

"I've seen your psych reports. We've drugged you, washed you out, taken your souls and bottled them in pickle juice. Why do you protest, Anthony? Haven't you ignored her on purpose? Used her for her companionship? Used her. You blinded yourself to her love. How could she love you, anyway? She's subhuman, not capable of love."

Anthony sighed and looked at Cynthia, still adorned in her Elvis face. "It was a beautiful try, love." Cynthia started to weep, and the makeup smeared. Anthony helped her take off the wig, the rhinestone coat and rubbed the makeup on her cheeks with his handkerchief. The Wizard aimed the remote at them.

"Do you deny it, Anthony?"

Anthony shook his head. "I accept it."

"She has loved you all this time, and you knew and pretended not to. You have used her for love. Used her for support. Always had her with you even though you loved others, made love to others and gloried them in front of her."

"I'm a monster," Anthony said. "I don't deserve my life."

"No, Anthony."

"Just let me die."

"To love you, though you won't love me," Cynthia said and let out a sob. She choked and swallowed. "I'll give you that in spite of yourself and weaknesses. I will be your soul when you lose it."

The Wizard of Walmart flipped channels, pressing his fingers along his magic wand. The visions on the crystal screen changed and swapped—showing the world, the life of the people of this planet, exposed and raw. He saw the worlds spin in this world. He witnessed all the life of the life of the people of foreign countries and the foreign countries in the American country. So many lived by artificial boundaries, and they watched them. They confirmed the Wizard of Walmart, invited his breed, lived

258

for his kind and sucked of his teat. He passed through the channels, slipping over the live feed of satellites spilling and spewing onto the Earth. Anthony couldn't help but think Andy Kaufman, perhaps his father, would have loved this. He'd occupy every channel, split it from his mind, circulate his many thoughts and be channeled into the many signal rivers that stabbed at the human occupants of planet earth. He could have defeated the Wizard of Walmart. Once again, the visions on crystal spun, portraying their intimate lives over the screen of the television. "We sell these thirty-two inchers for $210. Quite a bargain, really. You should get one. We do offer a payment plan."

Anthony longed for a television. Elvis wept in the corner. The tears broke his mind away from the need for the appliance. "Elvis! Baby! Don't cry." Anthony rushed to the weeping rock-and-roll idol. He held her arms and peeled the moustache from her lip. "Cynthia," he said. "You never need to be anyone but you to me."

"Anthony . . . I'll die. I will die."

"Shh. Don't talk about it."

The television spun to images of the store below. It might have been security cameras—perhaps it was the mind of God, the creator? Anthony could no longer tell. Perhaps the Creator stole from the inventions of humankind. He'd run out of imagination and create smaller versions of his Divine self, to think and work out things like the wheel, the printing press, the atomic bomb.

"God is a fraud," Anthony said. "Elvis is dead. You're a cruel being."

"And I keep America alive," The Wizard said, coming around the desk and holding his remote-control wand. The Wizard approached the television, and Anthony, holding Cynthia, stood before him.

"Turn back," Anthony said. "To the floor? Tolya. Go." Tolya slipped out of the manager's office, shut the door behind him. *Go Tolya. Do what needs to be done.* He could trust him. Tolya suffered for the truth, yet he hadn't revealed it. Anthony sensed this about him, but it would come in time.

"Trees blow in the wind. The crown of leaves turn brown." Anthony sang this to the Wizard. "Tune in your remote. See it below."

"You can do nothing that will wound me," the Wizard said. His tiny nostrils flared. He breathed through his mouth.

"I don't want to wound you," Anthony said. "There are slaves here, perfectly happy to be slaves. They don't want to think or feel. You free them of that. But look. I bet they are dancing."

"They do not dance," said the Wizard.

"Watch, my lord. And see."

He changed the channel on the remote, flipping through the networks, the cable providers, the weather and spurious news providers who reported on politics, channeling the information as they saw it. Finally, he found the live feed from the cameras scanning the workers below. They lined up, under the direction of Tolya, who had gone down to organize them. The music of Elvis still played over the intercom system.

"Do you see them below?" Anthony asked.

"I see . . . though it is a mirage! It burns in the heat of this story, country to humanity. Anyone with a free mind can see it."

"Yet, they do not," said the Wizard. "We offer prices cheap. We can clothe American children for the school year. We provide food so cheap. You will not destroy us."

"Man," Anthony said. "I don't want to destroy you. I

just want to find out if Andy Kaufman is my father! Just let us go."

"I cannot. You'll tell the world."

"Then look!" Anthony didn't see the screen. He didn't turn his back, but he knew what he'd envision. Anthony suffered faith in Tolya. He'd go down to the worker's floor, to the level of cheap merchandise—the last layer of ice hell according to Dante.

"They're dancing!" said the Wizard of Walmart.

"Yes," Anthony said. "They're waltzing to Elvis. He's the king of rock-and-roll! The prince of hip gyration!"

"This cannot be!"

"Oh, it can! It must be. Elvis beats all!"

Cynthia blinked then smiled. She started singing to the song playing over the intercom on the television, intruding on the security camera closed circuit system. Anthony witnessed it like a scene from a musical—like the Wiz when the cast broke its monstrous exteriors and danced. They danced to Elvis's "Burning Love". The lyrics changed, morphed as they listened, broadcasting over the loud speakers through the castle of Walmart.

"They're dancing," said the Wizard. Men had torn their shorts. Women tore their uniforms. Scraps of pants and shirts littered the floors like ribbons cut and decorating the air. The men found women. The women found women. The men found men. They danced, twirling among the aisles, the cheap merchandise. They danced to the song—the old Elvis master.

"They dance. They live."

"I'll fire them. I'll fire them all."

"And leave their town?" Anthony asked. "I adore you, Tolya. I'll adore you until the end of time."

And so it came to the end of their time, that Walmart shut and released its slaves. Elvis came and freed them all, and the town survived. If Walmart had grown for a little longer, it would have fed upon the town like a virus, as it had on many towns in America before. Tolya, Anthony and Cynthia had made enough money in their meager paychecks to fuel their car to Great Neck, New York, as the castle fell to dust and bits behind them.

"What if he is my father?" Anthony asked.

"What would it really matter?" Cynthia said.

"Both of you are insane," said Tolya. He spun the dial on the AM radio, refusing to listen to FM. A pre-recorded issue of the Cinderfield ministry broadcasted over the radio.

ANGEL'S DESIRE

Angel's new celebrity opened access to sexual delights he'd never imagined he would ever be allowed. Angel possessed a hunger, an overwhelming desire that burned constantly, in need. Angel longed to know all women, to taste them, feed on their spirits, their divine energy. Women always fascinated Angel, and he couldn't satiate his desire, fill the hole completely. There was always room for more, and when his fame and finances allowed his libidinous appetites to be fed, he found transmitter after transmitter, female and female and female, either through their own gift or salary. He hired prostitutes for weeklong marathons, daring himself to reach certain carnal frequencies.

Angel was cast on a weekly television show which allowed him the money to pursue his religion and sexual needs, to create beautiful singers like conga-man or darklords like Tony then bring them to his audiences. Angel became Latka, a lovable foreign mechanic, an extension of his Foreign Man persona. Latka was a discipline, a chore he cared little for, and he endured the filming of the sitcom, receiving ire from other cast members. He cared little.

Angel wanted more sex. He wouldn't be satisfied. Bodies just fueled the fire, creating a larger inferno that needed more fuel, burning a hell in him. The more sex he had the more he needed until it had become vapid, just strangers, flesh rubbing on flesh. And he wanted to do it live, to expose it to others, to the world, to show his sexual prowess and conquest through the live crystal screen. He enjoyed his private wrestling parties like his hero, Elvis, wrestling ladies in their white panties, and so he setup his first performances, pretending to be the bad guy wrestler, the incarnate of Tony, but this time Tony pretended to be Angel. It snapped his angel wings, and he wrapped himself around feminine bodies, pressing them into the mats, into the floor. He had to tape down his cock to hide his erection through his sweat pants, and he insulted women, calling them weak, acting on sexist attitudes then provoking them on stage. He always defeated them, humiliating women on stage then rubbing it in, rubbing himself in. He pretended it was a gag, but like Tony, the act served some dark nature within him, a terrible need to gratify himself. This was contrary to his kindness, his light, and Angel realized he also served a devil, that he was neither a host of heaven nor a denizen of the demi-plane of hell. He was a mixed creature, gray, both of light and dark. Angel was human, even though he created others, shaped the tangible illusion of reality. Angel had a name his father, angry Stanley, had given him.

He was Andy.

CINDERFIELD ASCENDS

August 11, 1984

The Great Ash-*King daydreamed of great rainbows of love and death that beamed from the sky.*
"I've just signed legislation that will outlaw Russia forever," the Reagan said, testing the microphone before his radio broadcast. "We begin bombing in five minutes." In a moment of jest, of spurious arrogance remarked at a time when he had raised Cold War tensions to the highest they've been since Stalin, he nearly induced Soviet paranoia into bellicose action. The Reagan of many dreams nearly burned the world with hellfire.

The Reagan, the great king of America, gave his speech then returned to his oval throne where he looked to the sky and dreamed of a giant magnifying glass that could catch and burn The Soviet Union like an ant hill. He'd cast rainbows down on the evil empire's weapons and cities in order to convince the Soviet people of America's greatness and love of peaceful times. He'd win their love with war and show them how wrong they were not to love the United States. Adoration could be compelled.

What was he doing again? His memory lapsed. He had plans to make, world leaders to call, but . . . what was it again? The Ash-King sat at his desk and daydreamed about great rainbows of love and death that beamed from the sky.

Cinderfield carried the wounded sparrow back to his shitty studio apartment. He bound his injuries with an old handkerchief and caught cockroaches on the bathroom floor then ground them up to feed to the tiny creature. No longer could he leave his apartment. The news aired the event. What should have been—Insane Egomaniacal Asshole Steals Monster Truck, nearly killing several to protest his own futility and insignificance in the universe became local man raises dead bird back to life after borrowing a monster truck to show the glory and goodness of the American god.

The American god dwells in underground silos, afraid of the light and throwing off particle poison, lethal neutrons that kill. This is what the apogee of species built with the great treasure and spirit granted to the country in heady salad days after Hitler and Togo. They set off their atomic firecrackers and marveled at the glow.

As the word of his miracle spread through Philadelphia, more and more potential pilgrims arrived at his apartment building. They lit white candles, brought their crosses and icons of faith, and worshipped at his ground floor window, pressing their faces against the glass—peoples of all cultures, all colors, all sharing the same desperation and frustration as trusted leaders readied to burn down their world as they watched helpless.

The carnival company at God Good Times and St. Mike's Church dropped all charges, especially when it turned out that the carnival vendor whose trailer Cinderfield had crushed—a shifty one-armed redneck named Slippery Sam—disappeared due to outstanding arrest warrants filed in three states for sexual assault on both humans and dolphins. The Levittown parents gathered for lunch in the next weeks as the news circulated.

Oh. Thank God for that lonely man who took the truck. Could you imagine what might have happened? Surely, God was working through him that day and compelled Cinderfield to put his own life and freedom at risk to protect the children.

To protect the children.

The community canonized him, though the act was not accepted nor allowed. And they would not cease until Cinderfield filled their needs. He had to sneak out through the cellar door to get to the state liquor store to buy dinner or collect his employment or attend the occasional play to watch the bad acting and remember back to days of light. One night, he came home, flipped the light on in the bathroom, paused to give the cockroaches time to scurry, catching one or two under his boot, and a young, naked woman with fat thighs jumped out of his shower stall.

"Bless my womb, fucker! My husband's seed won't take root."

"Fuck you, lady. You're not Wilma."

She slapped Cinderfield.

"Do it again."

She complied.

"Now across my ass." He bent over.

"Bless my womb first, you angelic asshole."

"Will you get the hell out of here?" he said. "And not tell any single person what I do?" She nodded and leaned forward on her legs, pushing her bush into the air. "Germinate, you motherfuckers. Find the egg. Bring one more useless person into the world. Who the fuck cares? It's all going to burn to ash soon, anyway."

The woman wept. "I can feel the baby growing now—a little boy. I'll name him Van Halen."

"What the hell do I care? Just leave me to my sparrow." She ran out of the bathroom, left his flat, running into the hall entirely naked then hopped into the parking lot among the growing congregation. "He raised life in my womb! He reached up my cunt and touched the head of my unborn child. It's a Christ child with the soul of an angel."

The crowd surged, and the weight pressed against the auto-locking door to the building, finally ripping the old portal off its hinges. The crowd of unwashed and weary folk flooded the halls reeking of bitter urine and the rotten vegetable odor of pot. The rats scurried from their path like running from a sinking ship; and the would-be congregation made short work of the apartment door—which had been broken into three times by junkies who stole his meager possessions, even his torn boxers.

Cinderfield had just put on an old porn VHS about blue women from the planet Penus Minor, dropped his dirty pants and was ready to jerk it. The desperate crowd of vacant souls didn't bother to knock, and Cinderfield threw a trucking magazine over his holy reproductive fruit just in time. Caught in that position, he decided to be polite and not draw attention to it.

"Would you kindly leave me alone?" he asked. People pushed into his apartment, squeezing into the cramped space. "I'm trying to jerk-off."

"Bless my warts!" an old woman said, holding out her talons. Warts dotted her skin up her limbs, up her shoulders and neck. "Don't heal 'em! I want more."

"Make it so I can have orgasms," asked another plain woman.

"Help me off the dope," said a teen wearing a torn White Snake shirt. "It's killing me, Mom."

Their requests for blessings and benedictions, for relative and pet resurrections, promises of an end to poverty or just the enrichment of hope ran together until the crowd begged.

Please. Please. Please.

"Get the hell out of my apartment! You're going to disturb Little Jim." He had named the sparrow that nestled and healed in a shoebox.

"Speak to us, prophet!"

"I'm not a prophet. I'm the devil, you asswipes."

They sighed in awe. Someone commented: "So humble. He understands his own weaknesses."

"I'm not a fucking messiah!"

"Praise him."

The more he denied the crowd's elevation to holy office, the more they declared him humble and worthy of their deification.

"You don't understand. Fucking monkeys. God threw me out of heaven. Now I rent a shitty flat I share with roaches. I'm quite misunderstood."

Speak to us. Guide us. Save us.

"Fuck me. Look. I'll be at Dunkin' Donuts tomorrow at eight. Just get the fuck out of my apartment."

"I knew a one-eyed whore once," Cinderfield began. "Rusty heart. She had a rusty box, too. If you fucked her, you had to get a tetanus shot at the free clinic."

The crowd had swelled, and he sat on the bench outside the Dunkin' Donuts down the Parkway from St. Mikes. "Praise God," someone yelled from the throngs. Cars honked, turning into the parking lot through the congregation.

"So, this whore told her clients that she could feel their sins through their flesh when they fucked. She could taste their betrayals, their evils, the every vile act they'd committed in a lifetime and never properly repented for. Some of the clients would hit her. Others would beg for forgiveness, and she'd create some appropriate penance for them."

The crowd listened absolutely dumbfounded. Cinderfield sipped from his coffee, found it lacking and poured in a drop of whiskey from a silver flask. Folk kept pushing money under the door, and he could afford to refill his liquor cabinet. So, maybe this wasn't a bad thing; still, it had to turn on him. It always did.

"I fucked her once."

I'm not charging you, she told me.

What's my sin?

Yours is the worst I've ever seen. You disgust me.

"Fucking Rusty Whore. What do you mean?"

"You have not sinned, but still you won't forgive yourself. You punish yourself because you've seen sadistic evil and injustice inflicted without punishment. It pains you so much that you can't make life unless there's balance. I feel sorry for you."

"Amen!" someone yelled.

A little asshole with a dirty gray beard approached the bench, handed him his card and offered him a timeslot on local Philly television for people to hear his sermons. "I'll build your church," the bearded dude said. Before Cinderfield responded, a gunshot fired from the crowd. It passed through the neck of a chubby woman, lost its lethal momentum and sliced through his shoulder, shattering bone and missing his heart. Slippery Sam, the carny whose life Cinderfield had ruined when he crushed his livelihood and exposed him to examination, thus exposing his criminal record, had returned for satisfaction. A huge black dude jumped him, knocking the .22 to the blacktop. The poor women fell over dead, and blood gushed from Cinderfield's shoulder.

THEY ALL HATE ANGEL

The world turned against Angel. He didn't understand why. Tony burned his audience, the people who saw him as a fun-loving rebel.

Why are they all mad at me? Angel asked.

He still had power through-influence, connections—and he decided he wanted to be a bad-guy wrestler. Tony could not satiate his father's anger in Angel, seeding, growing, rotting away in his soul.

Angel knew he could never wrestle professionally, and his desire for women absorbed him. He needed more, wanted more, hungered for the touch of a woman, to drive himself into their bodies and find a home. He could have as many as he wanted, and Angel needed more, to show the world his prowess, how they desired him. So he used his power to wrestle women on television, to demonstrate his sexuality. He taped down his erections, wore his long underwear and pressed their hips into his, doing it in public and defeating, dominating. He was the king. He loved being the bad guy, causing chaos, imploring anger in his viewers. His mother never protected Andy from Stanley's rages, always stood to the side and let it be between father and son.

"A woman's place is in the kitchen making me dinner!"

The women came to boo him, howl. He was only playing, though.

"Silence, when a man is talking!"

His anger, his own rage was no longer contained by his meditation, by the peace he sought, and he continued to act out his psychological issues on stage, turning his audience into his collective counselors.

Angel declared himself the Inter-Gender Wrestling Champion of the World. Then came the real hero, the champion of Memphis, the gentle giant, Lawler. In April of 1982, professional wrestler Jerry Lawler challenged Angel to his first same-gender wrestling match.

Angel sensed a kindred soul, a brute of a man with a gentle nature who loved the spotlight, ate up the applause of the crowd, personified their hopes and battles with poverty, starvation, destitution. The poor need heroes, underdogs who can fight their battles in spirit. The wrestling matches served as a pagan ritual to these needs. Angel would become his villain, the demon to his angel.

I come from Hollywood!

Jerry plays with Angel. They fight on the crystal screen, creating a staged battle between good and evil, the unknown and the famous, the rich and the poor, enacting the ritual. Angel knows how it must end. The hero must win and the pretender sent home. Then all will be right with the world.

This is soap. He holds up the bar to the Memphis audience. S-O-A-P. They jeer and scream. He stirs up the crowd, engaging their rage. Angel knows rage well, remembers his father. Tony whispers in his ear. Rage is the natural state of human life. We must strive to rise above it, channel it, exercise it like a possessing demon. Lawler and he engage, but it is all an act, choreographed, designed to tell a story, to keep the audience in suspense. He offers Angel a free headlock, giving him the advantage. Lawler can't take him down right away. It would be too quick. He needs to attack from a position of weakness, to rise above the tyrant like a fairy tale. Lawler prepares, giving the crowd time to build their expectation. He turns over Angel, grabbing his body and lifting his little frame, aiming to execute an illegal wrestling move—pile driver. It will lose him the match but make him famous in the sport. Angel floats in the air, loving the moment, thrilled by the chase. Lawler drops him carefully, giving the illusion of Angel's head hitting the ground. He falls over dead, playing just as he did as a child.

Death always yielded the greatest drama, the best reaction. If only he were dying—that would get them all looking at him. Angel wanted to be dying. He wanted to scare the people. He decided he would die.

DENYING DEATH, THE INEVITABLE

ANDY KAUFMAN
BELOVED SON, BROTHER, AND GRANDSON.
JULY 17TH 1949—MAY 16TH 1984.
WE LOVE YOU VERY MUCH.

Anthony ran his finger along the grooves of the letters. The moon bloomed nascent and cast no light to read the rectangular stone affixed to the grassy earth.

"Gravestones are an excuse," he said to Tolya. "We carve them to be ancient, to last so they can carry the burden of memory. We betray the dead and forget."

"At least there is a stone. We might just cast them out into the fields and let them be eaten by crows." Tolya surveyed the grounds and patrolled the hillside, looking down on the route below. At this time of night, few people would be on the road, but they didn't have much time until dawn. On Saturday, the living came early with offerings of flowers to their lost ones.

Anthony smiled. He knelt down on one knee and moved his hand along the grass. Numbness still spread up his digits—neuropathy from the chemo—much like a limb going to sleep but never waking. "Ideal," he said. "Toss me into a field of overgrown corn to be the feast of crows."

"Stop saying that," Cynthia said. "Just don't. Shit. Does none of this mean anything to you?"

"What do you think this is? I'm going to find out Kaufman was my dad and find the strength to survive? Such childish shit."

Cynthia's round face sucked up, and she choked back a sob. "I don't know why I try with you. I'm an idiot girl."

"Keep your voices down!" Tolya said. "We're trespassing now and in a few minutes you can add grave-robbing to the charges. And we don't even have shovels."

"So, what do we do now, Cynthia? It was your grand plan. You convinced us to do this."

"Fuck it," she said and walked off into the night, scaling a hillside into the lower area of Temple-Beth-El Cemetery. Tall memorial pillars concealed her outline.

"You fucked that up," Tolya said.

"She's too emotional."

"And you're a god damn moron."

He nodded. She appeared again over the hill, dragging tools behind her then dropped them in front of him—two shovels and a pickaxe. "Stole them from the shed. Well, borrowed." Tolya and Anthony just stared at her, a bit stunned.

"You magnificent bitch," Anthony said, smiling.

"Well, you're not dead yet, asshole. And you can still dig. Or should I dig for you, then pick up your dry-cleaning in the morning and make you breakfast, too? Goddess, men are difficult."

"You heard the boss," Anthony said, and pushed himself off the ground. He and Tolya grabbed a shovel and stabbed the protective earth, intruding on the cot of the slumbering boy deep beneath the roots, protected and

276

shielded from the pain of the living, of the old and caustic earth.

"I must be gone . . . " Anthony recited.

"Not yet." Cynthia cracked the earth with the shovel, disturbing the still sediment, waking the sleeping spirit that lay over the returned bodies, protecting them, keeping them from view so the living still might deny death the inevitable.

"The poem. Yeats."

I must be gone: There's a grave.
Where Daffodil and Lily wave.

"We read it in school," Cynthia said, swinging her pick.

"But, did you really read it?" Anthony said.

"I read it, understand it, but I won't find meaning in it until something relevant happens in my life. Give a girl a chance, Anthony."

He nodded. "Fair enough." Tolya grinned at them both, probably surprised that Anthony had conceded. Maybe, he didn't listen well enough—not that it mattered. There'd be no time to consider great and soulful thoughts. All that would have to be left for after.

After . . . He didn't quite understand the concept yet, and he knew it was egocentric; however, he came by it honestly. From his own viewpoint, he was the center of the cosmos. All energy, light, even matter flowed to him from equidistant points in space-time and flowed back from him. He beat the heart of his own world—an accident of consciousness, perspective, ears that heard in a sphere and eyes that saw coeval. He pushed the thoughts away. Be here. Be now. Why bother trying to contemplate what was impossible to contemplate? Regardless, he had no control. Cynthia didn't understand it, but he'd been taught, maybe the only lesson he'd ever let himself learn: control was an illusion. And if she didn't stop denying, hiding, running from Death the Inevitable, she'd eventually start to deny him, too. And then, he'd be lost.

Lights flashed by, somewhere down the incline along the highway—not much traffic at 3AM. They froze, waiting for it to pass, then when no police intruded on their grave-robbing party, the trio returned to their excavation. Anthony breathed fast, trying to keep the pace of his healthy friends, but it didn't take long for his body to give out. Cold sweat dripped down his face. The shovel slipped out of his numb fingers and collided with the memorial stone, then Anthony collided with the dirt. It just rushed up to greet him, and he laid his head on the final words given to Andy Kaufman by his family and friends.

What if we convinced people you were alive anyway? You wouldn't really be dead.

The trio of pilgrims had arrived in Great Neck, Long Island that Wednesday, two days before their graveyard expedition. Tolya pulled up to the Best Western to no fanfare or crowds applauding them like Lindbergh had just landed in France. The three had most of their paychecks saved from when they worked for Walmart. Two months had passed, lost to them, wasted, and Anthony could count his remaining weeks on his fingers and toes.

Tolya got them a room, and then they met at the Rocket Blast Off Dinner attached to the hotel—a restaurant themed from the 1950s, nostalgic and innocent. Pictures of Howdy Doody decorated the walls, and the seats up front looked like old Mercury rockets. A young waitress with dyed red hair seated them.

"Blast off?" Anthony asked the waitress, and she looked at him cross-eyed then took out her pad.

"What are we drinking?"

"Whiskey," Anthony said.

"You never drank whiskey in your life," Cynthia said.

"A possibility that is quickly disappearing."

She kicked him under the table and pouted like a child. She'd never really grown up, Anthony considered, and he growled silently, having little desire to censor himself and his reality because she couldn't deal with it. Still, he didn't believe it the time to confront his childhood friend.

"Coffee," Tolya said. "None of that decaffeinated shit." She scribbled it down.

"Tea," Anthony said. "Early grey."

"Chocolate milk," Cynthia said. "And none of that decaffeinated shit for pussies."

"Wild table," the waitress said. "Keep it civil or we'll call the police." Anthony smirked and wondered if she had a boyfriend. Smartasses always attracted him.

Hey, baby. You want to fuck death? It's in me.

"So, what the hell do we do now?" Tolya asked, looking at the menu. Grease coated the table and made Anthony's hand sticky. He took off his black blazer and folded it on the seat next to Tolya. Cynthia sat so close she might have been in his lap, and he inched over using inconspicuous increments so she couldn't take offense. He set her off constantly over the last few days, and he longed for peace between them. "Got any ideas?"

"We stick to the plan," Cynthia said. "We find Kaufman's family, explain the situation and ask them to volunteer a blood sample."

"It would be nice to be so young and stupid," Tolya said.

"Why can't that work?"

"Because celebrity is different in America. I understand this from my own experience, or at least the devil's. His family will be barricaded, away from the contact of strangers. They'll want their privacy. Cranks and lunatics have probably been bothering them for years."

"But we're a different kind of lunatic. We've got proof. Anthony's mother. The photos and letters. They'll want to find Anthony, to have some part of Andy survive."

"Grief doesn't work like that, and you don't understand because you've never lost someone."

Cynthia's eyes nearly burst, and she turned to study the bright yellow wall.

"It's just going to hurt 'em. The family wants to forget. I know what that's like, too. You tell them you might be Andy Kaufman's lost son, and a hundred lawyers will rain restraining orders down on your ass."

"We have evidence," she said.

Anthony remained silent.

"A couple of letters from Kaufman and a photo? You already told me. He wrestled hundreds of women. He used it to get laid. The guy's sexual adventures were legend. The only thing they might listen to is DNA proof."

"Why did you even agree to take us then if you don't believe?" she snapped.

The server returned and set down their drinks. "We ready to order?"

"We're ready to go fuck ourselves," Cynthia said.

"Cheeseburger platter," Anthony said. "Chocolate milkshake. Death is growing inside of me."

"Smooth," Tolya said, giggling.

"No point in holding back."

Cynthia shook her head. "I'm not hungry." She sighed and hunched in the corner. "Can't believe I gave up my life for you two assholes."

"Don't worry, babe," the server said. "There will be plenty of other assholes to take advantage of you."

Tolya ordered toast and a bowl of hot oatmeal.

"Move," Cynthia ordered Anthony. He got up from the booth. She pulled down her flowery skirt then got up, pushed by him and slipped out the door. He watched her pass by the window. He got up to follow, doing what came natural.

"Just let her go, for now," Tolya said. "Like I said. Grief. She's fighting the need to push you away."

"It seems counter-intuitive. Why isn't she pulling me closer?"

"Fear is stronger than love."

"I don't believe it. I don't want to believe it."

"Believe what you like, Anthony. You're blessed. You're not going to live long enough to have your faith challenged. You'll live young forever."

Anthony sighed and flicked ice water on his face. His back ached from the bench, and he just wanted to lie down. There'd be time enough for that later.

"That's what I like about you, Tolya. Your complete lack of sensitivity."

Tolya laughed then sipped his steaming coffee. It must have burned his lips, but he didn't notice. Chemo killed Anthony's nerves but still felt more sensation than the Russian ever would.

The server returned to the table with her pad. "Is she ordering or just bawling over stuff she can't change?"

"Is everyone an amateur psychologist?" Anthony asked.

"Human nature," the server said. "Your food should be up soon. One dead cow on bread. Yum. And slop."

"Do you have any idea where Andy Kaufman's family lives?"

"Christ," she said. "Not more."

Anthony spotted the lines of a tattoo on her shoulder, part of a face revealed just on her skin.

"More what?"

"Once a month for the last ten years, some fan boy shows up to touch the shrine of the almighty Andy Kaufman. He wasn't even that funny. I've seen his shit on YouTube."

Cynthia, refreshed from her anxiety, returned and sat down. "Yo. Can I order a thing of fries?"

"Steak fries?"

"Bitch, yes."

The server scribbled it on her pad.

"Wait. What happens when these pilgrims arrive?" Anthony asked.

"Most of them try to see the family, often with gifts, flowers. There's a lawyer in town, drinks at the bar at the Best West. Big dude. Bill. Takes up nearly two seats."

"And he's the man to talk to?"

"Dude, you're not getting it. He protects the family."

"This is different," Cynthia said, jumping into the conversation. "We think he might be Anthony's father. And he's sick. He has cancer."

"Everyone's dying," she said. "I'll go put those fries in for you."

As the morbid waitress had informed, a large wild boar of a man sat at the end of the bar, filling up space enough for three patrons, and drank beer out of a tall glass. They didn't talk to him, knew better than to disturb the guy after work. Anthony wrote him a note and asked the bartender—some chick with dyed platinum hair—to deliver it.

Destroying the Tangible Illusion of Reality

Dear Sir:

My friends have struggled and fought to bring me north so I can find my father. I will not take up too much of your time, and I'm trying because they have already given so much to bring me here.

Several months ago, I was diagnosed with a ravenous and bitter lymphoma that is now eating my body—a wild accident of chaos and nature. I don't believe in destiny or fate. I'd be really pissed if I did. I never knew my mother. She died in a car accident bringing me home from the hospital. I was but a day old. My mother died not as a result of the calculation of a deity or the plots of fate. She died as a result of metal liquefied at high velocities, of physics, momentum and pressure. I'm sure her last thoughts were not of a God punishing or delivering but of protecting me, which she did with her own bone and flesh. The EMTs found me wounded, silent and bundled up in her crushed arms.

I did not know my father, but I suspect I have one and was not the result of an immaculate conception. My grandparents raised me and forbade me to know anything about the causes of my past, of how I came to be. I have declined more treatment, a futile pursuit, and in those days of decision, we discovered evidence that the actor Andy Kaufman had indeed implanted the sperm into my mother's womb that then conceived me. Again, not an act of divine intervention: the act of a horny actor. I'd like to think they loved each other, if even for moments. I would like to believe this. I'm starting to believe a lot that isn't real. That's what happens when you die young.

I will enclose copies of the evidence including photographs with this note. I can produce the originals. I only ask for a bit of spit from a family member, and we will pay for any lab expenses. I expect nothing from the family and waive any inheritance. I will sign some device to this effect.

If you believe in fate, then perhaps believe that I came here because of the rhythms and inclinations of the solar winds. If you believe in God, then think it His will. If you need a fee, I can pay you what I can. I'll pay you in blood and tell you lies. Please contact me at your earliest.

Anthony Kaufman
Room 413

At 2AM, the three of them sat up in the room drinking hard cider and waiting for some indication as to their next move. Anthony sprawled out on the bed, his back aching. His head burned with fever, and he hid this from Cynthia who would probably insist he go to the hospital. What did it really matter anymore?

"There's an Andy Warhol exhibit at the local museum," Cynthia said. "I'd like to see it while we're in town."

"Who?" Tolya asked.

"Artist in the seventies. Redefined avant-garde. Got shot by a lesbian several times. Survived. Died in surgery several years later."

"Got nothing," Tolya said.

"You're just doing that to aggravate me."

"I can't remember much before 1984," Tolya said. "That's when I split in two."

284

Anthony popped two morphine down for his back then finished his bottle. Cynthia spotted his furtive movements.

"Anthony! Are you drinking with those painkillers?"

"Yuppers."

She folded her hands and sipped from her own bottle. "You're an adult. You can do what you like."

"Thank you for the affirmation."

She opened her mouth to slam him, but a note pushed under the hotel door shut her up. She got up too fast, probably a bit tipsy from the cider, steadied herself then reached for the note. She unfolded it and moved into the sickly light of the room lamp to read, first going over it to herself and sighing.

"*Make no attempt to contact the Kaufman family, or I will file a restraining order. Please return home. Sorry about your lot.* What the fuck?"

"Can we go home now?" Tolya asked.

Anthony felt kicked in the stomach. Tears wet his eyes, and he fought them, held them back. How had this become so important to him? "Yeah. Let's just go home."

"We can't. You'll. . ." Cynthia sat down on the bed next to Anthony and grabbed his elbow. She released the note and allowed it to flutter to the filthy rug.

"Nothing is going to stop that."

She sighed. "Don't be such a . . . pussy!"

It stunned Anthony, and his tears stopped. "What did you have in mind?"

"We need a smidgen of DNA. I've seen *Law & Order* reruns. We can get it on a coffee cup or a cigarette."

"We don't even know where the family lives," Tolya said.

She paused, cogitating then hunched over. "We have to do this. We're above the law now. What the hell does it matter?"

"It does matter," Anthony said. "You have to go on. I won't let you suffer for the mistakes of my family."

"I believe you're his son. I know it. It's true as blood. True as true north."

"The hell are you talking about?" Tolya asked.

"And once we get evidence, the family will have to believe it, too. So will the lawyer. We just need his DNA. So we go get some." Anthony borrowed her cider and gulped some down and waited to be enlightened. "They just abandoned him, stuck him in the ground to freeze and be lonely. They don't want it anymore. It's like when people throw out old couches. It's free game once it's on the curb."

"That's insane," Tolya said.

"Then you can stay in the hotel."

"I can't. I have to come."

Anthony finished his cider. "It is insane. What does it really matter?"

"What does it really matter?" Cynthia asked. "Reality is coming apart. Fucking idiot rules made by men who think they're going to live forever. We'll be fast. Holes can be buried. Forgotten."

"We're all holes." Anthony said, lifting his glass in a toast.

"And they're going to bury us."

Death the Inevitable lived in a small stone hut on the side of the Irish Sea. Seals honked and howled the night through, and he sat on a boulder at the ocean's edge, careful not to touch the lichen or clams, lest he cause their death, and contemplated changing his name, as it proved hard to shag someone if they knew you were Death the Inevitable.

Always the Inevitable.

Was death.

In his tiny kingdom by the Irish Sea where he could not touch anything living lest he'd kill them.

This made it even harder to shag anyone living, since he had to wear full body protection, or they would not survive the encounter. One touch, direct flesh-to-flesh, would compel his one-time mates into such an orgasm that they'd scream and bite their tongues clear off, then the Inevitable effect would occur, killing them stone dead.

Absolutely stone dead.

Inevitably.

"Fuck! Cock! Ass! Shit! My giddy aunt's red cunt!"

He swore into the sea, and the sea absorbed his curses and did not speak back sans to sing him into a light repose. He watched the sun die and felt kinship—not to the sun but to that last moment when the day's sun reached out to grip onto the earth before finally sinking into the dirt to suffocate.

And the seals howled.

"I have been the subject of so many movies. All books are essentially about me. Inevitably. All songs that sing of love defy me and thus glorify me. Shite. I need something warm to fuck."

The seals refused to answer back, not interested in his clumsy attempts to seduce them. In the pubs of the nearby villages—villages standing for thousands of years, built by the ancient societies of blue peoples of Scotland Death the Inevitable has seen rise and fall, yet always somehow the same—they drank whiskey by the cup and sang songs they knew of their youth. By-and-by, they'd come and see him.

He took some pot out of the top pocket of his leather jacket, cupped it in his palm, wrapped it in rolling paper then lit a match. Instantly, the flame doused, and he lit another and another. Still, the flame died.

"Shite." Fire always died in his presence, yet he kept trying, hoping for a different result. For millions of years, fire eluded him. "Yet, you give it to them! Motherfucker!"

Death the Inevitable had no mother, so he had never learned to be polite or clean up his language. He dipped his bare knobby feet into the water and let his fat belly—swollen from the souls that had passed through him on the way to the afterlife—and the lichen and clams died. He picked up the dead carcasses of both and chewed them with broken teeth, smashed from eating the hard shells raw. He felt little pain, at least physically; however, he did feel the agony.

On the earth, the homeless waited for their pain to end. Junkies shoved needles into their arms, pressed the plungers and waited for their consciousnesses to darken to oblivion. The old rotted early, the result of medical science perverting life, and they begged for release, not able to exact it themselves in a society that had advanced in science but not in reason or kindness.

Bad things happen for a reason.

Bad things happen for a reason.

Bad things happen for a reason.

"Fuck it. You lot can wait."

And he heard a prayer. He always heard the prayers to hold back death, to keep them a bit longer. A young woman appeared on the coast. She looked pudgy in her summer dress, not the ideal modern model featured in magazines and shows on telly.

"On the mainland, they're drinking whiskey. What are you drinking, love?"

"Love," she said.

"Then you're a foolish young thing. What's your name?

I be Death the Inevitable. Terrible I am. I exist to release, to cure pain, to end the suffering of the world. I serve a necessary function. Want to fuck?"

"I'll pay anything to keep him here."

"Then let's deal."

They waited until the next night, spending the day hanging around the hotel, watching movies, ordering room service, and drinking cider. Cynthia postponed until the evening to tell them about the nightmare:

"I dreamed of death."

"What did he look like?" Anthony asked. "I don't want to get conned by some flimflam artist."

"Please, don't talk like that," she said.

"Of course. Why should I speak about it? The inevitable?"

"That's what he called himself: Death the Inevitable."

"Catchy title."

At midnight, they left their hotel room, sticking a Do Not Disturb sign on the door handle. Tolya, Cynthia, and Anthony had stopped in the bar to have a stiff drink before heading off to the cemetery.

They got into Mr. Snowballs, and Tolya pulled out onto the highway—the nondescript highway he couldn't perceive the number, just another one of America's routes, built long and now decaying. Cynthia held the packet of evidence, the letters and photos they had found that lead them to this course. She couldn't read them again in the flashing of highway lights and sparse car headlights. They drove by diners, used car lots, closed shopping centers, and she caught words in their illuminations, saw the grainy colored photos of Kaufman in his obnoxious outfit and splendor.

"Do you see that?" Tolya asked.

"What?"

"That black Sedan just pulled out behind us. It's going slow, but I swear it's tailing us."

"You're paranoid," Cynthia said. "Just get us there."

SOMEONE TURN THAT GOD OFF

Is that a rock?" Tolya asked.

"Could be river stone or glacier deposited," Cynthia said.

"I didn't need a geology lesson."

Anthony scraped through the loose soil with his shovel, standing about five feet down in the awkward hole they'd dug with axes, tools, nails, and guilt. The soil cooled his fever, relaxed him. He could fall into the soil, merge with the particles, fuse into the living metal spirit of the hot and churning world. Going home. He raked away more loose soil.

"Throw me the torch," he said, and Tolya tossed it to him. "It's concrete."

"Shit. They capped it. We'd need a jackhammer to break through. Well, we're fucked."

"Can't we dig around it?" Cynthia asked.

"We're already pushing this close to dawn, and someone's going to know we were here when they see the grass dug up. Expect this to be on the news tomorrow, maybe even nationwide—not that too many people remember who he was."

"But it's perfect," Cynthia said. "This is what you'd expect from Andy Kaufman. Maybe people will remember."

Anthony toyed with his shovel, poking at the cement seal. Chunks of the aggregate broke off with minimal effort. "Something odd about this concrete." He slammed the shovel down on the surface, and the seal crumbled, breaking off into pieces that fell away, exposing soft dirt beneath it. Tolya jumped down with the pick and drilled into the concrete.

"It's thin. Shouldn't be this thin. Someone fucked this up."

"Or it was intentional," Cynthia said. "Who fucks up concrete? You just pour."

They cleared away most of the seal and dug away the dirt below, exposing the blue silver surface of the vessel. Anthony knelt in the dirt, and the rough concrete dug into his knees. He touched the surface with his palm, stroking the cool metal and brought the cooled skin to his forehead. Tolya dug around the sides of the front lid, around the hinges looking for a catch. He yanked on the frame, expecting it to resist, but the lid easily lifted. He dropped it and stepped back in the dirt wall.

"I need a cig'," Tolya said. "Don't touch this until I get back." Anthony cocked his eye at the Russian, but Tolya knew he'd wait. He climbed up out of the pit, digging up through the dirt wall with mole paws, and jumped onto the grass then strolled over to a quince tree now in bloom. He lit a cig'.

"Don't you open that box now," Cinderfield said.

"Why won't you leave me alone?" Tolya asked.

"Those things will give you cancer, but they can't take away someone else's."

"I'm a fucking monster," Tolya said. "Way it goes. I'll probably outlive all of them."

"God's granted you a long life. Punishment."

"I'm doing what I can. Fucking Beelzebub."

Tolya held his palm up to the moonlight and studied the heavy scar—coeval on the back of his hand and his palm. A deep fissure of scar tissue decorated both hands. Sometimes he'd forgotten the nails; sometimes, he could still feel the spikes being driven into his flesh.

"Don't open the box."

"Why? He should know the truth." Tolya finished the cig' and flicked it into the tree roots.

"Primitive brain matter. Not more than a step above ooze. You don't have the gray and roots to understand true truth, just what you perceive. Do you really think it's going to give that boy comfort? Anything you do now is just going to extend his pain and make it harder for him and the girl."

"There can be truth."

"Oh, ho, ho? Really? Want another cig'? These things will kill ya." Tolya lit up another cancer stick. "And you want some truth. How about this?"

"Oh, joy. Shocking revelation time."

"Shut the fuck up and listen," Cinderfield said, and rubbed his pointy chin. His eyes glowed in burning crimson coals, the hot cigarette tip aflame. "This isn't about you. Shit like cancer, it's never about the poor asshole dying. It's always about the people around him. They make it about themselves, absorb in their own pain. This is your guilt, Tolya. Your guilt for Wilma."

"That wasn't her name, you freak. Why do you even call her that?" Tolya finished the second stick, gave Cinderfield the finger, and strolled back to his friends. They waited at the grave. Anthony still toiled in the pit, clearing more soil. "Open the fucking thing." Tolya stood over the hole and guarded. Cynthia leaned down to jump into the pit, but the Russian held her back.

"So I just . . . open this? Like in the movies?" Anthony

gripped the edge of the lid. "Do you have the jar?" Tolya tossed him down the plastic cup and then dropped the knife. Anthony missed it, and the knife rattled on the metal coffin. He set them by his feet. Cynthia shone the flashlight down on the coffin, and it reflected off the surface. Anthony hesitated.

"Why do you wait?" Tolya asked.

His fingers froze to ice, touching the freezing coffin. Ice crystals, buried low in both this hole in the earth and deep in Anthony's mind broke free and spread through his body, down his neck and legs and feet. The ice crystals merged and flattened, growing into a looking glass, a magic mirror that emerged over his ribs. Anthony petrified, and he watched the scene unfold on his chest while the players above the graves took their parts.

Death bathed in the moonlight, entirely naked and without wearing clothes, too!

"So, you want me to leave this chap alone?"

"Not entirely," Cynthia said. "I wouldn't disturb the laws of nature like that."

Death the Inevitable strummed his own belly then tapped it like a drum. "Tum-ti. Tum-ti. Tum."

"Tum-ti. Tum-ti."

"Don't sing. Just hurts my ears."

"Sorry."

"Why do you care so much about this breather?"

She averted her eyes but did it slowly so as not to offend him.

"Oh, go ahead and look away. I know I'm ugly."

"It's not you. It's my perception of you."

"The fuck?" He burst into laughter. "Errant shite. You don't think I've heard it all? For thousands of gonebys that go by, your kind has cursed my name. *Damn you, Death the Inevitable? Why are you so Inevitable?* That's what they say, all right. Fucking spinning ol' ball of spider webs and dead uteruses."

"People are often unkind to you."

"They can be terribly cruel."

"What's the most unkind thing anyone ever said to you?"

"Musician Suzen Juel. She said, Death the inevitable. Fucking IV sucking junkie. I don't have a fecking idea what that means, and if I can't understand it, then it must be a kick to the bullocks."

"I'll tell you if I figure it out."

"Dealio."

"What about Anthony?"

"Out of my hands. I didn't make the clocks. I just clean them."

"I don't believe you." She sighed, sitting on the hard rocks along the Irish Sea.

"I'll lie to you if you want: Oh aye! Of course I'll let him live. Death the Compassionate! Death the Charitable."

"Death the Asshole."

"Just once, I'd like to be understood."

"Shh. He's opening the box."

"Look for the prize! Like at the bottom of crackerjacks."

"A box of crackerjacks," Anthony said.

"Anthony. Open it."

A car pulled up into the side parking lot outside the gate to the memorial grounds. Its headlights sliced through the dark and warned, accused. "Time's up," Tolya said. "You look now or forever be a pussy."

Anthony grabbed the lid and threw it open, exposing the interior of the forever-box buried in rocks. "Shit!" It wasn't a rotting corpse that surprised him, nor a collection of bones. A pale white visage greeted the world with stoic eyes carved from plastic. They held a single glance, frozen forever in the vision of the artist who carved it. White cloth sealed the rest of the vast face and decorated with swollen red lips. Musical instruments—bongo wood, trombone bones, violin necks—formed a skeleton and a fat suit filled out the elegant white outfit decorated with sequins gleaming in the torch ray. They glittered, and Cynthia tittered. Anthony couldn't breathe. He collapsed on his bum onto the coffin, and the ersatz body shook.

Anthony said an improvised prayer for the undying, for the empty body, the symbol in the coffin:

I need to drink to be sober.
And I need to stay awake to sleep
Someone turn that God off
Keeping me up.

"Those fuckers," Tolya said, studying the coffin.

"It's the same outfit the ghost of Elvis wears."

"Shit," Cynthia said.

"Come on. We've got to haul ass," Tolya said.

"It doesn't make any sense."

"Sure as shit it does," responded Tolya. "Those crazy, crazy fuckers. They're laughing at us right now."

"Bob Zmuda. Andy Kaufman. What devotion. Biggest hoax of the century. No one will ever top this, not for a long, long time."

"But it still doesn't help us. Where the hell are we going to find the DNA now?" Anthony reached his hand up, and Tolya took it. "Tolya, where did you get these scars from?" Anthony asked, feeling the raised tissue on the Russian's palms.

"From glory everlasting."

A beam from a flashlight assaulted the trio. Anthony needed to catch his wind and couldn't run fast. Cynthia and Tolya hiked but turned back for him, giving the stranger time to accost them.

"Tolya," Cynthia whispered. "Run. Get to the car. You know what to do." The old fox nodded and slipped behind the tree. The stranger didn't seem to notice. In the dark, he had only caught Anthony and Cynthia with his flashlight. Anthony saw him leaving and realized they only had to play for time.

"Who are you people? Do you realize what you've done?" The stranger wore a black overcoat and held the flashlight on his shoulder like a cop. His voice sounded soft, and from what Anthony could see, his head rounded off, mostly balding and what may have been a ponytail.

"Who are you, sir?" Anthony asked, adding an element of authority to his voice.

"Don't tell me my business, boy!" He raised *boy* at the end with a high pitch, twisting the sound. "I'll fuck your life! Reprobate!"

Anthony looked over at Cynthia who studied, pondered, cogitated on the voice and stranger. "Something really familiar about this."

"Shut up!" the stranger yelled, sneering. "Now, what are you . . . doing here? Looks like you dug up a body!"

"They're lazy asses," a gaunt man said, climbing on the hill, leaning on a shovel like a cane to steady his walk. He limped up the incline, below the tree and stood next to them. "They're supposed to be working. Got an early funeral tomorrow. A'yep I do." He spoke with a sharp New English accent, overdoing it a bit.

"You're a gravedigger?"

"Got to move them around. Took on some seasonal help. College students, but all they know is how to live off their parents and smoke that wacky weed!"

"Can we go get high now?" Anthony asked, and Cynthia kicked him.

"Dude. Shut up. It's the cops."

The stranger shone the light onto the coffin. The lid still hung open. "What the hell is that? This is Kaufman's grave right? What the hell did you do with the body? You are in a lot of trouble, folks. I'll have you thrown out of here."

"Something off about this dude," Cynthia said. "And so damn familiar."

"Can we see your badge?" Anthony asked.

"No! You . . . may not! But I salute you, sir. Finally, someone had the balls."

"I beg your pardon," Anthony said.

"Now, you get this hole filled in. I'm letting you off with a warning! This time. Next time, you can bite my fat big one!"

"I'd really like to see your badge. Arrest me if you want."

"It is back in my car."

The trio watched as the stranger turned around, walked back to his car. He'd left the engine idling. They waited, and he got into the car, shut the door, and the car pulled out.

"What the hell?" Cynthia asked.

"Who gives a god damn?" Tolya, no longer playing the gravedigger, turned and took off. Cynthia waited for Anthony, and they hauled ass back to Mr. Snowballs parked behind the gate. They didn't bother to fill in the hole, and tomorrow, if it went public, the world would know that Andy Kaufman had not really been buried in Temple-Beth-El Cemetery in 1984.

I DON'T BELIEVE IN HELL, JUST NEW JERSERY

Tolya pulled the truck up to the only place open before dawn where they could nurse their wounds and figure this crazy shit out. Captain Spizzie's Pizza and Church of the Reformed Faith offered pizza, cheesesteaks, hot wings and slaw by day and at night they converted it into a local church for the non-denominational folk to worship, hold weddings and bury their dead and veneration.

"Like throwing ashes out to sea, where you'll never have to think of them again," Tolya muttered. He checked to make sure no one followed them, not that black sedan that had crept behind them while driving. He thought he'd spotted it when they pulled up to a streetlight on the vacant roads at 4AM, but he gunned it. No one followed.

"I haven't had a good slice since we left Philly," Cynthia said.

"Is it a church or a pizza place?" Anthony asked.

"Probably both. Americans are insane."

"I love it."

Cynthia reached for the packet of love letters and photos where she'd slid it under the seat before getting out to engage in sacred desecration and grave-robbing earlier that night. She searched the carpet, dug around in the detritus of a road life—fast food wrappers, old fountain soda cups, empty plastic cylinders of tobacco.

"Did either of you move the love letters?"

Anthony and Tolya shrugged.

"Shit. Where is it?"

They got out so she could dig around under the seats, down the sides, in the corners. Still, she could find nothing. "I had them before we went digging."

"Then someone took them," Tolya said.

"Who the hell would?"

"Let's go inside and figure this out," Tolya said.

They slipped inside. A tall Hindustani fellow wearing a white tunic and a wreath of pink flowers swept up, and some of the staff stacked chairs. "Namaste," he said, dropping the boom stick and folding his hands in front of him, bowing forward.

"Namaste," Cynthia said, returning the greeting in kind and smiled.

"Will you be wanting a blessing, a cleansing, or breakfast?"

"A blessing," Cynthia said.

"A cleansing," Anthony said.

"Breakfast—whiskey! In a tin cup," Tolya said.

The Hindu priest smiled, bowed again, averting his eyes. "I am sorry, my fellow seeker, but we do not serve spirits of any kind here."

"Well, what's the point of faith, then, if you can't have a little drink afterwards? Nothing to seek forgiveness for."

"No, sir," said the priest. And he took his forefinger and pressed it into Tolya's sternum. It twitched and pulsed, and a nail shot through his ribs. "You think you have much to seek forgiveness for." He didn't know how to respond. He considered grabbing the guy's hand, but his touch paralyzed Tolya's body. Finally, he lifted it, releasing the Russian. "Let me get you seated," the priest said. "A booth and nirvana okay?"

"Sure," Anthony said.

"Delightful." He grabbed three day menus and led them to the corner. The trio sat down, and the bench creaked from their weight. "I'll be right back to take your orders and bring you enlightenment." Anthony held his giggles until the priest left the table.

"Don't laugh," Cynthia said. "He's one of the faithful."

"It's like an old Peter Sellers's film," Anthony said, and Cynthia joined his giggle.

"Goddess. It really is."

How can they know? Slick Phil slipped into the kitchen and threw off the wreath of flowers. He'd been acting the holy man role for years now, and it made good money, a pretty good racket. Sam, their blind cook, baked rolls in the long oven in the corner.

"I say, Sam," Slick Phil said. "Sam?" He'd gone mostly deaf after an unfortunate incident crossing the local country route at the same time a horny female moose crossed the other side. He never spoke about it, and most of his paycheck went to therapist bills. "I say, Sam, I'm a complete and utter fraud, you know. I'm not from Lhasa. I'm from New Brunswick, New Jersey. I used to steal hubcaps and car accessories and con short-change in Trenton. There are still three county warrants out for my arrest. And if you've got a moment, bub, I can go get my shell game. And we'll have some fun. We'll have tons and tons."

Sam, the deaf and blind cook, paid him no mind and slid the next tray into the oven, focusing on his work, probably driving away thoughts of the moose's eyes from his head.

Slick Phil found the bottle of Kentucky Whiskey in the linen cabinet, uncapped it and drank from the bottle. He needed it—another long night of prayers, of reading memorized prayers and venerations from real holy men through history. There had been enough inspired men and women and vats of fallow ink to record a thousand prophets for whom no one knew any regard. He did them a service by bringing them to life, recycling their words— mostly, the same concepts repeated—and then collected donations. The prayers held no value to Sam, but they comforted his flock; thus, it wasn't exactly a con.

Phil didn't think Cinderfield recognized him. It astonished him that the devil-gone-messiah-gone-fraud had survived the spontaneous nail-up at his last performance as a televangelist. The money Phil embezzled hadn't lasted long, blowing it on blow, drinking it on drink and shoving five-dollar bills, rolled up and sweaty from his palms, into the g-strings of stringy strippers— dreaming of something more and lied to by the dancers. Everyone conned everyone. People betrayed to fulfill their natures. You just had to know when to leave the party, preferably before the check came.

Phil pulled out the .45 from under the bottom stack of linens, checked to make sure he'd loaded it and spun the chamber. With what Cinderfield knew, they'd put him away for a lifetime, and he wouldn't last long in prison, not before stringing himself up with a bed sheet and hanging a sign around his neck that read:

NO! I WAS NOT TRYING TO GET OFF BY AUTO-ASPHYXIATING. GO FUCK YOURSELVES—CRUEL WORLD.

Phil put on an apron and slipped the gun into the pocket—just deep enough to conceal it up to the handle. Then he sighed, bowed, returned the flower necklace to his neck and gulped more whiskey.

"I don't believe in no heaven or hell. Just New Jersey. So what the fuck is a man's life?" Sam made no comment or judgment and kneaded more dough on the counter.

Tolya couldn't place the Hindu holy man—so damn familiar. Perhaps he had a racist mind and just recognized his mannerisms from a movie. Still, he watched the guru, careful of the fellow, trusting his instinct. Tolya had witnessed and participated in darkness, and somehow, this Hindu priest of light had been attached to his shadow.

They ordered, and the priest bowed, collecting their menus then wobbled back into the kitchen. Something weighed down his apron, anchoring his pocket.

"So, that wasn't a real cop?" Cynthia asked.

"Never a cop," Tolya said, stirring his coffee. He sipped it. "This is shit."

"Was it just some dude fucking with us?"

"Probably the same one who took the photos. Some shit is going on here."

Anthony ripped at the edges of the paper tablemat. It displayed a map of the Northeast, outlined in green with drawings of silos, tiny cities, and natural features, such as lakes or mountains. He opened a box of dull crayons and filled in the lines with contrary colors: yellow for water, orange for land, blue for the dead or abandoned. He drew wee stick figures.

"So, what's the great truth here?" Cynthia asked. "Andy Kaufman was secretly buried somewhere else?"

304

"Or never buried at all," Anthony said. "The greatest hoax of the 20th century."

"For years, there have been reports of his return to life. I never believed it. He's been my hero since my father told me about him, and I've read or watched everything I could find. If Andy Kaufman ever came back from the dead, it wouldn't be reported by a friend or family member. He'd jump out of a coffin on the David Letterman show. He'd have to be at the center of attention, especially for something this grand. Making fools of millions of people like this would be an achievement of religious significance."

Anthony took a bite of his pancakes, chewed it, tried to swallow, and his face pinched. He spit it back into his napkin. Cynthia frowned, looking worried, but she didn't admonish him. As the days progressed, and Anthony's sickness manifested upon his face and body—storm clouds growing gray, etiolating his skin, draining the light from his stars—Cynthia had restrained her care, pulling further back. Tolya knew exactly what she was going to do next, and most likely, she'd make it Anthony's fault. People excelled at generating excuses to protect themselves.

"So, Andy is alive?" Anthony asked.

"Whatever he's doing now, it has to be something in the public eye, but local, not national, so no one would recognize him." Cynthia drank some chocolate milk. "This tastes like soap."

"You can't read his mind," Tolya said. He crossed his thumbs and furry eyebrows, annoyed at her presumption. She couldn't really know.

"But, I know his kind—especially Andy, in such need. It's how he processed emotional issues: on stage in front of an audience. I've studied this, wrote a paper on him for my psych class. His characters enacted scenes from his

305

childhood. Many of his characters were a catharsis about his father's anger."

"From what you've shown me, he had a lot of buried rage."

"He'd be devoted to this hoax. He was a zealot, a fanatic for his art, so he'd still be hiding, but hiding in plain sight."

"Or a fat suit with a fake moustache," Anthony said.

"And they'd be watching. Bob Zmuda, his old partner, had to be on it."

"He's in California, isn't he? Writing another book on Andy?" Anthony asked.

"For something this important, he'd fly out."

"The lawyer," Anthony said.

"They've been following us," Tolya added. Now he understood why the black sedan had been following them even in the middle of the night: probably a private dick, paid to shadow them, keep tabs.

"I knew I recognized that fake-cop," Cynthia said. "It had to be Bob Zmuda." She searched on her phone and found a near-current picture of Andy's old writing partner then showed it to her crew.

"Shit," Anthony said.

Death the Inevitable found a shell washed up on the stony beach. He polished it on his fat stomach, cleaning off the bits of dark sand, grit and slimy green fronds of kelp. The white shell glowed in the moonlight. Seals howled in the distance, in the darkness, down along the coast and cliffs.

"Why does it have to be him?" Cynthia asked, still pestering the stocky embodiment. She'd been there for the day and frustrating him, interrupting the seal song and the singing from the pubs up the road from the sea.

"Well it doesn't, not really. It can be any of you, some random soul out there. The dice are thrown. The whip cracks. The world spins on and someone takes the slot. Humans fill up the world, saturate it, fill up the surface until the earth nearly cracks in two like hammers dropped on an egg."

"Please. Someone else."

"Are you sure?" he asked. "I am Death Inevitable. I am mighty and cruel. I will inflict and scratch you, cut your flesh, for I resent you and the living."

"Aim and miss," she said.

"It may not work, or worse, it may. You can live with it . . . but you won't be able to."

Before leaving, it finally hit Tolya where he'd seen the Hindu Priest—from Cinderfield's ministry. It cracked him in the head as they were getting up from the bench, and Tolya knew he had to step carefully. Wanted men often proved dangerous, and he'd built a comfortable life here. He looked so different, giving off the aura of a holy man.

"How do we do this?" Cynthia asked. "Find him? A man trying to hide for thirty years is going to be hard to dig up. We have no idea what he even looks like now."

"He's going to be in the public eye," Anthony said. "Exposed somewhere, not hiding in a cabin in the woods in some god forsaken lost world."

Tolya got up with them, moving fast, bumping into Anthony. In his weakened state, Anthony teetered. Some commuters and truck drivers had come into the restaurant-church for a quick breakfast or prayer on the way to work their livelihoods or run from their lives.

The holy man, who had been previously known to Tolya and Cinderfield as Philip, came out, carrying a tray of food. He bowed to the new customers, saying his customary phrase of greeting, then he turned to say goodbye to the trio. Tolya looked away, but the holy man had seen his eyes anew, recognized the recognition, thrown petrol onto the fire. He did nothing, and the trio quickly slipped by him, making their goodbyes. Anthony and Cynthia absorbed into this new problem, unaware of the drama unfolding between the two men.

They left the dinner-temple and walked across to Mr. Snowballs. Tolya heard the bell over the door ring behind him, and he turned around to see Philip-Holy Hindu step out of his place, raise a small pistol, and pull the trigger. The sound clapped his ears, and a shockwave knocked Tolya back. He tripped over a curb and collapsed onto a truck, knocking his head against a tire. He touched his chest. Dark blood dripped down his fingers, and his head spun. The sun came out to warm him, but he shivered. Philip-The Holy Hindu shed any remaining illusion of his pious faith, jumped into his car and drove off, nearly hitting Cynthia.

Death the Inevitable aimed and missed.

Cynthia screamed.

"It's my fault," she whispered.

As Tolya bled out, Cinderfield whispered to him the past, about the end of his time as a messiah, to torment what were probably his final moments. Cinderfield would never stop. It's why Tolya had created him: to always punish the Russian since he'd been the one who had survived the truck accident that had killed Anthony's mother when it should have been him.

Destroying the Tangible Illusion of Reality

October 20th, 1984

The crowd spreads the word of Minister Cinderfield.

He waved the bullet away.

No instrument of death or destruction could penetrate his holy aura.

God protected his holy ass. Cinderfield had a purpose.

"Of course I have a fucking purpose. I'm the bloody devil. Lucifer. Beelzebub."

Rusty, the whore of his past, cleaned the gunshot wound in his shoulder, dabbed it with rubbing alcohol then changed the bandage. She helped Cinderfield put on the rhinestone cape—the one that glittered in the stage lights. His arm still ached, and he adjusted the sleeve.

"You still haven't forgiven yourself," Rusty said.

"It's none of your fucking business. I pay you to open your mouth, not open your mouth."

She detailed his eyes with the liner, outlined the lids with storm clouds—enough to draw out the darkness in the crowd of petitioners. He had to summon them with his eyes. His words would be shit compared to the gaze he'd give the crowd.

"You want me to blow you before you go on?" Rusty asked.

"On your knees," said the devil. And she knelt down before him, made the sign of the cross then unzipped his zipper and pulled his cock out. She went down on him, taking his small sparrow between her lips and slurping. This was Rusty's trademark. It didn't take him long to cum, and she swallowed it down with blessed wine and holy water.

"The devil's juice," he said.

"You're so fucking full of yourself."

"And now you're full of me, too."

The stage manager ran into the waiting room. "They're waiting on you, boss," the squat fellow said. Cinderfield had never learned his name. What the hell was the point? He'd be gone in a matter of weeks. This couldn't last that long.

And he had been right. In three weeks, a crazy drunk bus driver would drink too much vodka and drive his SEPTA bus into the stage manager's ass while he crossed Walnut Street. The bus driver would keep driving, singing old show tunes and would switch on the windshield wipers to clean off the crimson rain spraying up on the glass. Cinderfield could perceive this happening but didn't want to admit this.

"It's time for me to go fuck over the masses," he said.

She swallowed the rest and zipped him up. "You taste like lemons," she said.

"I was born way down south," Cinderfield said.

"Be nice if you went way down south sometime," Rusty muttered.

"What the fuck, whore? Are you paying me? This isn't a relationship. I write your ass checks, and you absolve any guilty."

She sighed. "I might be in love with you."

"Then you're not just a whore. You're a stupid whore."

"Fuck you, Jeb," she spit. She grabbed a knife off a plate of old steak from the night before, from Cinderfield's late night show, and lunged at him.

His stage manager grabbed the whore and dragged her back. She dropped the knife.

"Please," Cinderfield said. "Let her. Fuck it."

"We can't let you, Rev. Cinderfield. We need you far too much."

"I'm so tired of living with this guilt."

310

"You will do as you're told," he said. "Now, here. How about a little god juice, drained straight from His toe." Cinderfield hadn't seen his long black beard before and smoky red eyes. "Oh, God."

"Wrong zip code," the manager said. "Now, take a sip." He held up the syringe. Amber dripped from its stainless steel tip into his vein; spirit tripped into stainless steel heaven in vain. "Christ, it's really you."

"Andy Kaufman died, and I came home to the world. Now, don't you feel better? Bring his coat!" Cinderfield's vision warped from the good shit. All his worry drained away.

"I'm a pretender; I feel fucking awesome."

The stage manager grinned, and his smile slit up his face, touching each burning-coal eye. Two of his minions carried in a heavy overcoat woven of golden threads and lined with quarters hanging from chains. The jacket weighed him down to earth.

"I can bring him back," Cinderfield said. "It was a trick. A hoax. Any day, Kaufman is going to jump out of a coffin on *Letterman*."

"There is no coming back." He polished some of the change.

"I brought that bird back," Cinderfield said.

"You start agreeing with the people, and they will crucify you. It happened before, though it's been edited for content. A nice bedtime story. I warned that asshole, too."

"Who? Jesus?"

"Kennedy."

"Shit, man."

"Now, go on like a good boy," the stagehand said.

"Your soul," Rusty whispered. "Save your soul."

"It's not worth the trouble," the stagehand said.

"I'm your angel," Rusty said. "I can help you relieve the pain. Your vanity."

"Shut your fucking mouth, whore," the stagehand said. "Or shall I entertain you with a story about a scared little girl who hid the baby growing in her from her minister father who beat her until her bones ached? And she hid in the alley behind his church and pushed out her deepest sin and shame, but the child was born cold and blue—blue like the sky and cold like that winter day. Where did you bury it again?"

"It is Scratch," she said, reaching for her holy medal.

"WHERE?" he growled.

She whispered: "Above my mother's grave."

"And coyotes came in the night and dug up the shallow hole. You found the bloody swaddling cloth in the wood."

Rage grew ice down her eyes, coating her face in snow. Then, she fell back into the wall of the dressing room, taking down a cake shaped like a cross that had gone stale on the table. The stagehand polished his heavy jacket. The coins jingled and rattled. The crowd transitional petitioners cheered and feared from the showroom.

"Help this weak asshole," the stagehand said. Two of his minions, who appeared to Cinderfield squat and gray, demonic things not of nature, grabbed his arms and carried him out on stage, throwing him into the center of the amphitheater. Before he left, the stage manager leaned over and whispered to him almost below his hearing. "My caveat." Thousands of humans filled cement slabs circling the stage and cheered Cinderfield like a rock star. House lights switched on and shot bright lasers at Cinderfield. His jacket ignited in a fulgent spectral display that would convince any primitive mind of his divine status, as if God had reached down and shoved a burning sparkler up his ass. Cinderfield raised his arms, adoring the adulation. He

312

couldn't help it. Who could? And he had a mission. He'd do something with this power. A silver crucifix lowered behind him, and blue neon lights outlined the cross, glowing to match his contrived brilliance.

"My brothers and sisters. I am a fraud!" The crowd cried out, adoring the idol they had set on high in the heaven and down low on the stage floor. They loved him for not wanting their love. This validated him as their messiah.

"Reagan will burn the world. I have seen it. I have dreamed it. The wall of Berlin will grow a heart then stretch across Europe, the ocean, America. We are lost."

We are lost! The crowd chanted. Green bills floated down from the seats, littering the stage like a poisoned snow. Cinderfield had no idea where the money went to as long as someone got his hotel rooms, cigars and fresh whores. He had done this show at least twenty times across the country, even sharing a stage with Billy Graham. He told the Rev. he should forgive Larry Flint, the editor of *Hustler*, for the satirical article he wrote about him. Who would believe that shit, anyway? People needed a sense of humor.

Cinderfield found his silver flask, snug in his pocket. He knew it was probably a terrible idea to mix whiskey and the dope, and the self-destructive thought just encouraged him. He looked up and Rusty stood in the aisle way just out of sight of the audience. Her naked and heavy body glowed in the side glow. Written on her two tits that sagged like water bags, was his benediction: "You are worth saving." The stagehand stood just off stage and watched. His crimson eyes glowed like twin cigarette coals, burning through the dark, the flashing lights, searing into his flabby chest, through his heart. The crowd cheered and screamed.

"Shut the fuck up!" Cinderfield yelled. "Christ. You yell so much, you can't hear anything." The crowd shut up, waiting for his wisdom. He looked over again at Rusty and decided . . . for her tits. Why does a man ever do anything?

"Today, I will bring the performer Andy Kaufman back to life."

The crowd didn't cheer, though he held his hand up, expecting them to go wild with hysterics. They sat dead silent, so quiet, Cinderfield could hear the dead whisper. "I said, with the power found in me, I will bring the dead back to this life."

"Fuck that!" some male voice yelled from the audience.

"You don't believe me. I brought that sparrow to life. That's why you believe in me!" The stage manager shook his head. Cinderfield could read his genuine eyes. He recalled the words whispered to him before the show.

They only loved you when you denied their love. The moment you accept the power, they will tear you down and rip out your heart. That is America.

The crowd's jeers amplified, shunning him on the stage.

"You elevated me. You clothed me in robes of money and silver. We need our angel back."

They don't want the dead raised, you idiot. The people don't want their parents returned or friends brought back. Death is their relief. It's why they believe in heaven.

"I believe in hell," Cinderfield yelled. "I am the devil. I was. Believe in me. Love me. Need me! I will bring Andy Kaufman from the wormy earth. I will raise him back to this world and return him to the people. His time was not yet done. I want to give you his joy—" The crowds, his previous congregation, now turned, jeered and sneered him, drowning out his sermon. Some of the more offended left their seats and rushed the stage. Workmen had left toolboxes along the aisle, and in a fit of divine inspiration, the elected executioners grabbed the boxes and emptied their nails along with hammers. The stage manager directed to the crew that the heavy plastic crucifix be lowered to the stage, made accessible to the mob.

"It happened so fast," Cinderfield said.

"Nail up the pretender!" the stage manager yelled.

"Nail him up!" yelled some of the mob.

"Nail him up!" cried out Cinderfield, feeling the social mob pressure. They grabbed his arms and flattened him out on the glowing plastic cross. A bulky woman aimed the first nail into his palm and hammered it deep on the first blow. The nail missed Cinderfield's bones and pierced right through to the plastic cross. The next blow drove the nail in deep, and she moved to the other hand. At first, pain shot up his arm, and Cinderfield bit his lip to keep from crying out. He'd be crucified with dignity. Ahh, shit. He started to sob. She drove the nail into the other hand, this time cracking bone. "You've broken my hand," he said.

"I have not. That's not what that was." She hammered the spoke, and nausea overwhelmed Cinderfield. His head spun and he vomited down his pretty outfit. Some of the dope must still have been working, or he would have been driven mad by the agony. They left his feet, and the stage manager spoke into his walkie-talkie to the crew. The plastic cross elevated, carrying Cinderfield to his new place. The mob cheered. The nails dislodged some lighting, blowing a fuse, and white sparks blew from the side of the cross then rained down onto the stage. The crowd applauded, and Cinderfield grinned. Blood drained down his arms and pooled black on the stage. He still served his purpose. It had all gone exactly as it should have. This was America, and this was the modern version of a nativity play. Cinderfield blacked out.

When he awoke, Rusty stood on a ladder and worked a hammer to yank out the nail. His arms ached. The crowds had left. She still wore no clothing except her holy medal.

"I dreamed of Andy Kaufman," he said. "That's what started all this shit."

"What did he say?"

"He wouldn't stop laughing. The whole thing was funny as shit. He said I really played the crowd, one of the best bits ever. Genius."

"Let's get you to the hospital. We'll take the back way, hide in the alleyways. I know how to keep to the shadows."

"Was that a dream?"

"Let's get you a tetanus shot, darlin'."

Tolya survived and his congregation forgot him—always a new messiah, a nascent saint popping up from the drug dens or sewers of the city to lead the leaderless, to take them across the sand to the holy land. Tolya had sucked the last of the milk and honey from his teat, and he realized he'd been distracted from his true mission, lost in hubris, attention and all the sex with the crazed nymphomaniacs that queued up to be blessed by his cock. Tolya still had some money left and used his remaining influence and money to track down the last son of Andy Kaufman. He traced the baby out to a suburb of Philadelphia.

He moved slowly across the country, heading back home. The old actor lived along the tracks, sleeping in old shacks and eating at soup kitchens. No one recognized him. No one cared. Finally, he hiked the Amtrak highspeed corridor down from Boston to Philadelphia. He moved by an abandoned junkyard. Gaps had long since rusted through the fence, and no one tended to the garden of chrome and steel. The old monsters slumbered, dreaming of old days on the roads. People loved their cars more than they loved their pets, even their kids, and tended to the soulless machines with such time and care that any alien species would think the human race existed in a symbiotic relationship. Tolya laughed about the absurd idea until he saw Mr. Snowballs.

"Steal this ice cream truck, and every American kid will worship us," Cinderfield said. "He's possessed by one of my demons. Mr. Snowballs is his name." Rust concealed most of the van, though some white paint still clung onto the sides of the cabin. Much of the silver grillwork had fallen off the front, though he found most of it in the dirt and leaves. Chevrolet stamped the hood in chrome letters, and the bodywork swept back over the wheel rims. He got up inside the cabin and chased out a couple of raccoons that'd taken up residence in the freezer bays. The glass window on the serving shelf had long since shattered, but the frame still slid easy, once he'd dislodged the dirt. He even found a plain white uniform bunched up in the corner along with a suicide note:

Big C. Curled up inside the main freeze and went to sleep. Nice and cool.

"So, that's how this boat ended up in dry dock," Cinderfield commented. "Think someone will ever tell his story?"

"No one's going to tell ours," Tolya said. He started gutting the truck, working on it through the night until his hands bled. The scar tissue ached, but he'd gotten used to it and finally, he curled up and slept inside, listening to the electric train roar by on the track. He'd found himself a home, and soon he'd find his charge, searching Philadelphia and its suburbs. People talked, gossiped, and they'd certainly have noted a boy living with his grandparents.

So, his life went on. He dreamed of Shakespeare, of the family he'd lost until they no longer felt real. All that mattered was his charge now. If he ever felt the urge to forgive himself, the devil was always there to remind him of his sins. When he wasn't eating out of town soup country, reading at the library, he rebuilt the truck with parts he scrounged, sometimes taking odd jobs to cover the costs. He painted an obnoxious orange devil on the hood with eyes swollen like moons. No child would ever have the balls to buy ice cream from him.

At night, the wounds in his hands bled, and he bound them up in old newspaper. By day, he watched over the baby he'd saved and his friend. The baby had grown into a boy, Anthony, and Anthony had a friend, Cynthia. He followed him to school, keeping out of sight, watched over his classroom, recess, then hovered over him walking home. At night, he sat across the street eating stale Lucky Charms out of old boxes and watched the pristine house that belonged to Anthony's grandparents. At night, his grandfather always yelled at him before bed.

"He can survive it," Tolya said to Cinderfield. His cigarette coal burned red in the shadow of the tree, watching the bay window like a messed up Boo Radley. Anthony stood in plain view, blocking the television. His grandfather towered over him. He gripped his fists, binder under his arm, and raised his hands over the blond-headed boy. Grandmom sat on the couch, watching her Wheel of Fortune and ignoring her husband as he conducted paternal business. She'd grown so accustomed to his violence that she just tolerated it as background noise.

"Which one is worse?" Cinderfield asked. "Who is the

darker shade of shadow? The one that hurts the child or the one that is capable of ignoring it."

"Both must exist for evil to function," Tolya said. "Fuck 'em both."

The bellow of the grandfather's rage passed through the five rectangular plates of glass, hummed about the Japanese maple plants and bounced off the mulberry trees until it reached the sidewalk. Kids rode by on bicycles, driving without care up the drive and avoiding his Mr. Snowballs parked along the curve of the suburban avenue. He followed his routine, walking Oberon, using the dog as cover for his nocturnal spying. It played out like this at thrice a week, except over the last month as stresses increased at the old man's job, his voice had amplified, so much so, that neighbors shut their windows or returned from relaxing on their porches. Anthony's grandfather possessed a vocal quality that stabbed fear in all those who overheard him yelling, sending them back to days of helplessness, when adults easily overpowered.

Tolya watched the routine, knowing each moment.

"You're a screw-up, like your mother," the grandfather yelled. "I don't know why we didn't just give you up. You weren't worth a drop of milk from her teat. Useless. Frickin' waste of our energy."

Anthony had grown to seven years and possessed no words yet that he could use to counter his grandfather's rage.

"Pussy," said Cinderfield. "You should go in there and knock his ass down."

"Fucker deserves it," Tolya replied.

"Then why don't you?"

"Because the cops will find me," Tolya said, keeping his sense about him. He remembered the vigil he'd kept, all the years he'd spend watching this house, watching

Anthony grow up since he'd first seen him as an infant. He had known Anthony for a long time, though the boy never knew that the mad Russian was there in the shadows, protecting, keeping himself. He peddled ice cream in the summer, patrolling this section, then worked in the Turkey Hill packing factory in the winter, hiding his real name, his past. He kept quiet, didn't cause any trouble and nobody cared. "They put me back into that laughing farm, then who takes care of the boy? I break my promise, and no one takes care of Anthony."

"That shows foresight," Cinderfield said, then cackled. "Fucking tit." The old man slammed his fist against the windowsill, and the solid wood prevented a dent.

"And what do you have to say for yourself?"

The little kid was too terrified to speak; Tolya could see it in his gentle face, yet he had to, or the old man would rage more.

"I'm doing my best," the child said, and Tolya held his breath, hoping tonight's rant had ended.

"Fine, then," the grandfather said. "Let's pray then and go to sleep." Little Anthony held up his hands for his grandfather to hold so that he might pray. "Oh, Lord. Please teach my grandson to be different from the follies of his mother who left us—" He never finished praying; instead, he punched the boy in the face, hitting his temple. Anthony yelped, and the force of the blow knocked him into the wall. Grandmother turned off the television and started up the stairs for bed, leaving the little boy on the living room rug.

"And what are you going to do now, Mister Patience?" Cinderfield taunted. "You promised to protect him? You're failing!"

Tolya returned to his reclaimed ice cream truck and unlocked the back. He leapt up into its guts and emptied the contents of the deep freeze into a sack. "He'll be wound up," Tolya said, " and need to walk off the stress so he can sleep."

"I dig ya," Cinderfield said. "A cool treat on a hot night." Tolya wiped off the cartoon devil sucking on a cone that had been painted to the side of the wide truck then tossed the old shirt into the drive. Tolya walked back into the housing section, spinning the sack of bars, pops, ices and candy. The Russian watched from the street, standing behind a Mulberry bush. He waited for the living room light in Anthony's house to go off then crouched down behind the dirt. He kept to the shadows and always stayed to the old man's back. The retired Navy officer exited the house wearing a pair of khaki shorts and a Phillies shirt, sporting his navy blue cap. Tolya waited until he walked back, stepping in arrogance, assured in his complete ownership of the country around him. Tolya's heart thumped. He tasted bile rushing up his throat. Fireflies pulsed bright, and moths burned white in the moonlight on the clear night. A car turned down the drive, flooding the street with its high beams, and Tolya leapt with a tiger's ferocity, swung the bag of hardened ice cream sandwiches and cracked the sailor in the back of his skull.

"Chocolate or vanilla, motherfucker!" The deep freezer had cooled the ice cream into cement, and Tolya swung it around for another hit. The old man turned to defend himself and collapsed into an oak. He stumbled, falling into a yew bush. Tolya returned to the shadows while the man tried to collect himself. "You ever touch that boy again, and I'll stab your heart out with a waffle cone."

"Come out where I can see you," the man said, struggling with the evergreen fronds to get to his feet. Tolya didn't wait. He didn't have to. His message was delivered.

"I'll be watching, you shit. And go ahead and call the police. They catch me, and I'll tell them what I've seen."

"Who the hell do you think you are?"

"Anthony's devil and angel." He ran off into the night, heading for Mr. Snowballs.

Throughout the years, Tony kept a relationship up with the boy and his friend Cynthia, often volunteering or doing odd jobs at the theater where she eventually worked. He spoke to them of poetry, of the stage and the art he had loved so before tragedy possessed them all. He offered Anthony magnetic north where as his grandparents summoned him south, giving him another way to look in life.

He never spoke of Anthony's mother. It wasn't his place, and he couldn't suffer the shame.

"But you shall dwell in such shame," Cinderfield always reminded.

POWER OF FAITH

By night, Anthony and Cynthia sat vigil, mostly in the lounge. The chairs assaulted Anthony's spine. He tried nibbling on a tuna sandwich, but food swallowed like wet cement and locked his stomach after only a few bites. Cynthia sat with her knees folded. She couldn't even look at Tolya, and every stray noise—the sound of the intercom calling for a doctor or the tap of nurse's shoes like dropping tennis balls—caught her attention like a frightened and wary animal.

"Are you watching for angels?" Anthony asked.

"I don't believe in such things."

"You used to. Remember when I'd sneak up the street and climb the tree? We were ten. You'd be sitting in the window seat at midnight and watching for angels to fly to Earth. You were convinced that the reason no one saw them during the day was because they cloaked by night. If you kept a sharp enough eye, you might see one."

"I did."

Anthony sighed.

"I still can't believe all that about Tolya. He never told us."

"He bled. It wounded him."

The intercom called a code blue, and Anthony ran from the lounge, looked through the double doors' window and watched the team assemble, pushing a cart. They sped into another room, not Tolya's. He strolled back. "Someone else leaving the Earth," he said.

"How the hell can you be so cavalier about this?"

He shrugged. "What do you want me to do? Howl until my tongue falls off? What will it change?"

"You could fight for me, you selfish asshole."

"This, again." Anthony sighed. "I fought. I let them butcher me."

"You talk to me like I'm an idiot," Cynthia said. "I see what's happening. I'm watching the man I love ripped away from me, piece-by-piece. You're losing so much weight. Getting sicker. I'm watching you die, and you're so lost in it you can't think of anyone else but yourself . . . and fucking Andy Kaufman!"

"He could understand," Anthony said. "How can you understand? You're not facing this."

"Neither are you," she said. "You're just pretending it's not real."

He sighed. "Let me comfort you!" she said. "It might help you cope."

"There is no coping. I don't want to be angry."

"You are very angry."

"You don't see shit," he snapped. "Angry? I don't feel anything. Ice grew in my heart. It spread to my skin. Ice crystals stabbed my hands and organs and feet. I'm an ice angel, and my wings have cracked. A glacier grows over me, layer by damn layer. Comfort? I can't feel you."

"You probably wouldn't even notice if I was gone, would you?"

"I wouldn't know until you were gone."

"Asshole!"

She got up to leave, to run outside, get some air and maybe not come back—not that she had anywhere to go.

She'd ended any links to her past, sawed off all the roots. One great gale would push her over and pull her up from the dirt.

The gal entered the lounge. She dyed her hair magenta and dipped the ends in grape. Her breasts swelled through her heavy metal shirt, depicting the band Angel-Slayers. She looked so tiny and light, sans the weight and bulge of the fetus growing. Her blue jeans, torn at the knees and stained with brown paint, clung to her tiny legs. She wore shit-kicking boots to kick the shit out of someone.

"Probably never wanted to see me again," Manhattan said.

"You're here," Anthony said.

"She's here," Cynthia said. "Wonderful."

Manhattan rushed and hugged Anthony, nearly slamming him with the woolsack she carried over her shoulder. Paintbrushes sifted to the top of the bag, nearly dropping. She wrapped her arms around his shoulders, pulling him down to her five foot two height—even with the shit-kicking boots. "Hello, my angel. I've thought about you so much."

"Something's different," Anthony said. "You, umm . . . changed your hair."

"I did! Isn't it wild? It's like the *Rocky Horror Picture*." She modeled her hair. "Oh. Hi, Cynthia. Didn't see you."

"I'm sure you didn't." Cynthia stabbed at Anthony with a look that not even shit-kicking boots could kick off. Manhattan flinched then returned her attention to Anthony, whom she still had pulled to her.

Finally, she released him. "Young Ginsberg is with my mom. I named him Young Ginsberg, that way, even when he's old, he can still feel young."

"Damn brilliant," Anthony said.

325

"I'm sorry about Tolya. I saw it on the news, and I drove up. What's the word?"

"Tolya's going to be just fine," Cynthia said.

"He's unconcious," Anthony corrected. "No one knows if he'll come out of it."

Manhattan leaned into Anthony's ear and whispered: "Did you dig up Andy Kaufman's grave?"

"Yep."

"Fuck. That's hot."

He smirked. "That's what I was going for. Sexy grave-robber."

"And his body wasn't there?"

"Nope."

She giggled. "Fucking brilliant."

Cynthia sighed and got up, not guarding her irritation. "I'm going to see Tolya now," she said. "Remember Tolya. And he's going to be fine." She left the lounge and slipped out the back. They'd discovered a second stairwell downstairs that allowed them access to the room. The staff had grown accustomed to strangers being in the room since this had been an assault with a deadly weapon, so they ignored them. Anyway, he had no family, and the nurses felt sorry for the Russian geezer.

"Oy," Manhattan said. "She . . . doesn't like me."

"She's pissed at me," Anthony said.

"What did you do, besides get cancer and start dying?"

Her bluntness kicked him in the chest, but he needed it. At least she looked at him, but was it because she didn't understand or because she didn't care. He didn't know whether to trust her, and Anthony hadn't realized how much he'd been thinking about Manhattan until he saw her step into the lounge of the hospital where his friend slept dying. For a moment, he poured his vision over her, and she curled up her fists over her face, looking away in a frisson of innocence. "Shy." She hid like a child in tall grass.

Anthony realized he might be making her uncomfortable and changed the moment. "Want to go see him?"

"If I'm not in the way," she said. Manhattan took his hand. "Lead the way, Angel." He could feel her palm and fingers through the numbness, the nerve damage. Her hand chilled his skin, and he gripped it tight to warm her.

"Angels live forever," he said, walking her to the back entrance of the ICU. The staff conducted a shift change, passing orders, changing out nurses and doctors.

"I can hear the sick people," Manhattan said. "The ones who can't speak, trapped in their own heads. I died once. Overdosed."

Anthony desired to believe her, to give some evidence to a greater world beyond sight, an ethereal plane he longed to understand and find within reassurance. He sighed, thinking of the ever-black void, and he swallowed back on a petrified throat, nearly choking. He couldn't help but worry for himself. He longed to feel more, to know sensation—joy, pleasure, pain, loss. He hadn't known enough. Maybe there was still time.

They walked into the room. A nurse attended him, changing his IV bag, putting another O-negative. "He's going through too much blood," the nurse said. Mascara smeared her eyes, and her gray, tired face belonged to a zombie. "The surgeon wants to open him back up, but his vitals are too weak. There are no instructions on file, so, legally there's not much we can do."

"He looks peaceful," Manhattan said.

"He's woken up a few times," the nurse said. "He just did when the girl was in here."

"Did he sing an Al Jolson number?" Anthony asked. The nurse eyed him.

"Asked for someone called Rusty. Did he have a dog named that?"

"I think she was his priest," Anthony said.

"Right," she said. The nurse left the room.

"Where did Cynthia go?" Manhattan asked. She looked at the tiny body asleep in the bed, hardly strong enough to exist in this world or the next.

"This is Tolya's room?" a deep voice asked. Rusty stepped in, uncertain, afraid of disturbing. Her coat bulged from her hanging breasts, hardly contained by a wire bra. A floppy red wig hung half off her head, rolling over her forehead. She wobbled into the room. Light reflected off the crucifix charm she wore, and her spicy-sweet aroma reminded Anthony of church, of the incense they burn, the red sticky power. She possessed a certain reverence. "My Tolya," she said. She approached the bed and rubbed his cheeks.

His eyes opened. "I knew you'd come."

"Of course. I came as soon as I could." She kissed his forehead.

"My sins."

"Forgiven. Forgotten."

"Anthony. Such a fine, young man. I tried looking after him for Wilma. I wanted to take the dark seed into me. I deserve it."

"Sshh, now, my love."

"What is your real name, Rusty?"

She hesitated, then answered: "Mary Magdalena."

"I don't blame you," he said. "Will you walk with me to the shadow?"

"Yes, my love." And she kissed him goodnight.

A million years ago, a kind actor driving a truck to pay the bills spotted a woman walking in the parking lot of a highway rest island and gas station. He'd had a few drinks but he felt clear. Knives of ice slit the air. He had to get home.

"You need a lift?" he asked.

She bundled something precious to her chest, shielding it from the winds and freezing rain, wrapped in blankets.

"I'm too tired to care if you're a pervert," she said. "Yes." He helped her climb into the cab one-handed, and she bounced across the seat.

"Who is he?" she said, pointing at the passenger in the back of the cab.

"Just the devil—very misunderstood."

Cinderfield smoked his cigar, filling the cab with acrid smoke, and giggled.

"You need help with that bundle?" Tolya asked, starting the engine. The truck growled, and he put on the radio. "The Impossible Dream (The Quest)" played, and it brought tears to his face that tasted sweet.

"Not anymore," she said. "Just carrying a lot of loss now." She unfurled the bundle and revealed it empty.

Tolya drove to the onramp and into the darkness. He smiled, glad he didn't have to make the trip alone. "What's your name?"

"Umm . . . Wilma."

"I'm glad I finally found you."

They left the room to let the nurses prepare the body ready for transport to the morgue and stepped back into the lounge. Cynthia took off the wig and removed the stuffing and oversized bra.

"Shit," Manhattan said. "I knew she looked bad. It was

you? You guys do this a lot, don't you? Preachers and old whores."

"It's how we've survived. Took our strategy off Andy Kaufman."

"It was so obvious, too," Manhattan said. "But Tolya bought your shit."

"Because he wanted to believe it," Anthony preached. "That's the power of faith." He looked at Cynthia. "Where's the real Rusty? Do you know?"

"I did a search for her on the internet. It was in a police log; at least I think it was Rusty. She was found at the end of a box cutter."

CALM DOWN, LUCIFER, IT'S NOT YOUR MORNING STAR

The three of them returned to the hotel room that night and finished off the cider. Manhattan conned the old man at the liquor store into selling her a free bottle of Jameson's, hinting that after a few drinks, she'd be waiting in the alley.

I just love older men.

Cynthia refused a sip of the ill-gotten liquor. She'd choke on the bitter taste. So she drank the remaining ciders, anything to drown out their little comments, their flirts and motions that caused her to swing between dripping eyes and yanking at her hair. Manhattan sketched with charcoal stubs on a blank canvas book, and the drunker she got, the more she smeared the black down her face. She didn't dare look at the portrait, remembering how the macabre girl loved to draw people aging then dying. She got off on it, and Cynthia nearly sat between her, not for just personal reasons but because she didn't want her influencing Anthony. Cynthia loved him for his life; Manhattan lusted for his death.

The cider put Cynthia to sleep, and she woke up alone in the double bed. Anthony and Manhattan had fallen asleep above the covers still in their clothes. Cynthia washed her face, got dressed in an ankle-length skirt and black shirt then undressed Anthony to his boxers and got him under the covers. Her body required coffee. Her tongue dried out from the liquor and air.

She slipped out of the room, shut the door and took the lift to the lobby. The Best Western had not yet setup for breakfast and an out-of-order sign hung on the hot beverage vending machine. She looked for a night auditor and found a dude wearing a nametag that said "Max" typing on a laptop at the front desk.

"Is there fresh coffee?" she asked.

"Fresh fucking coffee?" Max asked. "I'm writing my masterpiece. Shit. Go fuck an owl." So she left him to his opus. The night before, she'd seen some shops down the street, so she decided to check them out for a café. Smaller towns in America always boasted coffee shops. The 1950's diner would offend her senses this early.

The sun hunted her as she walked the avenue—low in traffic—passing by a few row-homes and a muddy field, walking in the dirt and rubbish littering the ditch. She tilted down her vision, and the near-star hunted her, stalking her from down its blue fields, firing fulgent arrows into her skull. She rubbed her eyes, and pressure built behind her face. Ache radiated through her right temple and forehead. It blinded her, burning out her metal seals. The ache spread into her stomach, incorporating the remainder of feelings from Tolya: the way when people spread inside you, wearing you like a glove, and when they're gone, you deflate and flop, empty.

Cynthia marched to the first shop in a row of buildings that housed a shut candy maker, chemist and church. She stopped outside a convoluted shop and nearly bumped into a human-sized statue of liberty wearing a wreath of flowers and a nun's black habit. "Excuse me," she whispered, and darted up the steps to get out of the unrelenting, acid-pouring, eye-ripping sun.

Costume jewelry filled counters—fake jade, gems, painted metal. Children's magic tricks from the seventies lined the shelves along with *Star Trek* toys still in the original packaging. A giant pig bent over wearing dotted bloomers, exposing the creases of its giant pork ass. The store sat on various levels, connected by few steps here and there like a board game. Her head fired in pulses like a potato gun. Though she'd fled into shade, her eyes still seared red, and she could see her heart pump blood through stringy capillaries in her sight.

"You my delivery?" A chubby hippie came out from a back room. He chomped down on a quarter stogie, and brown tobacco juices dripped down his chin.

"Were you expecting a delivery?" Cynthia asked, still dizzy.

"I never try to expect anything." His voice whistled like an old-fashioned child's play ring.

She strolled through the store, up and down the levels and found shrines to various dead celebrities: temples to Elvis, Marilyn Monroe, Bob Hope, and yes, even Andy Kaufman. He had a few *Taxi* lunchboxes below his picture. Most of them from his youth and on stage. Bob Zmuda wore his monochromatic striped referee's shirt in some of them, while Andy wrestled various women, wearing his obnoxious long johns and black shorts. This was, after all, his hometown.

"Are you Jerry Garcia?" she asked.

"He's dead and buried, on a plate to the almighty."

"Shit."

"Have you lost something? A pet maybe? We get lots of those." He gestured to flyers stapled, tacked, glued and secured to the wall by the front door. Hundreds of

333

'Missing' signs piled in layers. The ones toward the top of the walls had faded. Many of the older ones had been hand-designed with photos attached. The windows of the past showed children playing with cats, dogs, birds, beloved owners walking their pets, both happy and alive. No one ever looked melancholy in photos with animals.

"What's this place called?"

"Heaven's Lost and Found."

"I've developed an allergy to the sun. It burns my eyes like acid. I need a hat or something to block it."

He came out from around the counter and led her to one of the shelves then lifted up a pair of glasses. A pair of kaleidoscopes were attached to the lenses. "This should help!" He held them up to her face so she could gaze through then twirled the lever, spinning the spectral madness and matrix. "Don't hide from the burning light. Embrace it."

"I'm not running from anything," Cynthia said.

"Of course not."

"How about that?" She pointed to a black, wide-brimmed riding hat. A plastic orchid hung from the ribbon that wrapped above the brim around the round top.

"That'll block the sun."

"That sounds ideal."

"Not so. Once you start, your eyes will start hurting forever. You'll have to live in a cave, and your skin will shrivel up and your hair will fall out and you'll be alone forever, running from the light."

"I can't take anymore light."

"I don't sell wishes. Just crap." He set the kaleidoscope glasses on the counter by the antique register.

"You should take down those signs. Most of those animals would have died decades ago."

"I like to live in hope." He chewed on the cigar. "They're not dead if they're alive in our heads."

"It's cruel to the families. I wouldn't be able to take it if I were them. I'd just forget and move on."

He sighed then started going through some mail.

"I'll take the hat."

"I shouldn't sell it to you, but if you insist."

He ran it up, and she handed him cash. "Don't blame me when you end up alone," he said.

"I'm sure you're a nice man."

The hippie shrugged then left the counter to arrange some boxes in the back. She eyed the funny glasses, considered it, not quite ready yet to abandon them. She couldn't buy them, not after all that. She went to leave, stole them off the counter then slipped out of the store, heading back to the hotel. The long brim of the hat served to block the sun, and her headache calmed.

Regional gossip drove the new trio from the Best Western. Newspaper reporters intruded on their privacy, and they knew the local police kept someone in the bar, watching their comings-and-goings.

"They're going to arrest us if we draw attention to the search," Anthony said. Cynthia agreed, and she hoped Manhattan would be less affectionate in public. She'd snapped a few times already for the stupidest things—something about her voice just tore up Cynthia's spine.

They slipped out the back entrance of the Best Western. The room had been in Tolya's name. Anthony had stopped caring about such things, especially with no long-term consequences. He was pretty sure, anyway, Tolya had been ahead with cash. He didn't care for debts, and as Anthony had just discovered, Tolya had been trying to pay him a life-debt for his mother all this time.

"Do you have a car?" Anthony asked.

"I took the bus," Manhattan said.

"There are shops on the back road," Cynthia informed. "Some small shops and a mall parking lot with a Barnes and Noble."

"We've got to figure this shit out," Anthony said. As they strolled in the ditch, passing by row homes, old garages, and the shop Cynthia had just visited, Anthony updated Manhattan to the progress. Walking stressed his body, and he struggled to hide the weakness overwhelming him. Since coming to Long Island, his body had changed, developed some kind of fault. Clockwork jumped its path and slowed, rubbing, gnawing on the metal teeth and gears. He'd compensate, push harder, forcing his legs to walk steady.

Manhattan walked next to him on the left. Her thighs worked her fishnet stockings, flexing tight in the tall Dr. Martens black shit-kickers. Her tits bulged through the concert T-shirt, and she kept checking her phone, probably talking to her mother who was taking care of her baby.

"I can draw him," Manhattan said. "I've got an eye for growing old."

"You mean dying," Cynthia said. Manhattan didn't respond. "We could go to the bookstore," Cynthia suggested, skulking behind them.

"I'll need to log in to find the most recent pictures of your dad."

"Still too public." Anthony coughed, working his lungs out from a pressure. Blood smeared his fingers, and he quickly wiped it off on his handkerchief then put it back into his brown suede vest pocket. As they walked, Manhattan slipped out her canvas from her wool bag and started going through previous sketches. She wasn't watching her step and stumbled over a rock. Anthony caught her arm, and she folded it around his, holding onto him. Anthony heard Cynthia sigh behind them, and he held back comment. It just wasn't her place. He made no promises to her. Why would she want to deny him this? You'd think a friend would want him to know all the love he could before . . .

Before.

He'd banish all thoughts of death and references to the inevitable from his mind. If he had to cogitate or speak of it, he'd call it, Before.

Cynthia, Manhattan, the world would be After.

But not Tolya.

As they approached the parking lot of the chain bookstore, Anthony spotted a quarry fenced off behind the buildings.

"Watch your phone," he said to Manhattan. "There should be free internet from the bookstore. We just need to find a place in range." Anthony led them both around the side of the chain link fence. Machinery growled and plowed in the background, somewhere down in the pit by the artificial lake. Warning signs advised against trespassing, but Anthony didn't give a damn. Someone had spray-painted over one of them:

Chain the land. You chain yourselves.

"Fucking A," Anthony said. They passed through a gap in the fence and scaled the sandy decline, using the pines for cover. The sun beat warm on the exposed boulders. Heavy equipment moved and pulverized on the other side of the quarry, pouring powdered pumice down a conveyor belt for construction as humans dug up, compiled and re-organized the raw flesh and life-blood of the earth. They walked several feet along the lake surface. Its shore led to deep and black waters, and a sign reaffirmed the rule about private property, no trespassing, and to beware of dangerous undertows in the lake—just in case someone decided to violate the first two commands and go for a swim. Beer cans littered around a dead fire pit. Manhattan sat in the sand, leaned against one of the smooth boulders and unpacked her paints, brushes, paper. She searched and studied pictures of Andy Kaufman on her phone. Anthony sat on the rock above her, casting shadows down on her paper, and Cynthia paced behind them.

"I'm getting sand in my shoes," Cynthia said. "I hate nature."

Anthony repressed the urge to fire back at her, tired of her bitching. He adjusted any anger in his voice and said calmly, "You can always go sit in the bookstore."

"It's fine." She sat on the rock next to him then flattened out her flowery skirt. She fidgeted with her tight collars and wrists in the hot clothing. The sun burned like an early summer day and beamed off the water. She maneuvered her new hat. He had no idea where she'd gotten it, just appearing at the hotel room with the gaudy headpiece.

"Think I've hit this shit," Manhattan said. "This is the last photo before he died, and I can see time in the edges of his eyes, aging his face, stealing his youth. She took out a box of pencils, sharpened one of them with a little kit and scratched with raven's talons at carrion. Andy's face materialized in the forest of graphite bamboo and brambles.

"I have to sketch it first, but I'm inspired."

"What is inspiring you?" Anthony asked.

"Shouldn't that be a mystery?" Cynthia said. "All artsy and shit."

Anthony grimaced, and Cynthia smirked.

"Does it feel cold inside you?" Manhattan scratched, finished her first sketch then turned the page and applied greater precision to the next edition.

"The hell do you want to know that for?" Cynthia asked.

"Inspiration. And . . . it's sexy."

"It's all right, Cynthia," Anthony said. "I try not to think about it."

"I'd be thinking about it all the time. It would fuck me up."

Anthony leaned back on the rock, and his shoulder rubbed along the back of Manhattan's head. She leaned into him, and her black hair draped down his limb. He held his fingers back from touching it, just at the edge of the dark locks. Manhattan sighed, perhaps feeling the energy from his fingers and labored on her sketch, advancing Andy Kaufman forward. She possessed acumen for the human form, the morphology and structure.

"I love how you draw people," he said.

"I learned how by drawing myself . . . naked."

Cynthia huffed. "I'm sure."

"Do you need any new models?" Anthony asked.

"If you don't mind me drawing the death in you."

"Anthony, can I talk to you?" Cynthia said.

"You are talking to me."

A boulder crashed across the lake in the yard, shattering and thundering over the plain. It shocked Anthony, surprised his heart and set the damaged organ racing, stealing his wind. Cynthia's eyes looked pissed, and Anthony knew she was going to declare her thoughts in private or in front of Manhattan. "Let's go for a walk," he said.

"Oh?" Manhattan asked, looking up from her work. "Be back soon?" She touched his leg through his khakis.

"Goddess," Cynthia said and led him into a thicket of evergreens. An old tire stuck out half-buried in the sand.

"We're close," he said.

"What the hell are we going to do with a picture? Put him on the back of a milk carton?"

"There's pattern recognition software online, services that help you find lost people. It's a pixel search. If she's as good as she says she is, and I think so, we can scan it in at a stationary store and pay one of the services to search the ocean of data."

Her eyes lit up. "Holy fuck."

Anthony nodded.

"I just don't like it, the way she keeps talking about death."

He sighed and leaned against the tree, feeling spent. The fire kept dying down into blue flame then burning bright again.

"Anthony? What's wrong? You're sweating." Cynthia placed the back of her hand against his forehead. "You're burning. Cold sweat."

"It's just been a hell of a trip."

"We should get you to a doctor."

"Up here? Fuck it." He tore back from her hand. "She's almost done. She's brilliant."

"You just met her!" She gripped her palms. "I'm trying very hard to stay calm. But you can be a real self-centered prick."

"I like her . . . a lot."

"I have been here the whole time. Not once have I left your side since we were kids. But I get it. I'm fat and clumsy. You were never into me because I'm a big chick."

"Don't do that."

"What?"

"Put words into my mouth. Make me defend myself. I

340

never saw you as fat. You were always my . . . " Fighting with her had weakened him, and his head inflated with helium. He stepped away out of their private thicket and returned to the boulder where he lied on the surface, allowing his head to turn and churn with impunity.

Manhattan composed her third sketch, this time drawing life-like blemish and nuance, almost like she printed a photograph with her hands and pencils.

"How do you do that?" he asked, ignoring his symptoms.

"It's easy. I'm just basing part of it on your face. You're growing old so fast. It's really hot."

"Oh, fuck that," Cynthia said, coming back. "I'm getting some goddamn coffee. You two have a lovely time together." She scaled the hill, heading for the bookstore. The machinery across the lake growled and worked, and she left his sight.

"What is her problem, anyway? She doesn't own you."

"It's been hard on her since I got sick, and she was close to Tolya," he said. She reached up and tugged on his arm, then Anthony followed her pull, sliding down next to her. He opened his arm, and she laid her shoulders in his embrace.

"You saved my life that night," she said. "The angel."

"I don't know if that was me."

"No," she said. "This isn't you. You're far more than this, too much for this world. You'll shed your flesh and ignite like a firebird, a phoenix. I used to dream of phoenixes when I was little in Arizona. I was afraid they'd fly into my window and burn me up." She kissed him, tasting his dry lips, and he feared she'd gag on his blood. "I can taste the death in you."

"That's freaky."

She dropped the canvas into the sand and broken

green glass from beer bottles. Her mouth moved over his, devouring, pressing her lips wide over his mouth. He joined the kiss, and she reached blindly for his hands, moving them down her shoulders. He squeezed her thin muscles, and she sang into his mouth.

"Fill me with it," she said. "We'll throw ourselves into the lake, naked, joining each other, the currents dragging us down into the black ink. Our lungs will explode as we struggle for breath, and we'll claw at each other's bodies, trying to kick and fight to the surface. But, too late."

Her darkness stunned him, but he ignored its implications, just needing her, not turning her into something she wasn't but just focusing on those elements of her personality that meshed with his own. That wasn't a fantasy. What did fantasy matter now?

Anthony's head throbbed down his left temple. He worked against his fatigue, the soreness moving up his back. His erection pressed against his trousers, and she grabbed it, felt it through the fabric. Manhattan pulled down her leggings and panties. "Just do it now," she said. "Murder me."

Cynthia climbed the hill, nearly running, struggling to get away as fast she could—away from that self-righteous ass and the little death whore. How could he not see? Manhattan nourished the darkest spirit in him. His cancer turned her on. Fine. He'd have his fun. She was going to rip him apart, and Anthony deserved it a little. Had she really put him up so high on an altar that she'd forgotten all the girls he'd dated in high school, flaunting them, then crying in her arms when he got hurt? She swore every time that it would be the last, but it just nourished hope in her.

He wouldn't see her before the end.

Walking through the parking lot, tears obscured her vision. A delivery truck nearly slammed into her, and she jogged ahead. She leaned against the brick wall behind a stone garbage can. A dark-haired woman reading Tolstoy, lying out on the pavement, smoked. "Hey. You got one?"

"Sure." She handed her up a cigarette then a light. Cynthia had smoked for a year before Anthony convinced her to stop; of course he's the one that got cancer. Cynthia stepped to the side of the building to hide her eruption. She leaned and slid down on the wall then cried into the sleeve of her dress. Silly little girl. Useless. Tolya had left. In the coma, during brief moments of awareness yet still sleeping, he spoke to a man called Cinderfield, the man who had been the televangelist, who had brought a sparrow back to life.

"Run away, little girl," Cinderfield said.

"I can't watch it happen, not again. I'm not strong."

"Not your fault," the devil said. She puffed on the cigarette. Her lungs warmed to the comfort of the tobacco—a silent urge filled again. "Aren't you afraid of getting cancer?"

"I don't give a fuck," she said. She checked her purse to see how much money she had leftover from the job. Some of it she'd deposited into her checking account, and she had her cash card.

"You're going to run far."

"I'm not leaving him. I just need some space."

"Sure you're not, young one. Just some time."

"Anyway, he has her."

Cinderfield cackled. "Because she's not going to abandon him to his sickness."

She put out the cigarette, flicked it into the parking lot, and turned the corner. "Hey. There a bus station here?"

"You need a ride?" the woman asked. "You look like

you need a ride. I can tell with people. You're all hollowed out."

"I'll be back," Cynthia said. She'd picked up a cell at Walmart, and she get it out to text him, but she'd wait until she was actually on the bus. She doubted the two would even notice her missing. "I don't abandon people."

ANGEL'S STORY

If enough people believe your story, does that make it real? When do you lose control of a story and it turns on you? His joke worked too well. His wish manifested and became his punishment.

Three months after their match, the gentle giant, Lawler, and Angel attended *The David Letterman Show*. He went to apologize, to lay his soul down for the world, for his audience and beg their forgiveness. Most of them were willing to forgive, to take Angel back into their hearts and restore the balance in their fantasy lives. Americans don't want the truth in their entertainment. In American movies, the hero must always win. The American defeats the alien invaders or the Nazis from across the sea. The underdog hero always endures, survives and comes out the winner. The American drone looks to Angel to fulfill this myth, to vicariously lift their lives from the vapid vagary of vocation. Angel promises such diversion, but he misleads them, offering that relief, the drug of fantasy but instead, throwing them, shattering their complacency. He can't help himself. It's not a malicious act. Angel is not cruel. He only seeks his own relief and wants people to know that they shouldn't take reality so seriously, that it is all an illusion, that fear is an illusion. People get too comfortable, and he thrives on making his audience cringe, to spin in turmoil. His concerts and performances are always a ride on a Coney Island rollercoaster.

Angel comes out, wearing a neck brace, and cautiously sits next to the giant. He looks terrified, a bullied victim. Dave shows a series of Angel's fake sneers, his antagonism, winning over the sympathy of the audience:

"I am a Hollywood star! Back to the kitchen where you belong. I am from Hollywood! I have brains!" Dave Letterman pours petrol onto the flames, stirring up a confrontation. Lawler plays his role, insulting Angel, insulting his manhood. Then he plays his part, slapping Angel, knocking him out of his chair. Angel falls over in an exercise of slapstick, rolls on the ground, playing up the force of the blow, then stands back up. The audience gasps. Dave tries to play it off, worried he's lost control. He never had it. Angel screams profanities at him on live late night television, slamming his hands on the desk. Their live apology backfires, turning into more conflict. America joins them in the chaos, mortified but captivated. Alas, the effect stimulates, jolts, but it's short lived. Once the shock ends, the audience is left with a poisoned feeling. They feel betrayed. Their mutual redemption and forgiveness has been thwarted.

Of course, it was all by design. Angel and the giant choreographed their fight, timing it for maximum effect. The two love each other as brothers and enjoy playing the crowd. The audience, however, isn't in on the joke, and that dark energy feeds back onto Andy.

"Lately, it's become a pretty popular thing to say that Andy Kaufman isn't funny anymore . . . Andy Kaufman should not be allowed on television, and that he should be banned from television." Dick Ebersol, one of the creators and gods of *Saturday Night Live*, calls a vote, a phone-in on whether Angel should be removed from the late night comedy show, the venue of his national birth—a bit recently belonging to a lobster named Larry, to determine whether it would be boiled. The audience turned against Angel but saved the lobster. Angel could boil. The world on the other side of the crystal screen turns against Angel, convicting him then nailing him up on a cross. They once loved Angel, enchanted by his innocence, his antics, but they've seen his anger, his face of rage. Enough anger invades their lives, and Angel no longer provides that escape. Angel never understood that aspect. To him, television, the stage, was a playroom, that secret spot in the woods, an imagined broadcasting station. Angel continues doing the occasional show, but after his television show is canceled, he loses even more appeal. The shooting star burns out. He's no longer funny. Was he ever funny? His old routines are tired. Everyone has seen him turn into Elvis, over and over again. All he has is his anger. Rage fills Andy, overpowering him, burning off his wings. He fills his life with acts of anger or humiliation, never satisfying the debt for both in himself. His energy turns dark, no longer controlled by his meditation, his mental powers that he has developed. The characters possessed their own life, spirit, and they overpowered him, abusing him. He lived in fear of the rage, and it burned him up, a fire burning sans control, devouring with impunity. It ate him up, growing inside of him—a malignancy of soul and mind. His transcendental meditation provides a balm with diminishing effects. Angel employs prostitutes several times a week, hiring the women to be what he needs, sometimes even playing dead for him while he mounts them, fulfilling his lust, needing the release. He loves them all but doesn't truly love any of them. He can love no woman or man, nor give of himself deeply to any—not until Lynne.

347

WE'RE ALL BROKEN

The number 10 bus pulled out of the Staples parking lot. Scanning Manhattan's artwork had taken the last hour, especially to get the level of pixilation required for the pattern recognition software to prove effective and reliable. She had worked fast, exacting the kind of detail a master artist created, while sitting partially naked by the quarry. She had taken a swim, even though he warned of undertows, and he joined her, not caring if the waters swept him under to the frigid depths.

I wish the currents would pull us under, freeze us fast, our bodies entwined forever. That would be so much easier. She'd said that while swimming, and it worried Anthony.

Aren't you staying?

Let's go get dry.

They boarded the bus sans destination, needing time to consider, time for the person location service to process the pictures and comb the images through the Internet. They said three to five business days, but Manhattan had emailed one of the service representatives and explained Anthony's precarious situation. An email had been quickly returned:

Tell the guy to hang in, and we'll make this a priority.

"There are nice people in the world," Anthony said.

"Don't count on it," she said, adjusting her outfit. Her dark hair dampened onto her shoulder, drying. She took out a plastic brush from her bag and worked it out. Her hair curled over her forehead, and she tied it back, appearing innocent, childlike; and Anthony felt stars burning in his stomach for her, growing hot.

This was moronic. Still, he needed it—a black rose growing out of his stomach, no matter the thorns that cut him when he gripped it. He reached out and took her hand, and she laid her head on his shoulder, curling up into him. The bus reached its first stop.

"I should go home soon, see my son."

Anthony had forgotten she had a child, attachments, or maybe he'd blocked it, resenting she had a life elsewhere, a life he had preserved a month and century ago. He'd never expected to see her again after that night on the cliff, never knew she'd grow in his chest like a juniper tree. She closed her dark eyes and slept.

"Can't you stay? Bring your son here?"

"Anthony . . . I'd love to. I need my mother's help with him. I'm not natural at being a mother."

"We can talk about it tonight." Pain drilled behind his eyes, getting worse from the motion of the boss. His morphine bottle ran low, and he swallowed two pills then chased it with some water from her bag. The headache had lingered for days, growing steady in intensity. He tasted blood in his mouth.

"You look ashen," she said. "Turns me on so much." She whispered this in his ear, and Anthony's heart accelerated. He considered this dark woman sitting next to him, lying on his shoulder, pulling him closer, yet he sensed the distance growing, too. She prepared herself for the future, yet he still had little conception of his own personal destinations, the places his body would travel and then his soul. He'd grow sleepy, soporific then perhaps sleep for a time, but he couldn't believe he wouldn't wake up. It wouldn't hurt, though.

Anthony pushed the thoughts from his mind. They'd be together forever. He fell in love, or at least he convinced himself that he had. He knew he had to do it fast. Humans spent years analyzing whether what they felt was real life, often running from it. Most people believed they had the time to waste, and Anthony couldn't help but resent them for their ignorance. Still, he didn't want to be bitter. He'd love in the time he had left. Manhattan obviously felt deeply for him, and with some initiation, she'd act on it. They couldn't be together, and he needed her in his life, especially now that Cynthia had run off, protecting herself. The hell with her. If she couldn't be here for Anthony right now at this time then he was better off without her. That was unkind, but he ached. Without his dear friend, the raw world terrified him. In Cynthia, he had sought out a friend most of the time, a protector at some and a mother in all, and she had accepted the position, enhanced it, and supported his views of her. He always suspected she possessed deeper feelings, emotions, a need for him, but their friendship prohibited any amorous views of her. He just didn't see her that way. It may have been different if he'd met Cynthia for the first time in recent years, but this was the relationship they had built. He couldn't be blamed for that, and he couldn't be forced into a love he didn't feel.

"I could love you," he said.

"Man. What is love?"

It shot him through the stomach. "I don't know. I just expected . . ."

"I can't figure this shit out," Manhattan said.

"It's not hard. You just love someone."

He held her shoulder, but she started supporting her own weight again. He sighed, suddenly feeling the loss that overtook him: to never take care of a wife or family. He felt the candle burning down, and he drowned in his own melted wax. He possessed an innate instinct, sensing the curtain falling.

"I don't feel emotions like normal people," she said.

"I don't believe that."

"That's because you're dying and see what you want to see."

"Don't we all do that?" He leaned his head against the bus window. The coach rocked; throwing him to and fro, tide coming in and out. He felt himself flowing away on the white surf of her eyes, losing himself to both his body and his soul. He didn't think he could withstand a broken heart and hold onto the last attachments of life. "It's all an illusion, and I want to tear it all down. I'm weak. My fingers will break off. It's the illusion that will make you run. I can feel it now. It's tangible, easy to shred. A delusion. I want to destroy the fucking thing."

"You'd rip the world apart," she said. "Chaos. Who would love anyone if we truly believed we were going to lose each other?"

"Isn't that what you're about? Anarchy? Chaos? Tearing assholes down?"

"I was before my son was born, and now I'm his mother."

He breathed out hard, enduring the vertigo. Scenes of shops, used car dealerships, churches and stores rolled by, reminding him of that night on the bus with Cynthia. They had traveled hundreds of miles far, yet, had never left the familiar place. His right temple ached.

"Does that mean you have to be alone?"

"It does. I have to do this on my own, to show myself I can." Her words set him to sail far out to sea, beyond the silver veil. The seizure hit fast. He suffered tremors, ignoring them, blocking them, but his body ripped into ribbons. Space blurred then blacked out. The force tore Anthony out of time, and he fell back into the seat, his eyes gazing upward. Elvis, wearing his Hawaiian white outfit with lay wreath necklace.

"Hey, man. Take it easy. You look like you're freaking out."

This is not the time, King.

"You ready, yet? We're holding the door open for you. Huunka Huunka Heaven."

Just a little more. I need to find him. To let him know I exist.

"Let who know?" Manhattan asked, not yet aware of his condition. "Andy Kaufman? Fuck me. Anthony? What's wrong?"

The seizure overtook him, and he shook in the seat. He felt Manhattan grab his arms, but she laughed. "It's so beautiful," he heard her say, before vanishing.

People panicked on the bus. The driver kept turning his head, distracted, and drove the coach right into a BMW making a left turn just at the transition of a yellow light. The bus slammed forward and threw its girth at an angle, tossing Manhattan out of the seat.

"Wild, man," Elvis said above. "Earthbound dreams and wild insanity."

Cynthia's coach drove straight through New Jersey, following I-95 and stopping in Bristol. Her father lived in an apartment here on Mill Street, working as a security consultant for a warehouse company and living off his police pension. She kept his number in her cell for emergencies but had never called it once.

The bus pulled up in a parking lot by the onramp for Business Route One and dropped off its passengers. A garden center displayed marble statues in the lot of all sizes, shapes, species—all in stasis, trapped forever, never moving. She envied the stone ones.

She held the cell in her hand with her father's number up and considered her options. There had been no time for the consideration of living. Death held highest priority. She'd sacrificed everything in her life to save Anthony—a futile battle, probably—and it kicked her in the chest. She nearly hunched over and held back her sobs. She just needed time, some rest, distance to clear her head. Anthony didn't need her, anyway. He had his Manhattan. She'd been replaced, upgraded, deleted, and she didn't want to interfere.

She should have stayed. She was going to rip Anthony apart. Cynthia knew the type—the fleeting woman in black. She had no strength to handle him. She'd run. She'd run to Anthony, from her son, and soon she'd run back, or do something flakey, like meet some dude online then move out to live with him in California, promising to send back money for her son who had now been transferred without regard or consent to her mother's care.

Cynthia just needed a place to crash for a bit until she figured her shit out. She'd always wanted to go back to school, maybe write another play, try her hand at professional acting. Beyond Anthony, she had a world of potential; and being so far from him clawed into her stomach. She couldn't see him, though. Shit. She just needed some time to figure this out.

And she bitched about how Manhattan was going to leave him. But what the hell did the Goddess expect? No one dealt with their mortality. People didn't confront cancer. She knew even Anthony had denied it. The moment you accepted the inevitable end of your own consciousness you'd go insane.

Clouds moved in, and rain spit. She sighed; standing amongst the statue gardens then dialed her father. She let it ring.

"This is Dave."

"Daddy?"

At the same time she phoned him, another call beeped over the line. She ignored it, afraid of hanging up by accident on her father and setting them off on another long silence. She forgot entirely about the phone call, and the caller left a message on her voice mail. The charge on her phone died.

Anthony woke on the cot in a generic and ubiquitous stall in a generic emergency room in a ubiquitous hospital. The raw reek of paint burned his nose, and buzz saws screeched in the nearby ward. When he lifted his arms or legs, checking his limbs, gravity held tighter. Water filled the fish tank of his head. A filthy grey curtain hung between him and the stalls on either side, but the front of his private hole had been left open for nurses to watch him from the desk. He spotted a doctor in a checkered shirt writing on a chart, yawning and rubbing his sleepy eyes. He'd probably been on call the last few nights, a family at home, young children, a life. Clones of this doctor worked in clones of this hospital across the country, and Anthony had been subject to the reluctant care of this physician for most of his cancer patient career. Anthony's mouth had filled with cotton. An IV hung from his arm and ran up to a pump that pushed fluids and medicines into his system.

The icy saline froze the sensitive inner flesh of his arm, and he shivered.

"No," he yelled. "No. Not yet!" A nurse raced over from the desk: a large African American with a large busy and maternal aspect. He recognized this also as part of the standard hospital setup, customary staff, as if the whole place had been built from a kit and the personnel cloned over and over.

"What's the matter, honey?"

"This isn't what I wanted." His head cracked, and he rubbed his temple.

"EMTs brought you in a few hours ago, after you had a seizure. You caused a bus accident. I don't know why they hire people who can't drive. My husband drove a bus for twenty years—and never one accident."

"I had a friend." Anthony's heart dropped when he didn't see her waiting. She had to have run.

"The girl all in black like a funeral director?"

"Yep."

"I'll go tell her she can come back."

Anthony relaxed onto the cot and lifted his heavy arms to adjust his pillows, trying to support his neck better. A knot in the muscle above his shoulder pinched him, probably from just being dropped and left in this position like a fallen ragdoll.

He waited, and finally the curtain parted. Relieved, he looked to Manhattan. A fat man wearing a white beard and turban raised his fists and played with his eye patch.

"You cheap piece of shit!" he yelled, loud enough so the denizens of the ER heard his ire. "You die on my bus? I lose my job now. I have six kids to feed and two wives."

At first, he just stunned Anthony into silence. He reminded Anthony of a goofy pirate from some kid's show.

"Dude. What the hell do you want from me? It's not like I planned it."

"And now the bank will come and take my shitty house. Shit. Shit. Where are my eight kids going to sleep? I feed them what? Rat shit from the streets? You try to feed rat shit to my children? Fuck you!"

"You're one of my doctors, right?"

His nurse joined them and admonished him with her eyes. "Sir. You are going to have to keep it down."

"I'll keep down his fat ass!" the pirate yelled. Something felt off about him. He yelled in fury, but his eyes studied Anthony, especially his face. His tone felt forced, and he just sounded too absurd to be serious. Anthony giggled and sucked on his upper lip. Light flashed in the pirate's eyes. "Candy striper!" he yelled at the nurse. "I drove that bus, and this young shit-fart tried to kill me. Now I take my ten kids, and we go live in his shithole."

"I don't know who you are, but you are not the driver. He came in for minor stitches and went home an hour ago."

"Fucking fart-ass shit! This is a Medicare conspiracy! Fuck y'all. I am out of here."

"I'm getting security . . . Jerry? Jerry's my son. A quarterback. He's going to throw your sorry butt out of here."

"I'm going to sue all of you for malpractice and sexual harassment!"

The nurse's son, Anthony guessed, a bulky dude wearing a standard blue guard's outfit, came over and imposed himself between the bed and the imposter driver.

"You don't throw me out of here. I have you fired, bum sucker!"

The guard grabbed him by the shoulder, but the pirate

didn't struggle. Something seemed so familiar about the performance. The pirate glanced one more time at Anthony, and he swore he sighed. Then Jerry dragged him out of the hospital as he kicked and screamed and threw fake punches like a pantomime boxer.

"Are you all right, honey?" she asked.

Anthony stifled his giggling. "What was that all about?"

"Just a loon probably off his meds looking for attention."

"He was looking for something."

She closed the side of the curtain, blocking off light from hurting Anthony's eyes. "I'm going to get you some tea to calm us both down. I hate working this shift. Oh. Your friend is here." She left, and Manhattan took her place. She sank into her body, and in the raw light of the ward, Anthony spotted hoary strands growing out of her black hair that had been partially dyed. She carried her woolsack.

"You okay, babe?" she asked. "You scared the fuck out of me. Turned me on a bit. I know. I'm fucked in the head."

"I thought maybe you'd be running," he said. "After that."

"You crashed a bus, Anthony. It was awesome." A bruise swelled on her cheek.

"Shit. Did I cause that?"

"The crash caused that. But I made sure they took you to the hospital. I'm sure your friend Cynthia would be glad."

"She's not here," Anthony said. "I doubted she would be."

The nurse returned, slipping through the shut curtains. "Don't mean to be interrupting time with you and your girlfriend." Manhattan didn't correct the nurse. Anthony grinned like an idiot, a chump.

"Hello. I'm Doctor Hanson," a lanky doctor said, stepping into the cubicle. "It's good to see you awake. You were a mess when the EMTs brought you in."

"What will it be like, Doctor? Will it be an ocean of darkness? Will I even care?"

He referred to his chart, ignoring Anthony and laughed shyly at the assertive questions that this ER doctor probably had small desire to answer or even cogitate upon, at least not today. Got to get out of this fucking ER. "You weren't talking when you came in, and we had to call Penn to get your records. Some good doctors there. Your oncologist is Doctor McKenna?"

"I suppose he still is."

"When's the last time you had a follow up? Are you undergoing chemo, radiation?"

"A road trip to find Andy Kaufman," Anthony said.

"The *Taxi* guy?"

"I don't know if my oncologist drives a taxi. Is that the sort of thing that oncologists do in their free time?"

"What free time?" the doctor asked. "So, when's the last time you had any kind of imaging done?"

"A fortuneteller read me in a crystal ball recently."

"I'm going to order a CT scan," the doctor said. "Are you allergic to contrast?"

"I contrast reality constantly."

He scribbled something down in a manila folder. "We'll get you right up for that. In the mean time, can I do anything for you? Have the cafeteria send you up a tray?"

"Are you hungry?" he asked Manhattan.

"Cat's blood, please."

"Tuna sandwich. Okay. Sit tight." The doctor walked out on his Italian leather loafers.

"He wants to dump me so bad," Anthony said. "I'm his worst nightmare handling the ER today."

"He did look like a deer in headlights," she said. "Oh. Do you have an email for the pattern recognition people?"

"I don't have a working phone," he said, a bit perplexed.

"Well let me get it anyway, just in case. We can always find a café with computers or the library."

"I do have a Gmail account I don't often use. I'll write it down for you." He found a napkin, and she handed him a pen from her bag.

"So, you're staying? I thought you'd be freaked out."

"I think I'm going to stick around. You're worth fighting for."

She leaned over the bed and kissed him. Her lips tasted of cotton candy—and he had visions of walking fairgrounds with her, holding her arm, taking the rides; and a dark nebulous cloud lingering on the horizon, moving rain over the fair.

"You'll . . . stay?"

"Of course," she said, smiling, her dark hair falling over her eyes. "I'm going to go try to bum a cigarette off one of the nurses. I'll be back." She kissed his hand.

"They might take me back for the CT scan. Did you eat? I don't even know what time it is."

She slipped away, closed the curtain behind him. He waited, listening to the drone of televisions in other cubicles but not turning on his own. A cafeteria worker brought up a tray—a tuna sandwich wrapped in plastic with a diet ginger ale. He sipped at the soda, spitting at the faux-sweet flavor. Finally, they came back to get him for his CT scan—a process he knew well. In a frigid room, kin to winter, they carried him over to the table that slid through the hoop. All through the spinning scan, he

359

convinced himself Manhattan was coming back. She'd be there waiting.

The nurses had changed shift when he came back.

"Is my friend waiting outside?"

"Who is your friend?" said a blond male nurse.

Anthony described Manhattan—the basics, black hair, outfit, the woolsack.

"It may not have been her, but I think I saw her trying to get a ride out on Route 1 when I pulled up to the hospital. I may be wrong. Dude. Looks like someone just kicked you in the ribs. It probably wasn't her."

"No," Anthony said. "That was her."

THE ITCH IS THE BITCH

A certain peace comes with knowing. It's when you don't know, when you're being tormented with promises of life, of time, of living, that aches and drills and burns you. Waiting tortures. Anthony lived each day sans the awareness he required to plan. How could he start anything of duration, not knowing if he was really going to be able to finish it?

The ER doctors admitted him; of course they did. They weren't letting him back out onto the street, and Anthony didn't fight it, at least for the night. He had nowhere else to go, and at least it was a roof over his head and a couple of meals, even if they were being shoved up his ass through tubes.

"I'm Doctor Kahn, one of the oncologists here at Saint Mary's."

"Is that what this hospital is called? No one told me. I just woke up downstairs. Is all this really necessary?" He pointed at the tubes and bags hanging from the IV pole. Pain pierced behind his eyes, but his doctor had ordered him morphine.

"Are you in pain?"

"I can deal with it."

"We do have special hospice service. I can order you a morphine pump."

Anthony clenched the side of the bed; the plastic railing that secured it. "Don't be so god damn dramatic."

"We have several options to make you more comfortable."

"What the fuck is happening?"

"I have reviewed your scans from earlier this afternoon and the radiologist concurs. You've been having headaches? The grand mal earlier?" The light gleamed off his bald head, and he ran his fingers through his black beard, clearing out crumbs, perhaps from a blueberry muffin.

"Quit covering your ass and tell me."

"Your malignancies have metastasized to your central nervous system. You have a tumor on your frontal lobe."

Anthony never quite understood the consequences of his condition until that moment. He'd always had time, which he worried he'd wasted, and he didn't quite comprehend the science; however, he realized the oncologist's tone, the way he kept justifying his diagnosis.

"I'd like to consult with a neurosurgeon. We have some of the best in New York. With surgery and an aggressive energy therapy, I believe we could extend your life."

"How long?"

"In these cases, there are conditions unique such as your age, and it depends on how deep the tumor has grown into your frontal lobe. We won't know until we get in there—"

"And start cutting?"

The doctor folded his leg and activated the screen on his tablet. His leather loafers gleamed as bright as his bald head. They'd put Anthony in a double room like most of the rooms in the ward, but he had the place to himself. By the window, an empty bed, fully made with covers, waited to take a patient. He enjoyed the peace.

"Of course we can contact your case oncologist, get his recommendation, but I think you have an excellent chance of—"

"No."

"Beg your pardon?"

"Go spin your bullshit elsewhere like some carnival barker," Anthony said. "I've lost every person I've ever loved, even the day I was born. I've . . . had . . . enough."

"I think it's too soon."

"Fuck it."

The good doctor and stranger got up from the chair. His shoes—new and not broken-in—stretched and creaked as he turned his foot. "We can discuss this tomorrow. Please ring the nurses if you require anything. I can write you something to help you sleep."

"When you're dying, you run towards the fire; when you're watching someone die, you run away from it."

He slipped out of the room on brand new leather shoes, and because he wore them on the late shift, to the hospital, on the night when he told Anthony he was going to leave this world, he detested the doctor.

The doctor evaporated from the room, passed into the stream. The stream would go on. He left Anthony alone in his silence, in the dim yellow light from the flat lamp hanging over the hospital bed.

The stream would go on.

Tiny Kimmie—so tiny she nearly didn't reach the face of the burning machine—sat in the lounge, spreading out her coloring books and crayons. Her black crayon had nearly worn to a stub, and she peeled back the paper and pinched it with her fingers, maneuvering it into the lines of the horse. She loved to color, animating the outlines, the hints and impressions of animals, to life. She didn't know if she wanted to be an artist or a veterinarian when she grew up—if she grew up. Mom promised her all the time she'd grow up, and Kimmie hadn't doubted it until her mother said she was going to pray all the time.

Freaking the poor kid out.

Her stomach squeezed and ached. She couldn't even swallow ice cream, but at least the radiation felt better than the awful chemo. She threw up for days; and Kimmie wouldn't cry. She refused.

"Is that a walrus?" the angel asked. His face glimmered white in the faint light of the lounge by night. Sometimes the nurses came to smoke here after midnight, and Kimmie hid behind the couch.

Tonight, Kimmie had hurt so bad in her stomach, that she tried praying like her mother. Usually when she went to Mass, she told stories to herself in her head while everyone else prayed on their knees. Now she tried praying, too, because the medicine the doctors gave her didn't help. Finally, it released, and she disconnected herself from the tubes—having learned how from watching the nurses—and snuck out of her room to draw. She hated being in bed all the time. She'd spent the summer in bed while her friends played.

The angel sat down on the floor with her. "I like your robes," she said.

"They're hospital linen tied around my neck."

"Nope. They're white robes like silk. And your face is beautiful."

"Talcum powder."

"No. No. The touch of God."

"Sure. The touch of God."

"And this is a horse," she said, filling in the neck with the black.

"My apologies. I really thought it was a walrus," the angel said. "Why are you making it all black?"

"Cause that's what's inside."

"Inside you?"

"And the world. The sun."

"I see," the angel said. "May I help a bit? I do love purple."

"Yeah. You can add purple to the hair." The angel found the violet crayon and stroked curls along the neck of the walrus-horse.

"Do you have an angel name?" she asked, joining him in the strokes.

"Anthony."

"That's not a proper name for an angel."

"Oh, yes?" he said, moving to color in the tail. "Let's give it eyes on its bum."

Kimmie giggled. "No. Your name needs to be . . . umm."

"Tell me before I go?"

"You have to go? Don't go!" She grabbed his arm.

"I felt that way, too. I didn't want to go home. You never want to go home when you're having a good time."

"Yeah, but I'm glad you came to see me. I'm very sick. I might die. My grandfather got cancer and it made him really tired. Then he went to sleep."

"Can I ask you something?" he said.

"I guess."

"Are you happy you're here, even though you might have to go home soon?"

She considered this for a bit, then she switched her black crayon to blue. "Blue's much better now, I think. I feel like blue. Like the sea. And, yeah. I'm happy for my life."

"I am too. Now I got to find my dad."

"Angels have dads?"

"Yep. Jewish ones."

"I told that Doctor Zmudea to go fuck his own ass with cactus," said Anthony's new roomie.

Anthony listened from bed, riding out another migraine. The pain split down his forehead, into his eyes, and Elvis sat on the edge of his bed, just watching. *Not yet. I have something to do.*

"I said, and if some of your other rich asshole doctor friends come along, make sure to go fuck yourself with cacti. See that? I made it plural."

The nurse holding the enema bag sighed. "I'll go call the doctor."

"Please pass along my message, kindly. Thank you, sweet tush."

She huffed and slipped out the door. The new rubber of her shoes squeaked like mouse farts. Anthony snickered in bed, trying to keep his joviality from the attention of the nurse. She'd been late all day with his meds, snapped at one of the other nurses then complained that her husband's Porsche needed to go back to the dealer.

"Hey, brother," Mr. Cactus said. "Didn't see you there." A bandage was wrapped tight around his foot. His brown beard grew like ancient oaks in northeast forests, wrapping him in a tight bark. So far, he had no visitors, no phone calls, and he'd bitched for an hour about the coffee.

"It's cool," Anthony said. "I didn't see me there. I thought I was haunting this place."

"Haunting this place. Might be so. Might be. That's good. Love it. Last roommate I had broke down and screamed at night. Then he thought Jesus was coming to save him. After three days of that, I started seeing Jesus, too, and I'm an atheist."

"Why are you in?" Anthony asked.

"Fast women and slow drinking."

"Shit."

His roomie fiddled with the television remote wired to the side of his hospital bed. Carts rolled down the hall, rattling on the tiles. Phones rang at the front desk. Life dripped through the cracks like leaky pipes. "Nah. They're cutting pieces off of me. Shit. I don't eat sugar. Never could stand the sweet stuff. But my blood still can't take it. Fucking McDonald's. Fast food. Can't get away from it. Know what I think?"

His silver hair fell over his forehead, and he looked through Anthony with hollow eyes, like a trick painting in an old house where the murderer stares out through a portrait at his guests and intended victims.

"Fast food is shit?"

"Aliens. Hungry aliens. They ate up all the food on their planet, and now they're fattening up the Earth. Makes sense, doesn't it?"

"It's the most fucking logical thing I've heard all my life," Anthony said. His head had begun to lighten, and the pain meds raised him to a high. Feathers grew and flapped in his skull.

"Give it about twenty years. They're going to fly their flying saucers down on the planet with huge nets to sweep up all the lazy-computer-game-playing fat asses. There's going to be a culling."

"All so clear now," Anthony said.

"So, you're dying?"

"Guess so."

"Sooner than the rest of us then?" he said. "I'm David."

"So they tell me. I still don'tbelieve it, but it's getting closer."

"You make peace with it, yet?" He sipped from a plastic coffee cup then set it back on his tray.

"That's just a lot of shit cancer patients tell the people around them to calm their asses. So they won't die alone. Really. I can't figure it out. I'm not equipped for it. How can there be a world without me in it? And then the world begins to melt. The walls flow into water. I pour into sand. I'm going mad."

"Shit, man. Let's break out of this place and get a drink."

"Could I actually use your phone for a moment, check my email? I saw it on your table last night."

"Don't got internet," David said. "Aliens use it to infiltrate our brains."

"Are you a lunatic?"

"Nah. I just like freaking people out with that shit."

Anthony grinned. "I'm waiting on an email that will tell me if my father is still alive, organized by a morbid chick who fucked the death in me then abandoned me."

"Sounds hot."

"Man."

Dave laughed. "All right. All right. I'll wait until you're on more morphine to ask for details about the sex."

"Dave, are you a dirty old man?"

"Yes. Yes, sir, I am. Very proud. Very proud."

Patient ringers sang and rang at the nurse desk. The night shift came on duty. Night fell, and in the night, the patients felt death closer. Life drained from the hospital, leaving a vacuum. Sans the sounds of heartbeats and blood rushing, the warmth of their bodies, the motion of the applications of treatments and diagnostics, the hospital settled into the land, into old time, and the silence exposed the sound of their own sicknesses: the wheezing, coughing, groans of pain, yells of the demented old, returned to childhood, lost and afraid with no understanding of their environment or why these strange people pierced them with needles. No one slept in hospitals. You stayed up with your suffering and longed for the comfort of God. Dave scratched his fractured foot, poking at the bandages. "The itch is a bitch," he said.

"It drives me insane," Anthony said. "My body itches. I need to keep scratching. I'm not tired of life yet."

"Itch is a bitch."

"Itch is a bitch."

"The front desk should have a computer you can use to check your email. They won't let you use it, though. I have a plan."

"This sounds damn dangerous, Sundance."

He thrummed his nose and smiled. Then he got his crutches from the side of the bed, unplugged the IV from his arm, and pulled himself out of bed. "Be ready to move when I do. It'll be a short window."

"Let's do this, baby. Let's dance!"

David crept on his crutches, dragging his foot, careful not to put weight on it. Soon as he hit the open hall, he yelled:

"There's a dirty old man in here with me! And he's touching me in bad, bad places." He had to yell a few more times, and Anthony stepped to the threshold of the room, watching as the few nurses on duty came running from their various duties. One had been smoking in the lounge, and the other was going through patients' rooms with a cart to check vitals—as was the nightly routine.

"Now what is the problem, Mr. Finnegan?" A nurse spoke with a Dominican accent. She wore a flowery uniform and a pair of blue scrubs.

"I told you . . . my roommate is a dirty, dirty fiend! He's not even that cute, and he talks about doing diabolic and demented things with roosters. I hate roosters! They bring me out in hives."

"Oh, Lordy," she said. "We got'anodder one. Let's get you back to bed." The other nurse watched, and he threw a fight, smacking at the air, trying to wrestle an imaginary opponent. Anthony slipped out behind them as he turned their backs, drawing away their views. Anthony fought his laughter, breathing hard. His head shot with pain when he walked, and he made it to the nurses' desk and sat at the terminal. Someone had already logged into the Internet and played online poker. She was down about three hundred dollars. He opened the browser, finding his email.

"Cynthia" was his password.

The email from the Missing Person's company was buried in six months' worth of spam and dating site offers. Also, he recognized an email from his grandmother's account. The subject read: "Anthony Please". It had been posted three weeks ago. He'd read it later. He didn't want to suffer the loss to his energy and morale. For a moment, Cynthia's absence pinched his stomach. He pushed the thoughts away, but her vacuum gnawed on him.

The itch is a bitch.

Somewhere out in the hall, Dave yelled again, almost answering the chant: "The itch is a bitch!"

"The itch is the bitch," Anthony whispered, and read the screen:

Dear Customer 5204. After an exhaustive search on our servers, we have identified several potential subjects that were above a 60 percent match to the approximation you scanned us and the photos of the subject's youth. Because of the celebrity status of the subject, we received many false positives from before his death. However, our researchers have acquired three images posted in the last two months that match above our required level. These images and their associated web addresses are attached to this email.

He ignored the rest of the long email, the disclaimers and pleasantries, the offer to take a survey, and clicked on the links. Dave had finally run out of material, and the nurses had threatened to call Big Joe.

"Who the fuck is Big Joe?" Dave yelled out. "He a dirty old man, too? This hospital is filled with god damn dirty old men!"

"Dave. You magnificent son of a bitch. The bitch itches."

The first two pictures looked like the sketches Manhattan completed, but they lacked the twinkle. One was a cop in Alaska . . . marked as "last whereabouts unknown, presumed dead". The second picture showed a college professor who had written some book on whales. It couldn't be Andy Kaufman. He hesitated the cursor over the last link, knowing they had no leads or resources beyond this. The trail would die—and so would he.

"Hey! What are you doing over there?" The other nurse spotted him at the desk. He clicked on the link, throwing all hope at the screen, and the Internet slowed. The link cycle, trying to open. The nurse approached. "Get away from there! That isn't for patients."

"Elvis damn it!"

He hit the reload button, and finally the link opened, revealing a familiar face, a twinkle, a growl, almost perfect to the drawing. He recognized the face, the chin, the eyes, their color and hair. The quick scan of the history looked appropriate. His background vanished a few years ago. No previous references. It was a profile shot from some sort of production, a play produced in nearby Rustytown, New York. That just couldn't be a real place—sounded like the name some hack author would make up on the spot, panicking and hoping it sounded witty. The name of the play was:

WARHOL TRAPPED IN BOOB-TUBE.

What the hell was that? Rusty Town Community Playhouse.

The nurse turned off the monitor. "You can go back to your room now. You both probably think you're pretty clever."

"A lot smarter than you," Anthony said, getting up. "And you suck at poker. I doubt that's something you're supposed to be doing at work—you know, while your patients die. Not the best bet."

"None of your business."

He shrugged and walked away from the desk. A patient sounded his call alarm, only one, a single light flashing at the desk. The blonde nurse ignored it, wasn't even disturbed by this cry for help. Fucking medical staff.

Anthony tried to ignore it, but as he walked to his room down the empty hospital corridor, counting the wiry telemetry antennae sprouting from the ceiling but growing no foil leaves.

He passed an empty room three doors down. At least when he had gone to the front desk, the room had held no patients. A voice, a breeze through a scarecrow's mouth, called out from through the flooded aphotic depths, harboring no light, the bottom of the ocean filling the chamber:

"Help me."

"I'll get one of the nurses," Anthony said into the room, hesitating at the edge of the portal, fearing the sharp shadows slithering at the edge of the doorway.

"Now. You! The nurses won't answer. You hear me." His voice rattled in a bag of autumn leaves. Anthony swore he heard the soft tones of a piano playing, perhaps a radio. "Would you abandon me?"

He sighed. Pain pierced his head, and nausea turned his stomach. He'd just go in and see what the guy needed. The recent revelation of the search played in his head as he worked the permutations. Could Andy Kaufman really be alive? He'd never really believed it or that Andy was probably his father. That had been for Cynthia, for something to do, to occupy his time. He stepped into the room, crossing the boundary. Pressure hit him, and he nearly toppled over, catching himself onto a hospital bed without its covers. A curtain stretched around the other bed, concealing its occupant.

"I'm here," he said.

"But for how much longer?" the voice asked.

"Life goes on."

"But it don't mean a thing if it ain't got that swing." The voice scatted and said, "Doo-ah, doo-ah."

"Who are you?" Anthony hesitated at the curtain.

"I'll be seeing you real soon, boy," and it cackled. Anthony's heart thumped, and he fell to his knees. Elvis sang from the hall:

"Get up, man. Don't run. Walk. Don't let 'em see you scared."

"The itch is a bitch."

Anthony pulled himself up, holding his hand back from the curtain. He turned, fighting for his balance. His temple throbbed, and he walked to the door, pausing to lean on the wall at times until he could go on.

"Doo-ah. Doo-ah. Doo-ah. Scat tat tat . . . "

A DREAM OF A DREAM

A jail break is required," Dave said.

Anthony sipped at some cool cream of wheat. "Intelligence has been gathered. Time for a tactical withdraw."

"You're going to die, right?"

"Is that a problem?" Water filled Anthony's head from the morphine. The tide flowed over his thoughts.

"Nah. Just wanted to make sure. I probably won't be long behind you."

"I wouldn't mind a little company."

"What a terribly selfish and human thing to say," Dave said. "Let's do this shit."

Anthony knew it was time to go. The pain pierced his temple, drilling into his eyes, and he could feel the shadow spreading over his thoughts. His mind would dissipate. The doctors discussed transferring him to hospice care if he wasn't going to try treatment. They were done with him; and he, with them.

"You sure this is what you want, sport?" Dave asked, parting his silvery hair. "I heard what Doctor Quack-in-bush said this morning. They could extend your life. Don't you want a couple more—"

"Weeks? In this pain? What will I do?"

"Sing a song. Plant a tree. Fuck a whore?"

Anthony unplugged his IVs. He couldn't remember agreeing to have the meds. He hesitated, knowing how bad the pain would get. He'd experienced nothing yet, just the nascent storm. Other patients at the end writhed in the destruction of their bodies, usually not from the cancer but the treatment; often, the radiation or chemo destroyed them. Their bodies played host to toxic drugs and invisible rays, and it burned them away. Even if they had survived, the treatment would have diminished their lives to painful existences. Why had they chosen to go on like that? They had appeared so far away from his place at that time, and now he had met them on the road—reaching for ghosts.

"I'm not choosing to die," he said. "It's not like that."

"Seems like it," he said, pulling out his brown jacket with tweed elbow pads. He tied a bowtie to his collar.

Anthony washed in a pink basin. He left the IV port in his arm, not having the guts to yank it out. The tape tugged on his arm hair. "I'm just choosing not to suffer the treatment. My body will die on its own."

"You're very calm about this," Dave said.

He paused, breathed in and let the water drip from his face into the pink basin. "That's because it's not real to me. It never will be. How could this be happening?"

"I wouldn't believe it if it was happening to me; and it is, just not as up my ass."

Anthony dressed and found his wallet and personal stuff in the drawer. He kept checking the door to make sure they weren't interrupted. He wasn't sure if they'd just be able to walk out of there without at least signing something, but he didn't give a damn.

"The human condition."

"But aren't you mad about all the shit you're going to miss?"

"Furious. But what am I supposed to do? Throw my

fist at the heavens? I would like to live the next day. I'm curious. I got the itch."

"The bitch is the itch," he said.

"I just met you," Anthony said. "And I'm trusting you with the rest of my life. How do I know you're not a morphine hallucination?"

"Nobody wants to be alone when they die. And you've fucked that up. Who cares if I'm a dream?"

"Shit. Okay. Let's rock."

"And blow this fucking Popsicle stand."

They walked, fully dressed, civilians again, past the front desk. Nurse Gretchen spotted them, dressed and obviously incongruous to the environment, and she looked up from her computer, staring at them through bifocals.

"Are you gentleman off for lunch at a fancy restaurant? Off for some nice tea? Uh-huh?"

"Should we keep going?" Anthony asked.

"Move your ass."

"Gentlemen. You can't just leave." She got up and headed them off. Anthony's head throbbed as he walked, but he managed to break into a jog. Dave tugged on his arm. The nurse jogged after them, her sneakers squeaked after them.

"Fuck it," Anthony said, hitting the silver square button hanging on the wall by the double doors. They swung open just in time, and Dave hit his leg, banging his black aluminum cane, trying to keep up. The lift doors opened in the hall between wards, and they both hobbled in. The element of surprise had worked, and the doors shut to nurse Gretchen complaining.

"The bitch is the itch," Dave said, and they both cracked up.

Once they'd escaped the hospital, the two friends

crossed the highway and found a payphone. Anthony still had some cash on him from his last Walmart paycheck, enough for these last few days, and he found a local cab company in the phonebook. The cab picked them up ten minutes later.

Anthony did not read the email from his grandmother, and it might have gone unread, unless Cynthia went through his personal emails and effects to look for names and addresses that she'd need to notify. This is what his grandmother wrote:

Dear Anthony:

I'm not sure I'm even doing this right. You'd probably laugh if you saw me. The old lady trying to figure out the computer. I'll probably press a button and send a letter to Timbuktu. Do you remember when you were a boy and we'd take out your grandfather's atlas and point out all the places you wanted to visit?

I want to tell you I'm sorry for what has happened to you, but I can't. I wanted so much for you. I'm not good with words or talking about how I feel. I need you to understand that. And your grandfather can be overwhelming.

I have to inform you of sad news: your grandfather suffered a stroke two weeks after you left. Since then, he has been severely disabled. He has not spoken a word in months. Doctor Hanson believes he can, but he is very depressed. He's lost most of the mobility down the left side of his body. I have to feed him, bathe him, change him, and I am planning on selling the house and moving into a proper support place.

I believe your grandfather would like to see you. I know you both did not part on the best terms, but you have to understand him. He is prideful. He grew up in a family of eight siblings and was sent to work at the steel mill when he was twelve. They lost their father to liver disease soon after, and he became the man of the house. It was a different time for us. The world is so different now.

I'm sorry we drove you away. It wasn't our right to withhold your past from you. All I have left are the memories of my daughter, of the happy times before it went bad between us. Then I had you, and I always blamed her lifestyle for killing her. She was so smart and beautiful, your mother. She was the best of me, and we drove her away too.

Please at least tell me how you are. I know your condition was advanced the last time you went to the oncologist, and I can't imagine you're getting treatment wherever you are. If that's what you've chosen, I can't say I won't be angry at you for it. I'm going to outlive my family. But please know you are welcome to come home.

I love you, Anthony.

Please take care of yourself.

Anthony swallowed two more white morphine pills and rattled the orange bottle—only a few more remained. They dropped into his palm like the remainder of sand grains in an hourglass. He felt time ticking over, and he expected to recycle like a time bomb; however, he became calmer. Time stretched like he'd fallen into a black hole, and he wondered if at the moment of his death, would the clocks freeze on the last second to midnight, time dilated, wormholes opened. Perhaps life lived forever.

"This is it? What a shithole."

A marquee over a porch read "Rus-T Community Play". Some smartass had come in the night with spray paint and written over the faded letters after "Play: With my Dick, Honey". A hand-painted sign hung below: WARHOL TRAPPED IN BOOB-TUBE.

The cab parked in a side spot.

"They met, once."

"Kaufman and Warhol?" Dave asked.

"Both shy. Meeting each other in a restaurant. At first not talking. Then they really hit it off. Both were leading voices in a new movement. Cynthia told me about it."

"Oh, yes. The mysterious Cynthia. You should call her."

"I can't. I don't think she wants to talk to me."

"She probably thinks the same thing about you," Dave said. "Love is like that."

"No. I don't think I was in love with her."

"At least you were never old enough to realize it. And you never will be. That sucks."

Anthony thought he might have found Dave's honesty abrasive, but actually he felt refreshed to be treated like a person again. Everyone treated him like he'd landed from a different planet.

"You summed it up with such precision. Sucks."

"Are we doing this? Or just going to sit in this cab and avoid your father like a bunch of pussies?"

"Umm. Hmm. Oh, what the hell. It's probably all a lot of shit, anyway."

"Just get out of the damn car."

"Thanks for the ride," Anthony said, and handed the misty driver some cash. Then he got out of the cab and stepped onto broken green glass from shattered beer bottles in the parking lot. A threadbare cat, diseased and pocked with sores, ran out from under a sickly evergreen then crouched by his feet and hissed. "I think that's the ghost of my first wife come back to haunt me," Dave said.

"How many times have you been married?"

"Just twice. First one left me, but I deserved it. I could be an asshole."

"No . . . never."

"I like you, kid."

A few cars filled the spots in front of the derelict vessel. The playhouse had obviously been built with hope and vision of the art, but America had chewed at the edges: peeling off the roof tiles; growing weeds, vines in the walls; cracking the windows; and smothering the building in dirt. Squirrels lived in the rain gutters, and the rotting wood stank. An open sewer pipe overflowed in the adjacent lot, and Anthony gagged on the stench. "Yep. This is the place I meet my destiny."

"That always seems so important at the time. It means shit. Only matters what comes next. The itch."

Show times listed tonight in an hour, starting at the time of 5:34. It had taken them a few hours to drive from the hospital, and they'd stopped to have something to eat on the way.

Tape secured the glass of the ticket window—built into the front of the playhouse. A sign on the window read:

Closed Minded People Forbidden. Smartasses Welcomed.

The lights glowed from the cubicle, and Anthony knocked on the wooden counter. They waited. An older lady rose from below his sight and sipped from a bottle of whiskey. She studied Anthony and Dave for a moment, then her eyes exploded.

"Holy Fuck. We've got people. Real people." She looked at the bottle, probably wondering if she hallucinated the two of them. "You are real, aren't you? It's a day for hallucinations. You know we can still function even when we're crazy? Our minds just reconstruct reality."

"I've been wondering that for the last few months. You wouldn't believe the journey we've had to get here. I apologize. There should be more of us, but many of them broke off along the way, following their own destinations. I suppose that's the way this works."

"And you're here because you want to see the play?" Hair curled out of a black mole down her face.

"We would like to see the play," Anthony said.

"It's a piece of a shit," she said. "A real dead and melting rat-assed rat."

"Sounds charming. Two tickets, please."

"Six dollars and sixty-six cents. Cash money. None of that card shit."

Anthony handed her a few dollars—the remainder of his Walmart money. He treated Dave to the show and handed him a ticket.

"Don't expect a blowjob later," Dave said.

"You're quite welcome."

They slipped in through a set of double doors on the front and passed through a lobby. A concession stand displayed candy in wrappers at least a decade old, and a popcorn popper sparked and popped, blowing hot air. Watermarks stained the gray carpet, and ropes frayed leading an empty queue to the theater. Smoke clung to the edges of the lobby, masking the walls, flowing a fog into Anthony's vision.

"You see that?" he asked Dave.

"What?"

"The fog. There are ghosts in the fog."

"You're going insane," Dave said.

"I have brain cancer. It's attacking my head. I feel like I'm moving backwards in evolution or ahead."

"Do you have to bitch about it all the time?"

Tendrils of mist spread out and led Anthony along the ropes, phantom ushers taking him home, to the stage, to the place where reality and dream meet, soul and body, the in-between places, the threshold of life and perception. "I am not worthy," Anthony sang. The haze poured through his vision like the building burned. Was this place real? Was he real? Perception could not be trusted. The tangible illusion of reality thinned, and fog clouded his mind. Only pain sharpened his sight again, and he grabbed Dave's arm. His friend carried him into the theater, through doors once emblazoned with vibrant bronze fixtures—now gone dim and dull.

"Come this way, man," Elvis said. "Right through here for the show. Best show on earth." Elvis opened the door to reveal the chamber of a small theater. Only ten rows of seats filled the room, and the stage couldn't hold more than a small throng of actors before collapsing.

A mock and encompassing television screen sealed the stage, forcing the audience to view the stage through thin wax paper and plastic wrap. Several large buttons decorated the side along with a numbered rheostat near the top. It reminded Anthony of the old television from the 1960s his grandfather kept in his workshop—black and white, mostly faded, good for listening to the game.

They sat in the second row of seats and waited for the play to begin. Time paced fast. Pain stabbed Anthony's forehead. He tasted blood. His vision blurred, and he struggled to look sharp, to wait for Andy Kaufman—long dead—to appear on stage.

The actor, Samuels, sat in front of the mirror in his mini-dressing room—really a closet just big enough for a chair, desk, and mirror. Another mirror on the back wall reflected into his dressing mirror, establishing an infinite tunnel, of mirror thresholds flying out a trillion times in either vector—a trillion times a trillion times a trillion. He applied his makeup on top of skillful makeup, the layer atop the layer, face worn on face—a trillion times a trillion.

He had done this for years since his death: worn a face upon a face. He had carried the burden of their last plot together, their final hoax, the hoax of a hoax. He'd waited so long for someone to take the variations to heart, to demand satisfaction to the riddle. Finally, it had come, and so, perhaps, had a son, a last link to his great love.

Tonight they would play the bad play, recite the terrible lines, and secrets would finally be revealed, illuminated, and killed. Then he could put it to rest. He'd carried the burden long enough, lived with the anger for decades, angry at his friend, at his own inability to cure with weak hands, at a God he'd never believed in, yet blamed. He'd kept his vows, worn the face over the face.

If the world doubted your death, then were you really dead?

Makeup itched his face, and he adjusted his moustache.

THE PLAY

KAUFMAN & WARHOL TRAPPED IN BOOB-TUBE
Act 1—Scene 1
A Play by A Skull-Cracking Fuck-Up
Me

Brought to you by . . .

The talented and sexy and too-good-for Hollywood Caspiar Players in conjunction with the genius and brilliant and darling work of Zoo MOO Dah Productions.

The curtain rises. Stage lights shine on the stage. They illuminate the plastic of a television screen draped over the stage, obscuring the audiences' view through slightly waxy paper. It is a television screen covering the entire stage, an old 1950's television. Andy Warhol and Andy Kaufman walk on stage and enter the four walls of a large elevator. There is a lever and gears that control it, like an old fashioned elevator.

Warhol: Hey. Man. I hate being stuck in this elevator.

Kaufman: Tank you Veddy Much

Warhol: What, man?

Destroying the Tangible Illusion of Reality

Warhol moves into the elevator with Kaufman. The doors shut, closing them off to the audience. The lights darken. Then the stage parts, revealing a confined space where the actors had stood in front of the mecha-industrial doors.

Warhol: You're Andy Kaufman? The song and dance man? Who does the Foreign Man?

Kaufman: Yes. Yes I am. The cow goes moo . . .

Warhol: Far out!

Kaufman: But we can't take off without Howdy Doody. We've got to find Howdy Doody! Where is he?

Kaufman makes a child-like face, searches for him.

A marionette of Howdy Doody steps from stage left. Its strings glimmer in the stage lights. The puppet walks to the manual lever to control the flight of the lift. It looks back and smiles at Kaufman.

Doody: (Spoken in classic Howdy Doody voice.) Hello Andy. It is good to see you.

Kaufman: (Runs up to hug the puppet at the left controls.) I love you! (Acts childlike and smiles.)

Doody: I love you too, Andy! (Puppet raises its arms in a mock hug.)

Warhol: (Pokes at the fake television screen.) Man, I knew it. I just knew it.

Kaufman: That our life is on television. I knew that as a little boy. There's a big screen in heaven where God watches the earth.

Warhol: I've always seen it that way. Someone shot me once—a lesbian feminist with a manifesto. I supposedly died later, but I just wanted some peace. Before I was shot, I always thought that I was more half-there than all-there—I always suspected that I was watching TV instead of living life. People sometimes say that the way things happen in movies is unreal, but actually, it's the way things happen in life that's unreal. The movies make emotions look so strong and real, whereas, when things really do happen to you, it's like watching television—you don't feel anything. Right when I was being shot, and ever since, I knew that I was watching television. The channels switch, but it's all television.

Warhol finishes his diatribe about reality and television. A young man sits in the audience. He's dying of cancer and will die of a brain hemorrhage a few minutes after the play ends when he finds his destiny. Such is the timing of God.

Kaufman: Is that a banana in your pocket, or are you an existential artist genius who faked his own death? (Kaufman points at the obvious bulge in Warhol's blazer.)

Warhol: I think it's a banana.

Warhol fetches it from his pocket and hands the near rotten brown banana to Kaufman. Kaufman looks at it. A giant papier-mâché banana lowers from the stage behind Warhol and Kaufman, settling on the stage.

Neither of them seem to notice it. The large fruit is just part of the cosmos.

Kaufman: Wild cosmos! Can you heal the banana? I don't like that it's sick. Poor banana.

Warhol: Well, yeah, man. I keep banana Band-Aids. But I keep them on the moon.

Kaufman: On the moon? (Kaufman giggles like a child.) Well, we have to help the sick banana.

Warhol: Do you think this elevator goes that high? That would be wild.

Kaufman: Let's find out! (Kaufman walks silly over to Howdy Doody at the elevator controls.) Howdy, do you think you can take us to the moon?

Doody: (In classic voice) Sure I can, Andy! Hold on!

Kaufman: Hold on a minute! Okay? Okay. We've got another passenger. Hello, fellow traveler. Come on in!

Kaufman walks funny over to the edge of the stage and offers his hand.

Anthony takes Kaufman's hand and steps on stage, through a slice in the plastic of the television screen. On the other side, he walks through the ether of the second world like swimming in a fish tank.

Kaufman: We're going to the moon! And you're coming, too. It's going to be a party. Okay?

Anthony: Okay.

Kaufman: Ready, Howdy! Let's fly to the moon.

Warhol: Far out, man.

Howdy Doody: All right, Andy and Andy and Anthony. Hold on tight, now. Zoom!

(A rocket engine sound fires from speakers off stage. The players on the stage all reach to hold onto the walls to steady themselves. The puppet shakes and his strings wobble.)

Anthony: Will we need special suits to breathe? Helmets?

Howdy: Don't worry, Anthony. The elevator is airtight! And we're going fast. A trillion-Billion-Gogillion miles per second. We'll be there fast!

Kaufman: Wheee!!! This is fun!

Anthony: I think you're my father. Do you remember my mother?

Kaufman: Do you remember your mother? Was she ever real? Was I ever real? I once learned how to meditate and turn my body into energy and then levitate. I couldn't do it, though. I'd have to purify myself for a year, and I liked sex too much.

Anthony: Do you think you could do it? Was that reality for you?

Kaufman: All that matters, is I believed I could do it. What does it matter if I could or couldn't?

(*Sparks and lights flash from sparklers held off stage. Anthony shields his eyes. His body shakes. Kaufman holds him up.*)

Kaufman: You okay?

Anthony: Yeah. I'm okay.

Kaufman: Okay!

Anthony: Which side of the stage is real? Did I cross a threshold or never leave? Am I going home?

Kaufman: We're going to the moon.

Warhol: Nearly at the moon.

Anthony: How can I be in this play? It's impossible.

Warhol: Maybe you wrote it, man. (Warhol fiddles with the bruised banana from his pocket.)

Anthony: I'm not a writer.

Kaufman: I'm not a comedian. I don't know how to tell a joke. I'm a song-and-dance man.

Anthony: You look good for a dead man.

Kaufman: So do you.

389

(Scene change. Lights dim. Crescent moons show through cookie cutter patterns. Wheels of white cheese fall down on ropes and roll across the stage. Fog and mist waft in from dry ice off stage and out of sight from the audience—not that we'll get an audience. Light shift to violet and change the shade of the television screen. Eerie space music plays on a scratchy record, and the tape turns over again and again, restarting. The actors move as if no longer hindered by Earth's gravity, walking with their arms wide open and waving them about—under the sea.)

Howdy Doody: Welcome to the moon, kids!

Kaufman: Thank you, Howdy. (Kaufman goes over to the puppet and kisses him on the head, and Howdy lifts up on his strings and floats across the stage, vanishing. Kaufman looks to Warhol.) So, how do we heal the sick banana?

Warhol: Man. I'm not sure. We had to go to the moon. Maybe we should ask the moon people?

Kaufman: Moon people?

Warhol points off stage, and as Kaufman and Anthony watch, icons of American commercial culture, icons painted or depicted in Warhol's art, march out on stage in poor costumes like a school play. A dollar bill steps on the stage with hairy little male legs. Mushroom clouds painted on construction paper burst from the stage. A Coca-Cola bottle crawls on, its top shattered. The giant banana grows arms and legs and picks itself up.

Anthony: Is my mother here? On the moon?

Warhol: Yeah, man. Maybe. That would be far out.

Cinderfield: Hi, folks.

A devil man walks onto the stage from stage left, wearing a black suit that contrasts against his painted blue skin. He wears cell phones over his eyes as sunglasses.

Cinderfield: This is the last time I'm in this play. Just wanted to say Howdy.

Anthony: You're Tolya, my friend. You drove the truck that caused the accident that killed my mother. You're not real, are you?

Cinderfield: I'm in the play. The play is performed on stage in front of an audience. For the short time they sit before us, crowded in bad chairs until their backs scream, they surrender their understanding of reality and give us life. We step into the shoes, wear the souls, slough off our life and become something new, something created, stirring and tormented to torment. Are we real? For a while we are, then we piss off. So, I'm pissing off.

Anthony: Wait. I want some more time. Can't we talk a bit more?

Cinderfield: Sorry, kid. I've got to catch a bus to Jupiter. (Cinderfield steps off stage. Anthony reaches for him, then stops. So exits Cinderfield and Tolya for the remainder of the play.)

Anthony: I wanted more. I itch.

Warhol: The itch is a bitch, man.

Anthony: Am I dreaming this?

Kaufman: I dreamed of you. You look just like my Grandpa Paul in his photos when he was a young man. You look just like her, too.

Anthony: My mother?

(Bongos push from off stage. Andy puts on a Hawaiian shirt rich with yellow and red colors.)

Kaufman: Time for a song, a folk song from the harvest time on the moon. That's what will heal Mister Banana.

(Kaufman starts to sing in a made-up voice, contrived words that sound much like a typical foreign language while banging his bongos. The large banana dances to the song, and a bright yellow light shines on its skin. It finds salsa rattles on the stage and begins to rattle them to the song.)

Anthony: Will it heal me, too?

Kaufman continues to sing in his wild island language of his own creation.

Warhol: Far out, man.

Anthony: I'm seeing blood in my eyes. Then sunlight. The sunlight is drying the blood and turning it white. My blood is white. I see a bus. There's a bus to Jupiter, and I don't want to miss it. (Anthony reaches out to the bus. An actress wearing a mini-model of the Manhattan skyline moves on stage to him, reaches out to him. When he reaches for her back to steady himself, she pulls away.)

Anthony: You're here.

(The mini city-actress runs off stage.)

INTERMISSION

The actor playing Kaufman helped Anthony from the stage. He scratched an itch in his ear, first missing his face, then returned his fingers, dripping with black blood. His vision pulsed like looking through wavy lake waters. The theater melted. The world melted. The right side of his body dragged behind him. His fingers numbed. He felt no pain and felt grateful for that. The actor led him to a seat in the front row and helped him sit down. He took off his wig, revealing a mop of gray curls. Anthony recognized his wizened and grizzled face, his tiny smile, his ears and demeanor. His gut hung over his belt.

"Sit here, kid," the actor said. Anthony obliged and got off his feet before he collapsed. A clock had ticked over in his head. Bells rang—not marriage or Sunday bells. Still, he heard them chiming. The song would play to its finale—and no more bells would ring.

"I'm having trouble seeing you," he said. "But I know who you are. I've spent my last chimes getting to you. Seen dark and terrible things. I've come. Just to know you. You faked your death and live in the moment of the end. Immortality. You are Andy Kaufman."

393

"You're Andy Kaufman," the actor said.

"No. I'd remember something like that."

"How real do you think people are?" the actor asked. "You came in here with a friend. I heard you in the audience talking to an empty chair. You named the chair Dave. I thought you were just having us on."

"No. Dave's real."

"Is he? Where is he? Minnie out front said you bought an extra ticket then dropped it into the air. You were talking to yourself. She didn't care, figured you were an exiled avant-garde artist. She thought your lunacy was sexy."

"So did Cynthia, until it wounded her."

"You're all dangerous. Kaufmans!"

Anthony considered back to his hospital stay. How much of it had been real? Had he imagined the nurses who Dave had distracted? Had he manifested his friend—a friend he'd dearly needed after being abandoned by his friends in pain, fear or death—with other ghosts and figures to give him life and substance? Dave had served exactly what Anthony needed—a balm to his lonely soul. He knew he couldn't do this alone. He'd prayed, and Dave grew flesh and soul, like an angel come to save him. Perhaps that's all angels were—what people needed, dreams and desires made corporeal but never real beyond the mind. He'd created his own play in his head.

"Are you real?" Anthony asked.

"Not since my friend died."

The actor playing Warhol came down the aisle and reached for Anthony's hand. Anthony couldn't raise it, and the actor withdrew. "Thanks, man, for coming. This play is so wild."

"This is Andy Warhol," the actor sitting with Anthony said.

"Can't be. He still has his gall bladder intact. Cynthia told me how Warhol died during surgery."

"No, man. I couldn't take the art scene, anymore. I paid the doctors. I met Andy Kaufman once, and we stayed friends. I got the idea from him. Now, no one demands anything of me, anymore. I can just paint and write and make movies, and no one gives a shit. I live in Pittsburgh. I had to get out, man. After that woman shot me, I knew I had to get out."

"You're really Andy Warhol?" Anthony asked.

"Not anymore, man." And Andy Warhol climbed onto the stage and started setting the props and scenery for the next act. Anthony watched him for a time, trying to focus on him. He'd never really find out if he was Andy Warhol, but what did it really matter? He'd soon suffer no more earthly concerns—perhaps no concerns at all.

"You knew who I was?" Anthony asked, returning his attention.

"I recognized you the moment I saw you. Andy in his youth. So wild. So lost. Plotting ways to invade reality and get chicks. Andy would wrestle later just to satisfy his sexual cravings. And I helped." The actor took out a packet from below his chair, and Anthony recognized it as the bundle of notes and photos they'd liberated from his mother's possessions that day in ancient Egypt.

"Of course," Anthony said.

"I have private detectives under my employ. It's all part of the hoax of a hoax."

"You've been watching us?"

He paged through the packet, the photos and love letters. "I remember this one. He wrestled her at Berkeley. Had a real thing for her, too, for months. That was the longest I'd known him to be with a woman, well besides Lynne. He had a real thing for your mother. She wanted to marry him. Could you imagine Andy Kaufman being married to someone? He had his women. Couldn't be caught. Which one do you marry? Which Andy? No. He had his psychology play out on stage. He couldn't process his past, his pain and emotions, unless it was on stage. So much anger from his father."

"Which Andy was my father?"

"The boy. The young one. The one who played with imaginary friends in the woods by his school. The boy who snuck off from school to Coney Island to the freak show to see his friends. Your mother ran off, ran home. I never knew what happened to her."

"So, who are you?" Anthony asked.

"It's not obvious by now?"

Andy sat on the couch in the home he'd made with Lynne—the closest woman to ever come close to being his wife, the one who had understood. His weight had dropped. The hair had fallen from his head, leaving it shorn. Only his eyebrows had begun to grow back. Lynne heated him a can of Campbell's tomato soup and left the can on the living room table. He'd been tired since his trip to the Philippines, to receive the miraculous psychic surgery. He longed for more life—an addiction, a habit. There were so many more playhouses too, so many new people to create. He'd loved his time on the stage, though his acts had grown stale to his audience. Still, he kept playing, just as he had as a child.

His best friend and writer, his other partner, sat in the chair next to him. Bob Zmuda offered no comfort. Watching his best friend decay and diminish had killed the heart in Bob. Andy represented life to him, an ancient earth God. He'd given him joy, light, and the core of his existence. What would he become without Andy? How could he carry on their work, his legacy? He sat on the edge of the chair, ready to jump and run.

"I had this great idea," Andy said in a frail voice, yet the snark still remained. His fight still hadn't gone. Bob grinned, perhaps in hope. His ponytail trailed down his neck.

"Idea?"

"Wouldn't it be funny if no one really believed I was dead?"

"Yeah. That's wild. Yeah. And we can keep them guessing. Give them hints. No one would really know for sure." For a moment, Bob wondered if all of this had been an elaborate hoax, something to even throw his friends off. You had to expect that with Andy, and Bob had never entirely believed that Andy had cancer. Lung cancer? He never even smoked. He was one of the healthiest people he knew, eating all that lotus and vegetables and meditating. People that healthy didn't get a rare lung cancer. It had to be all bullshit.

"But, we do it all. I die. You bury me. But you leave hints."

"It's got to be subtle. And it'll take years."

"Then someone finally gets it and goes to dig up my body." Andy giggled, curling his top lip.

"Yeah! And then you can jump out of the grave and pass out milk and cookies and wear an Elvis suit."

"We don't bury me. You bury some Elvis stuff. At the funeral, you sneak my body out and replace the coffin. Then you bury the empty one. It's so good. It'll take years for someone to believe it."

"You jackass," Bob said. "You really are dying."

Andy nodded. "And you have to pretend to be me. You have to get makeup, a mask, play out my life as if I was alive. Pretend to be me pretending to be someone else. You'll know the name. You'll remember. One of my friends from childhood."

"You didn't have any friends as a child. You made them all up."

"I might have made you up, too."

"Then when you go, what's real in me goes, too."

Andy coughed.

"Andy, what do I do with the body?"

"What did you do with the body?" Anthony asked.

"We snuck it out of the funeral home and had it cremated there on the property. His family knows, though we didn't tell his mother for years. She figured it out, though."

"I tried to see them," Anthony said, slurring his words. Blood dripped down his ear.

"I know. That's how I found out about you. The lawyer, Gill. The fat man. He called me right away. We were up doing the play anyway."

"The play was another trick. Who wrote it?"

Bob Zmuda playing Andy Kaufman playing the actor Samuels shrugged, taking off his mask and makeup, revealing a man of different complexion from Andy, of salt hair. He put on his glasses. "Christ that feels better. I've been carrying that face for decades now, playing three men. I stopped being Bob when Andy died."

"I stopped being Anthony a year ago. I came apart. Cancer changes the way you see things. Dying does. Reality becomes tangible."

"The play? I don't know. I found it in the Philadelphia International Airport on a layover."

"Who wrote it, then?"

"Maybe someone you knew. Maybe a stranger. Maybe God left it. It's one of those fucking mysteries we'll probably never figure out. Others can discuss it."

"Sounds like something a bastard author would do to his readers."

"Whoever is writing this is a real bastard," Bob said. "Shit."

"So, Andy Kaufman was my father?" Anthony asked.

"I see him here, and I realize how much it killed me when he died, so much so, that I pretended to be him for years, never had a life of my own. Andy had a life force that outshone others, and you just wanted more."

"Will there ever be proof?"

"Why the fuck do you need proof? It's what you believe. Right? Did Christ ever die on the cross and come back to life? Who the hell cares? It was a long fucking time ago. People believe it. That's what we did. We created a new reality and showed people how fucking fragile their perceptions really are. Your dad loved doing that, fucking with people's heads. Destroying the false security they had. People can be created—and destroyed."

"You needed him to rise from the dead," Anthony said.

"Much harder in real life than in the Bible. Andy was a Jew, but Elvis was the King. But all we needed to do was create some doubt."

"You loved him," Anthony said. "You can't let him go."

"I still think he's out there laughing his ass off at us. The ultimate prank. Andy is an addiction I can't kick. Once you write for Andy Kaufman, you can't write for anyone else. I'm ruined for life, the fucker. Now, come on. The second part of the play is starting. It's short but important. Just be strong a bit longer. Call on old friends to help, if you require."

"I've been seeing Elvis," Anthony said. Fever burned his head. "He came at the beginning."

"Elvis is your angel of death?"

"Baby!" Anthony called out to Elvis. He manifested.

"Hey, man. Heard you're not feeling so good." Elvis walked down the aisle, holding his guitar. He wore the *lei* flower necklace from his Hawaiian persona.

"The King!"

Bob smiled.

"I'll help you on stage." Bob took Anthony's arm and carried him up to take his mark before the start of Act II.

KAUFMAN & WARHOL TRAPPED IN BOOB-TUBE

Act II—Scene 1
A Play by A Skull-Cracking Fuck-up
Me

Brought to you by . . .

The talented and sexy and too-good-for Hollywood Caspiar Players in conjunction with the genius and brilliant and darling work of Zoo MOO Dah Productions.

On the moon, Kaufman-Zmuda and Warhol both study the sickly banana. It begins to perk in his hands. The giant banana continues to dance and play the salsa rattles on stage. The plastic on the giant television screen glows bright in the house lights.

Warhol: Yeah, man. You healed my banana.

Anthony: I can't see either of you, anymore. It hurts. (His voice is childlike, and Kaufman-Zmuda has to carry him on stage, holding him up.) I'd like to go home, now. I miss my family.

Kaufman-Zmuda: You require the services of an angel! Angel! Where is that angel?

Warhol: Where is the angel I made? The American angel. So sexy. Commercial. The angels of modern industry and markets. The heart of America. Red.

A walking Campbell's soup can appears from stage left. A bent wire halo hangs over the top of the can. A pair of floppy and tattered wings hang on either side. She lifts a smoking cigarette on a holder to the can and smokes through a tiny hole, blowing out the smoke. A pair of striped stockings seal her sexy legs. She says nothing, just extends a hand to Anthony. A bus honks in the distance.

Bus Driver (In distance): Last stops: Jupiter and the cosmos. Then, end of the line. All on now or be stuck in stasis.

Anthony: That sounds just like my grandfather. (He stumbles on stage, his body obviously deteriorating. A bright light shines on his body from the stage. He hears laughter and clapping from the empty seats. His friend Dave cheers him on.)

Soup Can: It's okay, Anthony. I'll help you to the bus.

Anthony: And you're Cynthia. I didn't mean to hurt you. You may have been the great love of my life.

Soup Can: (In a voice similar to Cynthia's) Don't lie to me.

Please don't lie to me anymore. I'll do that enough to myself.

END PLAY.

LAST BUS TO JUPITER

The unique life form that played Anthony on Earth stopped.

GOODBYE ANGEL-FRIENDLY FRIENDLY WORLD

Angel has flown as high as he could. The world has changed on him. He only has one great act left, a last feat to close the curtain. All he can do now is die—and die well, entertaining, driving suspense, keeping them guessing. Death would make them all fill with sympathy again. If he willed it enough, could he use his mental powers to manipulate the universe, life, the chain of events? The darkness in his spirit could manifest in his body, grow as a tumor. He needs to get sick. Reality is tangible. He can make himself sick. If he believes it enough—if everyone believes it—then he must have cancer.

Everyone notices his cough. He doesn't have the flu or allergies. Angel is a vegetarian and insists on eating healthy, unlike Tony Clifton, who sucks down steaks, Jack Daniels and cigars. The medicine men push a television camera into his body and find his realized mass, his body's delusion and cut a piece off. Angel is giddy, excited about his disease. The medicine men put on x-ray glasses and shoot invisible beams into his body, and Angel snickers. Don't they know it's all an illusion? The cancer grows, hides in his blood, sucking on his arm like a lollipop. It would never kill him. The cancer is another character, a toy, a persona he's adopted to fake his own death. The malignancy was under his command. He can't help laughing. Bob and Lynne worry, and he thrives on the attention. It's like running away when he was a boy. The doctors won't operate. They say that radiation would just ease the pain, make it easier. It's all a new bit, a new game. Dying would be fun. Then he would be healed through roots or herbs or psychic surgery and be fine. Life couldn't end. It was Angel's. Life belonged to him and would never turn on Angel. It was all a trick, and he'd pull it off, die, then jump out of a cake or go on the *Letterman Show*. He'd rise from the grave, climb off the cross and be alive.

Papu Cy never died. He'd gone on a long trip. No one Angel loved had ever died. Death was a myth. It wouldn't come to him. It would be his most fun stunt ever, and no one would ever forget him. Angel could make it better. He'd wished his own dying and he could unwish. His spirit would overcome it. He was not his Papu Cy. No one really believed he had cancer. They would all laugh when they learned, and this would make it a fantasy.

If no one believed in it, wouldn't that make it unreal?

He ate his leaves and roots, shaving off ginger, filling bathtubs with it. He meditated his cancer away, using mental energy. The radiation drained him, but he pursued it, adding credibility to the joke, enjoying the stunt. It made him sicker, sucking out his marrow, and he played it, but it wasn't really real. Angel read his books and learned the true sources of his sickness:

"Chocolate! Chocolate is making me sick. I won't eat anymore chocolate, and then I'll be okay."

The rational mind tries to undo cancer. It cannot accept its own death and departs from reality. Angel was leaving the world, particle-by-particle, dissipating, leaking out his essence. His beloveds, Bob, Lynne, George and his family, watched it happening, and he wouldn't believe it.

Angel continues to play the game. He even brings out his beloveds to a mind-fucker, and they do a counseling session. It's all part of the joke, making it more real to make it unreal. That's how he'll beat it, pushing it so far beyond the realm of belief that no one believes it. That is how he lived, and this is how he won't die. They flew to the Philippines, Manila, and found a magician who could pull the cancer out of his guts, and everyday, he and Lynne went. This would cure it. His magical hands would fix it.

Angel grew sicker, weaker. His beliefs matter little. At the end of his time, he learned that he was always powerless. No magic or meditation in the world could heal his broken wings. In the end, he was but a small man punching and kicking the coming tide. His control was an illusion. Angel comes home. Bob, Lynne and his family come to see him at Cedar-Sinai. He sleeps, only waking briefly, and his vision distorts as if he gazes through a crystal screen. He's going on a long trip in the car.

They'll all cry and make a big deal out of it, then, in thirty years, he'll show up again. His audience will have forgotten the wrestling and all the bad energy, the darkness he created. He'll go back to singing "The Cow-Goes-Moo" and doing his puppet. The world will love him again.

Angel saw himself like he had so long ago on the screen. He passed through it.

EPILOGUE

Two months after the funeral, Cynthia worked at the Shop & Save up on Knapp Road, just at the intersection of 63 in Lansdale. Her father worked nights, and in the mornings he'd come home, she'd make breakfast, and they'd watch old *SNL* episodes he still had on VHS tape. She'd get him a proper DVD player for his birthday, though he claimed he didn't need one.

Anthony's grandmother had made all the arrangements when Zmuda had contacted them with the news of his death. The private detective had uncovered all of Anthony's information, and Bob made sure that the Kaufman family knew of his existence and bloodline, though very little could be done at this point but mourn and regret missed chances.

The day dragged like a dead raccoon run over and stuck to a truck tire, dragging it down I-95 until little flesh or fur remained, scraping it down the pavement. Each day, she struggled to end, to lift one more bag of potatoes or bottle of soda across the laser reader. She knew she had to continue, to go on, at least for her. On her break, she'd swallow a tranquilizer she'd bought off the girl who worked at the café and tried to cry less into her arms. She had never meant to leave him. She just needed time, a break to figure shit out. He should have called. The asshole should have told her. Cynthia would have come back.

She finished her break, feeling a bit mellow from the pill and returned to the checkout aisle that had become her domain, nearly bumping into a shelf of gum and candy and magazines. A queue of people waited, impatiently, believing their errands so important, burning through their time with little concept of the real nature of reality. A woman hurried her young daughter through. The child's fair hair had only recently started to grow back.

"Are you better now?" Cynthia asked, recognizing a cancer patient not only because of the physical symptoms but also her demeanor. She looked lighter, somehow, than other people, enduring an understanding of reality that few others possessed. She had glanced the same glance on the face of her friend, of her true love, now gone. When he died, he'd taken a part of herself with him.

The life force of some people is so strong that it outshines others. You become a component to them. Maybe I'll have my own life now. Bob Zmuda had told her this at the funeral. She'd lifted the lid just to make sure they weren't pulling anything funny—not that she'd mind, but she wanted to be in on it.

"I thought I was going to die," the little girl said. "Then an angel found me one night when I was in the hospital in New York. My daddy lives there, and I was visiting him when I got sick."

"What did the angel say?"

"I gave him a name, and it made me better. It was a promise to feel better."

"What was the name?" The little girl beckoned her down, and Cynthia leaned over. She whispered it in her ear—the perfect name. And Cynthia knew what had to be done. She'd just received late paperwork from the clinic, the bank where they had been on the first day of their adventure, that week when she lost her playhouse, lost her family, and they'd gone north—when she'd tried to save her love.

The clinic signed over the frozen samples. The treatment may have sterilized Anthony, so he put some of his swimming boys on ice and kept them there. She picked up the container and carried it home, to the apartment. She spoke to her father first about what she needed to do and to Anthony's Grandmother who loved the idea and promised to help.

Life goes on. The Itch is the Bitch. Last Bus to Earth.

She had no money, no future, no prospects, little family, and she knew this was a terrible idea. She let it thaw in the sink, careful, treating it like holy wine, communion wafers, the sincerest of divinity. Her holy of holics.

She knew the name of his child, of their child, and he and Andy Kaufman would live on in the lineage. It wasn't a standard name by custom, but they would make it so. Reality was shaped by the brave, the mad, the wild.

Acknowledgements

A book belongs to more than the author who wrote it. It is a journey with many friends and strangers who met along the road. I am grateful to so many.

I've got to thank Max Booth III for believing in this book and staking a fledgling Indie publisher to the word of a flaky author.

Marjorie Scharpf and Jeff Ledbetter, my wife's parents, have believed in me and given us the foundations to begin a real life. I didn't believe I could have one. They gave us the wedding of dreams, set in Scotland and by a stream. People are the only real force that can change destiny.

And of course to my new wife, Allison. She never doubts. Always hopes. And accepts me for all my flaws and damage, no matter the burdens on her. All my books are gifts to you.

If you enjoyed *Destroying the Tangible Illusion of Reality; or Searching for Andy Kaufman* don't pass up on these other titles from Perpetual Motion Machine . . .

TRUTH OR DARE
EDITED BY MAX BOOTH III
ISBN: 978-0-9860594-5-2
Page count: 240
$14.95

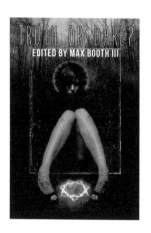

Halloween night. The freaks are out and having the time of their lives. The kids of Greene Point High School have organized a massive bonfire out in the woods. One drunken teen suggests playing a game, a game called Truth or Dare. That's always a fun game. Always good for a laugh. By the end of this night, nobody will be laughing. Alcohol, sex, deadly secrets, and oceans of blood await them. Do you dare to play? Truth or Dare is a shared-world horror anthology featuring the morbid writings of many prominent authors in the field today, as well as quite a few new kids on the block you're gonna want to keep an eye on.

DEAD MEN
LIBROS DE INFERNO: BOOK 1
BY JOHN C. FOSTER
ISBN: 978-0-9860594-7-6
Page count: 372
$14.95

Roaring south in a black Cadillac, John Smith is on the road trip from Hell through a nightmarish version of Americana, a place of rotting hollows and dusty crossroads, slaughterhouses and haunted trains. He doesn't know how he woke up after sitting down in the electric chair, where he got the black suit with the slit up the back or even the cigarettes in his pocket. All he knows is that there is a woman guarding a great secret and he's supposed to kill her.

"Frankly, I haven't been this impressed with an authorial debut since Clive Barker's Books of Blood. And no, that isn't hyperbole. John C. Foster really is that good."—Joe McKinney, Bram Stoker Award Winning Author of Dead City

TALES FROM THE HOLY LAND
BY RAFAEL ALVAREZ

ISBN: 978-0-9860594-0-7
Page count: 226
$12.95

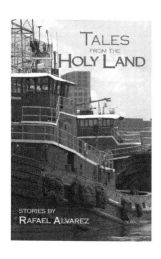

Tales from the Holy Land is the third collection of short fiction from the Baltimore author and screenwriter. The stories take place along the narrow streets and alleys of Alvarez's heartbreaking hometown, charting secret histories of the last 100 years through the difficult and hopeful lives of tugboat men, junk collectors, beautiful women, short order cooks and an artist who captures it all in house paint on the sides of abandoned buildings.

The Perpetual Motion Machine Catalog

Bleed | Various Authors | Anthology
    Page count: 286 | Paperback: $16.95
    ISBN: 978-0-9887488-8-0

Cruel | Eli Wilde | Novel
    Page count: 192 | Paperback: $9.95
    ISBN: 978-0-9887488-0-4

Dead Men | John Foster | Novel
    Page Count: 360 | Paperback: $14.95
    ISBN: 978-0-9860594-7-6

Four Days | Eli Wilde & 'Anna DeVine | Novel
    Page count: 198 | Paperback: $9.95
    ISBN: 978-0-9887488-5-9

Gory Hole | Craig Wallwork | Story Collection (Full-Color Illustrations)
    Page count: 48 | Paperback: $12.95
    ISBN: 978-0-9860594-3-8

The Green Kangaroos | Jessica McHugh | Novel
    Page count: 184 | Paperback $12.95
    ISBN: 978-0-9860594-6-9

Last Dance in Phoenix | Kurt Reichenbaugh | Novel
    Page count: 268 | Paperback: $12.95 |
    ISBN: 978-0-9860594-9-0

Long Distance Drunks: a Tribute to Charles Bukowski
    Various Authors | Anthology
    Page count: 182 | Paperback: $12.95
    ISBN: 978-0-9860594-4-5

The Perpetual Motion Club | Sue Lange | Novel
   Page count: 208 | Paperback $14.95
   ISBN: 978-0-9887488-6-6

The Ritalin Orgy | Matthew Dexter | Novel
   Page count: 206 | Paperback $12.95
   ISBN: 978-0-9887488-1-1

Sirens | Kurt Reichenbaugh | Novel
   Page count: 286 | Paperback: $14.95
   ISBN: 978-0-9887488-3-5

So it Goes: a Tribute to Kurt Vonnegut | Various Authors
   Anthology
   Page count: 282 | Paperback $14.95
   ISBN: 978-0-9887488-2-8

Stealing Propeller Hats from the Dead | David James Keaton
   Story Collection
   Page count: 256 | Paperback $12.95
   ISBN: 978-1-943720-00-2

Tales from the Holy Land | Rafael Alvarez | Story Collection
   Page count: 226 | Paperback $14.95
   ISBN: 978-0-9860594-0-7

The Tears of Isis | James Dorr | Story Collection
   Page count: 206 | Paperback: $12.95
   ISBN: 978-0-9887488-4-2

Time Eaters | Jay Wilburn | Novel
   Page count: 218 | Paperback: $12.95
   ISBN: 978-0-9887488-7-3

Vampire Strippers from Saturn | Vincenzo Bilof | Novel
   Page count: 210 | Paperback: $12.95
   ISBN: 978-0-9860594-8-3

forthcoming Titles:

2015

Crabtown, USA
   Rafael Alvarez

2016

Dark Moon Digest #22

The Violators
   Vincenzo Bilof

Live On No Evil
   Jeremiah Israel

Dark Moon Digest #23

The Train Derails in Boston
   Jessica McHugh

The Ruin Season
   Kris Triana

Lost Signals: Anthology

Dark Moon Digest #24

Mojo Rising
   Bob Pastorella

Quizzleboon
   John Oliver Hodges

Gods on the Lam
   Christopher David Rosales

Caliban
   Ed Kurtz

Dark Moon Digest #25

Speculations
   Joe McKinney

Night Roads
   John Foster

Website:
www.PerpetualPublishing.com

Facebook:
www.facebook.com/PerpetualPublishing

Twitter:
@PMMPublishing

Instagram:
www.instagram.com/PMMPublishing/

Newsletter:
www.PMMPNews.com

Email Us:
Contact@PerpetualPublishing.com

11694537R00249

Made in the USA
Monee, IL
15 September 2019